D0297392

4/13   MOR

MORPETH ASHINGTON

11 SEP 2018

2 8 NOV 2013

12 DEC 2013

3 0 DEC 2013

- 4 FEB 2014

18/4/18

THE
EDGE
OF
NORMAL

THE
EDGE
OF
NORMAL

CARLA NORTON

MACMILLAN

First published 2013 by St. Martin's Press, New York

This edition published in Great Britain 2013 by Macmillan
an imprint of Pan Macmillan, a division of Macmillan Publishers Limited
Pan Macmillan, 20 New Wharf Road, London N1 9RR
Basingstoke and Oxford
Associated companies throughout the world
www.panmacmillan.com

ISBN 978-1-4472-3069-4 HB
ISBN 978-1-4472-3803-4 TPB

1 2 3 4 5 6 7 8 9

A CIP catalogue record for this book is available from the British Library.

Printed by CPI Group (UK) Ltd, Croydon, CR0 4YY

Visit **www.panmacmillan.com** to read more about all our books
and to buy them. You will also find features, author interviews and
news of any author events, and you can sign up for e-newsletters
so that you're always first to hear about our new releases.

This book is dedicated to Colleen Stan and to survivors everywhere. Your courage is an inspiration.

THE
EDGE
OF
NORMAL

PROLOGUE

Seattle, Washington
Six Years Earlier

Her name had been out of the headlines so long that he was sure no one was searching for her when he fit the key into the lock for the last time. The door swung wide on its hinges, but he felt no need to secure it behind him. The steps groaned beneath his weight as he descended into the basement and ordered her to stand and face the wall.

First came the blindfold. Next, the handcuffs. He wrenched her hands behind her, tightening the cuffs until she flinched.

Then he bent close, inhaling her scent, lingering over her neck, admiring the pattern of scars that laced her skin. With a thumb, he slowly traced the crenulated edge of the newest one, still bright pink, which ran from her left shoulder blade, down and across her spine, to a sweet spot just above the waistband of her pink-and-black pajama bottoms.

"Turn around and open your mouth," he said, and when she did, he put a tablet on her tongue and told her to swallow. He'd calculated a dose that would make her sleepy enough for the trip, but not so drugged that he couldn't rouse her for what he'd planned for later.

Encircling her neck in a loose headlock, he licked his lips and whispered, "Now, my little cricket, we're going on an adventure. Don't dare even chirp."

Her old sneakers were much too small and he hadn't thought to buy shoes, so she went barefoot as he steered her up the stairs.

He paused at the door and snapped off the only burning light before moving through the kitchen toward the back, where he had everything ready. He peeked through the blinds. The neighborhood was quiet. The trees that shaded his backyard were in full leaf, obscuring the view of any neighbors. Better yet, it was raining.

He slipped a hooded poncho over her head, opened the door, and shoved her out ahead of him. The pair moved across the porch and down the back steps. The grass soaked his shoes as he walked her small frame along the path and through the back gate into the alley.

It was well past midnight and he had planned out every detail, but this was the risky part. A streetlight glared across one unavoidable stretch. In just three paces, they were back in the protective shadows, and in three more they were at the car.

The silver Mercury Grand Marquis was parked at an angle, with the trunk unlatched. He opened it, lifted her in his arms, and quickly placed her inside, muttering, "Lie down and be still."

He had lined the trunk with an old quilt earlier that night. This was mainly to dampen any sound, but it also gave her a cushion to lie on, and he planned to remind her of this act of kindness if she complained later.

Once she was locked in the trunk, he slipped into the driver's seat and settled behind the wheel, sitting in the darkness, scanning windows and watching for movement.

A cat skittered across the alley and disappeared into the brush. A breeze stirred the leaves overhead and fat raindrops spattered his windshield. Nothing else.

He waited another moment, stroking his thick, unkempt beard, then turned the key in the ignition and eased the car down the alley, where he clicked on his headlights and turned left. There was no traffic, but the rain was coming down harder now, and he scrupulously watched his speed, braking gently at two red lights before turning onto the road that wound through the arboretum. His tires made wet hissing sounds as he made the turns.

Daryl Wayne Flint smiled, glad for the added concealment of the rain, feeling certain that he'd managed it all perfectly.

The whole process of packing up and moving had been a headache, but everything was finally set. He would soon have her secured in his new house, a roomy place set far back from the road. Private and rural, with a big basement that made it all worth the risk. Its floor was flat and even, so that he could wheel his equipment around with no trouble. Its ceiling was high, and the overhead beams would be perfect for securing hooks.

But as shrewd as he was, Daryl Wayne Flint hadn't fully considered that even on a wet Wednesday night, Seattle's bars might be busy well past midnight. Or that some stubborn patrons could linger until bartenders had to shoo them out. Or that a few customers would stagger out too drunk to drive. Or that one particular driver would fail to turn on his headlights and come barreling down the steepest part of 23rd Avenue just as a silver Mercury turned into his path.

Flint barely glimpsed the coming collision and never saw the explosion of breaking glass glittering in the rain as the two cars smashed and spun.

ONE

Tuesdays are always a test, and getting to his office is the hard part, but twenty-two-year-old Reeve LeClaire has never told her psychiatrist about her route. It begins with a short walk to the Ferry Building, where she routinely orders a hot chocolate and carries it outside, sipping its sweetness while watching the ferries emerge from the fog. The boats come from Vallejo and Larkspur and Sausalito, trailing white foam and flocks of gulls before stopping to off-load a morning rush of commuters.

When the sun breaks through the fog, Reeve turns her face to it, shuts her eyes, and savors the red heat on her eyelids.

No one notices her in the flow of the crowd, and she feels almost smug about her anonymity. She's hardly recognizable as the schoolgirl pictured in the "Missing" posters, or the pasty waif heralded in the tabloids. Though still on the small side, she has grown an inch and gained sixteen pounds. Her teeth are fixed. She is clean and smooth and has plucked her eyebrows to precise arcs.

Her hair has grown back so nicely that it's almost a source of pride. She often changes its color to black or blond or, today, maroon. She wears it neatly cut, feathered, and always long enough to cover the scars that remain visible on the back of her neck.

When the clock tower begins its 9:00 A.M. chime, Reeve shoulders her bag. By the time its elaborate music is finished and it's pealing seven . . . eight . . . nine, she is out of the Ferry Building and crossing onto Market

Street. The street vendors and musicians are too busy to bother her. But the farther she makes herself walk down this street, the more cautious she must become.

She sets her jaw. Here comes the wooly-faced man with the tarp-covered cart. He's always here, hustling the corner by the bank, but she forces herself to look straight ahead as she hurries down the sidewalk, skin prickling.

Next comes the BART station, with its gauntlet of grubby people. She veers around them and comes face-to-face with the tall man in the smeared raincoat. She holds her breath and charges onward as he barks, "God bless you!" at her back.

She squares her shoulders. She's doing fine. Two more blocks and then she's nearly there. She feels the air on her face. Her legs are strong and she walks with purpose.

As she passes the sidewalk café, a handsome young waiter catches her eye and smiles, but she looks away. Why would she trust guys who pretend she's pretty? She knows very well that she is not, with her crooked nose and pointy chin.

She looks down at the sidewalk and follows the feet walking in front of her, then glances up and sees the safety of the Hobart Building, where the guard makes every visitor sign in. She waits at the crosswalk, balanced on the balls of her feet, watching traffic, scanning the last dangerous stretch. The light changes and she hurries across the intersection. The moment she reaches the other side, the filthy man in the wheelchair rolls into view.

Reeve stops, feeling her chest knot. She considers crossing back to the other side of the street and approaching the building from the far corner, by the flower stand. But the man is looking the other way. If he just keeps rolling forward, Reeve can slip past behind him, unseen.

She calculates, takes a breath, and hurries toward the building's entrance. She is twenty feet away . . . ten . . . five . . . when the man in the rolling chair works his wheels and pivots. His eyes blaze. His whiskers jut out like wire.

Reeve jumps back, swallows, and charges past him into the building, where she stops in the cool lobby to catch her breath. Next, she confronts the elevator. It's so old and small that it feels cramped with just three people. She knows she could do it; she has done so in the past. But not today. She opts for the stairs.

The waiting area of Dr. Ezra Lerner's office is always scented with citrus, and she is relieved to arrive early so she can enjoy the fragrance and cool down after climbing nine flights. She nods at the receptionist, a pleasant woman with a Cupid's-bow mouth, and slides into her favorite chair.

The walls are pale jade, and a white orchid blooms from a cobalt-colored pot on the coffee table. She picks up the latest copy of *The New Yorker* and flips through, looking at photos and reading cartoons. Sometimes she gets all of them, but today they seem obscure. She studies them for meaning and chides herself for not following the news.

At exactly 9:30, the receptionist says, "Miss, Dr. Lerner will see you now."

Patient privacy is strict office etiquette, another reason Reeve feels safe here. The receptionist never calls out her name, even if no one else is in the waiting room. Only her family, a few people in law enforcement, and Dr. Lerner know that Regina Victoria LeClaire, the girl who was kidnapped at age twelve and held captive for nearly four years, has legally changed her name.

She is no longer "Edgy Reggie," the feral girl who responded to media attention by whacking down cameras. She now thinks of herself as agile, not skittish. As serious, not grim. She has transformed into a composed young woman who is living a pleasant, structured life. She even has a job.

As Reeve replaces the magazine beside the orchid and stands, the office phone rings, which is slightly unusual, and as she walks down the carpeted hallway to Dr. Lerner's door, she hears the receptionist's bright greeting fade to a darker tone: "Oh no. . . . Oh no . . . Yes, of course, but the doctor has a patient and . . ."

Reeve puts her hand on the doorknob and pauses to listen, but Dr. Lerner swings open his door, saying, "Reeve, always so good to see you."

Dr. Ezra Lerner perhaps looks too young to be an expert of any kind, but he is in fact a leading authority on captivity syndromes, which is why Reeve's father first contacted him. He has the taut, compact physique of a gymnast. His face is clean shaven, his eyes observant. His little dog, a shaggy mutt named Bitsy, stands beside him, wagging her tail and looking up at Reeve with canine adoration.

Reeve stoops to scratch Bitsy's head. "It's good to see you, too."

She crosses the small room to take her usual seat on the sofa, pats the cushion, and Bitsy jumps up beside her.

Dr. Lerner settles into his chair, watching her, and asks how she's sleeping. He always asks this.

"Nothing to report. No bad dreams. No panic attacks. I haven't had a nightmare in so long, I'm starting to feel boring."

Almost normal, she thinks, though that's a term that Dr. Lerner would never use. During the early stages, she met with him for hours at a time. Then three times a week. Then twice a week. And now only on Tuesdays, a measure of her progress.

He asks a few questions about her new job, and with a slight smile, she retrieves a sheet of folded notepaper from her pocket. "Homework," she volunteers, waving the paper. "Right here."

She unfolds it, saying, "I thought about the reasons I like working at the restaurant. And even though it's only part-time, it's a pretty long list." She glances up, adding, "A good thing, but I'll try to keep it brief."

A smile flickers across Dr. Lerner's face an instant before his cell phone pings a muted note and his smile fades. "I'm very sorry, Reeve. Please excuse me a second," he says, checking the screen.

She stiffens. Dr. Lerner has never allowed himself to be distracted during their sessions before. "Is it an emergency?"

He scowls at the phone, shakes his head, and sets it on the corner of his desk. "I'm sorry, Reeve. Please continue."

"But do you need—"

"No, no, it can wait." He takes a breath, bringing his gaze up to hers. "You were telling me about the restaurant."

She hesitates.

"You were afraid you wouldn't like it," he prompts.

"Um, right. But just the opposite. And part of the reason I like it so much, I think, is that it has no emotional baggage."

"Ah. Meaning what, exactly?"

"Well, Japanese food is a long way from cold pizza and warm soda." She smirks, dimpling one cheek.

"That's a good realization on your part. What else?"

Holding the list in her right hand and stroking Bitsy with her damaged left hand, she tells him about the pleasure she takes in the simple formality of the Japanese, the ritual of bowing, the fresh clean smell of green tea. "And I'm learning the language," she adds.

"Excellent. It's a tough language." He steeples his fingers. "You were good at languages in high school, weren't you?"

She shoots him a cross look. "You're not going to start bugging me about college now, are you?"

"College?"

Rolling her eyes, she continues, "Anyway, on the topic of my homework, I've realized that sounds really affect me. You know, maybe after so much silence." She has written, *Dr. Lerner's voice is smooth as caramel,* but doesn't say this, and now recalls how his tone sharpened when he testified in court, how everyone sat forward, watching as a strange intensity rose off him like heat.

"Yes? What kinds of sounds?"

"For instance, Takami-san has this very soft voice, almost a whisper. And the sushi chef's knife clicks on the cutting board. And the music in the restaurant is almost Zen-like. Instrumentals, you know. No insipid lyrics."

"You enjoy it? That's progress."

She'd had trouble with music for years, complaining that it all sounded like noise to her. Dr. Lerner had suggested that she was suffering from anhedonia, the inability to experience pleasure.

She strokes Bitsy's head. "Now you're going to ask me about Thanksgiving."

"Right, good. You're having dinner with your family, aren't you? Any anxieties about that?"

She shakes her head, leans back, and tells him about her father's new live-in girlfriend. "She's going to cook Thanksgiving dinner, which will certainly give us all something to be thankful for."

Dr. Lerner is nodding and commenting as usual when his cell phone pings again. His gaze flickers to the phone and back. "I apologize again, Reeve. Please excuse me a moment." He picks up the phone, studies it, then glances toward the door.

She rocks forward, unsettling Bitsy. "Seriously, don't you need to answer that?"

His brow creases as he shoots another look at the door. "Not just yet."

"Are you sure?"

Reeve can't help but notice his pained expression as he sets the phone aside. She wonders if hostages have been released somewhere in Mexico or Iran, and again chides herself for not following the news.

TWO

Jefferson City, California

Otis Poe's size helps him. He sits a foot taller than any of these interlopers. One newscaster after another tries to edge him aside—here's that skinny bitch from Sacramento, that flashy dude from CNN—but no out-of-towner is going to claim his turf.

He owns this story.

Poe has been working it since the first day of the first kidnapping. He has written dozens of articles and countless blogs. These newcomers can shuffle and bump all they want, but damned if he'll give an inch.

He got here early, like he always does. He claimed a seat in the very first row. But word has leaked out. News vans are parking out front, satellite dishes are sprouting like mushrooms, and all kinds of newspeople are clamoring for a spot.

Some of them recognize him, of course. His shaved head, roughly the shape and color of baked bread, is hard to miss, especially in this small, vanilla community. A few reporters shake his hand and try to pump him for information, but he just chills. Poe has been sniffing out leads and covering news for *The Jefferson Express* for nearly seven years. He has earned his connections. And if these leeches want any news from him, they can buy a copy of the paper. Or better yet, read his blog.

The decibel level climbs as spectators crowd in and sidle along the rows of pew-like benches, wedging themselves into any available seat. The room would be plenty large for the usual press conference, but it's ill-equipped for this growing mob.

The bailiff turns away stragglers and shuts the doors. The crowd buzzes with anticipation, and Poe keeps his ears open, ready to jot down anything new as opinions are shared and rumors embellished all around him. Uniformed deputies and police officers file in and stand behind the podium, and Poe sits forward to watch a feminine officer who always reminds him of his curly-haired high school sweetheart. She looks pensive, talking with that muscle-bound FBI agent.

Poe smirks. He'd heard the FBI was back in town.

Three times Poe has watched federal agents charge up to Jefferson, hoping to be heroes. They arrive with speed and gravitas, but then slowly drift away. Because everyone knows that a child missing more than forty-eight hours is rarely saved. And Poe figures that the FBI doesn't like to wait around while days turn to weeks and months, that they don't like taking the blame for finding only decomposed remains.

Now that the story has changed, this steroid-infused agent and his buddies have made the long trek up from the Sacramento field office so they can help themselves to a big slice of glory pie.

Hypocrites.

Sheriff Mike Garcia, a stout man in cowboy boots, finally enters from a side room. Heads turn and the room quiets as the sheriff approaches the podium. Pens are poised, cameras are focused, lights glare, and the temperature rises. The sheriff adjusts his steel-rimmed glasses, bends toward the microphone, tests for sound. Television reporters cue technicians. News feeds are opened as Sheriff Garcia makes introductory remarks, acknowledging various civilians and law enforcement officers. At last, he stands tall and gets down to business, declaring, "It is my pleasure to announce to you today that thirteen-year-old Tilly Cavanaugh, who was kidnapped in October of last year, has been found alive and—"

A collective gasp surges through the room.

Louder, the sheriff continues, "Tilly Cavanaugh was rescued early yesterday from a locked basement in a residence on the outskirts of Jefferson County."

The crowd murmurs, but Otis Poe yawns. He already knows the address, a remote place west of town on Tevis Ranch Road. He drove all the way out there and was taking pictures at dawn.

"She was found alive," the sheriff is saying, "and was taken to St. Jude's Hospital, where, after a full medical examination and necessary treatment, she was declared in good enough health to be reunited with her family."

The crowd ripples with excitement. "Have you arrested someone?" a man yells, and reporters start barking questions.

"Quiet, please!" The sheriff's voice cuts through the hollering. "Hold your questions. Please let me finish." He glares from wall to wall and the crowd goes still.

"A suspect in the abduction of Tilly Cavanaugh has been arrested," he continues, and the room seems to collectively hold its breath, waiting for the name of the man they are all poised to hate.

The sheriff grips the podium. "Thirty-five-year-old Randy Vanderholt, a janitor at Three Rivers Mall, was taken into custody, and—"

"Hang him!" someone bellows.

"Shoot the pervert!" another agrees.

The sheriff scowls. "Quiet down, please. This investigation is at a preliminary stage. I'll have only limited comments today, but would like to outline some of the facts leading up to Tilly Cavanaugh's rescue."

"Please do," Otis Poe mutters under his breath. He posted this same news on his blog hours ago. Now he's on deadline, and his usual sources have come up short, so he's itching to hear something new. Ace detective work. Astute deductions. Eyewitness accounts, or perhaps overheard screams. Something dramatic.

"Will the family be speaking today?" a reporter calls out.

The sheriff ignores the question and gestures to his right, saying, "At this point, I'd like to turn the microphone over to Lieutenant Paul Stephens, who heads up the Joint Special Operations Task Force."

Poe sits forward and jots down: *Lt. Stephens, JSOTF gets the credit?*

A tall, reedy man approaches the microphone. His Adam's apple bobs up and down, but Lieutenant Stephens speaks in a deep, resonant voice: "Early yesterday morning, we received a call regarding possible evidence in a vacant house."

Poe's eyebrows rise. He has seen the house on Tevis Ranch Road him-

self, with the blinds open, the furnished interior exposed. He clicks his pen and writes: *What vacant house? A 2nd address?*

"A local real estate agent named Emily Ewing—" Lieutenant Stephens looks up and nods at a well-dressed, angular woman, who nods back "—discovered that the house had some, uh, suspicious features."

Poe sits forward, eager to absorb this new wrinkle in the case.

"Ewing learned that there was supposed to be an entrance to a basement, but it wasn't visible. So, with the owner's consent, a wall was removed, and . . ." Stephens flips to the next page, scanning past sections of the report before continuing, "and investigators discovered evidence of possible crimes having been committed. The owner subsequently confirmed that the residence had been rented for a period, but had recently been put up for sale, and he provided information about his former tenant, Randy Vanderholt."

Lieutenant Stephens clears his throat and looks up. "We located the suspect and under questioning learned that he had since moved to another residence in an unincorporated area of Jefferson County. The suspect cooperated in granting inspection of that premises, of his address on Tevis Ranch Road, where Tilly Cavanaugh was subsequently discovered alive—" the lieutenant's voice breaks slightly "—alive in a cellar under the garage."

The noise level rises and falls as Poe jots down: *Two addresses = Tilly was moved?*

Stephens continues, "The victim was thin but appeared alert. And when we asked her name, she confirmed that she was Tilly Cavanaugh."

Poe makes a note to himself to quiz his contacts at the hospital to see if he can find out more details about Tilly's physical condition, while Sheriff Garcia thanks the lieutenant and retakes the podium.

The sheriff adjusts his glasses, saying, "The suspect was arrested at the scene. Mr. Vanderholt was advised of his rights and is being held pending charges at our new county jail."

"Deluxe accommodations," someone snickers.

The sheriff ignores this jab about the outrageously expensive new jail. "The district attorney's office is preparing criminal charges, and we expect Vanderholt's arraignment will be scheduled shortly after the Thanksgiving holiday."

"Isn't it true that Vanderholt confessed?" Poe shouts.

Exclamations surge through the room.

Sheriff Garcia glowers at Poe and bends close to the microphone. "The investigation is ongoing. We can only say that we expect further charges to come from the district attorney's office next week. Now, we have time for a few brief questions."

The reporters explode with pent-up energy, waving and shouting, while Sheriff Garcia puts up his palms in a gesture more like surrender than a signal for quiet. He struggles to maintain order while handling one question after another.

But in Poe's view, the sheriff skirts past the most crucial information, recounting basic facts without sharing any juicy details. And isn't he trying to make it sound like Tilly's rescue was due to daring acts and clever police work rather than just dumb luck?

When he can't stand it any longer, Poe shouts, "How come Vanderholt wasn't found months ago? Why wasn't he questioned by law enforcement?"

Sheriff Garcia stiffens. "Every single one of the registered sex offenders in our county was interviewed. But since the suspect did not fit that category, he therefore was not previously investigated as regards this kidnapping."

"Isn't it true that Vanderholt has a criminal record?"

"It's true that the suspect was previously incarcerated for car theft." Sheriff Garcia's brow glistens under the hot lights. "But he served his time and was released from Folsom Prison more than eighteen months ago."

Spectators mutter. The reporters' questions become barbed. Garcia shifts his weight from one shiny boot to the other, denying that law enforcement botched the investigation, denying that they overlooked key evidence.

Otis Poe stands and his voice carries over the grumbling crowd: "Is there any evidence that Randy Vanderholt also kidnapped Abby Hill and Hannah Creighton?"

The mention of these other names sets a fresh wave of commotion rolling through the room.

"Yeah, what about those other missing girls?" another reporter yells. "Did you find any clues to their whereabouts?"

"Are these cases linked?" an anorexic television reporter demands, pressing a microphone toward Sheriff Garcia. "Three local girls have disappeared over the past two years. Do you suspect Vanderholt of serial kidnapping?"

The sheriff's expression darkens and he shakes his head like an old dog. "The investigation is ongoing, and as I've explained, we cannot go into any further details at this time."

With a sharp glance at Poe, he straightens. "That concludes our comments for today. The Cavanaugh family has asked me to thank everyone for the outpouring of support over the past thirteen months. They intend to make a public statement sometime next week. They are grateful to everyone involved in bringing Tilly home. And I'd particularly like to recognize the close cooperation between the FBI and Jefferson County law enforcement agencies, especially all those who . . ."

Otis Poe groans, writing: *blah, blah, blah.*

As the press conference concludes and Poe stands to leave, his bald head towering above the throng, all the out-of-town reporters start scrambling for interviews. Television personalities rally their camera crews, lick their lips, and prepare to give stand-up reports. Meanwhile, local citizens mill around, grinning at one another, murmuring words of praise, concern, and amazement.

"Unbelievable!"

"Thank heavens that child is safe!"

Several townspeople claim a special connection with the Cavanaugh case. Some have children who went to school with Tilly. Others helped with putting up "Missing!" signs.

"I helped with the search," one woman in a Harley-Davidson T-shirt declares.

"I did, too!" says a pock-faced teenager.

The businessman next to him rubs his palms together, saying, "A group of us tromped through the woods for hours and hours, but didn't find a scrap of evidence."

Backs are patted and hands are shaken as people share their stories and move toward the exits. Everyone is buzzing except for the tall man in the back who calls himself Duke. He has been standing very still, listening closely and thinking about damage control.

A white-haired woman with a cane squints up at him. "Isn't it wonderful?" she exclaims. "Now that poor little Cavanaugh girl will be able to spend Thanksgiving at home with her family."

Duke tips his head slightly. "Yes ma'am." He turns to go, exiting the double doors just behind the meddlesome woman who has ruined everything.

He's close enough that he could easily reach out and touch her. He imagines sliding his big, square hands under her shiny hair and seizing her scrawny neck. He savors the idea as they move down the wide front steps. Then the real estate agent pivots away, and he strolls along, watching as her high heels click down the sidewalk.

Duke slows to light a cigarette, keeping her in his line of sight. Half a block farther along, she lifts her keys to click open the doors of an amber-colored Lexus. He watches her climb in and fasten her seatbelt. As the engine turns over and she backs out, he makes a mental note of the license plate number, then turns and heads toward his SUV.

He climbs behind the wheel, sparks the ignition, cracks a window, checks his mirrors, and pulls into traffic. Heavy gray clouds are threatening rain. But as he heads toward home, he isn't thinking about the weather. Instead, he's wondering how to deal with Randy Vanderholt, now that the fool has gotten himself arrested. And he's worrying about the secrets that sweet little Tilly might spill.

THREE

San Francisco

Now, your father has a new love interest," Dr. Lerner says slowly, "and you said your sister and her husband will be there for Thanksgiving."

Reeve sits on the sofa, stroking the little dog's head, sensing that her psychiatrist is about to shift from safer topics to more tender areas. "But that's not a problem anymore," she tells him. "My sister has become super-mom. She's way too involved with her family to worry about me."

"Oh?"

"Really. *No problemo.* And the baby is so cute, he's like a gurgling am-bassador for world peace."

"So you're feeling more comfortable than last year?"

She rolls her eyes. "They're still going to bug me about the usual stuff, when I'm getting a boyfriend, all that. It's unavoidable." A shift in posture unsettles Bitsy, who moves away and begins licking a paw. Annoyed, Reeve continues, "But who cares? You said yourself that having a romantic in-volvement is not necessarily an indication of improvement and that I shouldn't rush into some kind of relationship just to prove to myself that I can, right?"

She knows he has heard the strained way she has paraphrased him, and expects him to respond, but when he doesn't, she gives a shrug and admits, "Okay, so I'm defensive."

"This is an emotionally charged issue for you. That's more than under-standable."

"Right."

"And there are good reasons for you to feel defensive."

"Exactly." She thinks about her scars and feels the heat flushing up her neck. "Besides, who's to say that the 'normal' male/female relationship will work for me, anyway? I know everyone talks about having a healthy sex life, but even on the off chance that I met someone I liked, and even if he liked me, how could I even begin to try to explain everything? So, what's wrong with being asexual? It's so much simpler."

"There's nothing wrong with remaining celibate if that's your choice, but what you just said is contradictory, isn't it?"

Her eyes narrow. "What do you mean?"

"On the one hand, you're expressing a desire for connection, and on the other, you're saying you want to remain asexual because it's too hard to work out a relationship. Do you see that contradiction?"

She fidgets, kneading the numb patch on her left hand. "Okay, so what's wrong with that?"

"If it makes you frustrated or angry—"

"Then I have unresolved feelings," she says curtly. "Yeah, I know."

Bitsy shakes herself, jumps to the floor, and crosses the room to curl up beside Dr. Lerner while Reeve frowns at her.

"Listen, you have worked very hard to overcome a traumatic past and reclaim your life," Dr. Lerner says smoothly. "You can take pride in that, and you don't need to be angry with yourself. There is no timeline."

Reeve places her fingertips against her temples, pressing hard, as if trying to force her thoughts into place.

"But you are the one who is having difficulty connecting with others," he continues, "and you are the one judging yourself for it, don't you see?"

"Okay, but the thing is," she takes a breath and says carefully, "I've been reading some of your studies."

"You have." He says this as a statement, as if he knew it all along.

"The one last month in the *American Journal of Forensic Psychology*, for instance."

"And?"

"And I think I've found myself in there."

He sighs. "Reeve, we've talked about this. You know I wouldn't write about you without your permission. My articles are based on other cases."

"Well, but anyway, I recognized myself, okay?"

"How do you mean?"

"In the part about being hypercontrolled. About being 'locked in a phase of arrested recovery.'"

"Is that what you think?"

She gives a small shrug. "Don't you?"

"Reeve, listen. That article is about a completely different situation, about a young woman who was imprisoned by her father. You were both young, you both suffered. But incest and sadism have very different psychic impacts."

"I know all that."

He's watching her, and she knows that he understands what she doesn't need to say: that even after all these years, even knowing that she is safe in San Francisco while Daryl Wayne Flint is incarcerated far away, the dark years of her captivity still linger like a bad taste. "Intellectually, I know it," she says, glancing around at the Persian rug, the framed art.

When her gaze settles back on Dr. Lerner, he leans toward her, saying, "Reeve, I know you read the studies, and I commend you for wanting to understand more about the long-term psychological effects of captivity." His voice is soft but heavy with emphasis. "But not everything in the literature applies to you."

She makes a face. "The curse of being self-absorbed."

He sits quietly, watching her.

"Okay. I know. I can't assume that every article on these subjects has bearing on my individual situation," she says, parroting his jargon. "But I just want to stop feeling like I have this ugly part of myself that no one can possibly understand. I want to have a normal life and be a normal adult." She glances at him and then looks away. "I know you don't like that word, but you know what I mean."

"Reeve, you *are* normal. But you've survived a uniquely traumatic situation. That's no small thing, and it's understandable if you're still having trouble adjusting, or if you're uncomfortable with men, or—"

"I'm comfortable with you."

"So give yourself some credit. And relax. Because you're still young, and you can't let your desire for self-protection preclude you from having any new relationships for the rest of your life."

"Why not?"

An elastic silence stretches between them. She knows this was a flip question, and that he is waiting for her to come up with her own answer. But she holds her breath, settles back on the sofa, and stubbornly says nothing.

He taps his chin with his thumb, studying her. "Okay, here's your homework," he says, as he often does when their session concludes. "Think about your own personal definition of a comfortable relationship: friend or romance, asexual or bisexual or whatever. Nothing is off-limits. And if you don't want to share the exact details with me, that's fine. Consider it private, and consider that you are in absolute control. But give yourself permission to at least think about making a true, intimate connection with someone, even if you're only fantasizing about it at this point. How's that?"

"An intimate connection?"

"Correct."

"Just try to imagine it, is all?"

He cocks an eyebrow.

"Okay, I guess that's nonthreatening enough." She looks down and sees that she has crossed her arms and legs. "I only look defensive. I'm actually a little chilled."

Smiling, he nods once in punctuation. "Good. I'll see you next week. And I hope you have a very nice Thanksgiving."

"You, too."

They're on their feet and moving toward the door when Dr. Lerner says, "Oh, have you given any more thought to getting a cat or a dog?"

"I know you think it would be therapeutic, but I don't need a cat or a dog. I have Persephone."

His lips compress wryly. "And how is the lovely Persephone?"

"She's therapeutic."

He chuckles and opens the door.

The moment they step into the hall, the receptionist hurries toward them, clasping her hands in front of her as if in prayer. "Excuse me, doctor," she says, "but you have an unscheduled visitor."

As the three come into the waiting room, a man wearing a crimped expression and a dark suit rises. "Dr. Lerner? I'm sorry to intrude on your schedule."

"You're here about Jefferson County?" Dr. Lerner steps forward to shake the man's hand.

"I'm sorry to barge in on you like this."

Dr. Lerner's voice drops to a low, serious tone while Reeve dawdles near the receptionist's desk, straining to hear. She retrieves the key to the restroom from its place in a floral dish, stalling, but can't make out more of the men's conversation. At the door, she turns to glimpse them disappearing into Dr. Lerner's office.

Out in the hallway, she passes Dr. Lerner's usual 10:30 appointment, a redheaded teen with fantastic freckles whose name, of course, she doesn't know.

When she returns from the restroom, the redhead is gone, and Reeve notices that the receptionist's face is clouded with a strange expression. Her Cupid's-bow mouth is a straight line. And as Reeve sets the key back in the dish, the receptionist looks up at her and says, "I'm terribly sorry, Miss LeClaire, but Dr. Lerner has to cancel all of next week's appointments."

Reeve blinks at her, realizing that this is the first time the receptionist has ever spoken her name.

FOUR

Jefferson City

By the time Duke turns toward home, he has already dealt with the first order of business. He has bought a new cell phone and transferred all the necessary phone numbers. He has dropped the new phone into the pocket of his leather jacket and placed the old phone in the colorful plastic bag with the new phone's packaging and receipt.

Now he is headed south. He turns off the old highway and drives parallel to the railroad tracks for a ways, then turns east toward the river, then right on Riverside Drive. For the first few miles, tidy houses are crowded behind manicured lawns, but the subdivision gradually exhausts itself, and then the road narrows. The few remaining houses squat on untamed lots of thick brush, old oaks, and tall pines. Street signs are pocked with bullet holes. Fences are thirsty for paint. Neighbors are scarce and make a habit of minding their own business.

Duke turns his Chevy Tahoe off the road and presses the remote control clipped to the visor. The heavy wooden gate rolls open and his SUV bumps along the uneven driveway. At the far side of the twelve-acre lot sprawls the ranch-style house that he inherited from his parents. It's riverfront property, so one problem is that there is no basement, but Duke prides himself on being resourceful.

He parks in the carport next to his van and climbs out, carrying the plastic shopping bag with him. He never leaves trash in his vehicle.

He climbs the steps at the side of the house, unlocks the deadbolt, and enters through the mudroom. The house is just as cold as outdoors so he does not remove his leather jacket as he heads straight through to the control room in back, where he unlocks a second deadbolt. He enters a wide room that has both a workout area with dust-free exercise apparatus and an office area with top-notch computers and displays, all humming like NASA.

He crosses the room to a metal file cabinet, unlocks it, and quickly finds the file he wants in the second drawer. He locks the cabinet back up, pockets his keys, and opens the file. Barely glancing at the pages, he plucks out a ziplock bag holding a silver flash drive, and slips it into the colorful shopping bag with his old cell phone. He then walks out of the room and down the hall, his boots striking heavily on the hardwood floors.

The living room has a brick fireplace with a wide hearth, where he sets the file and the plastic bag. Duke has been building fires since he was a boy. He opens the screen, selects kindling and firewood from the stack next to the firebox, and expertly arranges the paper, the kindling, and the logs. He strikes a match and watches while the fire flickers and grows. He waits until it is burning in earnest before adding the cell phone's receipt and paperwork to the flame.

After closing the screen, he carries the plastic shopping bag back through the house, through the kitchen, through the mudroom, and out the side door.

Clouds darken the sky as he walks back to his Chevy Tahoe and sets the plastic bag on the concrete behind the front wheel. Then he climbs inside, starts up the engine, and backs over it. The splintering cell phone doesn't even register under the treads.

Back inside the house, he checks that the SIM card is demolished before emptying the contents of the bag into the kitchen trash, where the synthetic debris disappears into a mix of cold coffee grounds and greasy chicken bones. Satisfied, Duke turns his attention to the next problem: Randy Vanderholt.

Vander-dolt had lied the whole time he was moving Tilly from one house to the other. He pretended he was being hypervigilant, claiming that he was scrubbing and cleaning, and that, as a final precaution, he was tearing out the funky basement paneling and replacing it with fresh drywall. He explained that he was painting everything, all of the interior walls, so that the freshly painted basement wouldn't stand out.

Instead, Vander-dolt took shortcuts. His cleaning had been minimal. And rather than gutting the basement, he'd decided to simply wall up the entrance.

Something only a moron would do.

This is the risk of working with someone like Vanderholt. Stupid people are generally easy to control, but they create problems when they try to be clever. Sure, Vanderholt had successfully moved Tilly from one basement to the other, but he was inexcusably sloppy. He left evidence behind. And worse, he blatantly and repeatedly lied to the one person he should never, ever offend.

Fool.

Duke's stomach growls, making a sound that approximates his mood. He stomps over to the fridge and rummages around until he has the makings of a sandwich. He slathers a mound of ham with horseradish and crushed garlic, adds slices of pepperjack cheese, then squashes it all between two slabs of bread. He eats over the sink while mulling his options.

The problem is that Vander-dolt is now behind bars, putting him in a position to cause even more damage. Because any cop with an ounce of brains will see that Randy Vanderholt has the IQ of a toaster. And then it's a short leap to figuring out that the moron had some help.

Clearly, the first order of business is to get to the dolt before some smart cop convinces him to start talking. That won't be easy, but Duke knows plenty of easily manipulated people in and around the jail. Guards. Inmates. He can pull some strings.

He recalls a recent conversation with an impressionable cousin—a longtime guard at the jail—and his mouth twitches a smile. Pedophiles are known to suffer all kinds of trouble behind bars. No one will be surprised if Randy Vanderholt bleeds.

The girl, however, poses a more difficult problem.

FIVE

The closer Dr. Ezra Lerner gets to Jefferson City, the worse the weather gets. Winds slap his Cessna Skyhawk about like a toy. He grinds his teeth and tightens his grip on the controls, keeping a sharp eye on his instruments.

He knew it was going to be like this, but he prefers to fly his own plane whenever he can, especially when called to places like Jefferson, places that have few commercial flights, places where the only other option would be hours of driving up a long stretch of freeway. Still, he could use a break. He glances at his untouched thermos, craving a quick dose of caffeine, but the plane lurches, buffeted by northeast winds, and he decides not to risk it.

Nearly there. He has flown to Jefferson before, and the landing pattern is clear in his mind. He radios the tower and watches his altitude.

The wind slackens as the plane descends into a layer of heavy, wet clouds. He's flying blind. The Cessna handles well, but he's relieved when he finally slips beneath the cloud cover at thirty-two hundred feet. Now he has a clear view. The river winds through the valley like a fat green snake. The airstrip appears below, rimmed by a horseshoe of snowy mountains that disappear into the clouds.

Dr. Lerner angles his Cessna toward the landing strip. With a practiced hand, he makes his turns, gliding lower, lower, making minor corrections as gusts strike the plane, lining up with the runway, settling into final approach.

This transition from air to land, from bird to vehicle, always gives him a visceral thrill. He adjusts the flaps, cuts speed, and straightens up, ready for the wheels to set down with a satisfying thump. A strong gust lifts and tilts the plane. He corrects, regains the center line, and abruptly drops down. The right wheel grips the runway, the left snaps down, and then gravity pulls tight and the Cessna shudders down the runway, shedding speed.

The plane eases almost to a stop at the end, and then Dr. Lerner turns and wheels slowly toward a cluster of buildings. He maneuvers down a lane and tucks the Cessna into a slot designated for visitor aircraft, where he shuts down the engine.

After making the appropriate notes in his flight log, he opens the cockpit and climbs out. He walks around, double-checking everything and securing the tail before grabbing his bag and heading across the tarmac toward a weathered building with a wall of windows.

A stocky, severe-looking woman in a raincoat and shiny boots comes out into the cold to greet him. She introduces herself as Jefferson County Deputy District Attorney Jackie Burke. Dr. Lerner shakes her hand, and they tip their heads together, conferring briefly before coming inside.

Only two men are waiting in the lounge, but Dr. Lerner would have spotted Gordon Cavanaugh in a room full of white, middle-aged fathers. He sits hunched over his coffee, wearing an expression that Dr. Lerner has seen many times: a mixture of shock, relief, and exhaustion.

Burke introduces Tilly Cavanaugh's father, who looks up at Dr. Lerner but says nothing. The man sitting next to him, a uniformed, athletic-looking young man, stands.

"This is Deputy Hudson," Burke says. "He's working closely with the district attorney's office on this case. I'll make sure he has the relevant files ready when you come by my office later. In the meantime, he'll be helping with logistics."

"Consider me your liaison with the DA's office," the young deputy says, gripping the doctor's hand in a friendly shake. "I'll be your driver and personal guide. Just call me for anything you might need while you're here."

Dr. Lerner thanks him, turns to Mr. Cavanaugh, and says, "If you two don't mind, I'd like to speak with Mr. Cavanaugh privately for a few minutes."

The pair nod and head toward the hallway leading toward the front entry while Dr. Lerner steps over to a coffee pot on a corner table. By the time he pours himself a cup and turns around, he and Mr. Cavanaugh have the lounge to themselves.

"My wife is at home with Tilly," Mr. Cavanaugh volunteers, staring down at the cup bracketed in his hands.

"That's good. It's good for both of them, I think." Dr. Lerner sips his coffee and waits.

Cavanaugh gives the doctor a long, appraising look. His eyes are weary and blue-gray. "Jackie Burke is a good attorney, and she says that you're the best there is at this sort of thing. That you've helped a lot of kidnapped kids. That you helped Beth Goodwin. And that other girl, too, Reggie LeClaire."

"That's right, those and others." Dr. Lerner holds Cavanaughs' gaze and speaks slowly. "Survivors of prolonged captivity are rare, so there aren't many in my profession who specialize in their treatment."

Cavanaugh snorts. "I found that out. Just so you know, my wife isn't crazy about having a male shrink in our house, treating our daughter."

"That's understandable. I'll do my best to respect your concerns. We'll take it slow and see how it goes."

A pause, an exhalation. "I guess that's all we can do."

"You've been through a lot. And now that you have Tilly home again, there's a lot of healing ahead of you. So we'll proceed at a pace that will allow you all to feel comfortable."

"Well." Cavanaugh glances away and then back again. "Okay."

"Good," Dr. Lerner says with a nod of encouragement. "You're acting very quickly to address Tilly's emotional well-being. I commend you for that. Not all parents are so enlightened in these circumstances."

Cavanaugh's eyes settle back on him. "So what happens now?"

"I'd like to meet your family—your wife and your daughter and your son, too—and then we can talk again privately and decide on the next step. And I assure you that everything you say will be considered confidential unless you indicate otherwise. How's that?"

"Yeah, okay. That sounds about right."

"Good. So tell me, how's Tilly doing?"

"It's hard to say. She's quiet. A bit jumpy, a little clingy, I think. She seems healthy enough, but thin, you know."

"She has been treated by a medical doctor?"

"At the hospital. The doctors there examined her, of course, and gave her some pills. But they're not, like, specialists or anything."

"Did they give you a diagnosis?"

"They said she's malnourished, and she has some minor injuries. Burns," Cavanaugh says, wincing. "They think she's probably suffering from post-traumatic shock, you know. But Tilly doesn't say much, and she doesn't seem to want to leave the house." He frowns at Dr. Lerner, adding, "That's to be expected, I guess."

"It is, sure. With your permission, I'll contact the hospital and check her records. In the meantime, you're just beginning the first phase of what may be a long healing process, for Tilly and for your whole family."

"Yeah, I get that."

"It's best if you don't press her for details. Let her volunteer things at her own pace, and don't let the legal process dictate that. She'll talk more as she feels more secure. For now, Tilly needs to be assured of your unconditional love and support."

"We went on that Web site—the National Center for Missing and Exploited Children?—and it had some good advice there."

"Excellent. Glad to hear it."

Dr. Lerner notes that Gordon Cavanaugh is sitting up taller, with his shoulders less hunched. As if by mutual agreement, they simultaneously raise their coffee cups and drink, a mirror image, men of equal stature facing each other across a table.

"There's something else, though," Cavanaugh says, setting down his cup.

"What's that?"

"I warned you that my wife has some issues."

"Yes?"

"She thinks Tilly might have a problem with you."

Dr. Lerner nods thoughtfully. "Because I'm a man, and Tilly was victimized and abused by a man, right?"

"Right."

"I understand. That's a legitimate concern, and I'm glad that you're empathizing with your daughter. But in my experience, it doesn't take long to overcome that hurdle. And of course it's important that you and your son will also be contributing to Tilly's healing process, so that she can again feel safe, so that she can feel that there are men in her life whom she can genuinely trust."

"Yeah, but there's more."

"What's that?"

"My wife . . ." Gordon Cavanaugh shifts uncomfortably in his seat.

Dr. Lerner watches him, saying nothing.

Cavanaugh clears his throat and starts again: "My wife wants reassurances."

"What kind of reassurances?"

"Well, you see . . ." He shifts again in his seat. "Well, I don't mean to question your credentials, doctor. I mean, you're clearly an expert, and the DA and the sheriff have checked you out, and what they've said is good enough for me. But my wife, well, she's protective, you know?"

"Very understandable, yes." Dr. Lerner waits a beat, then coaxes, "What kinds of reassurances can I give Mrs. Cavanaugh to help her feel more comfortable?"

"Well, the thing is, she wants to talk to one of those other girls that you helped."

SIX

San Francisco

Reeve is feeding Persephone when she misses Dr. Lerner's call. She drops in a live cricket, saying, "Enjoy your dinner, kiddo," then squats to eye level, watching through the glass.

Persephone lives in a terrarium that the guy at the exotic pet store calls "Persie's Resort." It has sand, rocks, and cactus-type plants that mimic the Mexican terrain of her origins.

Reeve had weighed the ethics of keeping Persephone for weeks before making up her mind. Dr. Lerner kept suggesting a pet, but how could she justify keeping a dog or cat cooped up in an apartment? A rodent or reptile was out of the question. And keeping any kind of bird locked in a cage seemed beyond cruel; it was criminal.

But she'd had a spider before. Nothing fancy, but it had been her sole company. And Anthony, the young guy with the tattoos who owned the pet store, had repeatedly assured Reeve that Persie had been born in captivity.

"She's not imprisoned," Anthony told her. "She's pampered and secure. She's fed. She has no predators. And she's living in the only habitat she has ever known."

Once Reeve had made up her mind to buy the Mexican red-kneed tarantula, she'd quizzed the shopkeeper about every aspect of her care and feeding, making certain that she understood everything.

Anthony maintained that Mexican red-knees are not social. "So it's not like she'll be lonely or anything," he said, pulling his earring and smiling at her. "See? She likes these nooks and crannies, where she can hide. She's a beauty, right? And she doesn't need much room."

Still, Reeve had insisted on upgrading to the largest terrarium in the store. It's a warm, well-conceived environment that rests on a low cabinet, and Persie seems content. She is a handsome, private creature who is finicky about her hiding places. Most often, she nests under one particular outcropping of flat rocks that Reeve carefully constructed in the southwest corner.

Persie stealthily creeps from the dark nook, darts out, and seizes the cricket.

Reeve watches Persie for awhile, then realizes that she, too, is hungry. She usually eats at the restaurant, but not today, with all that was going on. She goes into the kitchen and fixes a large cup of hot chocolate. Whole milk. European chocolate. The good stuff.

Pleasantly tired, she settles on the sofa and lets her mind drift. Which leads, inevitably, to the subject of sex.

Sex is a curiosity to her. She knows more than enough about its mechanics, but cannot fathom its intimacies. Being raped is not the same thing as making love. Clearly. But she has no experience of the latter, and has had plenty of the former. Repeated and brutal. Inventive only in the ways to cause pain.

She tries not to think too much about it. Still, no one wants to remain sexless, whatever their affliction.

She has experimented enough to know that she's capable of achieving orgasm. But when she tries to imagine approaching someone sexually, tries to conjure up a desire for physical intimacy with some particular individual, the idea makes her cringe. Which, she believes, is just one more thing that makes her a freak. And is surely the reason behind the homework Dr. Lerner has assigned.

Sexual intimacy would inevitably present two major problems: nudity and a locked door. Her worst fears.

She knows that, as a twenty-two-year-old American female, she is abnormal. Because, despite all the salacious media chatter about her demographic's wild behavior, Reeve has had sexual encounters with only three people, and only two as a consenting adult.

Neither was particularly satisfying. The first was a brief experiment with a boy in her driver's education class. She was eighteen, he was seventeen, and she was self-aware enough to realize that the small difference in those digits put her in the dominant role. Whatever the ethics involved, it was all tremendously stimulating to him, and premature ejaculation was a problem the first time. By the third time, the driver's ed class was over, and Reeve had lost interest.

The second relationship, if she thinks of it that way, was with a lithe young woman named Tasha whom she'd met at a New Year's Eve party. Reeve had never thought of herself as a lesbian, but she and Tasha had surprised each other with a kiss at midnight that led to a brief, heated encounter. She was astonished by Tasha's tenderness, having never been touched that way before.

In both of those encounters, Reeve managed to avoid being naked in a locked room. She and the teenager had grappled in the back seat of his car, which required minimal clothing removal. And she and Tasha had connected once, in a stairwell, almost fully clothed.

Reeve sits on the sofa, finishing her hot chocolate, remembering details, thinking about attraction and repulsion. Sex and fear fight in her skull like the polarized ends of magnets.

Maybe she can't have intimacy in the same way as normal people. Certainly she can't change the scars on her skin. But she should be able to control her fear. Because fear is paralyzing, pointless, and a stupid waste of emotion.

Her stomach gives a mild grumble, nagging her that she's still hungry.

There's not much in the kitchen, but she eventually comes up with a frozen burrito. She turns on the oven, which she prefers to the microwave, finds a metal pie pan in the cupboard, and places the burrito in the oven to heat.

"Who needs to eat sushi every day, anyway?" she mutters, her own voice sounding cheerless and unconvincing in the empty apartment.

She finds the remote control, clicks on the TV, and is heading back to the kitchen when a television announcer says, "—more about the rescue of a Jefferson County girl who was kidnapped and held captive in a locked basement for thirteen months!"

Reeve's muscles go slack. She turns toward the screen and folds onto the floor, hit by the cold certainty that this is why Dr. Lerner cancelled next week's appointment.

The news features a mug shot of the man who was arrested, a clip of the Jefferson County sheriff giving a press conference, followed by photographs of a pretty girl named Tilly Cavanaugh, and lurching videotape of the gloomy basement where the girl was found.

Each detail is like a knife.

The news pauses for commercials and Reeve turns off the TV, but images keep running through her head. Dark walls, locked doors, metal handcuffs. Swollen, purple bruises. Blunt hands holding sharp objects. Police. Glaring hospital rooms and dismal courtrooms.

She knows what's coming: the rabid news reporters with their relentless questions, the psycho-pundits rehashing old cases. They'll search for similarities, begin making comparisons, and she'll hear herself discussed and evaluated along with this new victim.

Something oily turns in her stomach.

They'll show pictures of Edgy Reggie knocking her fist against the camera lens. They'll show Daryl Wayne Flint, the celebrity kidnapper, acting crazy in the courtroom. Perfectly groomed newscasters sitting in well-lit studios will discuss the trial, pick over the details of her abuse, and speculate about the psychological effects of years of darkness and boredom and unending terror.

Reeve begins to hyperventilate. This isn't healthy. She needs to do something.

She looks out the window and sees that it's raining.

Never mind. She needs to go for a run.

She changes into her gear, puts on a waterproof jacket, and is tying the laces of her sneakers when she starts to sweat. Something sour rises in her throat. She jerks upright, dashes to the bathroom, and barely reaches the toilet before she starts to vomit. Once, twice, three times and her stomach empties. She rests, trembling, but soon the retching begins again, and she's powerless to stop. The heaving continues, over and over, until she slumps to the floor, exhausted.

Her stomach is tender and her muscles weak. She slowly sits up, catching her breath, fighting the spinning residue of sickness. She finds a tissue and is wiping the dampness from her mouth when she's jolted by a sudden noise: the burrito burning in the oven has set the smoke alarm screaming.

SEVEN

San Francisco
Wednesday Before Thanksgiving

Fog horns. One is harsh, the other is smoother, more distant. Reeve climbs out of bed, exhaustion clinging to her like sweat. She crosses the room to the window, feeling as if she is dragging hours of the sleepless night with her, and opens the blinds to a view so thickly fogged that even the Ferry Building is swallowed in white.

A flash of nightmare sends a chill shooting up her spine. She shivers, forcing Daryl Wayne Flint out of her mind, and grabs a robe that she draws tight.

She pads into the kitchen to make hot chocolate. Standing barefoot on the cold tile while the milk heats, she considers what to wear to work, then her mind strays to the next day's holiday, the coming onslaught of food and family. She dreads how Thanksgiving Day will play out. They will be falsely cheerful, tiptoeing around the news, wary of her mood.

Her cell phone rings. Her father. She ignores it, lets it go to voice mail, and a second later notices that Dr. Lerner called last night, as well. Twice.

Her fingers hesitate over the keypad while she fights a gnawing sense of obligation, then she sets the phone aside, resolving not to call anyone until she's utterly, thoroughly calm.

It's bad enough that Daryl Wayne Flint has returned to invade her thoughts. Like a ghost, always hovering behind her, muttering over her shoulder, slipping through the cracks into her dreams. She rubs at her hand, resenting that he is etched into her skin, that he is lodged in the numbness that stitches down her left wrist and through her little finger. Shouldn't she have moved past all this by now, after all these years, regardless of the news?

The news.

The television screen is a black hole that pulls her toward it. The remote waits on the coffee table, a numbered challenge. She hesitates, picks it up, holds her breath, and clicks on the morning news.

She's just settling down to watch when her cell phone rings again. Seeing Dr. Lerner's number, she answers with a curt, "Hello."

"Hello, Reeve, how are you doing?"

"You know how I'm doing."

"I can guess that you're upset."

She makes a nasal, unhappy sound.

"Any flashbacks? Nightmares?"

She sidesteps the question. "I'm singing songs, drinking piña coladas."

"You're angry?"

"Just pissed. At the media. At everyone."

"At me? I'm sorry I had to cancel next week's appointment. I hope you'll understand that I'm up here with—"

"With the girl and her family. Of course. I know they need your help."

"You understand that better than anyone."

"Yes, I do."

"But you're angry because . . ."

"It's just that the whole damn media machine is gearing up. And you can see what's coming." She inhales deeply and it all comes out in a rush: "All those talking heads, who have no right to be pontificating, who can hardly pronounce captivity syndrome, who haven't spent five minutes trying to understand a damn thing about what abduction really means, are already all over the news—" she is hit by a wave of anger "—reading off names of victims and their captors like some sick shopping list. Like we're celebrities with no privacy. While all those caged monsters are salivating in their cells, getting off on the fact that their sick psycho-brothers are out here roaming the streets and doing their disgusting, twisted, evil shit."

Her speech becomes faster, her voice shriller: "And they're already showing my old photos on the air and making comparisons and talking talking talking so that I'm back in the news and everything is back in the news and now I'm having to confront all those images and those memories of Daryl Wayne Flint all over again!"

There's a long moment of silence. Her eyes are wet and she flushes hot with embarrassment.

"Wow," he says. "That was good."

"Ha-ha," she says flatly.

"I mean it. Did you hear the fury in your voice?"

"Yeah, I know, I'm sorry," she says, wincing.

"But that's good. I mean, it wouldn't be good on a regular basis, but today it's completely justified."

"Well, I kinda lost it," she grumbles.

"Don't you remember how you were at first? That loss of affect?"

She swallows. She does remember. After being rescued from the trunk of Flint's wrecked car, life had unfolded in slow motion. The safety of being home, even the embraces from her family, had left her feeling disoriented. She'd emerged into a world that felt like an alien planet. No one spoke her language. Not a soul could understand.

"Do you remember?" Dr. Lerner asks again.

She had been raped, beaten, burned, whipped, starved, and nearly drowned. She had thought she would die. She had wished it. And when it was over, she had felt aberrant, as if something vitally human inside her had been crushed. "I was like a zombie. You said I had a flat affect."

"That's right. Nothing elicited much more than a shrug."

"I remember."

"Well, Tilly Cavanaugh is in a similar state now."

"She's in shock."

"You can think of it that way, yes."

"Post-traumatic shock."

"Absolutely, for starters, that's correct."

"Okay." Her breathing is under control now, and she sits on a kitchen stool with her elbows on the counter. "So, what exactly are you saying?"

"Just listen to yourself, Reeve. That anger you feel is understandable and healthy. It shows how strong you've become."

She says nothing. She remembers lying to him about the nightmares and decides it's time to end this conversation. She tells him she needs to go, but Dr. Lerner asks for one more minute.

"I know it's an imposition," he says, "but Tilly Cavanaugh's mother would like to speak with you."

"What for?"

"She would like some personal reassurance about my treating her daughter. And, well, she hopes you'll be honest about your own experience."

"That's weird. You mean like a reference?"

"Well, perhaps more like a mother-to-daughter-type talk. Do you see? Because you and Tilly suffered something similar? It's just that Mrs. Cavanaugh would like to speak with you directly, to help her feel more comfortable about having me oversee Tilly's care."

Reeve is speechless. Dr. Lerner's expertise seems self-evident, and the idea that she should have influence over someone else's treatment strikes her as bizarre.

"Remember how Beth Goodwin helped with your recovery?" he prods.

"Sure, she was like . . ." The memory rinses over her. "It sounds corny, but I always think she was like an angel or something."

"Yes, she was generous with her time, perhaps partly because your parents asked for her help. So can't you understand why Mrs. Cavanaugh might ask the same of you?"

"But I'm not . . . Why doesn't she ask Beth?"

"Her case was quite different, as you know, as well as more remote in time. So they're asking to speak with you."

"But I can't—"

"You don't need to decide right now. Just think about it, okay? Mull it over, enjoy a nice Thanksgiving with your family, and we'll talk again soon."

Reeve groans softly. This is classic Dr. Lerner. Somehow, he always manages to turn her arguments inside out.

His gentle voice continues, "I know it's asking a lot, but please just consider that these parents are struggling just as yours did six years ago."

"But how could anything I—"

"Just think about what you might want to say, and we'll talk when you're ready. How's that?"

EIGHT

At police headquarters Wednesday morning, the man who calls himself Duke strides down the long hallway toward the door marked "SURVEIL-LANCE," followed by a man nearly alike in coloring and stature, but younger, trimmer, with more spring in his step, more color in his face, more mischief in his eyes.

Duke turns into his office and has nearly shed his coat when the younger officer grips the door frame and swings in after him. Wearing an eager grin, Officer Tomas Montoya practically bounces on the balls of his feet as he asks, "Did you hear the news?"

Duke settles into his chair before responding. He always assumes the same jocular tone when dealing with Montoya, and it takes a second for him to slip into character. "Let me guess," he says with a leer, "you got laid?"

"That's not news," Montoya scoffs. "That's a daily occurrence. But this is news. Big news. About Randy Vanderholt."

Duke cocks an expectant eyebrow.

Montoya's frame fills the doorway. "You know, that pedophile, the one that kidnapped the Cavanaugh girl?"

"I know who he is, Montoya." Duke rolls his eyes to keep the anticipation from showing on his face. "What about him?"

"He hung himself!" Montoya sounds gleeful.

"No shit?"

"Yep, they found him this morning."

"Well, that didn't take long, did it?" Duke sits back in his leather chair and allows a smile. He can always count on Montoya, who works with him on various task forces, to stop by with the latest gossip. The guy's as chatty as a teen on Twitter. And this news is precisely what Duke has been waiting to hear.

"The perv did it early this morning, before breakfast," Montoya continues.

Duke leans back, stretches out his legs. "Really. How?"

"They're saying he knotted the legs of his jumpsuit together."

Another colleague, a petite brunette named Kim Benioff, comes in the door, nudging Montoya aside. Having overheard, she joins the conversation, saying, "Yeah, too bad Vanderholt didn't do a better job of it, eh?"

Duke's smile falters. "What do you mean?"

"He's not dead," says Montoya.

"Unfortunately," confirms Benioff.

"Close, but no cigar," Montoya says, crossing his arms over his chest.

"The guards found him just in time," says Benioff.

"Yeah, did their damn duty, brought him down," Montoya says.

"Got him breathing again," she says.

"Took him to the infirmary," he says.

"Now he's on suicide watch," she says, shaking her head.

"They should have let him hang. Done us all a favor."

"Yeah." Benioff grins. "Could have saved us the cost of a trial."

Montoya grins back. "Not to mention housing and feeding the asshole."

"The lousy, child-abusing asshole," she echoes.

With that, their banter loses steam. The two officers standing in the doorway stop smiling and remark that they need to get back to work. As quickly as they appeared, they head off in search of someone else who hasn't yet heard the news, leaving Duke to fume in silence.

Suicide watch will only make Vanderholt harder to reach.

He grabs his jacket and stomps outside where he can smoke alone and calculate the damage.

NINE

Reeve dips a polite bow at the sushi chef, who is intently sharpening one of his impressive knives. She pauses to study his technique, but moves on when Takami-san, the meticulous matriarch and owner, emerges from her office. Takami-san is a quiet, petite woman who somehow seems larger than anyone else in the restaurant.

Reeve bows with appropriate formality as she heads down the hallway to stash her things in the break room, a claustrophobic, rectangular space barely larger than a closet. She ties her hair back with a bright, clean Japanese scarf and checks her reflection. Satisfied, she crams her oversized bag into a locker, clicks it shut, locks it, and exits the break room, nearly colliding with Takami-san's teenage daughter. Reeve mumbles an apology and starts to ask about UCLA, but Keiko just blinks at her and hurries away.

What's this about? Takami-san told Reeve last week that she did not expect her daughter to be coming home for Thanksgiving. Reeve pauses, wondering about this, unconsciously massaging her left hand.

But she needs to get busy, so she starts preparing tables, setting out napkins and chopsticks, and has only a brief moment to survey her work before Takami-san unlocks the front door. The lunchtime crowd begins pouring in, filling the seats at the sushi bar and at the tables. There's a noisy, festive air, and the sushi chef's hands are a blur of artful slicing.

Out of habit, Reeve keeps watch on the three exits while she serves up steaming bowls of udon and beautifully prepared plates of sashimi. She can identify every regular customer, every new face. She remains alert for strange behavior, and keeps a sharp eye on any unkempt men, who are thankfully rare.

Reeve calls out orders for *unagi bento* and *toro maki* in perfect Japanese, and customers talk and laugh and order more. Today's crowds seem intent on satisfying their cravings for rare types of Japanese food, perhaps dreading the coming menus of turkey and more turkey.

In the midst of the lunchtime rush, while taking orders and carrying trays and refilling cups of green tea, Reeve is pleased that Takami-san's daughter is here with an extra set of hands. Still, she notices that Keiko does not look at her and does not smile.

At last, the orders dwindle. The restaurant quiets and feels cooler. Takami-san and her daughter head toward the back office, talking. The sushi chef prepares for the evening shift, honing and replacing his sharp knives. And while the final two customers linger over their desserts, Reeve begins the routine of refilling bottles of soy sauce and freshening tables.

She's not really listening to the couple's conversation, but overhears the word "kidnapping" and freezes. She tries not to eavesdrop, but their voices carry, loud as newscasters, and details start flooding through her. She shuts her eyes and sees the concrete walls. A siren wails in the distance and Daryl Wayne Flint's whiskers brush the back of her neck. She shivers, the siren grows louder, closer, and as the ambulance screams past she's back in the trunk of Flint's car, dizzy and spinning, noise slamming into her like blasts of heat, like physical blows that knock the bottle of soy sauce from the slippery fingers of her weak hand.

The glass bottle throws an arc of dark liquid as it drops, shattering on the floor.

Reeve stares, rigid, then sees Takami-san and her daughter in the back, watching.

TEN

Other inmates say the stink of fresh paint in the infirmary is enough to make anybody sick, but Randy Vanderholt, a doughy man with a pretty mouth, doesn't notice the smell. He's groggy and his neck hurts.

He blinks his swollen eyes, looks around, and sees that he's in a plain room with no window and little more than a hospital bed. The sheets are clean. The walls are bright.

He remembers being attacked from behind, knocked face-down on the concrete. Remembers rough hands lifting him off his feet, knotting something around his neck.

He rolls his tongue around the inside of his mouth, finds his teeth all in place, and decides that he was lucky. He has been through fights before, some pretty bad, during his four years at Folsom. But this is the first time anyone has seriously tried to kill him.

He struggles to sit up and realizes he can't move. He thrashes against the restraints, and it takes him a long moment to figure out what this means. He must be under suicide watch, tied down so that he can't try anything stupid with sheets or a stray pair of scissors.

This is a first, but it's fine with him. He raises his head and looks around at the narrow cabinets, the plastic dish of cotton balls, the roll of paper towels mounted to the wall. Everything is neat and clean and white.

He's glad to be safe and alone behind a locked door, but he wonders who attacked him. And it gradually dawns on him that maybe Duke was involved. . . . Because didn't Duke always say he would be watching? Didn't Duke always say he would come after him if he screwed up?

Vanderholt chews his lip, feeling stung by the unfairness of it. When the cops showed up, he took all the blame. He led them inside, unlocked Tilly's door, and said it was all his fault. And he kept his mouth shut about Duke, just like he promised.

But someone tried to kill him.

He settles down and tries to think about this.

What if Duke has connections inside?

What if everybody is calling him a perv and a kid-fucker?

He's got to think things through. This is a really bad situation. Child molesters are a target, he knows that for sure.

He tries hard to concentrate, but pretty soon his stomach starts growling. His attention wavers, and he begins to worry that—goddamn!—maybe he slept so long that he missed Thanksgiving dinner.

ELEVEN

If it hadn't been Thanksgiving Day, Reeve would have stayed in bed, snug in her nest of pillows. She has always dreaded social gatherings. And bad news sits at the back of her throat.

Still, the twin pulls of familial obligation and an outstanding meal are enough to get her dressed and out the door. She even manages to hit the street a bit early, which allows time for a detour to the park with the wild parrots.

She scans the treetops, listening for their distinctive noise. A pair swoops overhead, a squawking flash of green wings. They alight atop a streetlamp, and she cranes her neck to watch them preen. They seem enviably content.

She spots another pair, then several of the birds with their distinctive cherry-red heads. Sharp chatter flies overhead as she strolls beneath the trees, marveling that these South American parrots have escaped their cages to form this unlikely urban flock. She dawdles as long as she dares, watching them flit and glide, before trudging off to face her family.

Thanksgiving presents an unavoidable slog of emotions. She misses her mother. She loathes jolly questions about her nonexistent love life. And she is always treated like the damaged child, the weak link who is so in need of her family's meddling.

But by the time Reeve finishes a plate of turkey with cranberry sauce and hot biscuits, she forgets to be cranky. She licks her fingers, relieved that the newest family member is now the center of attention.

The star guest, baby Tyler, sits in his high chair and shoves Cheerios into his mouth with chubby hands. Reeve's new nephew is bracketed by her perfect older sister Rachel and her perfect brother-in-law Doug, who absently corrals stray Cheerios on Tyler's tray.

Henri LeClaire, Reeve's father, sits at the head of the table, smiling at his new girlfriend, Amanda, who has proven to be an excellent cook. All through the meal, the host and hostess have expertly shepherded the conversation toward football, films, fog, and similarly ordinary topics. Reeve has managed to navigate through Amanda's friendly queries, and now lazily watches the shared intimacies between the couples, the pats and murmurs. The baby laughs at her, his face crinkling with glee, and her family seems blissfully normal.

Her father pushes his plate away and leans back in his chair, declaring, "Amanda, this was very possibly the best meal I've eaten in my entire life."

Amanda grins at him while Reeve and Rachel exchange a look. This is Classic Dad. He has said exactly this at every shared holiday meal they can remember.

"And that pumpkin soup!" Rachel exclaims. "You have got to give me the recipe."

"I'll e-mail it to you," says Amanda.

"And that stuffing!" Rachel rises out of her chair and begins clearing the table. "Wild rice and almonds and what else?"

"Butter, butter, and more butter," Amanda says, rising to help.

Reeve stands. "No, no, Amanda, you sit," she insists, gathering plates.

"The cook does not do dishes," Rachel agrees. "That's the rule."

"No, Rach, you sit, too. You've done way too much already," Reeve says, waving her sister off.

"Really, let us take care of this," Reeve's father adds, putting a hand on Amanda's shoulder. He carries the platter of turkey toward the kitchen, saying, "We'll start the coffee. Who's ready for dessert?"

Everyone groans, laughing, while Reeve and her father disappear into the kitchen. They work together quietly, stacking dishes in the sink, wrapping leftovers, and wiping off countertops. It's a small kitchen, but they each know it well and work in efficient harmony.

Reeve wants to say something nice about her father's new live-in girlfriend, a smart, stylish woman who—to Reeve's amazement—her father met online. "Um, Amanda's great for you, Dad. You've been dating for quite awhile now, right?"

"Just about nine months."

The conversation stalls, and Reeve cringes at her inability to make small talk. She busies herself with filling Tupperware containers and stacking them in the refrigerator while her father loads the dishwasher. When it is nearly full, he asks softly, "How are you doing, kiddo?"

She freezes. "I'm fine."

He does not embarrass her by stopping or even looking at her. "I was hoping you would call me back last night so we could talk."

The subject they've been avoiding falls like a shadow. "Yesterday wasn't a good day," she says curtly.

"Well, I'm sure all this business about Tilly Cav—"

"It's not just that," Reeve interrupts. "I got fired from my job."

"What?"

She feels her face flush.

"They let you go?"

She hadn't meant to spill this particular bit of bad news—it's Thanksgiving after all, so she's supposed to be happy and thankful—but now it seems a convenient way to steer the conversation away from darker issues. "They tried to be nice about it," she says. "But still."

"I'm so sorry. What happened?"

"Takami-san, the owner, has a daughter who has apparently been kicked out of UCLA," she turns quickly to the sink and begins scrubbing a pot. "Or maybe she dropped out, because I don't think she ever wanted to study business. Anyway, she's home again, so she's back working at the restaurant, and I'm out." Her voice starts to crack and she covers it with a cough.

"When did this happen?"

"Yesterday."

"You really liked that job, didn't you?"

"Well, yeah. But I was really just replacing Keiko, I guess."

Her father puts an arm around her shoulders and gives her a hug, just briefly, because it's understood that Reeve doesn't like being touched.

———

After dessert, while the family sprawls around the television, Reeve slips away for a nap in the guest room. But when she sees the crib in the den, she stops and goes in for a peek at the baby. He's sleeping. She watches him, studies his soft, sweet features, trying to fathom the boundless peace of this exceptionally flawless being.

Something colorful on her father's desk draws her deeper into the room. A birthday card from Amanda. She checks the inscription and guiltily puts it back, then turns to browse the bookshelves, curious as always about her father's breadth of interests. Archeology, politics, art, literature, medicine, and a long shelf of computer texts, some with Henri LeClaire's name on the spine. Framed diplomas and photographs are neatly clustered on one wall. Reeve studies one of her father standing next to Bill Gates. Some people say they look alike, but she never could see it.

She yawns. The couch that faces the window looks comfortable. She has never slept here before, but the pale blue throw draped over the arm seems an invitation. She strokes it—soft—and pulls it over her as she reclines and stretches out.

She has just dozed off when she becomes aware of her sister's voice behind her. "He sleeps like a log during the day," Rachel whispers, "but he's a real party animal at three in the morning."

"You and Reeve were the same way," her father answers.

Their voices are soft. Reeve is unseen on the sofa. She closes her eyes, hoping they'll go away, and tries to go back to sleep.

"I wonder how Reeve is sleeping these days," he says.

Reeve smiles.

"Me, too. The news about this latest case has got to be awfully upsetting."

The smile disappears.

"She had such terrible nightmares, remember?"

"I'll bet this new girl is having nightmares, too." A beat. "Do you think they'll ask Beth Goodwin for help, like with Reeve?"

"No, I think they'll ask Reeve."

"What?"

Reeve is wide awake, partly fascinated, partly appalled by what she's hearing.

"She's closer, both geographically and in time," he says.

"Oh, right."

He sighs. "Anyway, I just hope they don't ask."

"Why not?"

"It would be too hard on her."

"Dad, she's an adult now, she can handle it."

"No, she was so traumatized."

Reeve considers sitting up and confronting them, but curiosity pins her to the sofa.

Her father continues, "You know she's still seeing Dr. Lerner."

"Still?"

"Once a week. She's pretty fragile, I think, beneath that aloof exterior."

"Dad, she's not made of china. She's got grit. She has her own apartment. I mean, I know you're paying some of her bills, but she's more independent now, isn't she?"

"She's just so isolated, Rach. She has no social life, as far as I can tell, and I worry about her. It's like she's locked up in a protective shell."

"But she seems to have adjusted pretty well. She's working and—"

"Not any more."

"What?"

"She lost her job."

"Oh, crap, another one? I'm sorry to hear that."

"I am, and I'm not. I still wish she'd go back to college."

Rachel scoffs. "I don't understand why she won't give Berkeley another try. She's the one with the fat IQ."

No one speaks for a moment and Reeve lies quiet, wishing they would go away.

"Besides, college would be good for her," Rachel adds.

"I know. But I guess she couldn't adapt."

"She didn't really try, did she? But it's what Mom wanted. Anyway, that was the whole point of the trust fund, right?"

"I know, but . . ." Her father's voice sounds far away.

"Of course she's socially awkward. But still."

"Well anyway, look at you, kiddo," her father says, changing the subject, his tone a notch brighter. "You're doing great."

Reeve hears what she imagines to be a hug, waits until they've gone, then goes to the window, thinking about her mother, about her life, about

Tilly Cavanaugh. The fog blows over rooftops, gray and dismal, curling like wet smoke, and she stands there for a long time, watching the chilly scene and weighing things, before going to ask her father if she can borrow his old Jeep.

TWELVE

Randy Vanderholt hears the lock snick open and hopes that someone is bringing him an early lunch. Instead, a guard who looks like Mike Tyson looms in the doorway. He grumbles, "Your lawyer's here," then steps aside and lets in a tall, thin guy with a stoop.

"Clyde Pierson," the lawyer says, extending a hand.

Vanderholt waves his fingers at the man, and Pierson calls the guard back to have the restraints removed.

Vanderholt sits up on the bed, rolls his shoulders and stretches. "Where's the other guy?" he asks. "I mean, I already talked to one lawyer, right?"

"Bradley? He was just getting the basic info, filling in while I was on vacation. I'll be your public defender from here on." Pierson seats himself on a plastic chair and sets his large briefcase on the floor beside him. He clicks it open, saying, "So, how are you feeling?"

"Hungry."

"I'll take that as a good sign. Eat and get strong. We don't want you trying to off yourself again, okay?"

Vanderholt starts to say something, but just makes a face.

Pierson extracts a folder from his briefcase and spreads it open on his lap. Without looking up, he says, "So, Mr. Vanderholt, you've been in prison before."

"Yeah, but that was just car theft, was all."

"Lighter charge, sure." The lawyer flips through a few more papers and grunts. "Listen, I'm not going to sugarcoat anything. The prosecution has your confession, plus a helluva crime scene, and a highly sympathetic young girl as a witness. Even your own photographs, man."

"But I took good care of her. You gotta understand that. You gotta give me some credit for that."

Pierson says nothing.

"So? What can you do to save me?" Vanderholt's tone is halfway between a complaint and a whine.

Pierson gives him a weary look. "Diminished capacity?"

"Hey, I'm not crazy."

Pierson shakes his head. "You tried to kill yourself, Randy. I'll have an expert come and talk with you, okay? That's standard."

"You don't really believe I'm crazy, do you?"

"I'm just saying that it's worth considering, seeing how it might pan out. It could be an option, okay?"

Vanderholt scowls at him.

"I've got to do my best to represent you." Pierson shifts in his chair. "But listen, you've got to work with me. They're going to scrape every last bit of evidence off the walls of both of those basements, you know."

"Yeah? So?"

"So, this is hot and they're going full-bore. They're planning your arraignment for early next week."

Vanderholt winces. "But we'll plead not guilty, right?"

"Sure. We'll make them sweat as long as possible. We'll look for mistakes. We'll work the angles. But I want you to think seriously about cutting a deal."

Vanderholt closes his eyes and mumbles.

"I think there could be an offer. That could be your best chance."

"But they'll crucify me."

"You don't really want to risk a jury trial, do you? Put Tilly Cavanaugh on the stand?"

"But she won't, ah, I mean—"

"And she's just your first problem. We're talking DNA, here. They're working damn hard to link you with those other girls."

"What other girls?"

Pierson squints at him.

"What other girls?" he asks again.

"Hannah and Abby."

"I don't know about any other girls. Only mine."

"You sure about that? Because if they find the least scrap of evidence linking you to Hannah Creighton or Abby Hill, we could be looking at a long list of very heavy, very serious, very ugly charges. Even the death penalty."

Vanderholt feels stung. "No, no, hand to God, I don't know what you're talking about!"

"Think hard about this, man. They're bringing in dogs. They're looking for graves."

"I'm telling you, I do not know any other girls. I only took one. Just Tilly. Just mine."

Pierson sits very still, watching him.

"I'm sorry I took her, okay? I know it was wrong, okay? But I never hurt her. I mean, not really. Not like you think."

Pierson sighs. "Well then," he says finally. "So a plea is our best bet."

"But if a trial could—"

"A trial will just give them an opportunity to grandstand. Think about it. Tilly Cavanaugh is a prosecutor's dream."

"But I told you, I took good care of her. I did. Good food, lots of water, a toothbrush. And vitamins. Really, no kidding, I did. I even gave her vitamins."

"Right," Pierson scoffs, studying the papers in his lap. "This is some sweet confession you handed them. You admitted that you kidnapped her. You described how you kept her locked up in your basement. Unless they screw up on a monumental scale, they've got you tied up and served cold. We're talking child abduction, false imprisonment, and multiple counts of forcible rape, at minimum."

"But you don't understand. When I, when she . . ." His eyes tear up. "She was my precious little girl."

Pierson grunts. "Listen, the DA is lining up a list of charges that will put you away for at least a hundred years. How sympathetic do you think a jury is going to be? A trial just gives the DA's office a chance to grab headlines. They'll make you out to be the Monster of Jefferson County."

The lawyer keeps on talking, but his words have sparked an idea, and now Randy Vanderholt is thinking hard. He's thinking about Duke, the man that his girl Tilly secretly called "Mister Monster." He's wondering if Duke had something to do with those other missing girls.

Because Duke sure seemed to know exactly what he was doing. So easy. So relaxed. Like he'd practiced everything before. And it was weird that Duke had pegged Randy for what he really was, first thing, when no one else ever did. "Takes one to know one," Duke had said.

Pierson is still talking, but Vanderholt is barely listening. He rubs his jaw, worrying about how much danger he might be in, trying to work how much he might suffer later. He's weighing his fear of Duke against his fear of spending the rest of his life in prison. It's a lot to try to figure out, and he's not good at this sort of thing, and the harder he tries, the blurrier his thinking gets.

"Um, I'm under suicide watch, right?" he blurts.

Pierson frowns, clearly annoyed at being interrupted. "You are, of course."

"So, um, no one can get to me now, right? I mean, I'm safe here, right?"

Pierson leans forward. "What are you saying, man?"

Randy licks his lips. "This is, um, confidential, right? Attorney-client privilege, all that?"

"Of course. Why?"

He checks the door, clears his throat, and lowers his voice. "There's another guy, okay?"

Pierson's eyebrows shoot up. "An accomplice?"

Randy sees the eagerness in the attorney's face and senses leverage. He sits forward. "But the guy's tricky, okay? He's smart." His eyes check the door again. "And dangerous."

"Yeah, okay, so what's his name?"

Randy rolls his tongue around his mouth. "A deal, right? I can get a deal?"

"If you're telling the truth, yes."

"So, uh, how does that work, exactly?"

"I'll set it up with the prosecutor just as soon as we know the charges." Pierson puts his hands on his knees and leans forward, intent. "So tell me about this guy. What's his name?"

Randy sucks his teeth, thinking. "Here's the thing . . . His name, uh, I'm not for sure about that."

"You've got an accomplice but you don't know his name?" Pierson snorts. "Don't jerk me around."

"His name is, you know, like a street name."

Pierson shoots him a skeptical look. "You've got to give me more than that."

"I'll give it all to you, I can ID him," Randy adds quickly. "I got his license plate number, too."

Pierson's face lights up. "Now you're talking." He balances a notepad on his knee, pulls a pen from his pocket and clicks it open. "Okay, shoot."

Randy rocks back. "Not so fast. How do I know I'll get a deal if I tell you?"

"I'm your lawyer. That's my job."

"But hold on just a minute here." Randy says, trying to line things up in his mind. "How can I be sure?"

"You've got to trust me on this."

"Trust you?" Randy's expression sours. People who ask for trust always mean trouble. And once he tells what he knows, his hand is played. Meanwhile, he's still a target and Duke is still a threat. He crosses his arms across his chest, suddenly clear on what to do. "That's it. I ain't saying another word until there's a deal on the table."

THIRTEEN

Jefferson City

Reeve carries a large hot chocolate over to a table far from the other customers. She sits facing the door, sips carefully, then fishes her cell phone out of her purse and taps in Dr. Lerner's number.

He answers after two rings. "Reeve, I'm so glad you called. How are you?"

She skips the pleasantries and says abruptly, "I thought about what you said, and I'm ready to help."

There's a pause, then Dr. Lerner says, "Good. That will be very much appreciated, I'm sure. I'll tell the Cavanaughs. Would you like their phone number so you can call them directly?"

"No, I'd like to see them. And I'd like to talk to Tilly. Can you come get me?"

"Oh, well I'm not sure when I can get back to San Francisco."

"But I'm here in town."

"What?"

"I'm here in Jefferson City."

"You're here?"

"That's what I said."

"How did you get here?"

"I drove. I borrowed Dad's Jeep."

"You *drove*?"

"Yes. I drove." Reeve had expected Dr. Lerner to be surprised, since he knows she has only driven a car perhaps a dozen times in her life, but now

55

she's getting annoyed. "I got gas. I parked. And I'm now downtown, sitting here at Starbucks, but I don't know my way around and I don't know where you are, so I'd like you to please come and get me."

"I see. Well, I'll be there in a few minutes."

The truth is, she's exhausted. She didn't sleep well, and the drive from San Francisco was just one more nightmare, with fog and traffic and white knuckles all the way. She purposely did not tell Dr. Lerner she was coming so that she could back out at any time without having to make excuses. But as much as she wanted to, she wouldn't let herself. Because years of therapy have given her enough self-awareness to see that she's not exactly the poster child for mental health. And because she's sick of having Daryl Wayne Flint's claws in her imagination, sick of being stuck on the same worn path of blocked responses.

And because Tilly Cavanaugh deserves at least as much help as she had.

She's finishing the last of her hot chocolate when Dr. Lerner comes in the door, trailed by a lanky young man in a uniform. She looks up and says, "Hi," trying to keep the confusion from showing on her face.

"Reeve, this is Deputy Nick Hudson," Dr. Lerner says. "He's our liaison with the district attorney's office and the Jefferson County Sheriff's Department."

"Which is a fancy way of saying that I'm the doctor's official guide and gopher while he's in town," Hudson says, stepping forward to shake her hand.

Reeve studies the tall young man, wondering—as she often does when meeting someone new—whether he knows who she is and what happened to her.

"We were just heading to lunch," Dr. Lerner says. "Care to join us?"

Several minutes later, at a nearby diner with a lumberjack theme, they consult the menu and make small talk until the food arrives on oversized plates, smelling delicious. Reeve tastes her soup and nibbles at half a sandwich. She is used to having Dr. Lerner's full attention and feels a bit irked at having to share him.

While she eats, she dodges questions and studies the exchanges between Dr. Lerner and this young deputy. Hudson makes casual conversation seem effortless. He volunteers that he grew up here, went to college in Los Angeles, hated the congestion, and returned. He says he plays "a little guitar, you know, in my spare time." And he gets animated when talking about the many pleasures of living in Jefferson County—skiing, kayaking, fly fishing—a litany of outdoor sports that seem as odd to her as space exploration.

"What drew you to law enforcement?" Dr. Lerner asks, forking up another mouthful of trout.

"Runs in the family, I guess. My dad was a highway patrolman. And I have a whole slew of uncles and cousins who work in law enforcement in some way or other."

"Seems like an unusual family."

"I used to think so, but a lot of my coworkers have similar backgrounds. Badges are contagious, I guess."

"You like what you do, don't you?"

"It's interesting work, and it pays a lot better than strumming guitar, I'll tell you." Hudson grins. "But eventually, I'd like to go to law school. Or at least, that's the plan. So I nosed around, and I caught a break, and I've been learning a lot in this position with the district attorney's office."

Nick Hudson's relaxed manner mirrors Dr. Lerner's, and while their desserts are served, Reeve studies his even features, his healthy skin, his nice teeth, and decides that he is handsome.

Dr. Lerner turns toward Reeve, his voice dropping to a softer tone. "I'm glad that you took the initiative to come up. The Cavanaughs are looking forward to meeting with you later this afternoon, okay?"

"It's great that you could come up and help," Hudson adds, confirming for Reeve that he knows exactly who she is.

She lowers her eyes and spoons into her chocolate ice cream, listening while Dr. Lerner fills her in on the situation.

"They're being gentle with their daughter, and they're not pressing for details about what she endured. Which is wise."

She nods, remembering.

"Right, but this is not the way the prosecution would normally want to proceed in building a case," Hudson says.

She stops eating and looks up.

"Understood," Dr. Lerner says, "but first we'll let her reveal things in her own time, as she feels more comfortable, more secure."

"What was that about building a case?" Reeve asks the deputy.

"I work with Jackie Burke, the prosecutor. She'd like to meet with you, too."

"Why me?"

"Because she needs to hear how things go with the Cavanaughs. Because she's hoping to accelerate the charges against Vanderholt."

"The kidnapper."

"The suspect, right."

She shifts in her chair. "So you're expecting that, as Tilly shares more specifics, the prosecutor will have what she needs for going to trial?"

"But understand that this will be a gradual process," Dr. Lerner says to the deputy. "We have to assure Tilly of some degree of confidentiality, help her feel safe, so she can start coming to terms with what has happened to her."

"And stop blaming herself," Reeve adds.

"Wait." Hudson gives her a quizzical look. "What do you mean? Why on earth would she blame herself?"

Reeve sighs. "It's common, with victims of abduction and captivity, to feel that you are somehow complicit, or that you have contributed to your own victimization." She shoots a look at Dr. Lerner, realizing that she sounds like her therapist.

"Really?"

She gives a shrug. "The media makes it worse by asking things like, 'Why did she stay?' As if it's a choice."

Hudson cocks his head. "You mean, like Beth Goodwin, when she was walking around in public with her kidnappers?"

"Like that."

"That's what they call Stockholm Syndrome, right?"

"That's the common term," Dr. Lerner says to him. "But it has become kind of a pop phrase, used to cover all kinds of hostage and captive situations, and it's imprecise."

"How's that?"

"Well, it's just one aspect of what is broadly called post-traumatic stress disorder."

"Sure. PTSD," Hudson says. "So, they're the same thing, more or less?"

"Not really. Stockholm Syndrome isn't actually in the diagnostic manuals, and post-traumatic stress disorder is such a broad term that it ceases to be useful at some point."

"I can tell you're a college professor," Hudson says with a grin.

"Forgive me for lecturing."

"No, listen, I'm not the smartest guy around, but I like to understand. So, why do we even hear about Stockholm Syndrome if it isn't in the—what?—diagnostic manual?"

"Good question. The term was coined years ago by a Swedish criminologist who was trying to understand the sympathy a group of hostages expressed for their captors at a Stockholm bank robbery."

"But they were held for just five days," Reeve interjects.

"Yes, and since then, a similar response has been seen in many individuals held under duress. Plane hijackings, prison riots, POWs—"

"But I thought Stockholm Syndrome was about captives falling in love with their captors," Hudson says.

Reeve groans. "It's a survival mechanism."

Dr. Lerner nods. "And it only scratches the surface, really, in trying to explain the psychological effects of prolonged captivity and profound coercion."

"Coercion?" Hudson asks, a forkful of pie stopping in midair.

"That's right," Reeve snaps. "Coercion."

"Or brainwashing, as it's often called," Dr. Lerner says, waving a hand, "though that's not a clinical term. Anyway, consider the different circumstances. Some hostages are held only a short time. Many are aware of ongoing negotiations, so they know that they're essentially bargaining chips, that their abductors want something in exchange, usually money."

"But sexual predators don't ask for ransom," Reeve says, gripping the sides of her chair. "There are no negotiations. The person taken is their prize."

"I'm sorry, but could we back up? Terror, I get. Rape and sexual abuse, I understand." He is addressing Dr. Lerner, but glances over at Reeve, who meets his eye. "But what I don't get is, unless it's a military situation, where does coercion come in?"

"Remember Patty Hearst?" Reeve's voice goes up a notch. "Remember how she was indoctrinated by the SLA? Remember how Beth Goodwin's captor spouted all that twisted, pseudoreligious crap?"

Hudson rubs his chin. "Same thing with that creep who took Jaycee Dugard, right?"

"That's right."

"Coercion is common in captive situations," Dr. Lerner explains. "It's part of the captor's strategy. POWs, for instance. A parallel situation, with coercion employed along with extreme emotional and physical deprivation."

"And torture," Reeve adds hotly. "The media always tries to make it sound titillating, calling it sadomasochism. But people who are kidnapped are not masochists. They're beaten. They're starved. And whether it happens to trained soldiers or to young girls, whether or not there's actual rape, torture is still torture."

The conversation lurches to a halt.

Reeve glares at her melting ice cream, excuses herself, and bolts from the table.

In the restroom, she washes the heat off her face. This is twice in the past two days she has allowed anger to overtake her. She makes a face in the mirror, muttering, "Well, Miss Sunshine, that went well."

After lunch, Deputy Hudson directs Reeve to a parking structure where she can park her Jeep all day for free—something unthinkable in San Francisco—and the three head toward the Cavanaughs' home. Having barely spoken since lunch, Reeve hunches in the backseat, watching the scenery roll past, telling herself to get a grip. What's the worst that can happen? The kid won't like you? You'll make her cry?

As the highway dips and turns west, they cross a long bridge. She stares out at the unfamiliar territory, the wide river that runs through town like a blue vein. What the hell was she thinking? It's not like she has an obligation to be here. It's not like she's a card-carrying member of the Pay-It-Forward Society of Kidnapping Survivors.

Nick Hudson tries to engage her in conversation, but she feigns trouble hearing, then pretends to like a country song on the radio, asking him to turn it up. She searches the mournful lyrics for meaning while they wheel through a residential neighborhood, where trees shed crimson leaves and early Christmas decorations line rooftops, sprawl across lawns, and crowd porches.

The moment they turn onto the Cavanaughs' street, she spots the TV vans. "Oh, crap!"

"Sorry about the welcoming committee. You might want to scrunch down," Hudson suggests, but she is already slipping out of her shoulder harness and gluing herself to the seat.

The vehicle slows as they approach a gate. She hears car doors slamming around them and voices calling out Dr. Lerner's name, begging for comments. Hudson keeps the tinted windows rolled up tight while Dr. Lerner calls the Cavanaughs on his cell phone, announcing their arrival.

She shuts her eyes. As the vehicle eases forward, past the clot of reporters and through the iron gates, she clamps down on the swelling apprehension that coming here was a mistake.

Tilly's eyes fix on Reeve from the moment they're introduced. She's a wisp of a girl with long wheat-colored hair and a pixie face. She wears a serious, unflinching expression, but looks younger than thirteen in her pink flannel pajamas and fuzzy blue socks.

Mrs. Cavanaugh offers coffee, but Deputy Hudson is the only one who accepts, politely adding that he'll take it in the kitchen, "so the rest of you can talk."

They sit in a pleasant room with high ceilings and logs flickering in the fireplace. The air is fragrant with the fresh, piney aroma of a tall Christmas tree, which stands unadorned in one corner of the room. Except for several unopened boxes of lights and ornaments, the décor is unseasonal and nearly bland, apart from several colorful oil paintings that appear to be the work of the same artist.

Tilly perches on the sofa with her parents, looking very small between Gordon and Shirley Cavanaugh, who are both tall and big-boned. An assortment of sweets sits untouched on the coffee table that stands between the sofa and the overstuffed chairs occupied by Dr. Lerner and Reeve.

"We're so grateful you decided to come," Mrs. Cavanaugh says. Her face looks damp, but her expression seems warm and open. She keeps one hand on Tilly's knee, as if reassuring herself that her daughter is really home, and this small shared intimacy brings Reeve a stab of longing. She recalls being in exactly that spot. The memory swims behind her eyes.

Mr. Cavanaugh apologizes that their son can't meet them because he's out with friends. After a few more polite comments, Reeve realizes that everyone is waiting for her to speak. The room suddenly seems overheated. Pinching the numb patch on her left hand, she licks her lips and begins, "I'm not sure how much help I can be, really, but I know a lot about what you're going through."

She meets the eyes of the family assembled around her and describes what comes to mind: the comfort and strangeness of being home again with her parents. The shock of seeing her older sister as an adult. The hollow realization of how much she had missed.

At first, she says, she wrestled with an absurd concern for her captor's welfare and worried that she would be punished, or that she would be blamed.

Tilly holds her with a steady gaze, and Reeve recognizes herself in those eyes.

Her story pours out. She describes the unreal quality of the trial, the constant presence of the media, the long wait for the verdict. When she mentions the insomnia and the recurring nightmares, they all nod mutely.

"My family tried to help, but still I felt that nobody understood me. I was very withdrawn." She exchanges a look with Dr. Lerner and continues, "There was no chance of any real connection with my former friends. I mean, I met with a couple of them, but I felt like a total alien because they had grown up without me, you know? They were all involved in high school, like normal teenagers. They didn't mean to be insensitive, but they asked such lame questions, and I'd been through something that they couldn't even begin to comprehend. I felt like my entire childhood had been sucked out of me."

While she talks, the parents sigh almost in unison, but Tilly remains motionless, staring with those serious eyes. The girl is so dwarfed by her parents that Reeve wonders for a moment if she might be adopted, wonders if that would make the least bit of difference. She checks Tilly's gray eyes, then her mother's. The same.

Reeve realizes that she's stroking the scar at the back of her neck and makes herself stop. "It took my father a while to find a good psychiatrist. First, you see, there was a doctor up in Seattle that I would go to, but she was . . ." She shifts in her seat. "I don't know, we just didn't click. So it was a relief when we found Dr. Lerner, because you could immediately sense this calmness about him, like he just *understood* everything, on multiple levels, without explanation."

She shoots a quick smile at Dr. Lerner.

"Anyway, he helped me right from the start. And he introduced me to Beth Goodwin, of course, who was absolutely wonderful and kind." She pauses, shifting again in her chair. "And then we moved to San Francisco, which helped. But then my mother got sick."

A long silence is punctuated only by the soft sputter of the fire.

Mrs. Cavanaugh clears her throat and asks, "How old were you, dear, when you were, uh, taken?"

"I was twelve."

Tilly stares. The girl's eyes are a mirror.

Mr. Cavanaugh asks, "And, if you don't mind my asking, how long were you, um, were you held captive?"

She swallows a lump of emotion. "Three years, ten months, and twelve days."

The sensation of being locked in the trunk of Daryl Wayne Flint's car comes back to her in almost palpable detail: the warm, oily closeness, the growl of the tires, the jarring impact, the spinning, and then the eerie stillness, with just the ticking of hot metal. . . . How many times had she fantasized about being rescued? And yet, when all the commotion began unfolding on the other side of the car's wrecked skin, she had stayed quiet, listening hard through the shouting for her kidnapper's voice, waiting for him to take command and order the strangers away.

Mrs. Cavanaugh's face puckers and she rises from the sofa, crosses the room and, in one quick motion, leans in and enfolds Reeve in an awkward hug, breathing, "Oh, you poor dear girl," into her hair.

Reeve flashes a pained look in Dr. Lerner's direction, and then the hug is over.

Before Mrs. Cavanaugh can reclaim her seat, Tilly shoots to her feet and asks, "Would it be okay if I show her my room?"

Her parents exchange surprised looks. After a moment, Mrs. Cavanaugh murmurs, "Of course, honey. That would be fine."

Tilly faces Reeve. "Do you want to see it?"

"Um, sure." Reeve gets to her feet and follows the girl down the hall. Tilly is quiet as a cat in her sock feet, and Reeve feels clumsy in her heavy black boots.

The girl's bedroom is all yellow and decked with frills, posters, drawings, photos, and knickknacks.

"Nice room," Reeve offers, noticing with relief that there is no computer and no TV. At this stage, the news coverage would be brutal.

Tilly picks up a framed photo. "This is when I went to Disneyland. I was seven." She shows it to Reeve, then takes it back and shows her another. "This is Christmas at my Aunt Becca's house. She made me this marionette. . . ."

Reeve trails after Tilly, watching as she picks up item after item, narrating her history. Reeve remembers doing this, too, remembers trying hard to recover any scrap of her lost childhood. She hopes that Tilly will have better luck, being so young, still small and flat-chested, while Reeve could barely recognize the child she had once been.

Tilly lifts a small jewelry box made of stained glass. As she hands it to Reeve, she studies Reeve's face and asks, "How old are you?"

"Twenty-two."

"So," Tilly says matter-of-factly, "you were in that dungeon about eighteen percent of your life."

Reeve considers this. "Yes, that's about right."

"That's more than me."

"Uh-huh. So you'll start feeling better pretty quickly, I think."

"Yeah?"

"I'm pretty sure."

"Do you have any scars?"

Reeve blinks, momentarily taken aback. "I do."

"Can I see?"

The girl is so straightforward that Reeve can only respond in kind. She takes a quick breath and peels her sweater off over her head, realizing that this is the first time she has undressed in front of anyone other than a medical doctor in years. She decides not to take off more unless asked. Even standing in a bra and jeans, she has plenty of scars.

Tilly steps in close, her face expressionless as she examines Reeve's skin. She tips her head from side to side, then slowly walks around Reeve to inspect her back. "What are these long ones?"

Reeve tenses. "I was whipped."

Tilly traces one scar that begins at the back of Reeve's neck and ends below her ribs. "They kinda look like leaves, don't they? Or feathers."

Reeve says nothing, holding very still as Tilly comes around to stand in front of her. The girl raises one hand and puts a fingertip on a flat round scar on Reeve's right shoulder, then touches the matching one on the left. "What are these smooth ones?"

Reeve blinks away a sudden image. "I was electrocuted."

"That must have hurt." The words are sympathetic, but the tone is utterly neutral.

Tilly gently grasps Reeve's wrists and turns her arms one way, then the other, examining the thin scars that bracelet each wrist. Then, with deliberate fingers, the girl touches a sequence of small, circular scars that run up Reeve's arms like the paw prints of a cruel animal. Tilly proceeds slowly up to her elbow, shoulder, and back down again, bending so close that Reeve can feel her breath.

Finally, she stands back and announces, "I have those, too."

In one easy motion, Tilly pulls her pajama top off over her head, an act so completely spontaneous and unself-conscious that Reeve realizes the girl is still accustomed to being naked.

"See?" Tilly says, raising her skinny arms toward Reeve. "Mine are still pink."

Reeve stares at the tight cluster of three fresh cigarette burns on Tilly's pale skin.

"These other ones are more faded," Tilly says, pulling down her pajama bottoms and baring a matching pattern of scars on her rump.

Reeve bites back a curse and mutters, "That sadistic scumbag."

Tilly opens her mouth to speak, then purses her lips and crosses her arms, hugging herself with her hands thrust deep under her armpits, as though holding something terrible inside her chest.

FOURTEEN

Surveillance is the perfect specialty for someone with voyeuristic tendencies, and Duke is an expert on such specialized technology that almost no one outside of Quantico—and certainly no one within Jefferson County law enforcement—can understand exactly what he does. They bring him a cell phone, he gives them the data. They ask for video surveillance, it comes streaming across their desktops. They need a wiretap, it's done.

It especially pleases him that he has received so much of his training compliments of local, state, and federal governments. Various framed certificates are displayed on his office wall. Whenever anyone congratulates him on some arcane aspect of his expertise, he modestly thanks the Department of Homeland Security.

He whistles, thinking about this, while he turns into the driveway of a two-story residence with fantastic views of the mountains. It's time for his second visit to the former home of his newest girl, the marvelously agile Abby Hill.

He's amused to note that Mr. and Mrs. Hill do, in fact, live on a hill.

Duke has been inside the Hill residence once before, and has since glimpsed the parents around town, but they didn't seem to recognize him. Even if they did, it would mean nothing. He was just another man in uniform who swam before their eyes during a time of intense strain, when they were suffering the shock of their daughter's abduction. Another nameless face, less important than the blustering federal agents who charged up from the Sacramento regional office to briefly run the show. The Hills might confuse him with any other officer who appeared during that brief, agonizing window between the day of their daughter's disappearance and the dimming of all rational hope.

At most, the Hills might harbor some lingering memory of him as the technician who installed the listening devices on their phones in case their daughter's kidnappers called demanding ransom.

No call came, of course.

So now Duke is back. He rings the bell and Mr. Hill, a listless man with a waxy complexion and dark-rimmed eyes, opens the door.

Duke introduces himself, and Mr. Hill's face betrays a wince, "Yeah, I got the message. We know why you're here."

Since there has been no sign of the Hills' daughter, and since ten weeks have passed without a ransom demand, the FBI has recognized the futility of monitoring their phones. So Duke, as a key member of the Joint Special Operations Task Force, has the job of coming through this door once again. His final mission is ostensibly to remove the remaining surveillance equipment.

He nods politely and comes inside.

Aware that the Hills are succumbing to the awful undertow of fear that they will never see their daughter again, Duke intends to get the job done mostly in silence. If pressed, he is prepared to voice sympathetic platitudes.

Mrs. Hill offers a cup of coffee, which Duke accepts, sipping while he steps from the kitchen, to the den, to the master bedroom. He moves according to plan, smoothly replacing the FBI's clunky listening devices with tiny elegant versions of his own. As he's finishing up, he returns the empty cup to the kitchen and asks to use a bathroom.

Just as he did at the home of Gordon and Shirley Cavanaugh, and at the home of Michael and Patricia Creighton.

He walks down the hall, flips on the bathroom light and fan, and then backtracks, quietly slipping into Abby's perfectly preserved room of sweetest pink to secure one more miniature device. He glances at the framed photos of a plumper, healthier Abby before hiding the device in the wall, beneath the light switch plate, where it pulses with a steady electrical flow. Far more reliable than batteries.

Certainly, anyone with an RF scanner would be able to find his devices, but Duke never worries about this. Except for some rare occasion when the

FBI might conceivably send someone up from the Sacramento office to scan for bugs, Duke is the only one in the county with any interest in that task. He snickers at the irony.

After bidding good-bye to Mr. and Mrs. Hill, he climbs back into his SUV. Back to work, where he will have to finish the day at his desk.

Despite his virtuosity, Duke finds the surveillance business often dull. Part of his time is dedicated to the electronic monitoring of escape-risk suspects. And criminals are, for the most part, pedestrian and dim.

Drug dealers—who unfortunately demand the bulk of Duke's time—are a particularly witless bunch. The names and faces change, but they appear as indistinguishable players in the same stupid soap opera, a never-ending loop. Duke has concluded that only fools fail to see that greed and drug abuse are futile in combination.

Only a select few drugs interest Duke. Rohypnol, for instance. He's found that "ruffies" can be quite useful.

Duke has been back in his office less than an hour when Officer Tomas Montoya appears in his doorway. Montoya grips the top of the door frame with the fingertips of both hands and hangs there, apelike and grinning. "Hey, did you hear the news about the dogs?"

Duke looks up from his computer. "You mean the ones you've been dating?"

"I date foxes, not dogs," Montoya quips, entering Duke's office and pulling up a chair. "I mean the dogs that are working the Vanderholt property. Actually, both properties: The one he moved out of, and the one he moved into."

"Cadaver dogs? They're searching for remains?"

"Yep, of those two other missing girls."

"Ah, Abby Hill and Hannah Creighton." Duke lifts his eyebrows, feigning interest, but he knows the dogs will find nothing. Abby and Hannah are exactly where they should be, and there is nothing to connect them to Vander-dolt, or even to sweet little Tilly. Duke is the only common link, and he is much too smart to leave behind any sort of evidence, other than some well-placed but untraceable marks on human skin.

"What's the news about Vanderholt?" Duke asks.

"Still in the infirmary, I guess. The DA is pushing for an arraignment early next week." Montoya pulls a face. "I bet Jackie Burke would have done it even sooner, too, if she could somehow push the calendar."

"So who's defending him?"

"Pierson."

"Really?" Duke scoffs. "I thought ol' Clyde was about to retire."

"Yep. Which is tough luck for Vanderholt," Montoya says, chuckling. "Because Pierson will just try to plead him out and go golfing."

FIFTEEN

A tall deputy named Mull has escorted Reeve into the office of Jefferson County Deputy District Attorney Jackie Burke, a smartly dressed woman with carefully styled hair. After introductions, Burke sends Deputy Mull out to fetch coffee, settles behind her desk, and points Reeve to a chair, saying, "You know, Miss LeClaire, I vetted Dr. Lerner very carefully before introducing him to the Cavanaughs. It seemed a smart and necessary move. But I fail to appreciate why my consulting expert has now invited an inexperienced young woman to question my primary witness."

Reeve blinks, trying to grasp the significance of this statement. "We were just talking. You know my history, right?" she answers stiffly, wishing Dr. Lerner were here.

"That you were kidnapped? Or course. And we're all quite sympathetic. All of us," she says with a tight smile. "But please help me understand how a patient of Dr. Lerner's in San Francisco has found herself in Jefferson, involved in my investigation." She addresses Reeve with eyebrows lifted high in expectation.

"I came up . . . Well, I'm meeting with Tilly Cavanaugh because I was invited."

"And your training is . . ."

"I, uh, I don't have any training."

"None?"

"Not formally, no."

"A college degree?"

Reeve shakes her head.

"And yet, Dr. Lerner believed it was appropriate to involve you in Tilly Cavanaugh's therapy?"

Reeve starts to answer, but Burke puts up a palm and keeps talking. "And today the Cavanaugh family brought you into their home and allowed you to spend nearly an hour, unsupervised, with their daughter. Do I have that straight?"

"Earlier this afternoon, that's right."

"Excuse me, but aren't you just one of Dr. Lerner's former patients, or are you supposed to be some kind of protégé?" Before Reeve can manage a response, Burke says, "I'll need a full report. Recorded, if you don't mind." She sets a small recorder on her desk, punches a button, and when a red light appears, faces Reeve. "Tell me everything, please, Miss LeClaire. In full detail."

Reeve shifts in the uncomfortable chair, which seems increasingly like the hot seat, takes a deep breath, and tries to keep the attitude out of her voice as she recounts the key points of her conversation with Tilly.

Burke listens with a pinched look, drumming her desk with manicured fingernails, until a point when her hands freeze. "Let me stop you right there." She frowns. "Now you're telling me that Tilly has revealed key evidence to you?"

"No, I'm sure there's nothing she told me that you don't already know."

"What makes you so sure of that?" Burke challenges, leaning forward. "How could you possibly begin to imagine what the DA's office does and does not know?"

"I said she showed me her scars. I'm sure you have all her medical records. I remember—quite vividly—being subjected to a thorough physical examination when I was in her situation."

Burke shoots a look at the thick file on her desk, crosses her arms, and is about to ask another question when Reeve adds, "She only gave me the message I just told you: That she is, and I quote, ready to tell you all about Randy Vanderholt. Unquote."

"Yet she refuses to come to my office."

"She didn't refuse, she didn't use that word. She just asked that you come to her house."

"I see." Burke sighs. "Underage girls are not legally required . . ." She waves away this thought and continues, "What else did she tell you?"

Reeve squirms, feeling as if she's being cross-examined. "That's it, pretty much. She showed me her room, some mementos, framed photographs, girly stuff."

"And then she just jumped up and said, 'Wanna see my scars?' That's hard to believe, Miss LeClaire."

"No, she asked to see mine first."

"Your scars?"

Reeve fights off a sickening wave of déjà vu and simply nods.

"Okay. The two of you compared scars. Then what?"

"Then she told me that she had a message for the lady lawyer."

"She used that term?"

"That's why I said it. That's a quote. She said, 'I've got a message for that lady lawyer.'"

"The message about Vanderholt?"

"Yes."

Burke's stare is unnerving. "Tell me the rest."

Reeve closes her eyes. She sees Tilly sitting on the bed, clutching her knees to her chest, watching her with that unflinching gaze.

"There's more, isn't there?" Burke prods.

Reeve sighs. "She asked me about my family, about how we moved from Seattle to San Francisco."

"What? Why? Is the Cavanaugh family thinking about moving?"

"They didn't say anything to me about it. I got the impression from Tilly that it was a new consideration, that she got the idea from me."

"You suggested it?" Her tone is incredulous.

"No. I just told the family, as a group, about some of my history. I was trying to explain that I understand what they're going through."

"You were establishing some kind of a bond?"

"I was trying to. That was the point."

"Dr. Lerner authorized this?"

"The Cavanaughs specifically asked to talk with me, I told you."

"And now Tilly wants her whole family to just up and move away?"

"My family did. The media attention was vile."

"What else did you two discuss?"

Reeve digs her nails into her palms, wishing she could have sidestepped this whole encounter. "Tilly asked if I thought she should change her name."

Burke opens her mouth and snaps it closed. After a beat, she asks, "Like you did?"

"That's right."

"And what did you tell her?"

Reeve gives a half shrug. "That it's up to her. That she should talk to her parents about it. What else could I say?"

Burke crosses her arms. "What's the whole story? What else haven't you told me?"

"That's it. Then she wanted a cookie."

"I need to know everything she tells you. Everything. You understand?" Burke gives her a long scowl, then gets up from behind her desk and starts pacing around her office. The heels of the prosecutor's shiny black boots click back and forth across the floor.

"Did she tell you any details about Vanderholt?"

"No, nothing."

"What? Seriously? Nothing?"

"Nothing."

"That's hard to believe."

Reeve purses her lips.

"What was her demeanor?" Burke asks. "Was she crying, upset?"

"No. She's stoic. Her affect is flat, meaning she's kind of blank and un-emotional. Dr. Lerner must have told you, that's normal for victims like—" *like us*, she thinks "—like Tilly."

Burke looks away and mutters, "Sure, but it will still seem strange to the jury."

Reeve now remembers the hard truth about lawyers: it's all about the case, it's all about winning. She's suddenly exhausted. She has been up since dawn, and the long drive from San Francisco was just the start of this draining day.

"So you can put Dr. Lerner on the stand," Reeve says wearily. "He's good. He can explain it all to the jury."

"Like with your case?"

"Like with mine, sure."

Burke scoffs. "I hope to do better than that."

"What do you mean?"

Burke crosses her arms and stands in front of her. "Well, Daryl Wayne Flint didn't quite get what he deserved, did he?"

Reeve looks away, pinching the numb spot on her left hand.

SIXTEEN

During free hours, Duke monitors his devices with the avidity of a teenage gamer. He has installed various types of surveillance equipment over the years—some state-of-the-art, some now out-of-date yet still functioning—and all of these are constantly transmitting to his well-appointed control room.

The programs that he's created for cell phones are his favorite. Given the opportunity, he can easily install a beautifully parasitic program that goes beyond merely eavesdropping on a limited number of calls and capturing a few phone numbers. Far better, the multifunctional program instantly turns ordinary cell phones into microphones and transmitters. Duke can then listen to any conversation within the vicinity of the phone, even when it is not in use, as long as the battery has a charge. Of course, he can also view photos and e-mails and text messages.

The problem with all this streaming information is that it's too much for any one person to monitor. So, rather than reviewing every single text or listening to hours of boring conversation about raising children or remodeling the house, Duke uses a brilliant filtering program called the Sniffer, which automatically monitors all the conversations on any given device and flags words or phrases that Duke deems to be of special interest.

The particular words, of course, are a challenge. Just as the Department of Homeland Security might zero in on a specific terrorist's name, Duke has to key in specific words that can bring him significant information, and he updates these words as situations change.

For instance, each of his girls has her own private name for him, which he has made a point of discovering and then keying in. For Tilly, the secret name chosen for him—one that she does not know that he knows—is *Mister Monster*. An obvious red flag.

Sadist, rapist, and *kidnapper* are some other terms that Duke has flagged.

So, if anything of concern has been said within several feet of any of his listening devices, the Sniffer targets those conversations, and Duke can later cue up the recordings to scrutinize them at his leisure. Usually, this is fairly routine.

But now things have changed, thanks to Randy Vander-dolt, who is currently lounging beyond Duke's reach in the infirmary at the new jail.

Duke has been thinking long and hard about what to do about this miscreant, and his plans are firming up, but there is nothing to be done at the moment. So, for now, Tilly Cavanaugh is his main concern. He pinches an earlobe, thinking that her rescue hasn't really put him in jeopardy. But what she does or does not say could trigger a very unfortunate series of events. A wasteful series of events. Countless hours of effort. Years of planning.

Luckily, Tilly is unable to disclose any truly significant information about him. Duke is confident about that, because he was meticulous. He took precautions. For one thing, she can't give an accurate description of him. She doesn't even know what he looks like, because his girls are always blindfolded before he even enters the room. The keepers are tasked with that. If he wants to see the girl's eyes, he secures his mask prior to removing her blindfold. Simple.

For another, Tilly is surely terrified of reprisals. During those sweet thirteen months when she was under his control, he made sure that she understood that any bad behavior on her part would have dangerous consequences. He stressed that he knew all about her family, including their schedules and their individual quirks. He dropped references to her brother's football practice, her mother's hairdresser, just to reinforce that he was continually watching everyone in the Cavanaugh household.

Tilly knew that her family would suffer if she misbehaved. And, for the most part, she had been smart; she had performed exactly as he required. But sometimes, when she became unruly, it had been necessary to use some force, such as a lit cigarette, to impress upon her that disobedience had swift and painful consequences.

This evening, the Sniffer has alerted Duke to a possible problem, so he laces up his sneakers, puts on his headphones, and begins listening to segments of recent conversations while running on his treadmill.

No reason to be lazy about it.

He has barely worked up a sweat when he hears something interesting. He's listening to Mr. C's familiar baritone, to Mrs. C's motherly clucking sounds, to Tilly's monosyllabic responses, and to that pompous shrink's irritating comments when a new voice arrives. He frowns in concentration.

The voice has a youthful, melodic quality.

She calls herself Reeve.

He slows his pace, confused. Why is she there?

He gets off the treadmill and resets the recording, hoping for introductions that might clarify her role. But everyone at the Cavanaugh residence clearly anticipated this strange female's arrival.

He sits down, listening with a scowl. He has missed something. He turns up the volume and now the girl accommodates him with a detailed narrative. He listens, rapt, and when she begins describing what she went through, he lets out a long whistle. He remembers this story.

But the girl's name was not Reeve.

He grasps for her true identity, closes his eyes, and then says it aloud, "Regina Victoria LeClaire," feeling the shape of her name in his mouth. "Edgy Reggie," he adds with a smirk. Leaning far back in his chair, he takes a deep breath, savoring a recollection of what he'd read in the news.

Yes, he remembers the case well. He was a big fan.

Duke had paid close attention to the kidnapper's trial—not for the legal outcome, but for the many salacious details, which he'd tried to imagine in their full splendor—and the genius of the girl's artful tormentor had become an early source of inspiration. The man was insane, of course, but clever.

Duke stretches out his long legs and begins to wonder whatever happened to Daryl Wayne Flint.

SEVENTEEN

She's a bully in heels," Reeve tells Dr. Lerner over dinner.

"Well, that's good, isn't it? That's what she's supposed to be. The prosecutor for your case wasn't exactly a wimp, either."

"Burke thinks he was," she says, picking at her salad.

"How's that?"

"She made a snide remark about Daryl Wayne Flint not getting what he deserved."

Dr. Lerner sighs. "Unfortunately. But it wasn't due to any failure of the prosecution."

"I know. It was an *unusual confluence of events*," she says with heavy emphasis.

"We weren't totally blindsided, but, yes, there were some unexpected maneuvers by that defense attorney."

"And that stupid judge." Reeve stabs a tomato. "And Dr. Ick."

"The evil Dr. Moody, yes." The sadness in Dr. Lerner's eyes belies his light tone.

Reeve's family had bristled at the testimony of Dr. Terrance Moody, the arrogant expert witness for the defense who had proven so persuasive in court. During the trial, the two LeClaire daughters had tagged the forensic psychiatrist "Dr. Ick." The name stuck.

"Plus Flint's mother," Dr. Lerner reminds her. "Your kidnapper's case might have collapsed without his mother's testimony."

"But she's as bad as he is! I can't believe anyone bought it."

"Agreed. But with her testimony along with Moody's, it was hard for the prosecution to prove malingering. Flint's attorney made his case, even if we're convinced it was all an act."

Glowering, she mutters, "Anyway, Flint is locked up . . . and a psychiatric hospital is just as secure as a prison, right? So I guess that's all that really matters."

"He'll stay locked up for an extraordinarily long time, if I have any say about it. You can bet that I'll keep flying up there every time a petition is sent to the judge."

"The next hearing is coming up, isn't it?"

"The Risk Review Board hasn't gotten back to me with the date yet, but they will soon. It's usually in January."

Reeve forces Daryl Wayne Flint from her mind, sets aside her fork, and looks around. They had opted for convenience, walking over from the hotel to a chain restaurant with pulsing music and a bar spilling over with a boisterous crowd. Regretting their choice of dining establishment, she tries to figure out what seems so different from San Francisco. The people here are more casually dressed, no surprise. But there's something other than the preponderance of flannel that's unsettling.

"How's your salad?" Dr. Lerner asks.

"Okay. But I kind of wish I'd ordered the salmon. How's your pasta?"

"Bland. And I definitely wish I'd ordered the salmon," he says, making a face.

Reeve turns her attention back to the singles scene churning around them, noticing two men dressed in camouflage, and several wearing baseball caps. Indoors. At night. It strikes her as odd.

"Are you okay?"

"Sure," she says, glancing away from a heavily bearded mountain man who grins at her from the bar. As she looks from man to man, trying to figure out what's nagging at her, it dawns on her that it's Friday night—date night—yet most of these guys have no apparent interest in razors or personal grooming. Maybe she's not one to judge, since it's rare that she would find herself out on a Friday night, but is there some kind of message in all this facial hair?

"So," Dr. Lerner says, interrupting her thoughts, "Jackie Burke intends to interview Tilly at home tomorrow."

"That's what she says. But I'm kind of surprised that any lawyer would want to work on the weekend, aren't you?"

"No, this is a big case, so everyone will be working nonstop until all the evidence is in and the trial is over. Anyway, the Cavanaughs want us to come, too."

"They do?"

"Since Burke is going to be interviewing Tilly, they'd like us to be there."

"Well, I'm sure Jackie Burke will be thrilled to see me."

"Tough. It's what Tilly wants." He studies her for a moment. "You don't mind, do you? I'm sorry to drag you into this."

"No, I get it. Talking to a lawyer is like feeding a crocodile."

"And you realize that it's a positive sign that Tilly has asked us to be there, that she already feels that kind of trust."

"Sure, I understand. It's just that I wasn't really planning . . . uh, but anyway, if Tilly wants moral support, I'll be there."

Another quick glance at the mountain man at the bar, and a connection snaps into place: He reminds her of the guy with the smeared raincoat who hangs out by the BART station. She looks around, thinking that most of these whiskered faces remind her of the scruffy guys pushing carts around San Francisco.

"What?"

"Nothing," she says, shaking her head.

"Ready to go?" Dr. Lerner pushes aside his unfinished bowl of pasta, and a few minutes later they're outside in the wintery night air. The pulsing music fades behind them as they walk across the asphalt parking lot toward their hotel. The cold bites through Reeve's clothes, and she jams her fists into her pockets.

"I probably don't need to remind you," he says, "but we need to take a back seat while Burke is interviewing Tilly tomorrow."

"Of course. Quiet moral support, no smart remarks, I promise."

"Although the truth is," Dr. Lerner says, "I'll be dying to ask about the dogs."

"What dogs?"

"The cadaver-sniffing dogs."

"What? You lost me."

"Didn't you hear? Crime scene investigators are searching both of the houses that Vanderholt rented, looking for those other missing girls."

She jolts to a stop. "What missing girls?"

Back in her hotel room, Reeve boots up her computer and does a search. Tilly's rescue and Vanderholt's suicide attempt dominate local headlines, and it doesn't take long to scan the news coverage and find more about the abductions bracketing Tilly Cavanaugh's.

Hannah Creighton disappeared more than two years ago, a few months after turning twelve and several months before Tilly was taken. She was last seen on a golf course near her home, in the evening, practicing alone at the driving range.

Fourteen-year-old Abby Hill disappeared just ten weeks ago while camping at Jefferson Lake with her family. A rescue team searched the surrounding terrain and dragged the swimming area, but found no sign of Abby.

First Hannah, then Tilly, then Abby. No wonder the prosecutor was being such a bitch.

Reeve scrolls through the newspaper's archives and reads everything she can find, hoping for some insight into how these three girls might be linked. They were all small girls, roughly the same in physical appearance, and vanished under similar circumstances. All three disappeared from an outdoor location, with no witnesses.

Most of the news stories were written by a reporter named Otis Poe, and Reeve follows a link to his blog. She scrolls down, skimming.

The guy seems obsessed with finding a connection between these three cases. He rants that Vanderholt is the obvious perpetrator, yet has not been named as a suspect in the abductions of Hannah Creighton and Abby Hill. And Poe eviscerates the copycat theories floated by an unnamed source at the FBI.

While reading, Reeve keeps flashing on Tilly's burns and is relieved that details of the girl's injuries haven't been mentioned in any articles. At least not yet. It's terrible reading personal facts about yourself in the news. But of course it's even worse reading lies.

Exhausted, she stands and stretches, easing the stiffness in her back. She opts for a quick shower, then turns out the light and crawls between the clean, crisp sheets. The bed is soft, the pillows are just right, but she lies there, wide-eyed and alert.

If Vanderholt kidnapped all three of them, where are the other two?

Dead, most likely. But if that's the case, why would he spare Tilly? Because she was the smallest? Because she didn't fight back?

She tosses and turns, but sleep won't come, so she gives up and finds the remote, hoping for some mind-numbing television. Instead, she finds the local news.

Here is a reporter standing outside taut yellow lines of police tape, gesturing to the house cordoned off behind her. "Crime scene investigators brought specially trained dogs to both residences where Randy Vanderholt allegedly held young Tilly Cavanaugh captive in two different basements."

The video changes to a German shepherd jumping out of a pickup truck, and then to a black lab, nose to the ground, with a police officer trailing after it. The voice-over says: "Sources confirm that these dogs will be searching for any sign of two other missing girls, Hannah Creighton and Abby Hill, whose disappearances may be linked to Tilly Cavanaugh's kidnapping."

Next, a man with gray skin and a bushy moustache is saying how shocked he is that Randy Vanderholt, the ordinary-seeming guy he hired to work as a janitor at Three Rivers Mall, is under arrest. "You just wouldn't think he had that kind of evil in him," the man says.

"Yeah, right," Reeve scoffs.

"Randy was quiet," the manager continues. "Maybe not the brightest guy around, but I saw him helping old folks, people in wheelchairs, things like that." He shakes his head. "It's awful creepy to think of him as a kidnapper. But I guess it's always the ones you least expect."

Next, a reporter interviews the girls' mothers, who are clearly distraught. Mrs. Creighton, a worn-looking woman with haunted eyes, says in her wispy voice, "We're still hopeful, of course. But any news would be better than not knowing."

A minute later, Mrs. Hill is saying essentially the same thing, but her face is tense and she stands with her fists clenched.

Reeve clicks off the news and turns out the light, but can't sleep. She keeps seeing the bald pain in those faces, picturing her own parents in that same situation: having a child missing for so long that even finding a corpse would come as relief.

EIGHTEEN

Saturday

Duke opens a thermos of coffee and pours himself a fresh cup. He was up early, pasting on a thick moustache before loading gear into his van and driving up into the hills overlooking the Cavanaughs' home.

Visual surveillance is another of his specialties, and the hilly, wooded terrain that rims the town of Jefferson makes it a watcher's paradise. Over the years, he has staked out several choice locations around town. He found this secluded spot, wedged between a thick copse of trees and a granite boulder, long ago, when Tilly was still a carefree kid, just one of a few select targets.

The heavy cloud cover that obscures nearby mountaintops gives the scene below him a flat, even light. No rain, just a damp, cold threat. He lifts his binoculars and peers down at the L-shaped house. No activity yet. And he's pleased that no reporters are congregating at the gate this morning.

He adjusts the volume on his earbuds, hearing nothing.

In Duke's experience, the distraught parents of a freshly kidnapped child are in a panic to cooperate with law enforcement. It had been almost as simple to take control of the Cavanaughs' cell phones as it had been to bug Tilly's bedroom. Regrettably, Mrs. Cavanaugh's cell has since been broken and replaced, but Mr. Cavanaugh's is still working like a demon. So, just in case Mr. Cavanaugh has carelessly left his phone in a coat pocket or on the charger, Duke now dials his number and listens to it ring. And ring.

"Hello?"

Duke says nothing.

A pause, a click, and next he hears footsteps, followed by Gordon Cavanaugh's voice muttering, "Another damn restricted number."

Duke smiles, sure the phone is being carried to where it will be close at hand.

Just then a white sedan pulls up at the gate. He lifts his binoculars as the gate sweeps open, and watches the car drive through and park at an odd angle. He gets a glimpse of Jackie Burke, looking crisp and stern, as always, accompanied by one uniformed deputy. They hurry to the front door.

"Here we go," Duke says aloud.

He hears a weak buzz, voices too soft to be distinguishable. Soon, the signal strengthens. Meaningless pleasantries are being exchanged, and Duke easily identifies the voice of each family member: Gordon and Shirley Cavanaugh, their son Matt, and then Tilly. The deputy, named Chris something, is tasked with recording Tilly's statement.

"Come on, Tilly-girl," Duke mutters. "Don't disappoint me."

He adjusts his earbuds and sips his coffee.

Another vehicle arrives at the gate, and Duke is so eager to get a good look at its occupants that he nearly spills his coffee as he grabs his binoculars.

The driver wheels through the gate and down the driveway. The dark SUV parks next to Burke's sedan, and Duke recognizes the young driver as Deputy Nick Hudson, no surprise. The wiry male passenger is clearly Dr. Ezra Lerner, that pseudosophisticated shrink.

Ah, and here is the famous Regina Victoria LeClaire. Edgy Reggie, all grown up and calling herself Reeve. He grins and leans forward as she comes around the SUV. He admires the tight curve of her ass and, with a pang of regret at not having his camera ready, watches her follow the others into the house.

In a moment, Duke hears more meaningless pleasantries, coffee poured and pastry offered. He waits impatiently, feeling bored until Jackie Burke's grating voice says, "If you don't mind, let's get started. Now, Tilly, would you prefer to talk with me privately?"

"Um, no. I want my mom with me. And Reeve and Dr. Lerner, too. Is that okay?"

"Of course," she says, but Duke chortles, because he can tell from her tone that she's displeased.

"Now," Burke continues, "before we begin, I want you to know how much we appreciate your cooperation." She goes on talking about legal mumbo jumbo, explaining what to expect in the weeks and months ahead, adding, "I know the news coverage is tough, but it should die down soon. And in the meantime, we'll do our best to guard your family's privacy. But, uh, do I understand that you're considering a move somewhere out of town?"

Duke sits up.

"Well, we're just in the talking stages," Mrs. Cavanaugh volunteers with a nervous laugh. "We do have family down in Fresno."

"That idea really sucks, if you ask me," declares a young male voice, clearly Tilly's brother.

"But, honey, it would make things easier on Tilly," says Mrs. Cavanaugh in a placating tone. "Besides, you might like it."

"But why move? I mean, everything that twisted perv did to her is bad enough. Why does the whole family have to suffer?"

"Don't worry, Matt," Mr. Cavanaugh says. "We would definitely wait until the end of the school year, after you graduate. It would be summertime before we'd even consider moving."

"Will the trial be over by then?" Mrs. Cavanaugh asks.

"It's hard to say for certain," Burke responds, "but that might be pushing it."

"Maybe there won't even be a trial," says the son. "Maybe he'll actually kill himself next time."

"Matt, that's enough," Mr. Cavanaugh says, cutting him off. "We'll have to see how events unfold." A pause. "So, Jackie, tell us: Do you expect that the public defender will try for some kind of plea bargain?"

"That would save Tilly an ordeal, wouldn't it?" Mrs. Cavanaugh asks.

"And then we wouldn't have to move," the son says.

"We have to go with the assumption that there will be a trial," Jackie Burke says evenly. "I realize it's an ordeal you'd prefer to avoid, but our first priority has to be building a case so that Randy Vanderholt is held accountable."

"And punished," adds Mr. Cavanaugh.

"But we can't plan our whole lives around this trial," the son complains.

"I'm working on this case exclusively," Burke says. "I'll do my best to keep things moving. And with luck, Vanderholt will be arraigned early next week."

"Okay," says Mrs. Cavanaugh, "but no matter how it all plays out legally, Tilly is still the one who has to deal with school, with her friends, and with everyone knowing who she is and what happened." She sighs. "Besides, Fresno might make a nice change."

"Oh, that's right. How stupid of me," says the son acidly. "Why would I think my opinion would count for anything in this family?"

The scrape of a chair, an awkward silence. A door slams, and Duke watches the teenager stomp over to a dented red pickup truck. A moment later, the truck is through the gate and speeding away.

For the next two hours, Duke smokes and listens while Tilly shares details about how Randy Vanderholt kidnapped and raped and abused her. She sticks with her story: It was Randy Vanderholt, and only Randy Vanderholt, who hurt her.

Several times, Duke smiles and murmurs, "Good girl."

Duke watches Jackie Burke and the first deputy come out of the house and drive away. He sets his thermos aside as Reeve, the shrink, and the other deputy emerge and head toward the dark SUV. He's hungry, and he considers following them, but decides that Tilly is the one to watch. From what he can hear, the family is making preparations to leave the house—Tilly's first excursion out—and he's curious to see her.

She comes out with only her mother, her face obscured by an olive-colored hoodie. The girl is so thin that, dressed in hoodie and jeans, she looks like a boy.

Duke turns the key in the ignition and quickly backs out of his surveillance spot. He takes a shortcut down the hill to the traffic light and, with perfect timing, sees them turn onto the avenue just in front of him. He follows their gold Infiniti SUV through town to a strip mall, where they park.

He circles the crowded parking lot while keeping an eye on them. They head into a beauty salon, and Duke parks nearby.

Looking for a good vantage point, he finds a Chinese restaurant with a perfect view of the salon. He insists on a seat by the window. When the waiter arrives, he orders a lunch special of hot-and-sour soup, egg rolls, and lemon chicken with fried rice, followed by some kind of yellow custard that he doesn't eat.

They're in the salon a long time.

He watches and waits.

He asks for the bill and is sipping jasmine tea when Tilly emerges with a very short haircut, dyed a burgundy shade not much different from Reeve's.

Duke lays cash on the table and reaches his van just as Tilly's mother is backing out of her parking space.

He follows at a safe distance, letting four cars in between as they drive down a busy street. When they merge into a turning lane and head east, the light changes and Duke is stuck, fuming. But luck is with him. He watches as Mrs. Cavanaugh makes a quick right turn into another busy strip mall.

Waiting for the light to change, he sees them get out of the gold Infiniti and head across the lot. As the light changes, he catches a glimpse of them entering a Jamba Juice.

He turns into the same parking lot and Lady Luck smiles: a space opens up next to their vehicle. Duke parks alongside. He climbs nimbly between the seats into the back, where he keeps most of his equipment.

By the time Tilly and Shirley Cavanaugh come out with their drinks, Duke has activated a highly specialized recording device attached to his driver's side mirror. As Mrs. C clicks her key fob, the Infiniti chirps, and Duke smiles. His device has just captured and recorded layers of electronic information, including the lock's encrypted codes.

NINETEEN

Sunday

Don't you love the smell of popcorn?" Tilly stands sock-footed in the kitchen, watching her mother shake the pot.

Once the staccato bursting of kernels slows, her mother removes the pot from the heat and gives two more shakes, popping the last few kernels before pouring the steaming popcorn into a big wooden bowl, which she hands to Tilly. She watches her daughter hold it beneath her nose and inhale.

Mrs. Cavanaugh smiles and asks, "You two know how to work the DVD, don't you?"

"No problem," Reeve replies.

"Of course, Mom," Tilly adds, rolling her eyes.

"Good, because I always forget."

Reeve and Mrs. Cavanaugh's eyes meet, and they share a smile. It's instantly clear to Reeve that Shirley Cavanaugh actually has no problem understanding the DVD player, and this is just a motherly ploy to build her daughter's confidence.

Today, the three of them have the run of the house. Mr. Cavanaugh is at the high school watching his son's basketball team either win or lose a tournament, so Mrs. Cavanaugh has invited Reeve over for an afternoon movie. For the day's matinee, Tilly has selected a popular film about vampires and heartache.

Reeve curls up on the couch beside Tilly, thinking how unexpected it is to be here, in such rare company. They are two survivors of very similar crimes. Ripped from everything familiar at a young age, both have traveled here from truncated childhoods, through prolonged captivity and unspeakable abuse, to this particular time and place: safely eating popcorn in a suburban living room, watching a movie on a wide-screen, high-definition TV.

It all seems so strangely normal.

After the film, while Mrs. Cavanaugh is in the kitchen cleaning up, Tilly grows quiet, and Reeve assumes she's mulling over their discussion of the themes in the film. Mrs. Cavanaugh has drawn comparisons with *West Side Story* and *Romeo and Juliet*. They've discussed gang rivalries, family dynamics, the need for love, and the problems of being the new kid in school.

It has been a surprisingly lively conversation, in Reeve's opinion.

Tilly fidgets beside her.

"Your mom's a smart lady," Reeve remarks.

Tilly hums a note of agreement, watching Reeve with her gray eyes. Then she sits up tall. "Could I ask you something?"

"Sure." Reeve inhales, anticipating some weighty questions about love or acceptance. As if she's got a clue. Dating is tough enough for most people, but nearly impossible for someone like Reeve, for whom answering the mildest query about her life is like choosing among sticks of dynamite.

"Sure," she repeats, trying not to grimace. "You can ask me anything."

Tilly leans over, grips Reeve's thigh, peers into her face, and whispers, "Would you help me convince my mom to let us move? I mean, like, *now?* Like, really, really soon?"

TWENTY

Duke's chair rolls smoothly across the hardwood floor. He is comfortable in his favorite chair as he monitors the various listening stations in his private control room. He's rolling and listening and congratulating himself for having thought so far ahead and having executed his plans so well.

Exactly as he had with the families of the other two girls.

It's a brilliant arrangement.

Finding the perfect mark was not always easy, but Duke is a patient man with unique skills. He perfected a method: investigate recent parolees, then target a few who just happen to spend a lot of time around playgrounds, water parks, and school yards.

He would wait and watch, which is exactly what he is trained to do.

Clearly, Duke would have the most influence over the particular ex-cons who shared some of his tastes, but had never been arrested for a sex crime. He had no interest in contacting registered sex offenders. Only a fool would want to pair up with damaged goods.

Upon identifying the proper target, he would track the parolee until some lapse in judgment and behavior provided enough leverage. Then, Duke would don a disguise, usually a full beard and glasses, and approach the man. He would first present evidence of the ex-con's recent transgressions and threaten him: "One photo sent anonymously to your parole officer, and you'll be back in prison."

Blackmail always worked.

He would watch his target flush and squirm. Once he was satisfied, he would back off and allow the parolee to catch his breath. Next, he would pretend to consider options. He would let the target hope, and then slowly, bit by bit, offer a proposition.

He would lay out the plan in simple, tantalizing terms. And then he would bring out the photographs and watch the man's pupils dilate.

No one ever turned him down. And it all worked perfectly, with minimal risk to Duke.

Each felon undertook the actual abduction. They weren't smart enough to put together the plan, but apparently enjoyed a sense of adventure in executing the task. And the beauty of it was, if anything went wrong, Duke was in the clear. No one in law enforcement would ever believe that the kidnapper was anything less than one hundred percent to blame, no matter what his story.

Duke's efforts remained in the background until the proper time. He found the girl, procured the location, prepared the basement. He refined every aspect of the kidnapping so that he was never in jeopardy.

Once the girl was secure, the keeper shouldered the dull, daily burdens of feeding and cleaning up after her. Duke had zero interest in dealing with messy routine. No, his special thrill came in establishing dominance over the girl, as well as her keeper.

He got to rape the girls first. The virgins were always his prize.

And his repayment was also monetary, because some nominal rent, of course, must be paid.

Later, whenever he wanted to visit, he just called and ordered the keeper to make preparations. Brilliant.

The ex-cons were his minions. The girls were his harem. Everything was working beautifully until Randy Vanderholt managed to screw it up. A flash of anger shoots through him. It has been days since he has allowed himself to indulge in a session with one of his girls. Instead, he must settle for the nominal stimulation provided by electronic monitoring.

Duke shifts in his chair and resets the recording to a preferred section. He hears Tilly's dispassionate voice. She is answering Jackie Burke's probing questions.

He settles back and gets comfortable, listening to Tilly's matter-of-fact descriptions. He sees the scenes exactly as they unfolded, because he was the one who was there, not Vanderholt. When Tilly describes how he pushed into her, breaking her hymen and making her bleed, he indulges the vision for a moment and relishes the stiffening of his cock.

Ordinarily, this would be the perfect time to pay one of his pets a call, but it is foolish to even consider acting on this impulse now, thanks to the idiotic behavior of Randy Vanderholt.

Tilly had been Duke's favorite—so petite, so moistly terrified—and now she is gone and the other two will have to be off-limits until things quiet down.

Picturing Vanderholt comfortably drugged and warm in the infirmary, Duke jumps out of his chair with a curse.

Time for a cigarette.

The control room has too much valuable equipment to risk smoke contamination, so Duke shuts the heavy door behind him and hurries down the hall, through the living room to the kitchen, where he keeps his cigarettes.

He strikes a match and inhales. His mind clears as he smokes, stepping over to the side windows that overlook his carport and yard. He likes this vantage point. He likes to stand and smoke while surveying his property. It's a large piece of land, stretching between the road and the river, a wild landscape of native oaks and resinous pines. It's not unusual to see deer, raccoons, river rats, or an occasional fox.

Today something else moves in the brush. Duke glares out the window at the big yellow tomcat slinking across his yard. Quickly stubbing out his cigarette, he sweeps up the air rifle that he always keeps handy, pumps it hard, and cracks open the side door. The cat has crouched low, watching a bird about twenty yards out.

Duke takes aim, squeezes the trigger, and the cat lets out a screech as it darts into the brush.

He throws the gun down in disgust. He could have easily killed the cat with a rifle, but can't risk gunfire. Especially now, with the suburbs encroaching on his acreage. Seems like there's always some busybody out walking a dog or repairing a fence. And Duke has no control over the river, so a stray bullet might ding a passing boat. All sorts of idiots are out there, just itching to file a report.

He retrieves the air rifle and sets it back in its spot, cracking the butt a tad too hard on the tile, feeling another stab of anger toward Randy Vanderholt.

TWENTY-ONE

Everyone recommended Gigi's as Jefferson City's best Italian restaurant. It is tucked down an obscure street on a poorly lit corner that isn't visible from the main drag. Thanks to the Cavanaughs' careful directions, Reeve and Dr. Lerner manage to navigate the route, and they find Gigi's parking lot crowded for such an unlikely spot.

Wonderful aromas greet them as they enter. There's a pleasant hum of conversation above the music—acoustic guitar—played by a musician near the back. They are promptly seated at a table beside a wall-sized mural of an Italian village. While they consult their menus, a well-dressed man who seems to be the owner moves from table to table, greeting customers, setting out baskets of fresh, warm bread.

The crowd consists mainly of couples, and the men are mostly clean shaven. Reeve sees only one baseball cap and a single man with a moustache. She dips a crusty bite of bread into a small dish of olive oil and tastes it, humming a note of appreciation.

After they've ordered, Dr. Lerner says, "We haven't had much chance to speak privately. So tell me: What do you think of Tilly?"

She has been gnawing at this very question. Tilly is the only person she's met who shares such a closely parallel history. In ways both simple and profound, Tilly's story seems to echo her own. "She's quiet, but she's a lot stronger than I thought she would be. Stronger than I was."

"Your physical and mental conditions were worse, and you were in deep shock, Reeve. Your captivity was much longer, and in many ways more traumatic."

Reeve strokes the numbness that starts near the scars on her left wrist and continues all the way to the tip of her little finger. She has never determined whether the nerve damage is from being cuffed and suspended for too long, or from breaking her hand when she tried to fight. "We have some similar scars," she says, "but I hated talking to the prosecutor, remember?"

"Which brings up the issue of the trial. That was a long and awful ordeal for you, so I thought it was extraordinary that Tilly asked for that meeting with Jackie Burke."

"I thought so, too. It's like she's in a rush to get it all over with."

"Maybe she is." He dabs a piece of fresh bread in olive oil and pops it into his mouth, looking thoughtful.

"Well, now that she has given her statement to Burke, maybe the worst is over. Or at least until the trial."

Reeve looks up as three new customers come in the door, then settles back and looks around. The decor is a warmly peculiar mix of Americana with rustic Tuscan. Each table has the traditional red-and-white checkered tablecloth with a quirky set of salt-and-pepper shakers. Their set is a cow and a moon.

Their food arrives and they address it in silence, with the reverence of the truly hungry. After several bites, Dr. Lerner asks, "How's your risotto?"

"Fabulous. How's your ravioli?"

"Outstanding." He lifts his glass of Chianti, and asks, "So, what do you think of Tilly's haircut?"

"She looks like a young, dark-haired Justin Bieber, doesn't she?"

"What do you think about the color?"

"That it's a lot like mine? Hard not to notice."

"So, you two had a good day today?"

"Well, we understand each other. But her brother," she adds with a sour expression, "he's another story."

"This kind of thing is hard on siblings, particularly brothers of that age," Dr. Lerner says, nodding. "You can bet he's getting all kinds of strange reactions from kids at school. He wants to protect his kid sister, but doesn't know how to act."

"You think that's it?"

"Even trained adults can have a hard time dealing with these kinds of situations. Which is why the Cavanaughs so appreciate your help with Tilly."

With a fleeting smile, she says, "It's kind of like we belong to the same tribe."

"You are both survivors." He takes a sip of his wine. "Any nightmares lately?"

"You know, it's funny, but I haven't had a single one since I've been up here."

"Funny how?"

"Well, I had a rough time when I first heard about Tilly. But since coming up here, since actually meeting her, I've been fine." She had expected recurrent nightmares, but except for a fitful hour or two, has plunged into pools of deep sleep.

"And why do you think that's the case?"

She squints at him. "Once a shrink, always a shrink, right?"

"Guilty."

"Okay." She sets down her fork. "It seems pretty pedestrian, but seeing her makes me realize how far I've come. Maybe I'm not as gentle and wise as Beth Goodwin, but I can assume that sort of role. I can help."

He smiles at her, tipping his glass in a toast. "You are indeed uniquely qualified. And you've been an enormous help." After a moment, he adds, "You know, Tilly's family has told me more than once how very grateful they are that you came up here. In fact, they'd like you to stay."

"What?"

"Don't worry, I told them that's not possible."

"Right. You're her therapist," she says, absently rubbing the tiny ridges of the healed bone in her little finger. "Why would they even ask?"

"They see that Tilly is bonding with you, and they'd like you to continue meeting with her, but I told them it's too much of an imposition, that these sessions raise painful memories for you."

"Well, sure." She cocks her head. "But do they really think I'm helping? She seems so . . ."

"It's going to be rocky for a while, of course. For all of them. Because the Cavanaughs are suffering through a painful adjustment. That's true in every case."

Reeve is hit with a pang of sympathy for Tilly's family, followed by a surge of guilt over how she had treated her own. How churlish she had been. How selfish. She had spent hours alone in her room, wrapped in a sulk, punishing them and herself with isolation.

He leans forward, his voice low but intense. "Tilly is just beginning to reclaim her life, and healing takes time, as you know."

"Sure. I mean, I understand what she's going through better than anyone else." A frown creases her forehead. "So if they want me to stay, maybe I should."

"Oh no, that's way beyond what anyone expects of you. You've done enough. Everyone underst—"

"Does Tilly want me to stay?"

"Well, of course, but—"

"Okay then. If I can help Tilly, I'll stay on."

He shakes his head. "I'm not sure that's a good idea."

"Why not? You just said I'm uniquely qualified."

"Well, it's a serious—"

"Weren't you just saying that Tilly's family isn't equipped to offer what she needs? That they're suffering through their own adjustment?"

"Reeve, you can't—"

"Listen, the main reason I'm here is because our cases are so similar, because Tilly and I were about the same age when we were taken, and we were both held captive by sadists."

He gives a shrug, conceding her point.

"But that's only part of it. We're almost like sisters. And I understand her also because I've read a lot of the literature. You know that, right?"

"Well, sure."

"I mean, I've read all of your scholarly articles."

He gives a half-grin. "Fishing for compliments?"

"I've also read Lawler, Auerbach, Zarse, and Ochberg."

His eyebrows shoot up. "Impressive. But I doubt you've read any of the profilers, the guys from the FBI's Behavioral Sciences Unit."

She leans forward and raps on the table as she lists the names: "Dietz. Hazelwood. Douglas. McCrary. Ressler."

"How about Cantor and Price, from Australia? And Favaro's study, the one about trauma among kidnap victims in Italy?"

"Please." She rolls her eyes. "Favaro's study was weak, at least in terms of captivity syndromes."

"You've read all that?"

"See?"

He laughs. "Okay, point made. You've practically got an honorary degree." He takes a sip of water, keeping his eyes on her.

"It's not like I'm trying to replace you or anything. You're still her therapist. But Tilly has no sister, no other girlfriends she can talk to."

"You're really sure you want to do this?"

"Absolutely. We survived similar ordeals, and how many people can say that?" She sits back, crossing her arms. "Besides, if the Cavanaughs want me to stay, it's a free country."

"Burke will spit bullets," he says, shaking his head.

"Why would she care? You're still her expert witness, you're still the name with the golden credentials. As long as I stay under the radar, what difference does it make to Burke?"

He exhales heavily.

"It's not like I'm going to *impede the prosecution of her case*," Reeve says, mimicking Burke's hoarse manner of speech. "I'll just be hanging around eating cookies with Tilly. Besides, I have no plans, no job, no life, and I'm embarrassingly free."

"If you're sure," Dr. Lerner says, turning up his palms in a gesture of surrender, "the Cavanaughs will be delighted. And on second thought, it might be good for both of you."

"Both of us? How's that?"

He says nothing, giving her an enigmatic look.

She studies him, sensing a deeper meaning. "Okay, I get it," she says finally. "Your suggestion that I establish a personal connection with someone, is that it?" She rolls her eyes. "I suppose it's better than having an affair with the hot guy at the pet store."

"Oh? You never mentioned anyone."

"Just kidding. Never mind. Anyway, if I'm going to stay, I guess I'll have to go shopping. I didn't bring enough clothes."

Back in her hotel room, Reeve sprawls on the bed and calls Anthony to ask him to take care of Persephone.

"When will you be back?" he wants to know.

"I don't know. Not long, I don't think, but I hadn't planned on leaving her alone for more than a weekend. Can you help me out?"

Anthony laughs. "It just so happens that emergency spidersitting is my specialty." He knows just what to do, and he lays it all out for her.

She listens carefully and agrees to call the building supervisor, a matronly woman named Helen, to arrange for brief entry into her apartment. Once they've covered the logistics, she says, "One more thing: You didn't mention how much you'll charge."

"Are you kidding? For a beauty like Persie? Just promise me you'll be back soon."

Next, Reeve calls her father to let him know she won't be coming home for at least a few more days. When she tells him she's going to be working as a kind of mentor for Tilly, the words feel foreign in her mouth.

"That's great, kiddo. It seems you're entering new territory, forming this bond with her." She can hear the pride in her father voice. Then he sighs and adds, "Does this mean you're not Dr. Lerner's patient anymore?"

She suffers a pang of regret. If she is not his patient she's—what?— his former patient? Is that even possible? Or is she like a recovered alcoholic, forever defined by her condition? "Well, yeah, maybe I've finally crossed over to some version of adulthood," she says begrudgingly.

When she explains that Mr. and Mrs. Cavanaugh have offered to cover her expenses, her father chuckles, but does she sense a relief that goes unsaid? Despite her father's generosity, she has felt more uncomfortable about her dependent status with each passing birthday.

They exchange the usual questions about how everything is going, a comfortable back-and-forth that has its own rhythm, until, during a lull in the conversation, he asks, "You didn't happen to see *60 Minutes* tonight, did you?"

Detecting a note of concern, she sits up. "No, why?"

"Well, uh . . ." He clears his throat. "They aired an update of that program about kidnapping and captivity syndromes."

"Oh, crap." She closes her eyes. "The one with Dr. Moody?"

"I'm sorry. They apparently dusted it off because of the kidnappings up there, with Vanderholt's arrest and all. Riding a new wave of interest at your expense, I'm afraid."

"And yours, Dad."

"Well, if it's any consolation, it was mostly old footage. There wasn't much new, really. And of course they don't have your new name."

"So, it was just some old stuff about Daryl Wayne Flint?"

"Um, yeah, but . . ."

"But what?"

"But they interviewed Dr. Moody again."

"That crackpot? Why? Can't they see he's a liar and an opportunist? They should pile up his damn books and strike a match."

"And roast him on top, I agree. But he's a crackpot with a Ph.D., unfortunately, so people are inclined to believe that he knows what he's talking about."

"Crap. Years of therapy, down the toilet." After a beat of silence, she adds, "Just kidding, Dad. Relax."

Her father coughs a laugh. "Anyway, I don't think anyone would recognize you now."

"Or Tilly, either." She tells her father about Tilly's new hairdo, then says good night and climbs into bed, exhausted.

But she can't help mentally replaying that familiar *60 Minutes* segment. It first aired during a brief phase of comfort—when she was free and back home, when everything was beginning to settle into place—before she learned about her mother's cancer.

She had almost forgotten about Dr. Moody's love of media attention. "Dr. Ick." She says the name out loud, groans into the darkness, and reflexively begins charting the internal geography of everything that has happened and how it has changed her. The long, deep pit of captivity. The dizzying high of being returned to her family. And then the trial and the cascading despair, punctuated by her mother's death.

It had almost sunk her.

But now she has an opportunity to turn it into something positive. Tomorrow, she will dedicate herself fully to Tilly's recovery. She vows to be attentive and compassionate, and to do her best to guard Tilly's privacy from those damn reporters.

She pulls the covers up to her ears, and drifts off to sleep, wondering if she can somehow help Tilly remember anything about those two other missing girls.

TWENTY-TWO

Monday

An arctic cold drops down from the mountains, and residents of Jefferson County bundle up, stoke fires, and worry about frozen pipes, but Deputy Nick Hudson's SUV is warmed up and waiting in the hotel's parking lot before Reeve and Dr. Lerner have had time to finish breakfast.

Reeve hurries through the cold and climbs into the backseat. They exchange brief greetings, but Hudson barely offers a smile, and the group falls silent. As they roll west toward the Cavanaughs' house, Reeve studies the mountains that ring the city, their bright, snow-covered peaks looking like diamonds cut from a backdrop of hard blue sky.

Oddly, Hudson doesn't turn on the country music he favors, and after riding in silence for several minutes, Dr. Lerner asks, "Is everything all right?"

"Sorry if I seem . . . I'm kind of distracted," Hudson says with a shrug. "There's a lot going on this morning."

"Anything you want to share?"

"Not really," he says, smoothly accelerating onto the freeway.

Reeve studies his face. "What about the dogs?"

He glances at her in the rearview mirror but doesn't respond.

"They were searching both of Vanderholt's residences," she prompts. "The first place Tilly was held, and the one that he moved to more recently, where she was found."

"Right. Well, the dogs came back with nothing. Nada. Zip."

"So you've got nothing to link Vanderholt to those other missing girls?"

"Apparently not."

"What about the DNA evidence?"

"It's not like TV, where DNA results come back in twenty minutes. That kind of work is sent out to experts, and the labs are slammed, so you send in cigarette butts, for instance, and it can take forever before you get anything back."

"So there's still a chance . . ."

"Yeah, maybe. But who says they'll find a match? And the district attorney isn't happy. He was all primed for a tight case, all packaged up and ready to go."

"So what now?"

"So he's yelling at Burke, who intends to hit Vanderholt with a fat list of charges tomorrow morning."

"But there's a pattern, right? In terms of timing?" Reeve pauses for a response, but Hudson seems to be ignoring her. "It just seems logical that since Vanderholt kidnapped Tilly, he took the other two," she mutters, looking out at the passing scene, where trees tremble in the wind, dropping blood-red leaves.

"Everybody's a detective," he says in a mocking tone.

"Same MO, obviously," she retorts. "Similar girls, same body types, all of them taken around dusk, while doing some kind of sporting or outdoor activity, no witnesses." When Hudson doesn't respond, she adds, "According to Tilly, Vanderholt never mentioned any other girls, so if there's a connection, you haven't found it."

"Not yet. Unfortunately." Hudson keeps his eyes on the road.

"But what do *you* think? Did he kill Abby Hill and Hannah Creighton?"

"Hard to say."

"Well, what do you think about the copycat theories?" she persists.

"They're theories."

"Can't you tell us anything?"

"There are lots of theories being pursued."

"How enlightening," she says flatly. "Well, your detectives better find some kind of evidence soon, because I'm sure those girls' parents are going nuts."

"It's got to be tough on them," Dr. Lerner remarks, "getting their hopes up, and then having no answers. No matter how bad the news might be, they've already been through hell."

"Of course they want answers, and we want to provide them." Hudson's tone sharpens. "It's just not that easy. And now there's a rumor about some new strategy coming from Vanderholt's attorney."

"What?" Reeve sits forward. "What kind of strategy?"

"Don't know. But he's bringing in his top investigator, a tough guy named Molland."

"But Vanderholt already confessed."

"Exactly. That's what's got us all scratching our heads. Because Pierson—the defense attorney—is a veteran public defender. He's smart. And he's not one to blow smoke."

"So what does that mean?"

"Who knows? Whatever it is, it can't be good. So whips are cracking. The DA is snapping at Burke, and she's barking at her investigators, and the whole department is screaming at JSOTF."

"Screaming at what?"

"The Joint Special Operations Task Force," Dr. Lerner and Deputy Hudson respond in unison, and then flash each other a grin.

"What exactly is this special task force supposed to be doing?" she asks Hudson.

"They better rev up their investigation, for starters. The goal is to put the HRT in action."

"The HRT?"

"The Hostage Rescue Team."

"You like acronyms, don't you?"

"Sorry. Anyway, I think they'll probably take another stab at rounding up registered sex offenders."

"Oh, great," she scoffs. "That approach sure helped find Vanderholt, didn't it?"

Reeve carries two mugs of hot chocolate down the hall to Tilly's bedroom, wondering if she's really prepared for this new role. The door is ajar. She nudges it open and finds Tilly sitting up in bed, wearing plaid pajamas, her new hairdo in a mess. She's busily drawing with a charcoal pencil, but closes her sketch pad and tosses it aside to accept the offered mug.

Tilly sips the liquid and scoffs, "Cocoa? Really? I'm not a little kid, you know."

"Sorry. I thought you'd like it."

"Well, I prefer coffee now. For future reference."

"The adult beverage. So noted." Reeve takes a seat at the foot of the bed and sips her hot chocolate before softly asking, "So, you had a bad night, huh?"

Tilly hums an indifferent note. Her eyes look almost bruised, and her skin seems very pale against her newly dyed hair. "I mean, I'm home in my own bed, with good food every day, with my family taking care of me. What could I possibly have to complain about?" She sips more of her hot chocolate, scowling.

Reeve looks around the room, letting the challenge settle. She sees that Tilly has added some drawings to her bulletin board.

"It's just that I'm not a stupid little kid anymore, okay?" Tilly says hotly. "But they're treating me like some kind of baby. So here I am, with no TV and no computer and no phone. Plus, I have absolutely no friends anymore, because whenever they call, they treat me like I'm some kind of freak." She takes a gulp of her hot chocolate. "But what do we have to talk about, anyway?"

"It's tough, I know."

"I mean, I'm glad to be home and everything, but I'm sick of how everyone is treating me. And I'm sick of being stuck inside watching Harry Potter movies." Tilly rocks back and forth, an angry woman-child with her knees clutched to her chest.

"I understand that."

"I mean, after spending, like, a year locked up in a dungeon, getting raped and sucking cock, do they really think I can't handle TV?"

Reeve absorbs the rough talk. She tries and fails to find any words of comfort to offer across the bed of twisted sheets. Standing, she carries her mug of hot chocolate to the other side of the room and looks at some artwork on Tilly's bulletin board. Charcoal sketches and watercolors.

"These are new."

Tilly glances over. "Yeah."

Reeve bends to take a closer look at a black, purple, and orange version of a famous painting. "This is called *The Scream,* right? By Munch? It's really good."

Tilly gives her an unreadable look, drains her mug, sets it aside. "Did you talk to my parents, like I asked?"

"About moving? Your folks sound pretty serious about visiting your aunt down in Fresno."

"Visiting isn't moving."

"Well, with the trial coming up—" Reeve gestures with empty palms.

"But I told that lady lawyer everything that I was, that I . . . I told her everything. So now she can just leave me alone, right?"

"I wish that were the case."

Tilly crosses her arms and scowls.

"Sounds like your parents might be open to moving after the trial."

"That's not soon enough."

"You could be homeschooled for awhile. That's what I did."

The girl shoots Reeve a look of disgust, snatches up the charcoal pencil, and grabs her sketch pad, holding it closed in her lap.

"Listen Tilly," Reeve approaches, sits on the edge of the bed, "I've been thinking about those two other missing girls. Can you think back a couple of months ago? Did Vanderholt start acting weird, or different in any way?"

"No. I keep telling everybody, he moved me to that other dungeon. That was the only thing that changed."

"Did he say anything about another girl?"

"I told you, he's not the one that took Abby or Hannah," she says, opening the sketch pad. "Now go away."

Reeve purses her lips and carries the two empty mugs out to the kitchen, where she hands them to Mrs. Cavanaugh.

"Thank you so much for your help, Reeve," the tall woman says, setting the mugs in the sink. "I can't tell you how much—" she chokes on her words, clears her throat. "Well, I'm just so glad to have your help in getting my little girl back to normal."

Reeve can only shrug, thinking that Tilly is no longer her little girl, wondering if any of them can ever hope to be "normal." She approaches the group gathered around the kitchen table: Mr. Cavanaugh, Deputy Hudson, and Dr. Lerner. They are silent, all eyes upon her, as if she has interrupted something.

"She dismissed me," she says, feeling like a failure.

Mr. Cavanaugh groans.

"Oh, no. I'm so sorry," Mrs. Cavanaugh says. "I don't know why she would do that."

Reeve puts up a hand. "Believe me, I completely understand. I was exactly like that, up and down, for a long time."

"She had a bad night." Mr. Cavanaugh shares a look with his wife.

Mrs. Cavanaugh grasps her husband's arm. "She woke up screaming."

Reeve feels their eyes fix on her. It's clear they're hoping for more, but her tongue fails to find a single adequate sentence.

After a beat, Dr. Lerner volunteers, "It's a difficult time, especially after talking with Burke on Saturday, having to recount all those details about what happened."

Reeve shoots him a look of gratitude.

"I can prescribe something to help her sleep," Dr. Lerner continues. "And there's no reason to rush today's session. We can postpone it until she's comfortable, but let's give her a few minutes. She'll come around."

And sure enough, Tilly pads into the kitchen moments later, saying nothing as she loops her arms around her mother's waist.

TWENTY-THREE

Reeve climbs into the front passenger seat of Nick Hudson's SUV and buckles her seat belt. The Cavanaughs are having an extended session with Dr. Lerner, but since Hudson needs to return to work, he has offered to take her back to the hotel. She scrunches down low in her seat and hides from the hungry eyes of the news teams clustered at the gate. But after the first turn, she sits back up, paying close attention to street signs, noticing landmarks and distinctive Christmas decorations. If she wants to go shopping, she'll need to learn to navigate around Jefferson.

He fiddles with the radio as they head into town, turning up the volume on country songs with forlorn, heartbreaking lyrics. Meanwhile, he keeps glancing over at her.

"You know," he says finally, "I've been wanting to apologize."

"For what?"

"For my lame comments about Stockholm Syndrome."

She scoffs. "Why? It's not like it's all that common in law enforcement."

"That's no excuse. I've studied some psychology, and I know a few things about PTSD, so I should be up to speed."

"Well, I'm sure you don't come across it every day."

"The thing is, I've seen some real mean behavior, where the husband beats his wife until she's as good as trapped and he's nothing but a jailer."

"Sure. Okay, so I forgive you." Her tone is so flip that she fears he'll think she's flirting.

A minute later, he says, "Um, if you don't mind my asking, whatever happened with your kidnapper?"

Her stomach tightens, but she says lightly, "He's in a mental lock-up facility."

"Not a prison?"

"Nope."

"That's ridiculous."

"That's Washington state."

He grunts his disapproval. "So, not guilty by reason of insanity?"

"You mean NGRI?" she quips. "See? I know some acronyms, too."

He tips his head in her direction.

"But that might have been better than what actually happened." She sighs.

"So, they decided he was culpable?"

"Right. Crazy, but culpable."

"So he was aware that what he was doing wrong, but . . . Tell me what happened. I mean, if you don't mind."

"Well, by the time the defense team had put on their whole song and dance, Flint's sentence was a lot less than we expected. And the truly bizarre twist was that once he was behind bars, the DOJ didn't know what to do with him, he's such a sick excuse for a human being. So, since he's *psychologically unsound*," she says, making quote marks with her fingers, "the prison ended up sending him to a mental hospital anyway."

"What? That's messed-up."

"Like I said, that's Washington state."

He brakes at a red light and turns toward her. "Hey, I've been meaning to tell you that it's pretty darn amazing how well you've adjusted."

"Well now, doesn't that sound condescending?"

"No, no, please don't take it that way. I just mean that it's amazing to see how well you interact with Tilly. I mean, you've been through so much, but look at you, you're so poised."

"Poised? That's a first."

"I doubt that."

She shakes her head, saying nothing. But the moment she resumes watching for landmarks, an idea occurs to her. Keeping her voice calm, she asks, "Is there any way I could take a look at Randy Vanderholt's file?"

"You're kidding, right?"

"I'm just thinking about those other girls, wondering if—"

"No way. It's an ongoing investigation."

She gives him a look.

"I can't believe you're even asking this," he grumbles.

"Why not? Dr. Lerner has seen it, hasn't he?" She crosses her arms. "It has been my experience," she says, taking a high tone, "that members of law enforcement are sometimes inclined to be helpful in unorthodox ways."

He snickers. "Nice little speech."

"And absolutely true."

"Really? So give me one single example. What has been your experience of unorthodox-type help?"

"You're skeptical?"

"One example," he repeats.

She briefly closes her eyes. "Okay. In Washington, after the trial, the investigator told me that there's a universal key that works on all handcuffs."

"Yeah, so?"

"So I asked him for one, and he gave it to me. As a gift."

"Well, he shouldn't have."

"So? Wasn't that unorthodox?"

"Okay, point made."

"All right. So, can I read Vanderholt's file?"

"No."

"Why not?"

"It's ridiculous to even ask."

"Why? It might help me with Tilly."

He drives on without answering.

"I'm trustworthy, I'm quiet, I'm anonymous. No one even knows I'm here."

At a stoplight, he gives her a sideways glance. "I'll think about it."

"Great."

"But I'm not promising anything," he adds quickly. "Because listen, I don't know what your arrangement is with Dr. Lerner, but I can guarantee that Jackie Burke would go absolutely ape-shit if she found out we were sharing that kind of information with you. Totally, unequivocally ape-shit."

The Three Rivers Mall looks like any American sprawl of franchises surrounded by acres of asphalt. There are no rivers nearby that Reeve can see as she circles around, searching for a spot to park. Finally, she angles her father's Jeep into a slot and makes a dash through the cold to the main entrance.

She's on a mission, her jeans and jacket being no match for the glacial temperatures sliding down from the snow-covered mountains. An hour later, her shopping bag is full of warm clothes: three sweaters, a scarf, a pair of corduroys, gloves, and five pairs of socks. She's wondering what she has forgotten when she spies Victoria's Secret. Usually, the lingerie-clad mannequins seem ridiculous to the point of surrealism, but today a stream of holiday shoppers carries her through the doors, and she reemerges thirty minutes later with a sack of undergarments that are all black, all practical, yet all more feminine than anything she has ever owned.

A rare memory of shopping with her mother strikes her. "Merry Christmas to me, eh Mom?" she murmurs, searching for an exit.

It's long past lunchtime, and when savory aromas from the food court waft by, she hesitates. Weighing the shopping bags in her hands, and eyeing the long lines of holiday shoppers, she decides it's crazy to try to juggle her purchases along with a tray of food and a drink. She spots an exit and hustles outside, noticing two smokers huddled by the door.

She darts out into the cold, stashes her purchases in the Jeep, and hurries back across the parking lot to the entrance, where she again passes the two smokers. She glances at the men, and somehow the stocky one looks familiar.

The notion tugs at her as she steps inside. She pivots for a better look, peers though the glass, and it clicks: She has seen him on television. This stocky man with closely cropped hair and a bushy moustache works here at Three Rivers Mall.

Randy Vanderholt's boss.

The man stubs out his cigarette and heads inside, and they are suddenly face-to-face.

She blurts out, "Hi."

He frowns at her. "Uh, hello. Did you need to see me?"

"Uh, no. I'm sorry. You don't know me, but I saw you on TV."

"Oh, that." He gives a shrug and puts out his hand. "My name's Quincy."

She shakes his hand. "I'm Reeve. A friend of Tilly Cavanaugh."

He groans. "God, I'm so sorry."

"Right. Well, it wasn't your fault."

"I just feel like I should have known, somehow." He wipes a hand over his stricken face. "I'm usually a pretty good judge of character, believe it or not."

She crams her hands into her pockets. "He never said anything that would, uh, I mean, he never struck you as strange?"

He shakes his head. "Maybe Randy wasn't very smart, but he seemed gentle, not like any kind of criminal. And I've got kids myself, you know? So it's just hard to imagine."

"It is, yes." She shifts from foot to foot. "During that television interview, you said he seemed pretty normal."

"You bet. Randy was always polite. The kind of guy that would hold open doors and help little old ladies. Kids, too, now that I think about it." With a grimace he adds, "I guess I should have made a point of getting to know him better."

"You two didn't socialize?"

"Nope, never did talk to him much."

"Not even during cigarette breaks?"

"Oh no, Randy doesn't smoke. Nasty habit, don't tell me. I'm trying to quit."

TWENTY-FOUR

Jackie Burke hates dealing with the press. No matter what she says, and no matter how carefully she phrases it, her words always seem to come back to bite her. And she holds a special grudge against Otis Poe, the local reporter who has made his name stirring up trouble. Lately, Poe seems to have made a crusade of making her look bad. Twice, she has given comments to Poe that were explicitly meant to be off the record, yet later appeared in *The Jefferson Express*. One such comment was even thrown back at her in court.

In the state of California, it is illegal to record a conversation without the other party's knowledge, so her office phone emits an intermittent beep to indicate that the conversation is being recorded. Today, when Otis Poe calls, Burke makes sure to hit the "record" button and to start the conversation by pointedly announcing: "This conversation is being recorded, Otis."

"Hey, Jackie, how are you doing this lovely morning?"

She loathes the false bonhomie in his tone. "It's lunchtime."

"Oh, right. So when are you going to let me take you to lunch?"

"What do you want, Otis?" It's no mystery why he's calling, but she's not going to offer him anything.

"Right. I know you're busy, but I'm calling to find out how your office is going to handle the kidnapping cases of Abby Hill and Hannah Creighton, now that the cadaver dogs have found nothing to link Vanderholt to those crimes."

She gnashes her teeth. "You know the answer to that."

"No evidence, no leads? Come on. You can do better than that, can't you?"

"You know better than to ask me to comment on an ongoing investigation."

"Nothing else to share? What about DNA evidence?"

"You also know that DNA takes time to process."

Poe grunts. "Yeah, that's a shame, isn't it? How long do you think it might take?"

"I'm busy, Otis, so if there is nothing else—"

"I just wanted to get your reaction to Clyde Pierson's statement."

Jackie Burke senses that Otis Poe is leading up to something nasty. She scowls into space.

Just then, Deputy Nick Hudson tips his head around her door frame, sees that she's on the phone, and raises his hand in a gesture of passing greeting.

"What are you saying, Otis?" she says, urgently waving a hand at Hudson, signaling him to come into her office.

The deputy steps inside and Burke jabs a finger at a chair until he takes a seat.

Poe is saying, "I understand that you've already hired a famous forensic psychologist. Who do you think Pierson will be hiring as an expert witness?"

Her answer comes in a rush: "The PD's office and Clyde Pierson have the luxury of hiring anyone they wish, and making any sort of claim they wish, regardless of the facts. But I have no statement at this time for either your paper or your blog."

Burke listens another moment, then barks, "No comment," and slams down the phone.

"What's going on?" Hudson asks.

"Even Otis Poe knows that Clyde Pierson is up to something."

"But Vanderholt confessed. There's a mountain of evidence, and we've got the victim's statement. Pierson has a loser of a case."

"Exactly. So why is he making statements to the press about mitigating circumstances?" Burke pops out of her chair and starts pacing. "He's not one for stupid posturing. But now he's got a hotshot investigator and apparently he's hiring a fancy expert witness. He's got something cooking."

Hudson turns his palms up in an empty gesture. "He has the same reports we do."

"Nothing exculpatory, by any stretch," she agrees. "So he has to have something new, but he hasn't sent me so much as a memo, the crafty old bastard." Burke stops pacing and faces Hudson. "I thought this case was solid. Hermetically sealed and going to court with a cherry on top. I've got a highly sympathetic victim who's willing to talk, and we're about to pull the trigger on fourteen criminal counts. I'll be damned if I'm going to be blindsided in court."

"So, what do we do?"

"I want you to go over to the PD's office and inform Pierson you're there regarding his new evidence."

"What new evidence?" Hudson asks, frowning.

"Hell if I know. Our investigators are clueless, but with all the noise he's making, there has to be something."

"But wouldn't he have to turn that over?"

"Of course. Don't be dim. If there's any physical evidence, even a scrap, it's discoverable." She stops pacing and crosses her arms across her chest. "Pierson knows damn well that he should have sent any new discovery over to me before strutting around in front of the media. Now the Hills and the Creightons are buzzing like wasps. Not that I blame them. We've got zip-all about their missing daughters."

Burke starts pacing again, the heels of her boots clacking across the floor. "This is only going to get worse. That damned Otis Poe is going to post a load of crap on his blog, no doubt."

"Can't argue that. But there's nothing we can do, is there?"

"Not unless we get lucky. But I'm not going to gamble. Since Pierson has Molland working with him, I'm going to have to sharpen my claws, too."

"What? You're putting Krasny on the case?"

"Damn right. If he's getting his best investigator, then I'm getting mine. I'm meeting with Krasny this afternoon. I'll have him turn this case inside out, send him over to grill that surveillance guy, Eubank, see if there's something we missed. But in the meantime, I need everything lined up for court tomorrow. So I want you to run over to Pierson's office and demand a copy of whatever the hell he's got."

"Yes, ma'am." Hudson unfolds from the chair and stands. "Anything else?"

"Yeah," she says, putting her hands on her hips. "For Christ's sake, act like we already know what it is."

TWENTY-FIVE

Every time she's about to tip over into sleep, Reeve jerks awake. Her eyes won't stay closed, and her mind won't stop ticking. She can't stop thinking about Tilly. There's something unsettling about that girl.

Is it that their situations are so eerily similar? Reeve had been older than Tilly when she was found, true. More damaged. But there were so many parallels: captors in jail and awaiting trial. Families intact, with one older sibling at home. Safe, suburban houses. Even a few similar scars.

Giving up on sleep, she opens her laptop, finds pictures of Randy Vanderholt, and studies them. How does a man transform from car thief to kidnapper?

She groans. Evil is a subject that has already occupied far too much of her time. Years. After her rescue, after the trial, after her mother's diagnosis, she spent countless hours in hospital waiting rooms, and instead of reading escapist fiction, she read academic journals. Studies on sadists and psychopaths. Theories about reptilian brain stems, about amorality and lack of empathy. Abstracts about defective genetic structures and childhood trauma, about bedwetting and an early tendency to torture animals.

There was no solace in any of it. Trying to divine some essential truth about evil is toxic, like inhaling fumes.

Reeve's mind wanders to the other two missing girls.

Did Randy Vanderholt kidnap and kill them? Or was it more likely that there are other predators out there with the same MO?

She climbs out of bed, finds the remote, and turns on the TV, clicking through channels until she catches a local news report. A windblown reporter addresses the camera from outside a low fence, her face glaring white against the gloomy house in the background. "This small home on Redrock Road is where Tilly Cavanuagh was first held captive."

Reeve clicks to another channel. A voice-over is saying, "—alongside a national forest, where Tilly Cavanaugh was ultimately rescued. Farther from town, and with a much larger basement, this second home seemed—"

Reeve clicks away again. Away and back. Away and back. Sampling the local news reports in small doses, while reporters reexamine Tilly Cavanaugh's rescue and try for fresh angles. One reporter coaxes words of outrage and despair from the mouths of ordinary citizens. It seems cheap, like the producer is filling airtime. Another speculates about the charges the district attorney's office will bring against Vanderholt at tomorrow's highly anticipated arraignment.

Both broadcasts show footage of search dogs straining at their leashes, dragging their handlers through the brush. A newscaster declares disappointment that the specially trained cadaver dogs found, "according to an informed source," no trace of the two other missing girls, Abby Hill or Hannah Creighton. The screen flashes the smiling photographs of all three kidnapped girls—scrubbed, cute, wholesome girls—while newspeople deftly mix fact with guesswork.

The bitter truth is that Vanderholt is now the nexus of attention, and over the coming months or years, he'll be the focus of a lot of experienced legal brainpower. Tonight, all the reporters steadfastly refer to Randy Vanderholt not as a vicious, sick rapist, but always as the "suspect" or "alleged kidnapper." Or simply as "the man who will appear in court tomorrow morning."

An anchorwoman addresses the camera and makes the smiling promise that "one thing is certain about this case: It's going to be a media circus."

Reeve clicks off the TV and falls back on the bed. Damn it! If Nick Hudson won't let her see Vanderholt's file, she'll ask Dr. Lerner for his copy.

Do the cops even know that Vanderholt doesn't smoke? And what on earth compels a man to burn a girl with cigarettes?

With his full lips and doughy features, Vanderholt looks nothing like Daryl Wayne Flint, but she imagines that Tilly's captor will try to use his twisted psyche as a defense, just as hers did. Images of Flint rise up and swirl around her like dust. His wiry beard and yellow teeth. His stained fingernails. His wild eyebrows and feral stare. She can almost smell the stench of his breath, almost hear his cackle, his dry cough. If anyone deserved to get cancer and die—

Reeve groans.

When will she be done with this quagmire? Her trial is finished; Tilly's is only beginning. And it's only going to get worse.

TWENTY-SIX

Tuesday

At twelve stories, the Jefferson County Jail is by far the tallest and most expensive structure within a two-hundred-mile radius. It is widely derided as "Moore's last erection," since the builder, Lester Moore (a man who battled "Moore is less" jokes his entire life), died the week of its completion, just a few hours after marrying his sixth bride.

Open for barely five weeks, the new jail sits on the corner of a two-mile stretch of recent development, a controversial sprawl of tax-funded buildings including an extravagant city hall with marble pillars and a huge fountain.

The front of the jail is as minimalist as the city hall is ornate: a concrete slab and bald ground spotted with a few sickly trees. The barren lot stretches around back, where workers and heavy equipment are preparing the cold ground for the next phase of building.

Years ago, this entire area was a pleasant park, but now the tennis courts and baseball diamond are gone, replaced by expanses of gouged earth. A huge bulldozer uproots trees and shifts tons of rock and dirt, busily preparing for the scheduled pour of innumerable cubic yards of concrete. It's a noisy project that seems to never end. The new county courthouse is scarcely underway, and has already fallen far behind schedule.

A short drive away in downtown Jefferson, anticipation runs high at the old courthouse, a functional but cramped and outdated structure, where Randy Vanderholt is due to be arraigned.

The throngs began lining up to get inside well before eight o'clock. TV vans with satellite dishes have staked out territory. Newscasters freshen makeup and rehearse lines. Seasoned reporters gather facts, making jaded comments, while younger ones grin and gossip over salacious details. Each one hopes to scoop the competition. With kidnapping, false imprisonment, rape, and other charges on the menu, this could be a career-making day.

No one expects Tilly Cavanaugh to appear, but everyone has heard the rumor that her father will be making a public statement on the courthouse steps at the end of the day.

The wide double doors swing open. Security guards stationed inside begin efficiently shepherding the agitated crowd through the metal detectors.

"Doesn't look like any guns are going to make it into court today," one citizen observes.

"And ain't that just too bad?" jokes another.

The guards scowl but remain unfazed. Variations of this exchange will surely be repeated. Kidnappers and pedophiles are universally loathed, always have been, and in earlier times these types of spectators would have cheered to see Randy Vanderholt hanged.

While the crowds jest and grumble at the old courthouse downtown, Randy Vanderholt is prepped for transport from the shiny new jail. He stands and watches as a deputy locks cuffs around his wrists and shackles around his ankles. The heavy chain linking them clinks as Vanderholt shuffles out of the holding cell, a guard on each side.

In the future, an efficient underground tunnel will lead from the jail to the new courthouse, but today Vanderholt is hustled down a hallway, buzzed through a heavy vault-like door, taken down another hallway, and shoved into a high-security elevator. It whines down to the ground floor, where more deputies are waiting.

"Transport's ready," one of them says.

By the time Vanderholt is escorted from the building, his entourage has grown to six. No one jokes. This is a solemn bunch. Four are fathers.

The group exits the building and is hit by a cold wind that blows across the bare lot, penetrating the thin cotton of Vanderholt's orange coveralls. He complains to the guards who are firmly gripping his arms, one on each side.

They barely hear his voice. The air is full of the diesel growl of the bulldozer.

The deputies shorten their strides to keep pace with Vanderholt, who shuffles forward in his shackles. The group proceeds along the new concrete walkway toward a van with the Jefferson County Sheriff's Department emblem proudly displayed on its doors.

The bulldozer angles toward them, drops its bucket, and chews a massive bite from the earth. The men turn their heads to watch, marveling like boys. As they walk together, studying the bulldozer's work, the air fills with the roar of the powerful engine and the smell of freshly torn soil.

No one is watching the prisoner when the bullet hits him, knocking a wet hunk from above his right ear.

Vanderholt sags to his knees, dropping heavily between the two confused deputies, who stagger and strain to support his body. Blood spills out on the ground. The entourage gawks in horror, then reacts as the guards surrender Vanderholt's weight to gravity. The lawmen spin, pulling their weapons, trying to identify the direction from which the shot came, searching for a sniper hiding in the brush, by a house, on a rooftop, across the street, or somewhere up on the hill.

Spinning and searching, they realize they are exposed on all sides to buildings and traffic and a hundred hiding places, smack in the middle of what used to be a baseball diamond.

TWENTY-SEVEN

CNN, FOX, MSNBC, and all the major networks would later scramble to secure images of Randy Vanderholt's shooting, but their disgruntled producers would have to settle for less interesting footage, because while Vanderholt was shuffling out of the jailhouse toward death, all the news teams and their cameras were downtown, focused on his attorney.

Clyde Pierson had paused to say a few words to the reporters gathered on the courthouse steps, unaware that his client had been shot. The television news cameras pulled in tight. And while Vanderholt's blood was soaking into the bulldozed earth just a few miles away, Pierson was saying, "You all have been jumping to conclusions. Maybe it makes for juicy headlines, but you need to slow down now and let the legal process run its course."

Reporters prodded him for details.

"Could you tell us about any evidence uncovered over the weekend?"

"Can you share the results of the cadaver dogs' search?"

Everyone was hoping for some confirmation of guilt, or some shred of news about the other missing girls, but Pierson merely smiled, pointing out that there was absolutely no evidence linking his client to anyone other than Tilly Cavanaugh.

"Why did your client try to kill himself?"

"Is it true that Vanderholt confessed?"

"This investigation is only just beginning," Pierson said, looking calm and comfortable. "I can guarantee that this case will prove much more complex than it might seem."

Even the out-of-town news teams sensed a coming shift in the story.

With a glint in his eye and the provocative comment that "an array of mitigating circumstances must be fully addressed," Pierson hurried up the steps, oblivious to the ambulance sirens screaming in the distance.

Minutes later, Clyde Pierson answered his ringing cell phone. He blanched, asked four brisk questions, and swallowed hard.

TWENTY-EIGHT

Duke's cooling rifle lies hidden in the back of his Chevy Tahoe as he enters his office carrying a shopping bag from Radio Shack and a half-empty cup of coffee.

Officer Tomas Montoya pops in after him, saying, "Hey, did you hear the news?"

Duke scowls, gesturing at his shirt front, which features a dark, wet stain. "I'm scalded." He tosses his Starbucks cup in the trash. "Not in the mood."

"This will make you feel better. Vanderholt is dead!"

Duke raises his eyebrows. "Say what?"

"Shot this morning, just behind the jail." Montoya says gleefully. "Heard it on the radio as I was coming in. Dead."

"Holy shit." Duke sits heavily in his chair, twisting his face into an expression approximating shock.

"Somebody took him out—*pow!*—right in the head," Montoya says, raising his hands to mime the shot.

"Friggin' amazing."

"Plucked him off clean, didn't even wing a deputy."

"Damn. Wish I could have seen that."

"Yeah, five minutes later, I'd've seen it, too." Montoya bounces on the balls of his feet. "Forget the jury trial, justice is done."

Kim Benioff swings into the doorway, eyes wide. "You heard already? About Vanderholt?"

"Montoya just said."

"How sweet is that?" she says. "One bullet, and he drops like a wet sack."

Duke just smiles. There were actually two shots, but only one bullet found its mark.

"Beautiful, right?" says Montoya.

"That shooter deserves a medal," she agrees.

Duke pushes his chair back and stands. "So, did we get the shooter?"

"Not yet," they answer in unison.

"Any suspects?"

"Yeah, my mother," Montoya quips.

"And mine," Benioff says, laughing. "Plus my grandmother, my sister, and my twelve-year-old niece."

TWENTY-NINE

Gordon Cavanaugh sits in Jackie Burke's office, sorting through a jumble of emotions. His initial shock has now bloomed into a strange, mean joy.

Randy Vanderholt is dead. His daughter is safe at home with his wife. His family will be spared the long, grueling ordeal of a public trial.

He feels both warmed and appalled. His eyes are wet. He has trouble focusing.

Jackie Burke hovers, grasps his elbow, and then she's gone. Men and women in uniform rush past, cluster in the hallway, barge in and ask questions, then hurry off.

A familiar woman whose name he can nearly recall appears in the doorway and gushes, "We are all so glad that horrible man is dead! This must be such a relief!"

He nods at her and tries to speak, but his throat is clogged with emotion.

Jackie Burke reappears with a burly deputy at her side. They loom before him, shoulders square. The deputy asks, "Where is your son, Mr. Cavanaugh?"

He looks at the clock on the wall. "In class, I think."

A rueful shake of the head. "I'm afraid we haven't been able to locate him, sir. Do you have any idea where he might be?"

"He's a senior at Jefferson High. He should be at school," he insists. The vengeful joy he felt only a moment ago is being nudged aside by some new emotion. "Maybe he's at home."

"Apparently not, sir." The deputy's tone is flat, but his stance is confrontational.

Gordon Cavanaugh frowns in confusion. His cell phone rings and he automatically checks the display. "It's my wife. I'm sorry, may I take this?"

Jackie Burke glances at the deputy, saying, "Of course, but . . ."

The Cavanaughs have already had two conversations since learning that Vanderholt was shot, so he addresses his wife with a slight edge of complaint: "Honey, I'm still at the DA's office."

"The police are here, Gordon! They're searching the house!" Her voice is sharp with panic. "They took your guns!"

And all at once, the last bit of warmth drains from Gordon Cavanaugh, replaced by a cold sense of dread.

THIRTY

Tilly Cavanaugh rocks on her bed, clutching her knees to her chest, while Reeve sits on the edge of the bed, watching her, trying to think of some way to soothe her, or even begin a conversation.

Mrs. Cavanaugh opens the door, gently sets a bowl of hot, fresh popcorn on the nightstand, and gives them a pained smile before returning to the knot of people in her kitchen.

The popcorn's aroma fills the room, but it remains untouched.

The assassination of the suspect in a high-profile criminal case does not decrease media attention. This is Dr. Ezra Lerner's observation as Deputy Hudson steers away from the house and down the driveway toward the clot of avid reporters waiting outside the Cavanaughs' gate.

If anything, there are more reporters than ever. The news machine is geared up and hungry because the day is winding down while deadlines are looming. Because everyone in law enforcement has cut them off without comment. And because they are stirred by the scent of blood.

"Lot of them still here," Hudson remarks, easing his SUV past the shouting reporters and turning onto the road. "I guess the only thing better than a pedophile's trial is a pedophile's assassination."

Focused on the messages on his cell phone, Dr. Lerner mutters, "The show must go on."

Everyone is tired. Hudson's usually erect posture has slumped. Reeve reclines on the backseat in her customary position, but makes no move to sit up once their vehicle turns the corner and heads back into town. And Dr. Lerner's face is etched with worry.

He sends text messages to his wife, his receptionist, his teaching assistant, and his dean at UCSF, then pockets his phone. He puts his head back and shuts his eyes, going over the day's events, trying to discern what is bothering him. Thoughts sluice past. Like a prospector working a stream, he dips and sifts, searching.

He has treated survivors and their families in a dozen countries on three continents, but he has never seen this. The entire Cavanaugh family is in a state beyond shock, beyond emotional overload. He has done his best, spending all day with them, individually and together, but feels he has missed something.

He considers how Gordon and Shirley Cavanaugh hunkered down in the aftermath of Vanderholt's shooting. Shocked by the event, stunned by the suspicion cast their way. Offended, of course. Angry and scared, waiting for their son to be cleared.

Matt had come home pretending to be defiant, trying to cover his embarrassment, like any kid caught skipping school.

Meanwhile, the law enforcement officers were walking an ethical tightrope. They seemed elated that their suspect was dead, but defensive because they had failed to protect him, had failed to bring him to justice. And now they had an assassin on the loose.

Gradually, tension had given way to a strained, dark humor. Gordon Cavanaugh brought out a bottle of whiskey and prepared generous mugs of Irish coffee, while his wife offered freshly baked cookies.

Had Tilly eaten any?

No. The cookies and milk had been refused. In fact, Tilly had barely left her room, responding to the news of Vanderholt's death with a stricken expression that soon hardened into something else.

What?

Shirley Cavanaugh had sent a bowl of fresh popcorn in to "the girls."

The popcorn had come back untouched.

Later, Reeve had come out of Tilly's room, unhappy and shrugging.

Meanwhile, Dr. Lerner had sat at the kitchen table, sipping black coffee while Gordon and Shirley Cavanaugh dipped cookies in their hot drinks. He had listened, trying to help them slowly work through a long day of overcharged emotions.

Mrs. Cavanaugh had said, "I don't understand why Tilly is so upset about that monster being killed. It must be Stockholm Syndrome, is that right, doctor? Is that it?"

And this is the bit that troubles him.

THIRTY-ONE

Duke's house amply serves his needs. Shortly after his parents died, he redesigned the entire place, knocking out walls, rewiring circuits, refitting doors and windows. He did all the work himself—why hire some interfering contractor?—and he's particularly proud of having transformed the useless, screened-in porch that ran the length of the south side of the house into functional space. Now the area off the utility room provides plenty of storage, plus a work space that perfectly suits his noncarnal, nonelectronic interests.

Firearms are a particular favorite.

He hums to himself while preparing to clean his rifle. He takes pleasure in this routine. The tops of the washer and dryer make a suitable work station, just the right height. He places a thick sheet of plastic atop the appliances to create an even surface, and a special chamois on top of that, then assembles his kit. He sets out the ramrod, cleaning cloths, nitro solvent, and gun oil. He hefts the M24, expertly extracts the trigger, and removes the bolt. He takes his time cleaning the weapon, using just enough solvent, gently pushing the rod down the barrel, repeating this step until a fresh pad comes out clean. Next, he puts on latex gloves, moistens a cloth with gun oil—just a little—and wipes down every metal surface, removing fingerprints.

When finished, he sets the bottle of solvent and the tin of gun oil next to the Dri-Lube on a shelf where he keeps turpentine and similar fluids.

He returns the cleaned sniper rifle to its case, which he built himself, and slides the case into a concealed spot above a specially designed gun cabinet, which he also built himself. The rifle case fits snugly into its spot.

He returns the unused bullets to their box on the shelf where he keeps most of his ammo. He takes pride in calibrating and loading every round, and has perfected combinations for every need, such as extra grains of gunpowder for more firepower, or lighter slugs for greater distance. He buys his powder and ammo in bulk.

Besides the sniper rifle, he owns two shotguns and six other, more ordinary hunting rifles. Four pistols—a Colt 1911 and three Glocks—are kept at strategic spots throughout the house, with extra ammunition stored close by. He also has two handmade suppressors, plus a .44 Magnum with a scope for recreation.

Duke keeps all his guns loaded and ready, just in case. But he has a rule against practicing with any of these firearms on his own property. Even in this sparsely populated area on the outskirts of town, discharging a weapon is prohibited, and he would never recklessly draw attention to his stash of weapons. An air rifle, which he keeps by the side door, is sufficient for everyday shooting, like eliminating cats and other pests.

Sometimes, he stashes his kill in the freezer. "You never know when you'll need some bait," he recalls his father saying.

Duke sets about reloading the air gun with .22 caliber pellets. He then wipes up residual spills, tosses the latex gloves in the trash, and thoroughly washes his hands in the utility room sink. He strips off his clothes, crams them into the washer, adds detergent, starts the wash cycle, then walks nude through the length of the house.

After a hot shower, he dresses in workout gear, unlocks the control room door, and sits in his favorite chair, facing a bank of four computers. He resets the Sniffer program, flagging words like *sniper* and *shooter* and *assassination*.

All day, he has wondered how Tilly Cavanaugh might react to her keeper's death, but has had to focus on his role at work, helping the dimwitted IT guys with a computer glitch, managing surveillance of two local drug dealers, writing reports about the clichéd activities of mundane criminals, wrapping up loose ends before taking his vacation.

Now he can replenish himself.

He decided years ago that he would never allow desk work to turn him soft. For this evening's workout, Duke selects the morning's recording from Mr. C's cell phone, then inserts earbuds, slips on lifting gloves, and settles onto the lifting bench.

As he begins a set of bench presses, he recognizes the unpleasant pitch of Jackie Burke's voice. Burke the Bitch.

He exhales as he lifts. His muscles warm.

He has just begun his second set when he hears that Gordon Cavanaugh's son is a suspect in Vanderholt's shooting. He chortles. This is sweet news. Matt the brat conveniently decided to skip class just as the crosshairs were finding Randy Vanderholt's ear.

Duke snickers, picturing the gawky teen forced into an embarrassing admission involving a moist and sticky cheerleader.

He has just begun his third set when he hears about the cops searching the Cavanaughs' home. When he learns that Mr. C is a veteran who owns three high-precision rifles, he laughs so hard he nearly drops the two-hundred-pound bar.

THIRTY-TWO

Wednesday

Budget cuts are not the topic of this morning's briefing, but Officer Kim Benioff can't help but curse them as she takes her seat. The room is freezing. Benioff sits with arms crossed, uncomfortably aware that her thick, curly hair is still damp from the shower, resenting the bureaucrats who decided to save a few bucks by curtailing heating costs.

Benioff checks the empty seats and stifles a groan. The Joint Special Operations Task Force has shrunk to puny numbers. Originally a group of eight police officers and eight sheriff's deputies, the JSOTF now totals only twelve. Staff cuts, disguised as "mandatory unpaid vacations," mean another redoubling of her work load.

Lieutenant Paul Stephens bursts into the room, followed by a burly man in a suit, and claps his hands like a basketball coach. "Listen up, people!"

The uniformed men and women in the room snap to attention.

Lieutenant Stephens scowls at a stack of reports he arranges on the table before him, then stands tall at the front of the room and makes eye contact with each individual. "You all know that we're under the microscope here, and the news is not good. Our primary suspect is dead, the shooter's trail is going cold, and we haven't got much in the way of evidence, so let's get cracking."

Signaling a hefty man with black-rimmed glasses, he says, "Howard, tell us what you've got."

Officer Howard stands. "Yes, sir. We've figured the trajectory." The ballistics expert clicks keys on a computer that projects a topographical map onto the screen at the front of the room. "It puts the shooter somewhere about here, at this elevation, probably in this wooded area," he says, using a laser pointer to indicate a hill overlooking the jail. "The problem is, this hillside is dense with brush and trees, and the area is approached from a blind curve. Also, it's adjacent to this semi-industrial strip. Cars come and go, but so far no one remembers anything significant."

Benioff studies the image. "What about those rooftops?"

He gives a shrug. "Could be. But that's some range."

"What is it, about a thousand yards?"

"A thousand thirty."

Someone whistles.

"Exactly. Sniper rifle, no doubt about that. Our shooter's an expert marksman."

"Well, that clears the Cavanaugh kid," someone snorts.

"That and the ballistics," Howard agrees, taking off his glasses.

Lieutenant Stephens points at a tall, slope-shouldered woman. "Myla, tell us about the crime scene."

"I'm afraid it's not great," Myla Perkins says, rising. She goes to the front of the room and frowns at the screen. "We found no shell casings, no footprints, no tire tracks, nothing."

"But somebody must have heard the shots," a deputy grumbles.

"Two problems with that. First, there's an auto body shop here, and another one here," Myla Perkins says, indicating two corners of the industrial area on the map. "Grinders, power wrenches, you name it. So you've got all that ambient noise."

"Okay, so we're talking major decibel levels," Stephens says.

"That's right. Plus the noise of the bulldozer working at the jail. But we do have reports—from individuals more remote from the scene—who say they heard two shots. Unfortunately, we haven't found a second slug." Perkins gives a shrug of apology, adding, "At least not yet."

Howard frowns. "Our shooter isn't just some cowboy with a truck and a gun."

"Ex-military?" Benioff wonders aloud.

Howard grunts. "That's a theory. Or could be law enforcement."

The room goes uncomfortably still as this sinks in.

Stephens puts his fists on the table and leans forward. "Listen, people. I know some of you were happy to hear about Vanderholt's death. I'll be glad to dance on his grave myself. But if our shooter's a vigilante, he's something unusual. This was an expert hit. And we can't let down our guards just because we approve of his target. We don't know his motivation. We're lucky he didn't take out one of the guards. Any one of us could be next."

He gestures toward the man in the suit. "You all remember Agent Coulter, from the Sacramento field office. Barry, you want to fill us in?"

The brawny FBI agent stands, clearing his throat. "You're right that this shooter is rare." Coulter's voice has a guttural quality that makes new acquaintances think he's getting over a cold. He clears his throat again, looks down at his notes, and begins laying out the scenario. "We need to start with Vanderholt. Why was he killed? Our profilers think it's because the kidnappings of Creighton, Cavanaugh, and Hill are connected."

He looks around the room. Heads are nodding.

"Our thinking is, the perp is a serial kidnapper. Note the timing, the approach: All at dusk, all unobserved. No sign of struggle. No ransom demand." The FBI agent coughs and goes on, detailing similarities between the kidnappings: that all three occurred on or around Labor Day weekend, that all three girls were active in outdoor sports, similar in stature, etc., etc.

How many times have they been over this? The police officer to Benioff's right is drumming his fingers. The deputy on her left is jiggling his foot. Everyone is anxious to get on to something new.

They know they got lucky with Tilly Cavanaugh. They know that kidnapped kids are usually killed in the first few hours and dumped at the first opportunity. The fact that Tilly was the second girl taken but was found alive has stumped them. Some have speculated that the kidnapper liked to keep the girls around, that maybe Abby and Hannah still had a chance, but with Vanderholt shot dead, that seems a faint hope.

Stephens raps the tabletop with his knuckles. "Could you get to the new theory, Barry?"

"Right." The FBI agent shuffles some papers. "The thinking now is that Vanderholt killed Hannah Creighton somehow. Maybe it was an accident. Or maybe she fought too much, or proved unsatisfactory for some reason. So he disposed of her body, and then he took Tilly Cavanaugh as his second victim. She was different in some essential way, so he kept her alive. Or perhaps he had perfected his technique enough so that he didn't need to kill her."

"But what about Abby Hill?" asks the deputy beside Benioff. "Are we supposed to believe that she's still alive somewhere?"

"We have no evidence of that," Agent Coulter responds, wiping a palm across his crewcut.

"Because where would she be?" The deputy's tone is acerbic.

"Our profilers think it's more likely that he tried to keep the last two girls together, but something went wrong."

"Meaning that he killed Hannah, kept Tilly, and then killed Abby?"

"Right."

A detective scoffs. "Is that the best you guys can come up with?"

"Hold on," Agent Coulter continues. "Let me clarify. The thinking is that Tilly may have been held captive with Abby. And that Tilly may have even seen Abby killed."

The task force members grumble and shift in their seats.

"If that's true, the kid must be terrified," Benioff mutters. More loudly, she asks, "Has Tilly confirmed any of this?"

"That's a negative, at least for now," Coulter responds. "An unknown. But the thing is, we have consulted with that forensic psychiatrist, Dr. Ezra Lerner, and he believes the victim may be withholding information, that she's not responding to Vanderholt's death in the way you'd expect."

"What does that mean?" asks Benioff, frowning.

"Dr. Lerner says the girl might be responding to Vanderholt's shooting as some kind of threat."

"Isn't that consistent with a Stockholm Syndrome–type response?" someone asks.

"The doc says it goes beyond that. He says the girl's behavior is atypical. And he's the expert, so let's assume for now his opinions are correct and work from there."

The door opens and Deputy District Attorney Jackie Burke tips her head into the room. She arches an eyebrow, giving Lieutenant Stephens a questioning look.

"I asked Jackie to join us this morning," he says, motioning for her to enter.

Burke finds an open seat by the door. She stands behind it but doesn't sit.

"You haven't missed anything that you and I haven't already discussed," he says to her. "This is a good time. Jump right in."

"We have a problem," she begins. She looks from face to face, just as Stephens did, before continuing. "We have a leak."

The room goes still.

"Maybe we got lucky before, but now Vanderholt is gone, and so far we have no evidence linking him to our other missing girls. Okay, that's all public knowledge. And by now everyone and their uncle knows that our search dogs found nothing. But from here on out, we need to tighten up. If anything else discussed in this room shows up on TV, or in the newspaper, or in Otis Poe's blog, I'm going to skewer and grill every last one of you."

Benioff glances around the room. Someone coughs. An officer shifts in his seat. A deputy squints at Burke and shakes his head.

"Listen up, people," Stephens says. "That damn blog encourages every crackpot in orbit to vent. Since yesterday, the Internet has been flooded with all kinds of crap, mostly congratulations to Vanderholt's killer."

"You can imagine the shooter's response to reading all that nonsense," Burke says. "You can bet he's gloating over his notoriety."

Curses echo around the room.

Jackie Burke crosses her arms. "Poe claims that the public defender's office found some kind of evidence regarding Vanderholt, that he had something proving him innocent regarding the two other abductions. Now, I don't know how Poe came up with this little theory, because Clyde Pierson certainly didn't turn over anything exculpatory."

"No discovery?" Stephens asks. "No additional physical evidence?"

"I talked to Pierson, and whatever he got, it wasn't much." She blows out air.

"Maybe the leak is in the public defender's office," Myla Perkins suggests.

"Could be," Burke says, "but we don't think so."

"The point is, people, it's a good bet that Vanderholt knew something beyond what he confessed to," Stephens says. "We need to work that theory. Whoever took him out needed to shut him up."

"Pierson sure seems to think so," Burke says. "And he sounds scared. He's leaving town."

Agent Coulter clears his throat. "Let's move on. We don't think the shooter was a vigilante. He could have been a partner of some kind, so assume he's our link to the other girls."

"That's how it smells," Burke mutters, frowning at the floor, "but we need something solid."

"Excuse me," says an officer in the back, raising a hand. "If you're saying all the kidnappings are linked through the shooter, are you discounting the copycat theory?"

"We're not discounting anything." Stephens snaps. "We're keeping our minds open. The shooter could have had a grudge against Vanderholt, who knows? No one has claimed credit, so let's work the theory that two perps were acting as a team. Meaning that our shooter might lead us to the other two girls."

"Or to their graves," someone mutters.

"We have a few cigarette butts, right, coming from Vanderholt's residence?" Benioff asks.

"Right," Myla Perkins responds, "but no DNA yet."

"We can't count on a match in our database, even then," Stephens says. "So keep in mind that we need a lot more. Keep after registered sex offenders; there are a thousand of those slippery bastards. Keep working the crime scenes. And pull the owner regs for high-precision rifles, the whole gamut of sniper models."

"That's half the force," an officer protests.

Lieutenant Stephens glares at him until he hunches down in his seat, then glances at Burke and continues, "Listen people, we need to find that shooter, and Vanderholt's the key. Turn his background inside out. Known associates. Cell mates. Cousins. Hell, find out who he hung with in grade school. And bring that guy from the mall back here, Vanderholt's boss. He's ex-military, and I want his whole goddamn history." Slapping his hands down on the table, he says, "So! The newshounds think we've just lost our only suspect? Let them. But things are heating up now, and you need to get creative. Get fierce. Find a witness. Find a lead."

"We owe it to those girls," Burke says. "They deserve more than lame theories and a dead suspect."

"And don't blab, people," Stephens warns. "We need to keep this guy upwind."

THIRTY-THREE

Tilly has specifically asked to be left alone. She is on the bed, curled in a fetal position.

Reeve sits on the bed next to her. "Are you okay?"

Tilly doesn't respond.

"Would you like to go to Jamba Juice? Or a movie? How about the mall?"

Tilly glares at the wall, shakes her head.

Reeve stifles a flash of exasperation. Sure, Dr. Lerner urged her to come and try to talk to Tilly, but what's the point of spending all this time in here if the kid won't even speak?

Reeve gets up and walks around the room, wishing she could talk to Dr. Lerner about what is really bothering her. Envy is a petty emotion. She tries to resist, but it burrows in: Tilly's kidnapper has been killed—how sweet that must be—and how many times has she wished that Daryl Wayne Flint were dead? She pushes the thought aside.

A few of Tilly's old pastel drawings have been replaced with dark, moody pieces slashed with yellow. Reeve bends close to look and notices Tilly watching her. "What?" she says, straightening.

Tilly glances away,

"What? Just say the word, maybe I can help."

Tilly exhales and sits up. "Don't I wish."

"What's going on?"

Tilly shakes her head. "I just wish you knew more."

"That makes two of us."

"But I think I've told you everything I can."

"Okay, well, how about Dr. Lerner? He's good. You can trust him."

"Dr. Lerner was hired by that lawyer lady, right?"

"Jackie Burke, right. He was hired as an expert witness for the prosecution, if that's what you mean. But that's a good thing."

Tilly frowns. "What about you? Are you, like, are you a witness, too?"

"God no, I'm . . ." Reeve mentally gropes for an answer. "I'm here as moral support. Because I understand what you're going through. On a personal level."

"But Randy's dead, so there's not going to be a trial, so what happens now? Are you going away?"

"Tilly, our relationship has nothing to do with the legal system. I'm your friend. And I'll be around as long as you want."

Tilly clenches her hands in her lap, wearing a strange expression.

"As for Dr. Lerner, if you want him to help you, he'll find a way to make that happen. He's very dedicated. He commuted all the way to Seattle to see me, and I would have been a mess without him."

Rather than soothe the girl, this seems to make her anxious. "But do you, um, do you talk to Dr. Lerner?" Tilly fidgets and averts her eyes. "About me, I mean?"

"Only in general terms." Reeve sits on the bed and adds, "So if you want me to keep quiet about something, I will."

"Really?"

"Yes, really."

Tilly considers her with wary eyes.

"You know, Dr. Lerner is very trustworthy. He doesn't talk to me about any of the specifics that you share with him, either. Not without your permission. That would be unethical. So, whatever you want to have kept private between us is kept private." Reeve hasn't actually articulated this before, but as she says it, it rings true.

"So you won't repeat anything secret that I tell you? It would be, like, confidential, just between us?"

"Unless you say otherwise, every word." Reeve instantly recalls the prosecutor's demand that she share every detail of their conversations, but to hell with Jackie Burke.

Tilly gets off the bed and stands in front of her, an intense woman-child with pain etched in her face. "Honest? Can I really trust you?"

"Of course."

Tilly closes her eyes briefly. Her body seems to shudder, like a pup shaking off water, then she opens her eyes and whispers, "So you totally, absolutely promise not to tell anyone what I tell you?"

"I promise. Totally and absolutely."

"Not anyone, not even Dr. Lerner."

"Not a soul."

"Swear it. I mean really, like, on your mother's grave."

Reeve blinks at her, then slowly raises a palm. "Yes, Tilly Cavanaugh, I do hereby solemnly swear not to tell a soul whatever you are going to tell me. On my mother's grave."

Tilly stares unflinchingly, and Reeve stares back, waiting.

Tilly swallows. "Randy Vanderholt wasn't the worst."

"What? What do you mean?"

"There was another man."

"Another man? You mean, another man at the house?"

Tilly gives one solemn nod.

"With Vanderholt? Or before that?"

"With Vanderholt."

"Someone else that hurt you? Another kidnapper?" Reeve's voice hits a high pitch.

"Yeah, but not like, when I was taken. He came later, after I was locked in the dungeon."

"Two men? God, Tilly, have you told anyone else about this?"

She looks away, shaking her head.

"Why not?" Reeve can hardly believe what she's hearing.

"Because he's out there. He's watching."

"But Tilly," she says, taking her by the shoulders, "you have to tell them. You're home safe now, and it's important that you tell them."

Till shakes her off. "No! I can't!"

"Tilly, you have to. The police will protect you."

"No! He said he would hurt us if I told."

"But—"

"You don't understand! He's a cop!" Tilly spits out, glaring at her.

Reeve opens her mouth to speak but chokes on the words.

"You promised not to tell." Tilly's voice is ragged. "You can't tell anyone."

"But you've got to tell your parents," Reeve says, shaking her head in disbelief.

"No! That would be the worst. They'd go straight to the cops."

"But Tilly, why do you think he's a cop?"

"Because Randy said so."

"What kind of cop? Police? Highway patrol?"

"I don't know."

"Did you see a uniform?"

"No."

"Or a badge?"

"No."

"Well, there are lots of different kinds of cops. And maybe he was lying."

"Randy said that he was a dirty cop and that I should do whatever he says or he'll make it worse on both of us."

"But Tilly, if you tell your parents—"

"Don't you get it? He's watching! He warned me, he said if I ever rat him out, he'll kill me and he'll kill my family!"

The terrible logic hits Reeve like a slap. The girl appears free but she's trapped. "Tell me about this man. What's his name?"

"I don't know. He made me call him Master." She scoffs. "But to me, he was always Mister Monster."

"What does he look like?"

"I don't know."

"What do you mean you don't know?"

"I was always blindfolded."

"What?"

"Before he came downstairs, Randy would always come down first and blindfold me, handcuff my hands. It was, like, Mister Monster's orders."

"You were blindfolded?"

"Usually. Either that, or sometimes he wore a mask." Tilly grimaces.

"He wh—What kind of mask?"

"Like a mask in the movies. Black, with eye holes."

Reeve inhales sharply. "Like a ski mask? Or like an executioner's mask?"

"Yeah, like that."

"Oh, god."

"It freaked me out. That's why he did it, I think. He liked to scare me. And he did these," she says, rubbing the pattern of scars on her arm.

"And Vanderholt didn't smoke."

Tilly looks down at her arm and stops rubbing. "Mister Monster smokes Marlboro Lights, I saw that."

"Okay, that's good. Is there anything else you remember?"

"Why? It's not like you can do anything," she says bitterly.

"Just watch me."

"What?"

"I'll do something," she mutters. "I've got to do something."

"But you promised! You swore on your mother's grave!"

"Yes, I promise I won't tell anyone." She grabs Tilly's hand and squeezes. "But that man has to be stopped. So I don't know what, exactly, but I'll do something. I'll figure it out. At least I can promise you that."

The room is charged with tension. "I can't sit," Reeve says, and begins pacing around the room. "How old is he?"

"I don't know. Old."

"Does he have gray hair?"

"No. I don't know. I was blindfolded, or he wore that mask. But he had dark hair, you know, everywhere." Tilly swallows. "But I'm pretty sure they won't find any DNA or anything."

"Why not?"

She makes a face. "Because he always used condoms, for one thing. Plus, he was, like, hyperclean. Paranoid clean. He always brought a sheet with him and made Randy spread it out on the bed before he came in. Then, when he was finished, he'd fold up the sheet and take it with him."

Reeve groans. He was smart and careful, this guy. "What else do you remember about him?"

"Nothing. . . . Oh, but he has brown eyes."

"Okay."

"And a mean voice."

"Like some kind of accent?"

"No, he just had a mean kind of voice."

"What about height and weight?"

"Tall. Taller than my dad, I guess. But not fat or thin, just, you know, with muscles."

"Bulky? Like a bodybuilder?"

"No, more in a regular kind of way. But really strong."

"Did he have any moles or scars?"

"I don't know why you're asking all this," Tilly snaps. "It's not like you're going to see him naked. You can't recognize him."

Reeve squints at her. "But what else do you remember?"

"Um, he smelled bad, like garlic and cigarettes. And he had a tattoo. Right around here," Tilly says, indicating her left bicep.

"What kind of tattoo?"

"Of barbed wire. It went around his arm, like this," she says, encircling her thin arm.

"That's good. What else?"

"Why are you asking all this? You can't do anything. You promised not to say anything!"

"He's your enemy, so he's my enemy," Reeve says, smacking a fist in her palm.

"No! I just want you to tell my parents that we need to move. That I need to change my name, and we need to move, like you did. You have to help me get out of Jefferson."

"Yes, I promise. I'll do what I can." Reeve glances around the ordinary-looking room, with its girly knickknacks and yellow wallpaper, which seemed so safe just minutes ago. This conversation cannot be happening.

Jolted by a sudden idea, she faces the girl and grabs her shoulders. "Tilly, listen to me. Do you think this guy had something to do with kidnapping those other girls?'"

Tilly shakes her off. "Maybe, but I can't help them. They're probably dead."

Reeve bites her lip and studies her for a long moment.

Tilly heaves out a sigh. "Randy said, 'Without me here to protect you, he'll kill you.' That's what he always said." Her eyes shine and her voice quakes. "And he said that if I ever tried to run away, if I—"

"But you didn't run away. You were rescued."

"It doesn't matter! Don't you get it? He's out there watching!" She turns away and scowls at the floor. "Who do you think killed Randy? It's like a warning. I'm next!"

Reeve reaches out, but her fingers only brush past the cotton pajamas as the girl collapses onto the bed and faces the wall, resuming her tight fetal pose.

THIRTY-FOUR

Winter cold reaches inside Reeve's jacket and under her sweater. She shudders and clasps her arms tight as she clicks the Jeep's locks and hustles away toward the trail. She has fled the Cavanaughs' house saying she needs to get some air. She evaded Dr. Lerner and bolted, craving solitude, needing to get away from everyone to grapple with Tilly's awful disclosures.

She jogs away from the road, across a footbridge, and finds the trail that heads upriver.

How could she have been so dim, so self-absorbed? All this time, while she's been missing her mother and envying Tilly's intact family, the poor kid was wrestling with a double dose of terror. Two kidnappers!

A lone runner darts past without making eye contact and Reeve hurries on, keeping a brisk pace, carrying Tilly's secret with her. The trail follows the rush of green water winding through the winter landscape. Thick, ominous clouds mass overhead and the twisted limbs of huge oaks claw the air. She pauses to catch her breath. A single duck wings low over the river's surface. The air smells of rotting foliage, of wood smoke.

She shivers and pushes on, following the trail farther along. Pines darken and sway overhead. The trail turns right, away from the rapids, climbs, then dips to where it crosses a swollen stream. She hesitates on the bank, choosing her path, then starts across, wobbling, navigating from rock to slippery rock, stepping unavoidably into the mud on the other side.

The path narrows and abruptly climbs higher. Her skin warms as the trail rises in steep switchbacks.

Tilly. Abby. Hannah. The girls' names echo in her head. Images of concrete walls and locked handcuffs swim through her thoughts. She has promised not to tell Dr. Lerner and cannot confide in Nick Hudson, but what if everything Tilly fears is true?

As she hurries upriver, something seems to breathe on the back of her neck. She senses what's coming and hurries deeper into the rough terrain.

Now the river has disappeared and she wheels around, disoriented. She steps off the trail. Dense foliage seems to crowd around her, and she pauses, breathing hard, searching for a way through the brush. She squats, drops to her knees, and crawls through a cluster of dry manzanita, branches scratching her face and catching her hair.

She rises to a crouch and emerges before a wall of granite. Scanning the rocky ridge, she considers turning back. But with a whiff of what's looming, she trembles, presses herself to the rock face, and begins climbing. She breaks a fingernail, sharp stones cut her palms, but she keeps climbing, scrambling upward. Her boots lodge awkwardly into footholds, her hands wedge into cracks. Sweating, balancing, she scrambles higher, cramming her toes into notches, searching for handholds in the lichen-pocked rock, thrusting upward until she emerges on top.

She stands unsteadily, exposed on a high, narrow shelf. The chill air whips around her as the icy river twists and pools below. She looks down at the gray-green water, lowers herself onto the rocky ledge, and hugs her knees to her chest, unconsciously stroking the tongue of her boot, seeking brief comfort in the secret spot where the handcuff key stays hidden.

Abruptly, the phantom she has been fleeing closes in. Tilly's captor morphs into another sadist with dark eyes, another criminal who covered his tracks. She smells his stink. She sees his wet lips, his filthy whiskers. She swoons slightly, and as Daryl Wayne Flint nuzzles her ear like a physical presence, she dangles her legs over the long drop to the rushing river.

Emotion knots in her throat. "You filthy bastard," she croaks, grabbing a handful of pebbles and flinging them into the void.

"Four years of captivity." She pitches a rock. "Six years of therapy." She throws another rock, and another, crying, "A whole fucking decade of my fucking life!"

She hurls fistfuls of rocks over the edge and watches them splash into the fast water, then gets to her feet and scrambles along the ledge, searching for more. She tosses anything she can find—gravel, fallen branches, stones as big as melons—and doesn't stop until every loose object has been pitched.

She stands there, hot and panting. A single raindrop hits her cheek. She frowns up at the sky, feeling as if she's just awakened from a trance, suddenly aware that she must get moving before she's caught in another storm.

THIRTY-FIVE

There is always cleanup after any crime, particularly murder. Which is why Duke's crimes are so brilliantly planned and executed. It's always best to have an alibi, for example, so Duke's coworkers believe that he's in Reno, gambling.

He put in his vacation request the same day that Randy Vander-dolt was arrested, and then took off the day after he was killed. Not ideal circumstances, but he looked at the vacation schedule and instantly decided it was necessary. A calculated risk.

Before leaving the office, Duke had made sure to flash a thick wad of cash. Everyone knew he'd inherited a fair bit of money, and after years of this sort of behavior, they weren't surprised by his last-minute "gambling trips" to Reno or Vegas. They imagined him to be a high roller. He enjoyed cultivating this image.

Years ago, when he was still a young man testing his appetites, he had in fact spent a fair amount of time in Vegas. It was his very own adult playground, where he could make up his own rules. He had exploited it to the fullest, finding all sorts of young flesh for sale. And during his experiments, he had attained new sexual peaks. But he soon realized that once he was finished, he preferred to relax and indulge in reliving the experience rather than having to deal with complaints or consequences.

One whiny whore provoked him so much that he had to strangle her just to shut her up.

He immediately regretted this loss of control. Murder is messy, he discovered. Killing a human is much more inconvenient than killing, say, a dog or a deer.

It still disturbs him to think how close he came to getting caught. He was reckless. And the risk and difficulty of disposing of the body was so distasteful that it fully negated the pleasure he'd gained up to that point.

While driving back from that hectic and overheated visit to Vegas, he'd reviewed the entire episode and revised his thinking. He needed a less hazardous way to enjoy his habits.

He smoked and drove and thought about this for hundreds of miles. He weighed risks and rewards. He already had a fine collection of state-of-the-art surveillance equipment at his disposal, but while watching was sometimes interesting, it was a poor substitute for hands-on experience.

In Barstow, he stopped for gas. And while he was filling his tank, another car had pulled in and stopped. A door opened and a young girl in a tank top and tight shorts popped out. As she bounced toward the mini-mart, Duke studied her tight little rump, then noticed another man watching her as well. When the pubescent girl disappeared inside, the man caught Duke's eye and grinned.

That was the seed. Over the next several hours, while Duke drove, the idea germinated, took root, and bloomed into a thing of beauty. By the time he pulled into his driveway, he was marveling at its perfection.

Over the next several days, he lovingly worked and reworked the elaborate steps that would ultimately lead him to his keepers and his pets. First came J.J. Orr and Hannah Creighton. Next, he found Randy Vanderholt and Tilly Cavanaugh. Months later, he arranged for Simon Pelt to capture Abby Hill. And now Fitzgerald is in place, waiting and eager for a future assignment.

In retrospect, it had been a mistake to trust Vanderholt. Duke had let himself believe that a keeper already living in a house with a basement was a bonus. But Vanderholt had pretended that he owned the place, and when the real owner had decided to sell the old dump, Vanderholt had turned the whole business of moving Tilly from one house to another into a fucking disaster.

But now Vander-dolt has been taken care of, and Duke's two other keepers aren't so stupid. Orr was convicted of fraud and embezzlement, not simple crimes. Plus, he managed to get away with it for several years, which took brains. And Simon Pelt had at least enough intelligence to get a degree before he screwed up and went to prison on narcotics charges.

Smarter keepers, Duke reasons, will not cause trouble. They can follow the news, they can read between the lines. So no further bloodshed should be necessary.

When things calm down, Duke will initiate the next phase of his plan with his new keeper, Fitzgerald. Once he has found the appropriate victim, he'll arrange for Fitzgerald to capture a girl to replace Tilly. But for next time, he's considering somewhere outside Jefferson County. Maybe Oregon. Or Nevada. Lots of runaways in Reno.

With Vanderholt eliminated, he can take his time. And thanks to recent budget concerns, he'll have many extra hours to indulge in his favorite pursuits. His hours at work have been cut. And his coworkers believe he wastes his inheritance on gambling trips, when in fact he stays put, because he has everything he needs close at hand. Disguises. Extra vehicles. Fake IDs.

He's not worried. Certainly he fits the classic profile of a predator, being a loner with private habits, a white male of a certain age, but so do uncountable other men, including dozens at work.

Many are ex-military. Few are better marksmen.

He smirks. Duke can understand the need of lesser men to join a militia, though he personally could never tolerate years of taking orders. So, after his father's death, he trained himself, long and hard and for years before even considering the benefits of joining law enforcement.

Being a highly disciplined individual, he takes pride in his fitness, making regular use of his home gym. And he rarely drinks.

Beer is for fat boys. Like his keepers. All of them: Pelt-blubber and Orr-ca and even Vander-fat. When Duke wants an alcoholic beverage, he opts for something more sophisticated: a single shot of fine scotch, no ice. One shot, no more.

True, he smokes a pack or two a day, but so what? This is another calculated risk. If he gets cancer, he'll man up and eat a bullet, far better than being eaten alive by chemo or disease.

Other than nicotine, his habits are clean. His few, select vices are well thought out, which is why the dogs found nothing.

Investigators will nurture some vain hope for a break, saying that DNA takes time to process, but they are fools, and he is not. He always brings a clean sheet for playtime with his pets, which he later takes away with him, then destroys.

Need heats his groin and he stiffens in frustration. But he won't let himself risk visiting either of his girls. Not yet. Not until the investigation cools and the FBI goes home. Not until he's sure that old Clyde Pierson has nothing to say and that Tilly Cavanaugh is keeping her nasty mouth shut.

THIRTY-SIX

Thursday

Trouble nudges Reeve awake. It's too early to get up, so she tosses and turns, worrying, feeling overwhelmed.

How is she supposed to keep her promise to Tilly if it requires lying to Dr. Lerner? He knows her too well. Even when she says nothing, her subconscious gives her away, tensing her musculature, shouting body language.

The truth is, she'd love to tell Dr. Lerner. He's like a rock. A smart and caring rock who always seems to have answers.

But a promise is a promise.

And that's the problem. Because, just as Reeve would never break hers, Dr. Lerner would never break his, and it's clear that he has already made quite a few promises of his own. To Jackie Burke, for one.

Reeve tosses off the covers and heads to the shower, where she soaps up and tries scrubbing away her anxiety. The hot water and steam work their magic, and she's feeling better when she towels off. She can make it through her regular breakfast meeting with Dr. Lerner. No big deal. She'll eat and nod and volunteer nothing.

But when she checks her phone, she finds a text message from him:

> We need to talk. Can we meet a bit early? I'm already here.
> Come down when you can.

Dr. Lerner is hunched over an untouched bagel and a cup of coffee, intent on his cell phone, when she slides into the chair across from him. "What's up?"

He holds up a finger, asking her to wait. A moment later, he sets his phone aside, thanks her for coming. "I hope my text message didn't alarm you."

"No problem."

"But I'm afraid we've hit a speed bump."

"Oh?"

"A few speed bumps, actually."

She holds herself very still.

"First, the Cavanaughs have asked for some time alone, a little peace and quiet."

She smiles with relief. "Understandable. After yesterday's joyride."

"Exactly. So, I hope you don't mind, but I need to fly back to San Francisco and take care of some important matters. This is my window."

"Oh, right. Obligations at UCSF?"

"That, of course." He sighs. "And a problem with my son."

She bites back the realization that she has been so self-absorbed that she has failed to even inquire about his son. What was he now, eight? Nine? Dr. Lerner rarely mentions his family, keeping their relationship on a professional, doctor/patient basis, but she has sensed, from time to time, that Dr. Lerner's boy has some kind of chronic health problem. "Nothing serious, I hope."

"Not a crisis, anyway," he says, yet his expression remains tight with concern. "But here's the thing: I realize that you might like to head home, too. So, maybe you'd like to pack up? Or, if you wish, I can fly you down with me. You could leave the Jeep here for the time being, and then return with me."

"No, I'd like to stay."

"Okay." He sighs heavily. "That's good, actually, because the Cavanaughs are in such a delicate state right now, emotionally. I think it would help Tilly if you could just spend some time with her. Not today, of course, but perhaps tomorrow, if you don't mind. You know, go out for pizza, take her shopping, whatever. Nothing intense." He peers into her eyes. "What do you think? Because if you want to go home—"

"And miss the rodeo? No, I'll stay."

"Well, good. Thank you. That's great." He gives her a weary smile, and he looks so exhausted that she almost asks whether he can safely fly.

"Don't worry," he says, as if reading her mind. "I'll be back in a couple of days." A message pings on his phone. He checks it, then looks back at her, saying, "I'm sorry, but there's more. I hate to impose on you, but since Vanderholt has been killed, my status has changed. Clearly, I'm no longer needed as an expert witness, so the district attorney's office has terminated my contract."

A small yelp of surprise escapes her lips.

"But don't worry. The Cavanaugh family and I have already discussed future arrangements, which will be handled through my office. And you'll stay on, if you wish, without interruption, with everything the same as previously discussed. Before I forget—" he reaches into his breast pocket, and sets a slim white envelope on the table in front of her "—this is from them, to cover your expenses, as promised."

She blinks at the envelope and mumbles her thanks.

"But there is one other thing, if you don't mind." He pulls a thick manila envelope from his briefcase. "I'm sorry to impose on you. The thing is, Jackie Burke provided this file, but now I'm pressed for time. Would you mind returning it to her office?"

His cell phone pings again, and as he turns toward it, she eyes the fat, sealed envelope, holding her hands in her lap, resisting the urge to snatch it up and rip it open.

"I have to apologize," Dr. Lerner says after a moment, setting his phone aside, "because there is one more thing that I have to ask you about." He folds his arms on the table and leans toward her, intent. "Things have been pretty crazy lately, but it seems to me that Tilly is having an unusually difficult time adjusting. That she's fearful, that she's begun withdrawing, emotionally. Tell me, Reeve, what do you think she's afraid of?"

THIRTY-SEVEN

His chin itches but Duke is careful not to scratch at the fake beard while he drives. He wears sunglasses, despite the overcast weather, plus a baseball cap, so he's confident that no one will recognize him. Or the white van, which he has rented using one of his fake IDs. He eases through traffic, following just a few cars back as Mrs. Cavanaugh winds her way through downtown traffic with Tilly riding shotgun.

Traffic lights seem to be in sync with his wishes, beaming green or red as needed. Things are going smoothly, but Duke realizes that, being tired and cranky, he might be prone to mistakes. He must remain vigilant. After listening to yesterday's recording of little Miss Tilly's detailed confession to Reeve, he decided to waste no time.

Mrs. Cavanaugh turns her gold Infiniti SUV into the supermarket parking lot, and Duke wheels in behind, steering left to her right, circumnavigating the lot until she has parked. He watches while the pair walks inside, then parks in a slot that opens up nearby. Perfect.

He turns off the ignition, puts on his black leather gloves, and fetches the plastic bag from the floor, glad to be getting it out of this vehicle before it begins to smell.

He climbs out of the van, just another guy in a heavy plaid shirt and jeans making a quick run to the store. But as he approaches the front of the supermarket, he stops and gently knocks his head with the heel of his hand, in that universal gesture of just remembering something. He turns, heads back through the parking lot, and raises his key fob, aiming it at a vehicle. The gold Infiniti chirps as the doors unlock.

Casually, he opens the driver's side door, climbs inside, and settles behind the wheel, placing the plastic bag on the floor. He glances around, checks the mirrors. No one is watching. In one quick motion, he opens the bag and spills the dead animal onto the floor, just where Tilly will be placing her feet. He shoves it far enough under the passenger seat so that only a bit of the tail protrudes. Dark tail, dark floor mat. Not enough to be noticed unless you really look.

Satisfied, he climbs out of the vehicle, purposely leaving the doors unlocked, and doesn't even glance behind him as he walks away. He'll toss the plastic bag in the trash, make a quick purchase of Marlboro Lights, and then head to the other side of town, where he has a date to keep with Edgy Reggie.

THIRTY-EIGHT

Reeve rationalized that she hadn't exactly lied to Dr. Lerner. She'd answered a question with a question, which seemed just enough of a difference to shade the ethics of the whole exchange. "Don't you think Tilly is freaked out by all the cops and all the reporters?" she'd responded, heart thudding, to his question about the source of Tilly's fears. "Don't you think that's why she keeps saying she wants to move?"

Luckily, Dr. Lerner had been under a tight schedule, so the conversation was cut short. Once he'd said good-bye, she wasted no time in taking the envelope upstairs to her room.

Reeve knew she shouldn't, but she couldn't resist opening the envelope and slipping out the pages. She flipped through quickly, then sat cross-legged on the bed and fanned them out before her, poring over every page. There were full descriptions of both houses, plus details about the searches, but most of what she found wasn't particularly helpful. The file was clearly incomplete, with sections blacked out and big gaps in sequence, so it was impossible to guess what was missing.

Vanderholt's "confession" was given verbatim, however, and she read it twice. But there wasn't a single mention of a colleague or partner. At one point Vanderholt had said, "I may not seem that smart, but this kind of thing, you know, it just takes dedication."

Was she imagining it, or did his words sound artificial? She rubs her eyes, wondering if Vanderholt had been coached.

And didn't Tilly also say something odd? What was it?

The notion flits away. Probably nothing.

She gets up, stretches, then hurries downstairs to the front desk, where the clerk provides a map of Jefferson. It's a ridiculously imprecise, cartoon-ish image covered with advertisements, but it will have to do. Back in her room, she boots up a computer search, studies the screen, finds some paper, and jots down notes starred with questions. A few minutes later, she slides Vanderholt's file back into its envelope, grabs her jacket, and heads out.

Cold needles her face as she exits the hotel, hustles around the building and across the parking lot. Turning the corner, she glimpses something odd: a bearded guy in a baseball cap standing next to her Jeep. The hair on the back of her neck stands up.

The bearded man is hunched, looking down at the ground, and then he disappears.

She hurries over. As she gets closer, she finds him crouched down in a squat with his back to her. "Hey," she says, hitting a note halfway between greeting and warning.

He stands up and turns around. A tall guy, squinty eyes, compressed mouth. "Oh, hey, sorry, is this your car?" He gestures helplessly toward the ground with his blunt, square hands. "Sorry. I'm such a klutz."

The man drops back down into a squat and continues picking up the coins that Reeve now sees scattered across the pavement. "I'll be out of your way in just a minute," he mumbles, turning away.

"Let me help." Reeve stoops to gather up change. She notices an odor of garlic and cigarettes while handing him several quarters, but forgets all about him the moment he walks away.

According to her map, Redrock Road is within easy driving distance, so Reeve cranks up the Jeep's heater and heads there first.

The house where Tilly Cavanaugh was first held captive is not hard to find: "Pervert" is spray-painted on the fence, and the house is cordoned off with yellow police tape.

Reeve parks the Jeep on the street, gets out, and pauses on the side-walk, getting a feel for the layout of the small, white house. It's an older home on a weed-infested lot. There's a fractured picture window and an official-looking notice posted on the front door. The house seems empty as a sucked-out egg.

A "For Sale" sign hangs near the mailbox, and the real estate agent's cheerful placard looks out of place.

Reeve steps off the sidewalk, slips under the police tape, and quickly moves around the side of the single-story house. Dead, dry twigs snap underfoot. It's cold and she has forgotten her gloves.

A small patch of concrete at the side of the house marks a side door. She approaches, tries the knob, finds it locked, and continues around to the back, studying the footprint of the house. There are no basement windows, not even any vents to indicate there might be a lower level.

Two steps lead up to the back porch. Reeve drops down into a crouch and peers between the wooden steps, searching the darkness. There's a dank, earthy odor. Something stirs behind her and she jumps to her feet, startling a bird that flies away. She turns back and mounts the steps.

A face gawks at her and she blanches, then feels foolish. She leans in and places her forehead against the sliding glass door, cupping her hands around her mirrored reflection and holding her breath to keep from fogging the glass. Just inside is a dingy kitchen, open cupboards, a dirty tile floor. Laying a cheek against the cold glass, she tries to see deeper into the interior. In one corner is a heap of what appears to be broken drywall, but a wall blocks her line of sight.

She grips the handle and rattles the sliding glass door in its metal track. The only thing keeping her out is an old-fashioned latch. She bumps the door back and forth, feeling for weakness. The latch taunts her.

She drops into a squat and studies the lock, hoping for a gap wide enough for a tool of some kind, but finds it too narrow. With a cluck of disappointment, she steps back. What would a burglar do? Her eyes travel along the frame, considering how the door slides along the track, the rollers at the top. . . .

Stepping close, she opens her arms wide, grips the handle in her left hand, the edge of the door in her right, and lifts, straining.

Too heavy.

She drops her arms, reconsiders, and steps in again. With bent knees, putting both palms flat on the glass close to her chest, she inhales and shoves upward. With one hard push, the door lifts in the frame and the lock clicks free.

The door glides open and she steps inside, wrinkling her nose at the smell of old cooking grease. Her steps seem loud in the empty house. She finds the entrance to the basement just off the kitchen. Broken edges of drywall surround the doorway and debris crunches underfoot as she approaches. Ignoring a beat of trepidation, she leans forward and peers into the blackness, then looks around, searching for a light. She finds the switch covered with black powder, the special talc of crime scene investigators. Carefully, with one knuckle, she prepares to flip the light, then freezes. A rustling noise.

She whirls around, stares hard, but sees nothing. Creeping back to the sliding glass door, she searches the yard and locates the sound: the bird is again flitting through dead leaves, hunting for grubs.

Exasperated with herself, she strides back and flips the switch. Light glares ahead, illuminating the basement stairs, and she heads down. Her boots make disturbingly familiar sounds on the wooden treads, and when they touch the concrete floor, she realizes this is the first time she has confronted a basement since Daryl Wayne Flint unlocked her door.

She stands swaying in the center of the room, absorbing the blank hideousness of the place. The room is tiny, barely the size of a walk-in closet. The concrete walls are painted not the gray of her own prison, but a sickly yellow.

She closes her eyes and begins to hyperventilate as the cruelty of this place registers in her bones. It's worse than any cell in any prison. There's no Geneva Convention, no time served. No chance to tunnel out with fellow prisoners, or to bribe a guard into helping you escape. No amnesty. No hope.

She shudders and opens her eyes, chastising herself: *Breathe normally. It's not as bad as learning to ride an elevator. It's not even locked.*

She turns in a slow a circle, studying the cramped space. When she has seen enough, she spits on the floor and hurries up the stairs, where she pauses just long enough to flip off the light and to wipe the blackness off on her jeans.

THIRTY-NINE

Perhaps it's logical that Buster Ewing Realty is located near a hospital, since real estate deals surely follow a good number of births and deaths. But the downtown area is a maze of one-way streets, and despite the blue signs directing Reeve to Jefferson Medical Center, despite the small, precise map on her cell phone, the address is seemingly impossible to reach. Each time Reeve thinks she finally has gotten her bearings, she makes a wrong turn and barely escapes oncoming traffic.

After the third mishap, she detours into a pharmacy parking lot.

Close enough. She'll walk.

She gets out of her car and a winter gust slams her door shut. She hurries into the wind, wondering what exactly she hopes to learn from Emily Ewing.

According to news reports that Reeve has pored over recently, it was this Realtor who first noticed something weird about the Redrock house, and it was her call that eventually led police to Randy Vanderholt's lair. The articles were vague, but still, Emily Ewing might know something significant that didn't quite fit into an article or sound bite. At the very least, she might supply a better map than the flimsy handout from the hotel.

Reeve fights the wind for two blocks to the south and two more to the west before spotting Buster Ewing Realty. The business is housed in a plain stucco building that was clearly built as a private residence and later converted into an office. A Lexus sedan is the sole vehicle in the small parking lot.

Reeve follows the sidewalk up to a heavy wooden door with an old-fashioned leaded glass window. The place seems so quiet, it feels appropriate to knock, but a tall placard declares: "WE'RE OPEN!"

The knob turns easily and a chime sounds as Reeve steps into a room smelling of fresh oranges.

"Hello!" exclaims an angular, stylish woman seated at a nearby desk. "Come in, come in! It's freezing out there, isn't it?" She stands, folding a napkin around orange peels and bread crusts and neatly tossing it into a wastepaper basket. She dusts her fingers, saying, "Pardon my lunch. I'm Emily Ewing."

Reeve introduces herself, and as they shake hands, can't help but notice Ewing's red fingernails, which match her red, extravagantly high heels. She seems very tall.

Ewing gestures toward a set of brightly upholstered chairs. "Please have a seat. I was just going to make some coffee. Would you like some?"

Reeve has no time to decline before Emily Ewing steps over to a counter and begins scooping coffee grounds into a filter. "I'm a total caffeine addict, I have to confess."

There are stacks of brochures and magazines, all advertising real estate. Spying a stack of maps, Reeve picks one up, saying, "Well, I guess I have to confess that I'm not really shopping for a house."

"Too bad for me." Ewing turns around and flashes a grin. "So, what can I do for you?"

"I'd like to talk to you about Randy Vanderholt."

Ewing's smile falters. "You're not a reporter, are you?"

"No, I'm a friend of Tilly Cavanaugh's."

"Oh, that poor girl! Can you imagine?" Her eyes go wide and she presses both palms to her breastbone. "I'm so glad that man is dead. My lord! What an animal!"

Ewing steps toward her and Reeve can't help but flinch, expecting a hug. Instead, Ewing lightly touches her shoulder and again motions to a brightly upholstered chair, saying, "Please, please sit down."

The coffee machine burbles while the woman continues talking: "I'm not really in favor of the death penalty, you know, but with sexual predators, I make an exception." She straightens up and flashes Reeve a bright smile. "I guess that makes me a hypocrite, doesn't it? Ha! Anyway, I'm glad that man's dead. Saves all of us from having to read about him in the newspapers and see his face on TV every damn day for god knows how long."

Reeve sits watching while Ewing pours two large mugs of coffee.

"Sugar? Cream?"

"Yes, please."

Handing her a mug on a saucer, Ewing says, "It's just shocking to think that, if I hadn't got that listing, that poor girl might never have been found! I mean, I can't really take credit or anything, but it was some kind of lucky fluke, because it wasn't all that obvious that the house even had a basement."

Reeve mutely accepts the coffee, takes a polite sip, and tries not to wince at the taste. She stirs in more sugar and wonders if coming here was a mistake.

Ewing sits across from her and continues talking. "The furnace and the water heater were in the garage. So it wasn't like you'd say, 'Hey, something's wrong with this picture,' you know?"

Hit with her own private vision of concrete walls and a heavy door, Reeve sets the coffee aside. "You mean, the furnace and water heater are usually located in the basement?"

"Heavens, no! There usually is no basement at all! None! I mean, it's common that the furnace and water heater are in the garage. But if they aren't in the garage, then you wonder, well gee, where the heck could they be! You see?"

Reeve frowns. "You're saying that basements are rare?"

"In this area, pretty much. I'll bet I've only listed a dozen houses with basements in the past decade."

"I see."

"And Vanderholt had it all walled up! Isn't that weird? Like some kind of horror movie, you know what I mean? Anyway, do you want to know how I figured it out?"

Reeve nods.

"It was a no-brainer, really. It was in the listing!"

"I'm confused. Didn't you just say that you listed the house?"

"Oh, that!" Ewing slaps her knee and pops out of her chair. "It sounds confusing, I guess, but it's not."

Reeve thinks the woman has already drunk way too much coffee.

"See, when I list the house for sale, I consult the MLS—the Multiple

Listing Service—which has a full description of the house. How many square feet, what kind of roof, how many bathrooms, all those details. *And,* of course, whether there's a garage or shed or basement. You see?" She leans forward, her eyes shining.

"You mean, you have to research all that before putting the house up for sale?"

"Oh, no, no, no. All the specs are compiled and put on file when the house is built. It's all recorded based on the blueprint and permits and such. You know, from the builder. The data is maintained by the county. The tax assessor needs to keep those property taxes coming in, you know." Ewing rolls her eyes. "Anyway, all that info is compiled, and then it just filters right into the MLS."

"Oh." Reeve sits back, thinking. "Well, if it's not too much trouble, could I see a copy of the listing for the house on Redrock, where Tilly was held?"

"Well, sure. Absolutely. I mean, it's not a big secret or anything." Emily Ewing sits at a computer terminal and pulls another office chair up beside her, saying, "Come take a look."

Ewing's fingers skip across the keyboard while Reeve watches the screen. A form appears with a brief description of the house. Emily Ewing scrolls down and then points to the word "basement" with a checked box next to it. "See?"

"That's it?"

"Yep. So, when I was writing up the ad, I called the owner and said, 'What's up with this? Where's the basement?' Because it wasn't obvious at all, you know, with no windows or anything to indicate there's another level to that structure. But it has that extra square footage, you know, so it's important."

"Okay. So the owner of the house confirmed there was a basement, and then—"

"Then I called in the home inspector, who told me that one whole freshly painted wall—the most horrible color, too—was actually newer construction than the rest of the house," Ewing says, waving her hands and talking fast. "Weird! So, we consulted the owner again and got his permission, and we had that wall knocked down and—dang!—there was the basement door. So I called the police!"

Reeve sits back. "So, all the houses in the county with basements are traceable?"

"Sure." Emily Ewing checks her watch. "Oh, lord! I've got to get going. My dog's at the vet, and if I don't pick her up in thirty minutes, they'll charge me extra. She's a pug. The cutest little thing ever, but you know dogs. You have dogs? You love 'em like your own children, but—"

"Just one more thing," Reeve interrupts. "What about the other house, the one way out of town that Vanderholt moved to, where he was arrested. Do you know anything about it?"

"Yep, that one's up for sale now, too."

"That was quick."

"Warp speed! But it's not my listing, thank heavens, 'cause it'll never get sold."

"How come?"

"Are you kidding? In this market? After such bad publicity? Ugh!"

"Would you have access to that listing, too?"

"Well, sure. Do you want a copy?"

"If it's not too much trouble."

Ewing turns back to her computer, clicks to another screen, scrolls for a moment, then makes a growling sound. "Grrr, my crappy machine is frozen." She clicks madly but nothing happens. "This damned old thing. I've been meaning to upgrade, but . . ." She checks her watch again. "I'm sorry, I really need to get going, but if you'll give me your e-mail address, I'll be happy to send it to you."

Reeve scribbles her e-mail address on a notepad while Emily Ewing slips into her coat, clicks off the coffee machine, and snatches up her purse.

As they head toward the door, Ewing hands her a business card, trilling, "Here's my card, because you never know when you might need a Realtor!"

FORTY

When Reeve returns to her Jeep, Duke turns the key in his ignition and follows at a leisurely pace. He's had no trouble keeping her in sight, thanks to the GPS locator, a good-quality, Raytheon-made device that emits a strong signal.

He wonders what the hell she's up to. He followed her to the first house where Tilly was held, where she apparently broke in. He felt sure there was nothing for her to see, but still . . . What took her so long?

Next, unfortunately, she'd made a visit to that damn real estate office.

And now, to his surprise, Reeve is cruising past the courthouse, parking in the lot adjacent to police headquarters. He drives past, then makes a U-turn and swings back around, parking across the street. He scans the entrances, thinking he has missed her, then realizes that she's still sitting in her car.

What is Edgy Reggie up to? Probably checking her phone. Kids these days, so tied to their electronic devices.

He fishes a pack of cigarettes from his pocket, and as he lights up, notices a group of smokers standing outside the building. He takes a long drag, studies them. Studies Reeve.

She's watching them.

He's smoking, while watching Reeve watch cops who are smoking. This is an irony that would ordinarily amuse him, but not today. He has been in a foul mood since listening to the recording of Tilly's stupid disclosures.

His Sniffer program had caught the reference to "Mister Monster," and he'd replayed the long conversation.

He found the whole "swear on your mother's grave" bit melodramatic. And then things got worse. Much worse than he'd imagined. So he'd listened again, more carefully, getting angry again at Vander-dolt for being so stupid, angry at himself for letting the dolt know that he was aligned in any way with law enforcement.

He rolls down his window, flicks out his cigarette butt, lets the chilly air fill the van, and considers his options. Killing Vanderholt had been a necessary task, but he'd hoped that, when things quieted down, he could resume his private activities. Now Silly Tilly has spilled too much, and her friend, this meddling cunt, is becoming a major distraction.

She had almost caught him in the act of securing the GPS device inside her bumper this morning, but he'd used the "oops, dropped my change" ploy after quickly fixing the small gray box in place.

He'd figured that tracking her would be enough of a precaution, that Edgy Reggie was no problem for him, still barely more than a kid herself. But he hadn't expected her to make that detour to Buster Ewing Realty. Which was irksome. Because even though that scrawny Ewing woman may not realize it, she could stir up serious trouble.

He lights another cigarette and smokes, watching while Edgy Reggie gets out of her Jeep.

Now what? If she sees a tall cop with dark hair, she'll rush up and demand to see what brand he's smoking? Ask to see his tattoos?

But Reeve walks slowly past the cluster of smoking cops, continues down the street. And damned if she doesn't stop at the door of the Jefferson County District Attorney's Office.

FORTY-ONE

Four people stand outside police headquarters, puffing away, huddled in their dark coats, stomping their feet in a recessed area that offers partial protection from the brisk winter wind. To Reeve, they look furtive as criminals, and she keeps a sharp eye on them as she walks past, wondering if Vanderholt was really working with a sadistic cop. Or was that just some ruse to scare young Tilly?

As soon as Reeve steps inside the district attorney's office, she wants to turn around and go. Two men just inside the door are arguing in hushed tones, and they glare at her as she enters, as if she's interrupting.

She approaches the receptionist's thick window, which seems designed to block any assault, and waits. After getting no acknowledgment, she says, "Excuse me?"

The woman behind the glass shakes her head, points at something, and looks away.

It takes Reeve a moment to realize what she means, but then she sees the dispenser, plucks out a numbered tag—forty-four—and finds an open seat beside a lump of a man with ugly tattoos on his neck. The two men by the door continue arguing. The artificial light buzzes overhead.

Last time she entered this building, a deputy met her and escorted her upstairs. Now she realizes how simple that made things. She perches on the plastic chair, careful not to touch anything and contract a disease while dropping off this file.

"Forty-one!" the receptionist barks.

No one moves.

"Forty-one!"

People glance around, someone coughs, but no one responds.

"Forty-two!"

A gaunt woman with a whimpering child rises, gathering her things. She balances the child on her hip and hurries over to the window, where she begins a lengthy complaint.

Reeve waits. More people enter the office. The envelope in her hands feels like kryptonite.

The woman with the whimpering child is buzzed inside a blank metal door.

"Forty-three!"

The two men arguing by the door abruptly turn toward the window. One speaks in short, clipped sentences. The receptionist shakes her head. The second man speaks to her sharply. She matches his tone. The first man begins speaking, and she slams her window shut.

The two men grumble at the window, at each other, and then stomp out the door.

Reeve tenses, expectant. "For Deputy District Attorney Jackie Burke," is written plainly on the front of the envelope. She will just hand it to the receptionist and get out of here.

"Thirty-nine!"

Reeve stifles a groan as the tattooed man next to her rises to his feet, saying to no one in particular, "Me again, sorry," and hurries to the blank door, where he's buzzed inside.

A minute later, the receptionist barks: "Forty-four!"

Approaching the window with a tepid smile, Reeve offers the envelope and deferentially explains that she'd like to simply leave it for Jackie Burke.

"You can't leave that with me," the receptionist protests.

"But I—"

"Nope. Just sit down and wait."

"But can't someone deliver it?"

The woman gives her a pained look. "If you want it delivered, why don't you just mail it?"

"Because I promised to get it to her today."

"Then fill out this form," the receptionist says, pushing a pink notepad under the window, "and I'll let them know you're here."

Done with being polite, Reeve makes a face and hastily fills out the form, using a pen leashed to the counter. She pushes the completed form back to the woman, who snaps it up and waves her away, calling out, "Forty-five!"

Reeve groans and resumes her seat. The last thing she wants is another encounter with Jackie Burke. The envelope has obviously been opened, and she can just imagine the grilling she's about to get.

A tall man in uniform enters the office, shedding his coat. Wasn't he just outside, smoking? He nods at the receptionist and walks past Reeve to the blank door. She studies his biceps, wishing she could see through the fabric, then glances up and finds him scowling at her. She looks away as he's buzzed inside.

Closing her eyes, she tries to think. Actually, if she were to buy an envelope and find a post office, she could mail the file to Burke. And what's the harm, really, if it doesn't arrive for a day or two? It would arrive by Monday, at the latest, and she could just explain to Dr. Lerner that—

"Hey, Reeve, are you okay?"

She opens her eyes to find Nick Hudson bending over her.

"Oh! Yes, I'm fine!" She scrambles to her feet and proffers the envelope. "I just wanted to deliver this to Jackie Burke."

"Okay, sure," he says, taking it from her. "But she's not in, and it's lunchtime, so I have two questions: Are you hungry? And do you like sushi?"

It's walking distance to the restaurant, so they hurry through the blustery weather, just making the front door as fat raindrops splash down around them.

The restaurant is bright and welcoming, and Nick Hudson suggests sitting at the sushi bar. Reeve assesses the layout and the clientele while taking a seat beside him. She eyes the sharpness of the knives, the freshness of the fish in the display case, then asks the sushi chef a couple of questions in Japanese.

"Well, aren't you full of surprises?" Hudson says, grinning.

"I used to work at a Japanese restaurant."

"So, what was all that about?"

"It's a good idea to ask the sushi chef what he suggests, that's all."

"Noted. So what's the verdict?"

"The yellowtail is especially fresh."

"Great. Let's start with that. Uh, and how about some pot stickers?" After placing an order with the sushi chef, he turns to her. "Any other tips?"

She hums a note, thinking, and adds, "Any sushi prepared with cream cheese or mayonnaise is a fraud and an abomination."

"Also noted."

She has been avoiding eye contact, since good-looking men always make her nervous, but now she cocks an eyebrow and gives him a long, appraising look. "You didn't invite me here just to flatter me. What's up?"

He sits forward, drumming his fingers on the envelope resting on the counter between them. "I wanted to ask how Tilly is doing."

The waitress brings cups of steaming green tea, and Reeve holds hers with both hands, warming them before answering, "You know, Dr. Lerner has been meeting with the whole family on a regular basis, and he should be back in a day or two."

"Right, but in the meantime, can you share any insights?"

She acts nonchalant. "Dr. Lerner is the professional. He's the one with the insights."

He studies her for a moment. "What about you and Tilly, the two of you together? How's that going?"

"There's not much to tell," she lies. The food arrives and she picks up her chopsticks.

"Come on," he scoffs. "With all the time you two have been spending together?"

"Actually, she's pretty reserved. More than I thought she'd be."

He exhales loudly. "Okay, you want to maintain confidentiality, right?"

She lifts a piece of sushi and says, "Mm, doesn't this look delicious," trying to change the subject.

He laughs. "Okay, the truth is, I have an ulterior motive for asking you here. I hope you don't mind, but Jackie Burke wants to talk to you."

"Burke? Why?"

"She wants to pick your brains."

Reeve chokes.

"Are you okay?"

"Too much wasabi," she croaks, grabbing her cup of tea and gulping so quickly she burns her tongue.

"She said she'd be late." He cranes around to check the door. "But she should be here pretty soon."

"Well, I can't tell her anything more than she already knows. At least, nothing that's, uh, pertinent." Tilly's secret seems to pulse inside her.

"Maybe, maybe not. She's pursuing a new theory."

"What theory?"

"Oh, here she is now." He stands and waves Burke over while muttering under his breath, "Just be helpful, okay? And try not to get us both in trouble."

Burke seems to bring the storm inside with her as she comes toward them, carrying a dripping umbrella. "God, it's pouring out there," she complains, stamping her wet boots. "Sorry I'm late. Oh, I don't like the sushi bar. Let's move to that table in the back where we'll have more privacy."

Taking charge, Burke signals the waitress, and with some effort the group shuffles toward the most remote table in the restaurant. Reeve sits with her back to the window, keeping an eye on both the front entrance and the side exit.

As they're getting settled, Burke says, "How about some of these rolled-up thingys with cream cheese?" She jabs a finger at a picture on the menu, adding, "My treat."

Hudson shoots Reeve a wry look, waits for the waitress to finish taking orders, then hands Burke the envelope, saying, "Vanderholt's file. From Dr. Lerner."

She inspects it closely. "It's addressed to me," she grumbles, indicating the broken seal.

"Sorry about that." He places a discreet hand on Reeve's knee, as though to keep her from jumping out of her seat, adding, "My mistake."

Reeve gives him a sideways glance and says to Burke, "I'm sorry, but I really need to get going. So was there something you wanted to ask?"

"Yes, Miss LeClaire, there are quite a few things I would like to ask. As you surely understand, there are numerous legal difficulties associated with having to interview children, a litany of difficulties that—"

"But Vanderholt's dead," Reeve interrupts. "So there's no case, right?"

Burke's eyes harden. "Okay, fine. I'll get right to the point." Putting her elbows on the table, she leans toward Reeve. "Has Tilly said anything to indicate that she has any knowledge regarding the whereabouts of Hannah Creighton or Abby Hill?"

"What? No."

"I want you to think very carefully."

"No, I'm sure. But if you'd like to talk to Dr. Lerner—"

"Right now I'm talking to you. Is there anything at all that Tilly has revealed to you that I should know?"

"Nothing." Reeve swallows, trying to maintain her poker face.

"Are you absolutely certain?" Burke asks, peering at her.

"Believe me, I wish there were something I could tell you, but I don't have a clue about those other girls."

"You'd better be straight with me, because if I find out she has shared important information of any—" Burke's line of sight skims past Reeve's shoulder. "Oh, shit, it's Poe."

"Otis Poe?" Reeve asks, craning to see.

A bald man the size of a football player comes through the door, his smile a slash of white across his dark face.

"Well damn, Burke," Hudson mutters, "did he follow you here?"

"One important thing you should know about Tilly and me," Reeve says to them, scooting back her chair, "we both hate reporters." She grabs her jacket and makes a beeline for the curtained area beside the sushi counter, where she finds the exit and dashes out into the storm.

FORTY-TWO

Friday

A few news vans still clot the approach to the Cavanaughs' residence late Friday afternoon, and reporters bark questions at Reeve, but she barely glances at them as she turns into the driveway and drives past. No one knows who she is, and she has nothing to say.

Mr. Cavanaugh greets her as if she is an old friend and invites her to join them for a snack. The entire family is clustered around the dining room table, where Reeve accepts a slice of pecan pie before announcing, "I come bearing gifts."

Setting a shopping bag on the table, she pulls out a selection of chocolate bars and a tin of gourmet cocoa mix, but these are just distractions from her true purpose. It had taken her awhile to find this particular calendar. She places it before Tilly, saying, "I hope you like it. I noticed you like art."

Tilly splits open the cellophane wrapper and begins flipping through the colorful pages, pausing to study works by Monet and Matisse and Gauguin.

Reeve takes a seat beside her, saying, "See? It starts with December, so you can use it right away." Turning to Mrs. and Mrs. Cavanaugh, she adds, "You know, for planning trips and things."

Everyone seems to gape at her, saying nothing. She gives Tilly a quick nudge beneath the table. "Didn't you say you have family in Fresno? I mean, you probably want to plan your trip, don't you? For Christmas vacation?"

Reeve steals a peek at Tilly, who is staring at the calendar with a kind of hunger. The rest of the family stops eating their pie and studies Reeve as if she has done something gauche.

Feeling awkward, Reeve is about to offer an apology when Tilly pipes up. "Yeah, let's go down to Aunt Becca's right away, okay? Please? Then we won't have all those reporters camped out on our doorstep."

"That's a great idea," Reeve says, her voice a bit too bright.

Matt glances at his sister and grumbles. "Yeah, we're practically prisoners here."

"Right! Just leave the media in the dust," Reeve says. "The scrutiny here is hard on all of you, I'm sure."

Tilly flashes Reeve a conspiratorial smile. "Mom, couldn't we stay in Fresno with Aunt Becca? I mean permanently?"

Mr. and Mrs. Cavanaugh look at their children.

"Please?" Tilly says, rising from her seat. "Please, please, please!"

"What do you think, honey?" Mrs. Cavanaugh says to her husband. "It is getting pretty bad here."

"Hey, Dad, why couldn't they just stay down there for awhile," Matt says, "and then you and me can come back here?"

"That might be a good idea," Mrs. Cavanaugh says.

"I don't know." Mr. Cavanaugh puts his head in his hands. "Split up the family?"

"We could try it out, you know, as a compromise." Mrs. Cavanaugh says. "Maybe Tilly could start school down there next semester."

"See, Dad? Everyone thinks it's a good idea." Matt sits back and crosses his arms, giving Reeve a rare smile. "Let her move if she wants, and then I can at least finish my senior year like a normal person."

"Could we go, Dad?" Tilly begs. "Please? Like right away?"

Mr. Cavanuagh looks from face to face and opens his palms. "I don't know. I'm not crazy about the idea."

"Well, but honey," Mrs. Cavanaugh says slowly, "there is, um, one other thing."

He exhales. "What?"

"Uh, well, someone put a dead rat in our car."

He gawks at her. "Are you kidding?"

"I wish I were."

"A dead rat? That's disgusting."

"Yes." She grimaces. "It was really disgusting."

"Why didn't you tell me?"

"Because I didn't want to alarm you."

"A *rat?*" Tilly says.

"Where? When?" Mr. Cavanaugh asks, frowning.

"I'm not sure. While Tilly and I were out shopping, I guess. I thought the car was locked, but when we got home, I was unloading packages, and—"

"A *rat?*" Tilly repeats.

"That's mega-gross," Matt declares. "I mean, why would—"

"There are sick people out there," Reeve says, staring at Tilly, who sits rigidly upright, looking pale. "It's not safe."

Reeve has no doubt the rat was a message for Tilly. Was it really from Mister Monster? Could he strike this close?

An hour later, Reeve and Tilly are curled on the couch watching yet another PG-rated movie, when Matt comes in and sits down beside them. He's not paying attention to the movie, Reeve notices. He's fidgeting, kneading his thighs, and keeps looking at his sister.

After a couple of minutes, Tilly sighs with exasperation and demands, "What?"

"Um, you're not really watching this, are you?"

"Not really," she admits.

His voice drops. "That rat creeped you out, didn't it?"

She stares at him for a long moment before giving a short nod.

"I thought so." He swallows, anguish showing on his face "Okay, can I show you something?"

"I guess."

Tilly reaches for the remote, but he blocks her hand, saying, "Leave it on," with a glance toward the door.

This earns Tilly's full attention. Whatever Matt has in mind clearly would not meet with parental approval.

He stands, saying, "Reeve, you can come, too," and leads them down a hall to a part of the house she hasn't explored. They enter a den that's twice as big as Reeve's father's, with a massive mahogany desk, paneled walls, plenty of bookshelves, and an elk's head mounted above a fireplace.

He shuts the door behind them, saying, "Okay, weird shit is happening, but this is the safest room in the house. So if anything ever happens, meet me here."

Reeve glances around, wondering what makes this room safer than any other, noticing the double locks on the door.

"If there's a real emergency, I just want you to know that I can protect you, if it comes to that."

Matt's snarky attitude has vanished, and Tilly nods at her older brother with solemn respect.

He crosses the room and stands beside the fireplace, saying, "Mom and Dad don't want you to know about these, so don't say anything, okay?"

He grips the vertical edge of a gleaming wood panel and slides it to the right, revealing a hidden compartment stocked with guns.

Tilly stares with a rapt expression, standing with her hands clasped behind her back and leaning so far forward that she's balanced on the balls of her feet.

"Don't ever play with these," he says, pointing. "I'm a pretty good shot, so if anything happens, I'll take care of it, okay?"

For an awful moment, Reeve is afraid he's going to take out a gun and hand it to Tilly, but then he slides the panel closed and she breathes out relief.

"Wait a minute," Tilly says, stepping toward him. "At least teach me how to shoot."

He glances at the door and shakes his head.

"What if you're not home? What if I'm here all by myself?"

"If you're home alone and something happens, come in here, lock the door, and call 911. Then just wait here, okay?"

"Come on, you showed me where the guns are, at least show me what to do."

Matt rubs his face, thinking. He slides the panel open again, and says, "These three are rifles and these two are shotguns."

For a moment, Reeve thinks she should stop him, but reconsiders. Maybe Matt actually knows what he's doing. Given the circumstances, maybe this kid's instincts are better than hers.

He takes down a rifle and hands it to Tilly, showing her how to hold it. "Now, this is just for absolute emergencies, okay? Grip it here. The safety is on, see? But always assume a gun is loaded. Don't even put your finger on the trigger or point it at anyone you don't want to see dead. You got that?"

"Yep, got it," Tilly says quickly.

For the next several minutes, Matt conducts his own version of a gun safety course, and Reeve watches closely while Tilly learns the basics of how to aim and fire a rifle. The shotgun, he says, "has stopping power, but it's too difficult for you because you to have to pump it."

Tilly frowns at the rifle in her hands and asks, "How do I know when to shoot?"

"The thing is, you don't want to shoot," Matt says, taking the gun from her. "You just want them to run away. And trust me, anyone staring down the business end of a barrel is going to be scared."

He fits the rifle back into its place and slides the panel closed.

The trio returns to the couch, and while the movie continues, they sit guiltily, quiet and watchful in the way of children trying to get away with something forbidden. Eventually, Matt slinks out of the room. Tilly chews her nails. And Reeve rubs the scar on the back of her neck, staring at the screen without seeing.

Later that night, Reeve is busy writing a last-minute e-mail to Emily Ewing when Tilly Cavanaugh borrows her father's phone to send a short text message:

> Dad says we can move. Thank you, Reeve!
> xo, Tilly

And just like that, Duke has captured Reeve LeClaire's phone number.

FORTY-THREE

Duke makes himself comfortable in his control room, opens his laptop, and in a few clicks is scrolling down Otis Poe's blog, a favorite place for readers to pontificate about local issues, about crime, and particularly, of late, about Randy Vanderholt and the kidnapped girls. Poe's coverage of the case has generated a growing number of followers, who simply click his link to join the discussion. For the most part, these postings bemoan the fate of the victims, criticize law enforcement, and condemn pedophiles. Several recent posts have heaped praise on Vanderholt's killer, an irony that Duke appreciates.

Now it's his turn.

Using two newly created identities, Duke sends both sides of what appears as a conversational posting:

kommonknowledge@jefferson.net	Everyone knows that Tilly Cavanaugh is being treated by that SF shrink, Lame Lerner, but who is that babe who's always with him? The hot one with the trendy hair?
streeter@jefferson.net	kommon, you aren't so knowledgeable. That's Reggie LeClaire, obviously. Remember her? Edgy Reggie? She's another patient of Lerner's.

kommonknowledge@jefferson.net	Reggie LeClaire? Isn't she that girl who was kidnapped up in Washington State a few years back?
streeter@jefferson.net	Yep. Looks like she's doing some kind of victim-to-victim consultation. Hope these sob sessions aren't paid for by our tax dollars.

Duke sits back and smiles, watching the conversation take off.

In no time, there are indignant responses, followed by long-winded expositions on post-traumatic shock disorder, plus a few good wishes—posted with lots of exclamation points!!!—that are intended for Reggie LeClaire, Beth Goodwin, Tilly Cavanaugh, and every other victim of every other sex crime ever committed.

Duke leaves the room, fixes himself a snack, eats it in the kitchen, follows it with a cigarette, then comes back and posts:

streeter@jefferson.net	Hey, guess what: Reggie LeClaire has changed her name, too. She calls herself Reeve. What kind of name is that?

Duke smiles, watching the responses. Some congratulate Reeve for moving on. Others rant indignantly that the poor girl's anonymity has now been ruined by this insensitive writer. Some call him an asshole. Others, for various convoluted reasons, are glad that he has outed her.

He follows the online chatter for only a few minutes. There are other, more important tasks competing for his attention.

It takes just a quick search to locate the proper address, a few minutes more for the correct inmate number.

He pulls on latex gloves, loads paper into his printer, and prints out a few choice selections from Poe's blog. Lastly, as a single line on a blank sheet, he prints out Reggie LeClaire's current phone number, which he has collected thanks to Tilly's recent text message.

He slips these sheets into a self-sealing priority mail envelope—leaving no saliva to trace, thank you very much—and addresses it to Daryl Wayne Flint, Inmate 44610906FP, c/o Olshaker Medical Hospital, Forensic Services Unit, South Turvey, Washington.

FORTY-FOUR

Saturday

The late Buster Ewing would have been dismayed to see the present state of the realty office he left to his only child. He had quit this world believing that Emily would inherit a thriving enterprise that would continue to grow, but the years have chewed away at Buster Ewing Realty. His contemporaries have grown frail and been eulogized, one by one, and the promising young employees whose careers Buster had cultivated and encouraged have all left for more lucrative endeavors.

Emily Ewing has been forced to downsize and then downsize again.

Just last month, her favorite real estate agent, a young guy named Skeeter, gave up and moved to Oregon. Now business is so slow that she has only one person working for her, a scrappy young woman named Nicole who opens the office on weekends.

But Emily Ewing's strength is her dogged optimism, and she breezes into the office this rainy Saturday morning with a smile that defies the weather. "Good morning, Nicole! Wait until you hear what we've got going today," she sings, as if this dreary day were brimming with opportunities.

Nicole welcomes Emily's sunny attitude and appreciates her tutelage. She loves going to networking meetings, updating ads, and working with clients. She is so young that she expects life will only get better, though she's beginning to sense how much she has to learn.

"Let me guess," Nicole says. "You have an open house scheduled for today."

"The Baker house!" Emily exclaims, hanging up her raincoat. "God, I love that house. The koi pond? The kitchen? And those beautiful floors!"

"Right. I did the open house there two weeks ago, remember? It was dead."

"But this is always the slow season, with the holidays and all. Just wait, things will pick up after the Super Bowl, you'll see."

"So why even bother with another open house today?"

She sighs, gazing out at the gloomy weather. "I promised the Bakers." Her smile hardens. "Besides, while I'm out of the office, you'll have the place all to yourself. You never know when a hot client will walk in. And anyone shopping in this kind of weather has got to be a serious buyer."

Two hours later, Emily Ewing is out in the rain, putting up her signs. Her heels are impractical, and the Lexus is not the ideal vehicle for carrying around so many cumbersome "For Sale" signs, but she has had a lot of practice lifting signs out of car trunks and placing them on strategic corners. Any kind of trunk, wearing any kind of shoes.

The signs are heavy, made of sturdy materials that withstand even strong winds, and each displays a flattering picture of her from an earlier, happier time. Despite the cold and rain, she's overheated by the time she drives up the steep driveway and parks outside the three-car garage.

She uses the lockbox to let herself in. She cleans herself up, tidies the bathroom, sets out a vase of flowers, polishes the kitchen appliances, starts cookies baking in the oven, arranges stacks of her business cards, sets out newly printed four-color brochures, and waits. This is her sixth open house here, not counting Nicole's. If nothing happens before the end of the year, she'll have to ask the Bakers to consider another price cut, but that's risky. The house is already worth much more than they're asking, and she's afraid they'll replace her with another agent.

She's fretting over this when she hears a car door slam, then two more. She uncovers the dish of freshly baked cookies and smiles at the family that comes in scowling.

Later, Emily Ewing checks the time and sighs. Is there anything she could have done differently today?

Yes, she should have downplayed the landscaping with the overweight family that complained about the small refrigerator, perhaps suggesting another fridge in the garage. And she should have come up with some kind of helpful response for the elderly couple that hated the koi pond, though it must have shown on her face that she was appalled by the idea of "filling it with concrete and putting a shed over it."

She looks around at the house. It's gorgeous. It deserves to be loved.

She throws the flowers away, knowing she may not be back here for days or weeks, and there's nothing more depressing than a vase of dead flowers. She puts the six remaining cookies in a ziploc bag and carries them out to her car.

The rain has let up, but the ground is soggy and the looming evening darkens the sky. Wrapping her coat tight, she makes a mental note to limit showings to earlier hours until the days start to lengthen in the spring.

She heads down the steep driveway to retrieve the "OPEN HOUSE!" sign and is muscling it into her trunk when a vehicle turns up the driveway. She stops and squints. The sedan parks, its headlights die, the door opens, and she watches while a man's cowboy boots find the ground. He unfolds from the car and nearly stands, but then leans back inside for a moment, and re-emerges, standing very tall while topping his head with a dove-gray felt cowboy hat.

He shuts the door and grins at her, saying, "Hey there, I'm not too late for the open house, am I?"

Duke can be charming when he wants to be. He smiles and flirts as he follows the woman into the house, telling her that he has just found this listing and the house might be perfect for him.

"What do you do?" Emily Ewing asks, turning on lights.

"I'm an engineer. From Colorado. Sold my business, and now I'm looking to kick back here in Jefferson. I want to live close to the mountains, but I'm done with having to shovel snow. Doesn't snow here much, does it?"

He trails after her while she assures him that snow is rare. She shows him the home's features, the Brazilian cherrywood floors, the imported tiles, the six-hundred-square-foot master suite.

In the kitchen, he admires the granite countertop without raising a hand to touch it. In fact, he keeps his gloves on and touches nothing.

"I like a lot of outdoor space," he says, peering out the French doors. "How's the back?"

"I can't wait to show you," she says, opening the doors. "This is a five-acre lot, and the landscaping around the house is one of its best features. They put in deer-resistant and native plants, and you'll see that it's just beautifully laid out."

He follows her clicking heels out onto the back deck. "A hot tub? This is great. And there are no neighbors, are there?"

She smiles. "No one nearby. It's very private."

They go down the stairs onto a stone path, and she leads him over to the koi pond. "This is my favorite part!"

A few colorful fish appear in the clear water. They rise and swim close, opening and closing their whiskered mouths. More join them until several white, black, orange and yellow fish crowd the surface, making hungry kisses, hoping for food.

"Are you kidding me?" he exclaims. "Are these, whaddya call 'em, Japanese carp?"

She beams at him. "Yes, Japanese carp. Or koi, same thing."

"Fancy that. And they come with the house?"

She confirms this, smiling while pointing out the finest specimens. "With those markings, some of these koi are really quite valuable."

"Well now, will you look at that?" He squats down by the fishpond and places one hand on a softball-sized stone as if for balance, carefully working it loose. "And how many do you reckon we've got here? Ten? Fifteen?"

She squats down next to him, studying the fish. "Gosh, two dozen maybe? I can ask the—"

Duke smashes the stone against the side of her head with such force it knocks her into the pond with a splash that drenches his boots. He stands quickly, watching, breathing hard.

She floats facedown in the water, a faint, red blush trailing from her head. The fish have disappeared.

He glances at his watch and looks around. The hillside setting remains still and undisturbed. Peaceful.

He waits a full five minutes—watching for any sign of struggle, just to be sure—then carefully replaces the stone in its muddy spot, the bloody mark showing on top.

FORTY-FIVE

Sunday

Fourteen-year-old Abby Hill listens hard for clues to whatever is going on upstairs. She closes her eyes and curls up on her side, listening, locating. There's a new sound, a repeating metallic noise that is somehow measured, but doesn't seem to be mechanical. The noise is not directly overhead.

She opens her eyes and tries to imagine what's above. Assuming the wall with the socket and night-light continues all the way up into the main house, the noise is coming from that room, on the other side of the wall.

Clunk, clunk . . . pause . . . *clunk, clunk.* . . .

The man grunts in relation to this sound she almost recognizes but cannot place. There's some kind of rhythm.

She counts repetitions—seven, eight, nine, ten—then a hard noise that's almost a crash reverberates through the floor.

Is he lifting weights? The thought makes her cringe. She doesn't want the man to get stronger. She wants him to weaken, and wither, and die, just like she is.

She runs her hands over her bare ribs and absently wonders why she ever wished to be skinny. She lies on her back, measuring the protrusions of her hip bones with her thumbs, and vows for the millionth time that if she ever again has the chance, she will eat as much as she can and will never, ever go on another diet. Visions of meals with her family appear, her mother serving up all her favorite foods: chocolate cake, rocky road ice cream, honey-baked ham with mashed potatoes. . . .

Her stomach growls and she stops. This is pointless. She'll die here. Either she'll starve to death, or the other man, the one she must call Master, will kill her.

She wonders idly if her body will ever be found, or whether she'll decompose and turn to white bones in this pitch-black basement, the little night-light long burnt out. Will she turn into a skeleton, like in the movies, forgotten here for a hundred years until the house collapses, timbers and dust raining down, burying her remains in rubble?

The noise continues above: *Clunk, clunk* . . . pause . . . *clunk, clunk*. . . . *Slam!* with a sharp curse.

She lies still, clasping her arms across her chest, careful of the burns, listening to the sudden stillness above, waiting for the repetitions to resume.

Nothing.

She waits, but hears only silence.

Maybe he died. Maybe he had a heart attack.

She strains to catch some hint of movement, holding her breath. The silence continues, and her pulse thuds in her ears.

At first, she thought she might be rescued. She imagined that she could scream and someone would hear, but the man always hits her if she screams. And the Master makes her bleed. The house must be far from other houses on the road, anyway, because she hears no traffic, and no one else ever comes.

Maybe he's resting. Maybe he's taking a nap.

She guessed it was daylight, but really has no idea of time. There's never much light.

She imagines a clock, the seconds ticking past. She imagines a calendar and wonders what day it might be. Today might be Thanksgiving, or Christmas, or her sister's birthday. She's mad at herself for not keeping track, somehow. But there is no way to do it, and really, what difference does it make? She sleeps as much as possible, just to pass the time. It's her only escape.

An eerie quiet permeates the house, and she feels a gnawing shame for wishing him dead.

He takes care of her. He is her "keeper," that's what the Master calls him. He brings her food; he removes her waste. As if she were just an animal in a cage.

If he dies, I die.

Her stomach growls again, and she pictures her mother's pot roast with all the trimmings for dinner, then shoves the image aside. She gets to her feet, and in two steps she's across the room, crouching beside the night-light, hoping for sound.

Move. Please move.

She closes her eyes, listens.

Don't be dead, don't be dead.

She listens hard, waiting.

Please.

She hears only her own thudding heart. The concrete floor is like ice beneath her bare feet and goose bumps prickle her skin.

What's that? A slight scuffing sound comes from above. She listens.

Nothing.

Then Abby hears the man grunt and she exhales, realizing only now that she's been holding her breath.

With a creak of floorboards, his heavy feet hit the floor. She hears his tread, hears a door shut as he exits the room. His footsteps thump cross the floor overhead as he enters what is clearly the kitchen. She hears water running, then stop.

She shakes herself, crosses the room, settles back down on her cot, and wraps herself in the thin blanket. She curls up tight and tries to warm her bare feet in her hands.

She hears the high-pitched squeak of what she has concluded must be the refrigerator door. Next, she imagines that she hears the subtle clink of glass. Given the frequent odor on his breath, he's probably getting another bottle of beer.

FORTY-SIX

Mornings are a peaceful time on Duke's riverfront property. Sometimes he takes a crossbow and creeps out before dawn in search of prey. On occasion, he carries tools and walks the fence line, fixing what needs attention. This morning, he carries a steaming mug of coffee down to the riverbank, absently checking for tracks in the mud while he carefully reviews the details of both recent executions.

He figures that no one can connect either Vanderholt or Ewing to him. There's no way. They're both clean kills, one a shooting, one a drowning. No apparent link.

Duke feels confident that Emily Ewing's death will look like a simple accident. A slip-and-fall, the insurance people call it. Too bad she wore those silly shoes. He warms his hands with the coffee mug, glad that trouble-making woman is out of the picture. Serves her right.

He takes a gulp of the fresh black brew and smacks his lips, sure he left no trace. No footprints, no witnesses, no risk. Twenty-five minutes after killing her, he dumped those tacky cowboy boots in a dumpster behind a liquor store. The hat he decided to keep.

Duke studies the gray surface of the river, so wide and deep here that it appears placid. A dangerous deception. The swift, cold water claims new lives every year. He drains his coffee and turns away, heading back toward the house, thinking that Vanderholt's killing was the more elegant of the two. Riskier, but all the risks were calculated.

He had entered the warehouse before dawn. The lock took only seconds. He climbed the stairs and got settled on the roof, setting up the small tripod, adjusting the scope. The roof was uncomfortable, but it was flat and he wasn't there to sleep. Best of all, he blended with the deep shade of the air conditioner as the sun rose to the east.

The sniper rifle he used was a sweet, army-issue M24 that he bought for peanuts from a junkie vet in Vegas. He had trained on it for many long hours over the years. Staring down its scope, perfecting his aim over incredible distances, timing shots between breaths, between heartbeats.

It's a seasoned, accurate weapon. He'll hate getting rid of it.

Using the warehouse was a no-brainer. It was vacant and for sale. Emily Ewing's former employee, Skeeter Jones, had shown it to him, along with five other commercial properties, plus twelve homes, four of which he'd bought. All great deals. All with basements. All legal and neat and hard to trace.

Duke had carried fake IDs, of course, when meeting with his attorneys in Reno. For the first three houses, he used an LLC set up by a baby-faced loser named Yow. Later, for Fitzgerald's place, he used an entirely different setup, judging it wise to use a different LLC for future purchases. Duke practiced the signatures in advance and signed each document with a flourish.

Dealing with attorneys is always dicey, but if pressed, Duke could get rid of Yow. The guy smelled like a gambler, and judging from his frayed suit and junk heap of a car, he had serious money problems. Guys like that disappear all the time.

Duke had considered ways of taking out Clyde Pierson, too, but that would cause major headaches. Besides, why press his luck? None of his keepers knew Duke's true identity. If Vanderholt had made noises about a coconspirator, if he'd been on the brink of handing over a physical description, Duke had hit him just in time, before Pierson had a chance to cut a deal.

Vander-dolt had spilled only blood.

Halfway back to the house, Duke stops to light a cigarette. He looks around, notices the fat, rotten stump of an old oak tree, and comfortably rests the heel of one boot on the stump while he smokes.

Being a man who appreciates irony, Duke allows himself a laugh, because it's ironic that, with so many cops crawling all over this case, the only living person who might even come close to guessing Duke's pattern is that snoopy little bitch. Untrained, and not even that bright.

He has been giving Reggie LeClaire a lot of thought, and has just about decided how to get rid of her. He has worked out a plan so that he can satisfy his appetites without having to coax or train or control another keeper. The risks are manageable, and afterward, he will dispose of the girl without raising the slightest whisper of suspicion.

It will be so ironic.

FORTY-SEVEN

Once again, Reeve has been vexed by the downtown maze of one-way streets. Having almost turned the wrong way into oncoming traffic, she has ended up parking far downhill and is panting heavily by the time she has hiked back up to the right block. Closing in on Buster Ewing Realty, she sees that the parking lot is empty, and the happy "WE'RE OPEN!" placard is gone. The building looks deserted.

Reeve stands on the porch, aggravated. She has left three messages for Emily Ewing, but has gotten no response. Maybe that's what happens when you're pestering a real estate agent for information rather than shopping for a home.

She pulls Ewing's business card from her wallet and again tries her cell. Getting no answer, she clicks off and punches in the office number. She hears the phone ringing inside and then, to her surprise, a voice answers with a flat, "Hello."

"Oh! Hello, are you open? I'm standing outside." Reeve cups her hand to the window and peers inside.

A woman turns around to stare at her. "What do you want?"

"Um, I'm looking for Emily."

The woman hangs up, and Reeve stands there feeling as if she's been slapped. But an instant later the door swings open, and she finds herself before a young woman with red, puffy eyes. "I'm sorry," Reeve says, "who are you?"

"I'm Nicole, Emily's assistant."

"Well, um, could I speak with Emily?"

"Emily's dead."

Before Reeve can absorb this, Nicole sways, staggers backward, and crumples, but Reeve swiftly catches her under the arms and begins maneuvering her inside.

"I'm sorry . . . I'm such a mess," Nicole murmurs as Reeve sets her down on one of the upholstered chairs. The young woman's face is pale and wet and streaked with tears. "I just heard the news." She shakes her head. "I just can't believe it."

"My god. What happened?"

"They say she fell. Hit her head or something."

Reeve feels dizzy.

"I don't know why she had to do that damned open house," Nicole continues, her voice quavering. "I should have done it. It was my turn, and if I had, maybe . . ."

Reeve looks around, hands Nicole a box of tissues, and sits heavily. "I'm—I'm so sorry."

"The coroner's office just called. Can you imagine? They were looking for relatives, but there's no one. Her father's dead," Nicole says, wiping her eyes and blowing her nose.

"How? I mean—"

"They said a neighbor found her. The neighbor who was feeding the fish, you know, for the owners?"

"Fish?"

"Yeah, they found her body in the koi pond." Shuddering, she takes another tissue and blows her nose again. "She loved that damn house." She looks up at Reeve with a miserable expression. "I think she wanted to buy it herself, actually."

The two sit in silence for a long moment. Reeve gets up and turns around, looking for something to do. She gets a coffee mug, fills it with tap water, and hands it to Nicole. "Have some water."

Nicole sips once, sets the mug aside.

"I'm so, so sorry," Reeve says at last, rising to leave. "I wish there were something I could do." She feels a need to say something of substance, but the words seem insignificant as dust. And she knows so little about Emily

Ewing that she can only add, "I only just met her, but she seemed like a very nice person. Really energetic. And kind. And helpful."

Nicole looks up at her, frowns, and gives a quick shake of her head. "Oh, wait. You're Reeve LeClaire, aren't you? I nearly forgot. Emily left an envelope for you. It's on her desk."

Driving along, Reeve feels hyperaware of the unopened envelope on the seat beside her. Traffic flows downtown and seems to carry her directly to a Starbucks, the very same place she stopped when she first arrived in Jefferson more than a week earlier.

She pulls into the Starbucks parking lot, stops, and looks at the envelope. It is marked in bright blue ink: *For pick-up by Reeve LeClaire.*

This was surely one of the last things Emily Ewing ever wrote.

Gingerly, she lifts the envelope and opens it. Inside are six pages of small print, along with a pink sticky note:

Hi Reeve,

   Per your request, I did a search. No problem at all! Here are the abbreviated listings of all houses with basements sold within the past three years.

   Nice meeting you, and please keep me in mind if anyone you know needs a Realtor!

Reeve pulls off the sticky note and sighs. Is this the way life always goes? The good ones suddenly die, and the evil ones just keep hanging on?

She glances at the list and sees a listing near the top, highlighted with yellow marker. The Redrock house.

A chill passes over her, and she's hit with the strange notion that Emily Ewing was murdered.

She considers this for a moment.

No. That's crazy.

She puts the papers back in the envelope and starts to get out of her Jeep, but the pink sticky note catches her eye. It's stuck to the seat and she plucks it off, considering Emily Ewing's cheerful handwritten message, which blurs around one phrase: *please keep me in mind.*

Clucking softly, Reeve fishes her cell phone out of her pocket and punches in Nick Hudson's number. He doesn't answer, and when it beeps to voice mail she can't think of any message that doesn't sound insane, so she clicks her phone off and climbs out of the Jeep.

Inside, she orders a hot chocolate. The barista blinks at her, unmoving, and Reeve repeats her order.

As she waits for her drink, she begins to feel that people are stealing peeks in her direction. She tells herself that she's imagining things, carries her cup over to a seat, sits down with her hot chocolate, and focuses on the real estate listings.

On the third page, she finds the house on Tevis Ranch Road where Tilly Cavanaugh was imprisoned, also highlighted in yellow. She sips her chocolate and briefly pictures Emily Ewing marking the pages. As she scans the list, searching for some insight or pattern, she realizes that the order is chronological. In terms of sales date? Apparently. Other than that, there's nothing obvious.

Remembering that she has left the map in the car, she starts to rise, glances up, and catches a couple at another table staring at her.

They quickly look away. But now she notices the newspaper spread open on their table, displaying a color photograph. Of her, walking with Dr. Lerner.

FORTY-EIGHT

Monday

Otis Poe waits in his car outside the Cavanaughs' gate, hoping to get an interview with Reggie LeClaire. Or Reeve, as she calls herself now.

He feels proprietary about this new angle of the story—it's a scoop from his blog, after all—but unfortunately, three other reporters are already here with him on this cold Monday morning. He watched each one arrive. They had raised palms in greeting, but opted to stay in the warmth of their individual vehicles.

Each time a car approaches, they all stiffen with readiness, then slump as it passes.

Poe has done his homework and prepared a list of questions. He doubts that he'll get answers to more than a handful. And he's mentally prepared, as always, to hear only the dreaded "no comment." But he's hoping to ask something that will provoke an answer, maybe add a fresh bit of meat to the stew he's cooking.

He has invested countless hours in this story. Evenings, weekends, so much of his time that his girlfriend is threatening to leave him. He has been working every angle from the very beginning, from the time the first girl was kidnapped. He has interviewed all the girls' friends and families. He has taken thousands of photographs, including several of Dr. Ezra Lerner, a psychiatrist of national reputation who was called to Jefferson by Deputy DA Jackie Burke. Plus, he has several photos of the girl he now knows to be Reeve.

Poe had pinned all his hopes on Randy Vanderholt being nailed for multiple crimes—three kidnappings, perhaps even murder—but with Vanderholt dead and any hope for a trial gone, this story has dried up like yesterday's toast.

Edgy Reggie, aka Reeve LeClaire, is the only new angle he's got.

He studies the picture printed with his article: fresh-faced and attractive in an enigmatic way, but with angry eyes. She stands several inches shorter than Dr. Lerner, who isn't a particularly big man. Poe has watched the way she moves—like a dancer—and even this still image seems to capture her posture, her grace.

He hears the white Jeep before he sees it, and he's out of his car the instant he recognizes Reeve at the wheel.

The other reporters and cameramen also rouse themselves and climb out as Reeve's Jeep stops at the gate. She rolls down the window to punch the intercom's button and announce herself to the Cavanaughs, but ignores the newspeople that surround her like barking dogs, shouting:

"Reggie, when did you change your name?"

"What can you tell us about Tilly Cavanaugh?"

"How do you feel about her kidnapper's death?"

Poe steps into an expectant pause following the reporters' questions, holds up his card, and says, "Otis Poe, *Jefferson Express,* and I'd like to ask your opinion—"

Her eyes flicker in his direction, but she ignores his card.

"—about what Tilly Cavanaugh knows about the other missing girls."

"Her privacy is important to her, obviously." She glares at him. "Just as mine is important to me. So step aside, Poe. I'm going to disappear."

Her window rolls shut, the gate rolls open, and she does exactly that. But not before the cameraman from Sacramento records a usable clip.

Reeve parks her Jeep and rings the bell. After a moment, Mrs. Cavanaugh shows her in, asking how she's doing.

"Okay," she says, coming inside, "but I just had a close encounter with the paparazzi at the gate."

"How delightful," Mrs. Cavanaugh says flatly. "Reeve, we were so sorry to see that photo in the paper. Do you know who the awful person is that revealed your new name?"

"No idea. Somebody on Poe's blog, apparently."

"I'm so sorry. Dr. Lerner is upset for you, too."

"Where is he?" she says, looking around. "With Tilly?"

"Yes. That investigator's got her pretty upset."

"What investigator?"

"His name's Krasny. You haven't met him? He's with the DA's office, left about an hour ago."

"Why was he here? And why is she upset?"

"Well, ostensibly, this investigator fellow brought Dr. Lerner over, as a courtesy. But really he wanted to interview Tilly."

"Interview her?"

"Or grill her is more like it."

"About what?"

"About her kidnapper. And about those two poor girls who've gone missing. You know, to see if she has any clues about what happened to them."

"But she doesn't."

"Sadly, no. Would you like some banana bread? Fresh baked this morning."

Reeve sits heavily at the kitchen table, weighing this new development, wondering if Tilly has finally cracked under the pressure. First the dead rat in the car, now this pushy investigator. The kid has been carrying around a secret that is almost too much even for Reeve, who is a champion at keeping things bottled up. She's thinking about this, swallowing a bite of banana bread, when Tilly and Dr. Lerner appear.

The girl's shoulders are slumped, her lips compressed.

"Dr. Lerner says I don't have to talk to anybody if I don't want to," she spits out, climbing onto a kitchen stool. "And I don't know anything that would help those girls, anyway." She shoots Reeve a fierce look.

Dr. Lerner has entered the room without comment. Now he steps close to Reeve, touches her arm, and murmurs, "Could I have a moment?"

She senses immediately that something is wrong, gets to her feet, and follows him into the next room, feeling guilty for having lied to him about Tilly's secret abuser, mentally preparing justifications.

He stops by the fireplace and faces her. "I'm sorry to tell you this," he says grimly. "It's not good. Sit down."

She does, crossing her arms defensively, but he remains standing.

"I don't know why they had to spring this on us at the last minute, and it's grossly unfair," he says bitterly, "but I just got the message. Daryl Wayne Flint's hearing has been moved up. It's tomorrow."

"Tomorrow?" she chokes.

"It gets worse."

"Oh." She inhales deeply, steeling herself. "There's no time, of course. You can't go."

"No, actually, I think I can make it. If you can give me a ride to the airstrip, I'll prepare my flight plan and leave right away."

"Wow. Okay. So then, how does it get worse?"

"I won't be the only forensic psychiatrist at Flint's hearing."

"What? You don't mean Dr. Ick is getting involved again?"

"Yes, unfortunately. But I'm afraid it's even worse than that."

"Well, crap, what's worse than Terrance Moody?"

FORTY-NINE

In preparation for his call to Kim Benioff—ostensibly from Reno—Duke turns away from the GPS tracking display and cues up the background noise that he has at hand: previously recorded layers of indistinct conversation and the incessant whirling, giggling music of slot machines. It's a forty-minute loop, punctuated by the occasional dinging of a jackpot.

Benioff is in charge of surveillance while Duke is on vacation. She isn't really qualified to do more than routine housekeeping, which made her Duke's best choice. Before leaving, he wiped all evidence of his personal projects. And from his control room, he carefully filters sensitive information, so that he manages what she can and cannot learn.

Still, he can't exactly bug everyone in law enforcement, so he assumes a casual tone and calls just to find out what developments he might be missing.

"Hey, Kim-bo, what's going on?"

Duke has no interest in office gossip, but he listens while she blabs, then steers her toward the Vanderholt case.

Benioff tells him what he already knows: "The roll call of registered sex offenders turned up a zillion suspects, but they all alibied out." She disses the profilers, saying, "And guess what, the Bureau says we're looking for single, white males between the ages of twenty-five and fifty-five. I can't think of anybody, can you?"

Duke chuckles. "How about the shooter? Any news?"

Benioff fills him in on the ballistics, snidely adding, "So, he's well trained. What a surprise."

When Duke doesn't respond, Benioff asks, "Late night playing black-jack?"

"Poker."

"Win anything?"

"Of course."

"Lucky you."

"Not luck. Skill."

"Whatever."

"So, anything else going on?"

"Let's see . . . oh, the deputy DA asked for Vanderholt's cell phone records."

"I provided all that already," he says, annoyed, "and there's nothing there. Nada. Zip-fucking-all."

"Yeah, well, Burke's on a tear. The other missing girls' families are going nuts. Understandably."

"That's not news."

"So, anyway, we're broadening our focus. Since Vanderholt wasn't even a registered sex offender."

"Right. So what?"

"So, he was an ex-con, a carjacker, so now we're looking more broadly at ex-cons who might have, you know, 'tendencies.' "

Duke grunts. "Must be thousands."

"Yep. We're having all kinds of fun."

"Hey, is Montoya around? Can you transfer me?"

"He's out, too, remember? Cashing in his vacation time before the end of the year, like you. So I'm here slaving away and covering for you two boys while—" The tone of Benioff's voice suddenly changes and she says, "Anyway, gotta go. Have a good time."

The line goes dead, and Duke switches off the background noise, then leans far back in his chair, mulling over the troublesome loose ends that must be taken care of.

FIFTY

Reeve pulls off the road again to consult the navigator display on her cell phone. No service. She is stuck in an area that seems vague on any map.

She rubs her eyes, cursing in frustration. After dropping off Dr. Lerner at the airport, she decided to tackle Emily Ewing's list, but despite her comment about the scarcity of homes with basements, the list details thirty-six such homes, all sold within the past three years. Reeve has studied the dates, hoping to connect the listings and sales with the kidnappings of Hannah Creighton, Abby Hill, and Tilly Cavanaugh, but found no discernible pattern.

After driving around for nearly two hours, she has physically located only four addresses, all of which were dead ends: vacant and still for sale.

She tosses the hotel's useless map aside and glares at the map from Ewing's office. The perspective makes the town of Jefferson seem tiny, a mere postage stamp of a grid fed by thicker lines: Interstate 5, which runs north and south, and the few arteries that run into surrounding wilderness. The mountain roads look like scribbles. Even loggers must get lost.

The wooded hillsides yield no clues to her location, and the few signs she has noted in passing seem to have no correlation to anything she can find on the map. Feeling defeated, she makes a U-turn and backtracks a few miles until she manages to locate a freeway on-ramp.

Jefferson City lies to the south, but she dreads going back, even if this whole expedition is pointless. Burke's investigator, Krasny, has called her twice, and Tilly's secret is too big to contain. The whole situation makes her itch.

She decides to take the next exit to see if there's any way to salvage this goose chase.

The Old Cedar Road off-ramp spills into the weedy parking lot of an abandoned gas station. She pulls in, leaves the engine running, and consults the map. With a pulse of satisfaction, she identifies two nearby addresses, gets her bearings, and heads east.

The road is nicely paved but narrow, and there's no traffic as it winds away from the freeway into an unpopulated area. Boulder-strewn hills with melting patches of snow climb from one side, pastureland stretches out from the other. Barbed wire fences sag and lean.

She checks the map, crosses a muddy creek, and prepares to make the next left turn. A smattering of old trailers bracket the corner. An ugly dog on a porch barks as she drives past.

Farther along, uphill, there are a few larger, newer homes, set farther apart. She slows to check each mailbox along the road, studying numbers until she finds the oversized mailbox for the address she's seeking—2133—brightly painted in a black-and-white cow pattern, with horns and a tail. She peers up the driveway at a modern, ranch-style home. There is a basketball hoop set up beside the long, wide driveway that leads to the garage. The yard is strewn with colorful toys, and the top of a swing set is just visible above the fence.

She stops the Jeep in the middle of the deserted road and marks 2133 off her list. She checks her phone, which again has no signal. Biting a knuckle, she studies the list, then references the map. After a moment, she locates another address in the vague tangle of roads.

But forty minutes later, she's on the opposite side of the freeway, lost again, searching for a spot to turn around. She has somehow ended up on a road that climbs in switchbacks up a steep hill, offering nowhere to maneuver. The late afternoon sun flashes through the clouds, blinding her, then disappears, leaving the hillside in deep shadow.

Tall pines crowd the road, which turns and dips and turns and rises like a crumbling rollercoaster. The asphalt is pocked with potholes. She passes a dead raccoon, lying swollen and rigid on a patch of dirty snow at the road's edge.

At the top of a rise, the road abruptly flattens and a gravel driveway appears up ahead. It doesn't give her much room to turn around, even in a vehicle as easy to maneuver as her dad's Jeep. She slows and turns in, cranking the wheel hard to begin a three-point turn, then stops.

Reeve sits in the Jeep with the engine running, smack in the middle of someplace with no marked roads. No cell phone service. Nowhereland. There's not even a number on the rusty, old mailbox, just a scrawled name: *Orr.*

A battered van is parked on a gravel driveway that stretches alongside an uneven yard landscaped with overflowing trash cans, a few old tires, and piles of brush. Wind blows trash around to where it catches against a sturdy chainlink fence. There are mesh-covered vents in the concrete foundation, and wide steps leading to a deeply shadowed porch.

FIFTY-ONE

Fourteen-year-old Hannah Creighton is glad she's bleeding. That pervert upstairs is squeamish about blood, so this is her monthly reprieve. Unless the other guy shows up. He's not bothered by blood.

They're both tall, both way stronger than she is, but Jay, who lives upstairs, wants her to think he's basically a nice guy. He brings her sweets and nail polish and magazines, as if that makes up for kidnapping her, for keeping her prisoner, or for raping her. He even gave her a teddy bear, which is pretty fucking weird when you think about it.

The other guy doesn't care if she bleeds or screams or cries. In fact, that seems to turn him on more, so Hannah tries hard not to respond to anything he does.

Jay is ugly and fat and disgusting, but at least he doesn't enjoy hurting her. He's quick about it, and afterward, he squats beside the bed and strokes her hair, like he's apologizing.

The other guy never makes a kind gesture. He's all business. He makes Jay bring down a special sheet first, and then handcuff her to the bed. It's his routine. Usually she's blindfolded before he makes his entrance. Either that, or he wears that freaky hood. Which is probably better than having to look at that sicko creep's face.

If she ever gets the chance, she'll rip off his dick and chop off his balls. She has pictured it a thousand times.

He'd kill her if she tried, of course, but that would be okay. Because he's going to do it sooner or later anyway.

She used to spend a lot of time imagining ways to escape, but every idea she could dream up involved tools and skills that were about as realistic as some dumb superhero movie. She used to beg Jay to let her go.

Now, when a new notion thrills through her, making her eyes open in the darkness, she squashes it. She makes herself face reality. It's better to stop dreaming and just give up.

The room has turned chilly, so Hannah slowly unfolds from her bed, takes two steps, and stoops to turn the knob on the electric radiator. While she's up, she checks the freshness of the Kotex pad affixed to her panties. Then she climbs back into bed, clutches the teddy bear to her chest, and settles under the covers.

Jay has tried to make her comfortable. Clean socks and underwear. A soft blanket. Two extra pillows. As if these small comforts could erase even two seconds of what has happened to her.

Still, it's better to have Jay tending to her than the other guy. Once, after he had beaten her two days in a row, Jay brought down ice packs for her swollen nose and lip, bandages for the cuts on her wrists and ankles, making clucking sounds the whole time in a way that reminded her of her grandmother.

The other guy had shown up the next night, banging on the door, hollering, "You there? Orr-ca, you dumb shit?"

Jay bolted up the stairs, shouting, "You goddamn asshole! How dare you do this to her!"

There had been a fight, it sounded like. Not long, half a minute, maybe. A scuffle. And when Jay came slinking back downstairs, carrying that damn sheet, there was a scraped place on his forehead that was starting to swell.

He wouldn't meet her eyes. He locked her hands in the cuffs, muttering that he was sorry, that it was "barbaric, three days in a row."

Now the room is too warm. Hannah gets up again and turns the heat down, comes back to bed and sprawls atop the pink quilt. She glares at the bright posters of Justin Bieber and Lady Gaga, at the stacks of stupid magazines. "It's all so fucking ridiculous," she says, peering into the toy bear's black eyes. "It's just fucking straw for this fucking cage."

FIFTY-TWO

Reeve is scanning the cabin's blank windows, weighing whether it's even worth the effort to get out and knock and ask directions, when the front door cracks open, revealing the shape of someone standing in the darkness.

The hair on the back of her neck stands up.

Get over yourself, she thinks, and punches the button to roll down the window. The cold air rushes in.

"Excuse me," she hollers, waving. "Could you please—"

"You're trespassing! Get the hell off my property!" the man shouts, stepping toward her.

"But I just—"

"I'm warning you." The man swings his arm up to eye level with the unmistakable glint of a gun barrel. "I have the right to protect my property. Now get the fuck off!"

She stomps on the gas, cranking the steering wheel hard, and the Jeep spits gravel as it lurches off the driveway and jumps over the ditch. The tires grip pavement and the steering wheel is slick in her hands as she looks back to see the flash and hear the crack of gunshot.

She races back down the hill, and as soon as she finds her way to the freeway, pulls over, shaking. She can't believe she's been so stupid. She grabs her phone, grateful to find service, and sends Nick Hudson a text:

Need to talk! Can we meet?

Relieved to see headlights zipping down the freeway, she sets her phone aside and accelerates up the on-ramp, out of the godforsaken wilderness. All the way into town, she keeps replaying what just happened.

But somehow, it doesn't come out right when she tries to explain it to Hudson.

"Let me get this straight," he says, interrupting her. "You asked a real estate agent to print out this list of houses with basements, and then you rushed off to do what, exactly? To investigate? Am I getting this right?"

"Well, yes, I guess that's what I'm saying."

"I can't believe you're telling me this. I thought you were charging down here to complain about your ID being leaked to the press."

She waves this off. "That's not the important thing."

"We didn't leak it, you know."

"Aren't you listening to me? I was shot at!"

He makes a face she hasn't seen before and shakes his head. "By a stranger in the dark, down a road that you can't identify."

She glares at him.

He looks away and blows out air.

"You have to do something. This is serious."

"Reeve, listen . . . I'm not a detective. I've been assigned a job with Jackie Burke's office, and I've been there barely six weeks. What is it you expect me to do?"

"I want you to do what cops do! I want you to investigate, find this guy!"

"You can file a report, but you just said that you don't know where you were. And if they happened to find this mystery man, it would be his word against yours."

"He shot at me!"

"Okay, but look, you weren't hit, were you? And your car's okay? So even if I believe you—and I do, okay?—but who else is going to? I'm sorry, but there's no evidence. You can't expect detectives to traipse around the woods and accuse every hunter with a gun."

"That's not what I mean and you know it."

"Okay, let's start over. Can you describe the man?"

She makes a growling sound. Then, reminding herself that the office is almost empty, and that he has stayed late to meet with her, she takes a deep breath and tries to calmly explain what happened, being careful not to mention anything about Tilly. But somehow, again, it doesn't come out quite right. And before she can fully explain, she makes the mistake of saying, "The point I'm trying to make is that now Emily Ewing is dead, and I think she was murdered."

"What?"

"To shut her up. Don't you get it? Emily Ewing was killed because she knew something."

Hudson sits down, puts his elbows on his desk, and cups his face in his hands. "I can't believe this. Now you're saying you have evidence of a murder?"

"Okay, I know it sounds crazy, but you have to listen, because I think—"

"You know we have a little thing called a homicide division, right?" He gives her an exasperated look. "You understand how that works? It might be hard for you to imagine, but civilians aren't invited."

She closes her eyes briefly, then tries a softer approach. "At least consider it, okay? Can't you please just look it up, or check, or something?"

With a shrug, he turns to his computer and begins clicking through screens. But after a few minutes, he shakes his head. "Here's the report. Emily Ewing's death was accidental. She fell, hit her head, and drowned. Weird. Sad. But accidental."

"But it wasn't an accident! You need to take another look at the crime scene."

He scoffs. "You need to stop watching so much TV. There's nothing to indicate murder, and I'm not about to second-guess the coroner."

"No, look, she gave me this listing of homes with basements," she says, holding up the pages. "And both of the places that Vanderholt rented are on this list."

Hudson snatches the list from her fingers and flips from page to page, scowling. "This is crazy. Don't you think this is already being investigated? Why are you even trying to get involved in this?"

"Don't be mad. I was just trying to . . . I was just intrigued by the—"

"This is dangerous, Reeve, and it's not your business. I told you, there's an entire task force already working on this."

"But can't you see? Whoever killed Vanderholt must have killed Ewing. And the killer's the link to those two other missing girls."

"Reeve," he says, shaking his head, "it's not your job to try to find those girls. We have a team of investigators working every aspect of the kidnappings, every wrinkle of Vanderholt's death. We've got experts combing the evidence, even the FBI."

She wants to scream that one of his colleagues is a stalker, a kidnapper, a murderer.

"They've looked at all the angles, believe me. We've got people working this, okay? And they're smart, trained professionals."

"Your point being that I'm not."

"Absolutely you're not," Hudson says, standing.

"Okay, okay, just give me back my list," she says, reaching for it.

"No," he says, snatching it back. "You have absolutely no idea what you're doing. Leave the investigating to the cops."

"You sound like Burke."

"Like I said, trained professionals."

"Okay, I get it."

He stops and scowls at her. "I don't think you do. You've been sniffing around this case since the day you got here, but this has to end. You're not armed, you're not a cop, and I don't want to see you get hurt. So just do your consulting thing with Tilly and back away before you stumble into something and screw it up."

"But the point is—"

"The point is that it's not your job."

"But I—"

"Back off, Reeve. I mean it. You're out of your depth."

FIFTY-THREE

Tuesday

At 5:44 A.M., Reeve gasps awake. Her crotch is wet, her skin is hot and charged. Was she dreaming about Nick Hudson?

She wrestles with the twisted sheets, wondering if sex and anger are forever linked in her psyche, worrying that she's deeply deviant, that she's cursed with the grime left by Daryl Wayne Flint.

Because sex is supposed to be gentle and loving and soft, isn't it?

She flips the light on, feeling overheated, and gets out of bed to pace around and cool off. She scavenges around for something to eat or drink, but finds only sodas, alcohol, and boring snacks. Nothing chocolate.

Remembering a vending machine in the hall, she pulls on some clothes and returns a few minutes later with a package of Oreo cookies. She eats them with a glass of tap water, then takes a long shower and climbs back into bed.

An hour later she's still hungry, still awake, still thinking about her fight with Nick Hudson. She tries to tell herself that she should just let it go.

But Emily Ewing is dead—*murdered!*—and Nick won't even listen to her. And he took her list. Meanwhile, the killer is still out there, Tilly is still in danger, and the other girls are god knows where. Maybe when Dr. Lerner is back in town, when he's back from Daryl Wayne Flint's hearing— she checks the time, calculating how much time must pass until the hearing, and flashes on Dr. Ick, the loathsome Terrance Moody, and on Flint's wacko mother. What the hell is she—

Reeve stops herself, takes a deep breath. *Get a grip!*

Maybe she should just go home. Tilly's family will be leaving soon. . . . And when Dr. Lerner is back in town, he'll have everything under control. Besides, he put the kibosh on that investigator, so at least he won't be talking to Tilly.

"She's too fragile," he'd said.

Where else has Reeve heard those words?

Stop it, stop it, stop it!

With no chance of going back to sleep, she tosses off the covers, gets dressed, and heads downstairs, feeling so distracted that she drives away without stopping to get something to eat.

The map is still spread out on the seat beside her. She doesn't need Emily Ewing's list, she realizes, because the address she seeks was the first place she marked. She heads west out of town, toward a ridge of snowcapped mountains. Just days ago, the house on Tevis Ranch Road had seemed too remote to try to find, yet now it feels wrong to have checked out the first place that Tilly was imprisoned, but not the second. Besides, what else does she have to do?

While she drives west, Reeve replays a conversation she had with Nick Hudson and Dr. Lerner—when was it? The first day she arrived?

They were in a restaurant, and Hudson had asked, "Do you mind if I bring up something about a similarity between your case and Tilly's?"

She had stiffened. "Of course not."

"I was thinking about the way you two were rescued. It was because of a move, in both cases."

"Right. I thought about that. We were found only because our kidnappers wanted better basements."

"Just a fluke," he said. "A random fluke."

"That troubles you," Dr. Lerner observed. "Because of the other girls? Because you're worried about the factor of sheer luck versus police work?"

"That about sums it up." Hudson frowned. "The thing is, kidnapped girls are rarely held captive. Excuse my saying so, but, statistically, well . . ." He glanced at Reeve.

"They're usually killed," she said blandly. "Tilly was lucky. I was lucky. That's a given."

This conversation nags at her while she drives.

Westbound traffic is surprisingly light. She turns left off the highway onto a two-way ribbon of blacktop. It winds into the foothills for several miles, passing lonely houses tucked into untamed lots. With so little traffic, she scarcely bothers to check her rearview mirror.

She's so preoccupied, she nearly misses the sharp turn onto Tevis Ranch Road. The corner sign is partly obscured by a tall tree, which has an old tire swing hanging from a low branch. A shanty stands a few yards back. She cranks the wheel and the Jeep bumps onto a road so narrow that it's hard to imagine passing anything wider than a bicycle.

Meanwhile, Reeve keeps worrying about similarities between her captivity and Tilly's. She has been reflexively linking the two, thinking that Randy Vanderholt and Daryl Wayne Flint were predators cut from the same awful cloth, but that's flawed logic. Daryl Wayne Flint went shopping for a better basement, but wasn't Vanderholt forced to move?

The road climbs past rugged hillsides of manzanita bushes, evergreens, and scrub oaks. At last, she spots the "For Sale" sign and turns into the driveway, recalling with a pang Emily Ewing's remark that the house was already listed, and that it would be a hard sell.

The place looks deserted. The house is a mud-brown color, ugly and squat, with cracked concrete sidewalks and a deep, screened, front porch. No reason to let it creep her out, but it does.

A dog barks somewhere far off, but otherwise it's so quiet that she wishes she hadn't come. She can picture the basement without seeing it. The dungeon, as Tilly called it.

She steels herself and proceeds up the front steps. The door to the screened porch has a big, heavy lock on it, the coded kind that real estate agents use.

She puts her face to the screen and breathes in the musty, metallic smell. The place looks dark and empty. As far as she can tell, someone has already gutted the house and hauled the trash away.

Thinking she might repeat her luck with the sliding glass door, Reeve moves around the side of the house, where she lets herself through a gate to get to the back. It's a neglected, weedy lot with a few broken terra-cotta flowerpots, the remnants of some overly optimistic resident. Only the chain-link fence looks new.

No sliding glass door this time, however; just a solid door painted the color of dried egg yolk. She climbs up on the concrete porch and tries the knob. Locked. She steps off the back porch and freezes as she hears the unmistakable sound of a closing car door.

She holds her breath and listens. Footsteps. She tracks the sound and her muscles tense.

The gate clangs and a huge man in a baseball cap comes around the corner.

They face one another across the lot and she feels her pulse jump. She has no weapon, but checks the distance to the closest terra-cotta fragments and instinctively takes a fighting stance. Her elbows are sharp, her boots are heavy. She summons up the basics of a self-defense class from years ago: eyes, instep, throat, groin.

"Don't look so scared," he says, coming toward her.

She checks the fence line and takes a step back, wondering if there's another gate behind her. "I didn't hear your car," she says, stalling.

"Prius. I know, they're creepy quiet." He stops. "You don't recognize me, do you?"

He's as big as a bear. She swallows, shakes her head.

In one motion, he sweeps off his baseball cap, revealing his bald head. "Oh, shit. Otis Poe."

He puts the cap back on and makes a face. "Well, nice to see you, too."

She scowls at him but says nothing.

He puts up his hands and jokes, "Okay, don't shoot."

"I was just leaving."

"Hey, I'm not some big, scary guy, okay?"

"Worse, you're a reporter."

"Come on, I'm not so bad. Look, I don't even have a notepad. No camera, no microphone, nothing." When she doesn't respond, he adds, "Listen, this is all off the record, okay? You were never here, I was never here. Deal?"

"Are you following me?"

"Just a coincidence."

She crosses her arms.

"No, really. I've been here . . . oh, four or five times now."

"Is that right? How come?"

"I don't know." He looks around. "Something I haven't figured out yet,

I guess, something I'm missing. My girlfriend says I'm obsessed." He gives a sheepish grin.

"Something you're missing. Like what?"

"I don't know. Maybe a link between Tilly and the other two missing girls. You know about them, right?

"Of course."

His eyebrows shoot up. "Has Tilly said anything about them?"

She scoffs. "Would I tell you if she had?"

"People tell me things you wouldn't believe."

"Yeah. Like my name."

He gives an apologetic shrug. "Somebody posted it on my blog."

"I put a lot of effort into avoiding the media, you know."

"Hey, I'm sorry. But Tilly's news, so you're news."

"You didn't have to splash my photo all over the paper."

"My editor did that," he says, opening his palms. "That's the newspaper business. Anyway, I'm sorry."

"Of course you are," she says with heavy sarcasm.

"Listen, I get it. You said you want to 'disappear,'" he says, making quote marks in the air, "so I assume there's no chance of getting an interview."

She puts her hands on her hips and gives him a sour look.

"Okay, well, just so you know, I think it's great that you're helping Tilly Cavanaugh. Who better than you, right?"

They study one another in silence. Finally, he says, "Listen, let me make it up to you. You like to avoid the press, guard your privacy, right?" He takes a step toward her, taking off his navy-blue baseball cap, and holds it out to her. "I think you need this, you know, to cover up your hair."

She blinks at the cap, recognizing it as a peace offering, wondering if an alliance with Otis Poe might be of use. After a beat, she takes a step forward, accepts the cap, and holds it with both hands. "So, am I supposed to trust you?" she asks, narrowing her eyes at him.

He crosses his heart. "Trustworthy, that's me."

"So I can be honest with you? And you'll be honest with me?"

"My middle name is Abraham. Honest Abe. No kidding."

"Then the truth is," she says, handing the cap back to him, "this is a really ugly hat, Otis. Take my word for it, you look better without it."

He accepts the cap awkwardly, folds it, and jams it into his back pocket, saying, "Well, since we're both here, do you want to look around? I know how to get inside."

"You do?" She frowns at the house. "How?"

"I have connections."

He steps up to the yolk-colored door, runs his fingertips across the upper edge of the door frame, and plucks off a key. "Voila!" he says, holding it up to show her. He fumbles with the lock for a second, and when the door swings open, she can't resist.

As they enter through the kitchen, Poe flicks a light switch back and forth. "Shit," he mutters, "no power." Even in the dimness, the house has a grimy, battered look. "For a guy who made his living as a janitor, Vanderholt wasn't much of a housekeeper, was he?" Poe remarks.

She trails him from the kitchen into the living room. Gray light filters through blinds that hang askew. All the furniture has been removed, leaving indentations in the mottled carpet. She walks around, opens a bedroom door, glances into the bathroom. This isn't what she came for, but can she really trust Otis Poe?

He's facing away from her, his big shoulders slumped. "Not much to see here, really. I don't know why I keep looking," he says, his voice soft with despair.

"Where's the basement?"

He turns toward her, cocking an eyebrow. "Seriously?"

"Seriously."

"It's pretty creepy, even with the lights on."

"You think I can't handle darkness? Where is it?"

He leads her down the hallway and out a door into the garage. "Jesus, it's dark," he mutters. "Watch your step."

She closes her eyes a moment, letting her eyes adjust, then looks around. Thin lines of dusty light seep in around the garage door. The place seems bare.

"Where's the door?"

"It's a trap door. Over here." Poe squats down and fumbles with hasps on the floor. Grunting, he lifts it open. Hinges squeak as he swings it wide and drops it heavily to the concrete floor. He stands to face her, dusting off his hands. "It's down these stairs, but you can't see anything."

"Move over."

"Hey, seriously. With the power out? It's pitch-black down there."

She drops down into a crouch, puts her palms on the edge, and starts lowering herself down the stairs.

"Are you nuts?"

"I'll just be a minute."

The wooden stairs creak beneath her feet. With her head at the level of his feet, she pauses. "Do you smell that?"

"Smell what?"

Without answering, she continues down. When her boots hit the floor, she takes half a step away from the stairs and squints into the darkness. Seeing nothing, she waves a hand in front of her face. Still nothing.

The distinct odor of bleach hangs in the bone-chilling air. She squats and drags her fingertips across the floor, recognizing the familiar texture of painted concrete. The floor is very clean.

With the stairs behind her, Reeve puts one boot in front of the other, heel to toe, and moves cautiously across the floor, her arms outstretched in front of her, counting the steps to the wall. Also painted concrete. Cold and hard and bare.

Yes, Tilly, this is a dungeon.

"You okay down there?" Poe calls.

"Wait."

She takes a deep breath, walks her fingers out in both directions and brushes her hands across the surface. No cracks or seams. She turns right and in six steps reaches the next wall. More featureless concrete. Questions flicker through her mind while she circumnavigates the rectangular room.

"Hurry up!" Poe urges. "I'm freezing."

"So chill," she shouts upward.

The concrete basement measures roughly twenty-four boot lengths long and fourteen boot lengths wide. Even on tiptoe, she cannot reach the ceiling to explore for beams with screws or hooks. There is no cot, no bedpan, not a trace of what went on in this dark pit. But she knows.

"Reeve? Hello? Could you please hurry?"

She shuffles across the floor, gropes for the stairs, and ascends, saying, "Okay, let's go."

"What did you find?"

"Nothing. It's scrubbed clean." She gulps in the cold air, still smelling bleach.

"Really? Well, they did that quick."

"When were you here last?" she asks, following him into the house.

"Saturday, I think. Yeah, Saturday."

"Was the power on?"

"Yep, and it was a mess. I was here with the real estate agent, Paul Walters. He said he was going to get it cleaned out, and he sure meant it, 'cause he didn't waste any time."

"When were the dogs here? Last weekend, right? And when did the police wrap up their investigation?"

"The police wrapped up the day after Vanderholt was killed, I think. Or, that would be last Wednesday."

Reeve grows silent while Poe locks up the house and returns the key to its hiding place above the door.

"Okay," he says, wiping his palms on his jeans, "we were never here, right?"

"Right," she says, heading back through the side gate to the front of the house.

He follows her over to her Jeep. "Hey, do I see wheels turning? What are you thinking?"

Careful of her promise to Tilly, she asks, "What do you know about Vanderholt's killer?"

"Word is, he's an expert marksman."

"Some kind of trained sniper?"

"Yeah, military maybe."

"Military, right." Keeping her eyes on Poe, she says slowly, "Or maybe a cop?"

He winces. "Wouldn't that suck?"

She lets this sink in, then asks, "What's your theory about the missing girls?"

"I don't know, but it's driving me nuts. I mean, the odds are that Vanderholt killed them, right? But there's no evidence. They've just vanished."

"So, you think he had an accomplice?"

"Yeah, maybe. Either that, or there's a copycat situation."

She cocks her head at him. "Okay, thanks for nothing."

"What?"

"The tour that never happened, right?" She gives him a wry grin and opens the Jeep's door.

Poe grins back. "Right! Sure. See ya." He starts walking toward his blue Prius, then stops and turns around. "Hey, Reeve," he calls out, "do you think Dr. Lerner would give me an interview?"

She waves as she drives away.

FIFTY-FOUR

The rolling leather office chair in the surveillance room at Jefferson Police Headquarters is not properly set for Officer Kim Benioff's small stature, but instead of messing with the height adjustment, she sits up tall, studying the data on the computer screen. She doesn't often use this console or this set of skills, except on days like today, when her coworkers are out of the office.

There are several types of electronic equipment that she doesn't recognize. Framed certificates and diplomas are displayed on the walls, but the room seems sterile, with no family photos or goofy knickknacks to soften or personalize it. It's clean and dust free, yet she can't quite get comfortable. There's something about this spot that reeks of testosterone.

She tucks her dark curls behind her ears and puts that out of her mind, focusing on the task at hand, pursuing a lead spawned just this morning by her father.

The two often meet for breakfast, and, like a lot of people of his generation, Benioff's father loves to bring a copy of the local newspaper to the table so that he can berate the editors and debate the issues. It is also his habit to read the obituary column, scanning for the names of anyone stored in his elephantine memory: classmates, teachers, colleagues, Rotarians, golf club members, or any of the thousands of Jefferson County residents that he has ever chanced to meet.

It creeps her out, but her father insists that it makes him appreciate each day and reminds him that he's lucky to be alive.

"Isn't that a shame?" her father had declared this morning, setting his coffee aside and tapping on a headline.

Kim Benioff had barely blinked, having become somewhat hardened to hearing about the deaths of her father's wide-ranging acquaintances.

So, he leaned in and stressed the point: "Buster Ewing's daughter died," he repeated. "It's tragic."

"Well, clearly, she wasn't shot, strangled, or stabbed. Otherwise, I would have heard about it," Kim quipped, cutting a slice of ham.

Her father jabbed a finger at the article. "It's the end of a dynasty, you need to realize. The end of another local business. Remember Buster? He was a character, bigger than life. Got us a good deal on our house, and on your grandmother's, too. He died about, oh, six or eight years back, I guess it was. And now his only daughter is gone. Emily Kay Ewing. Only forty-one, no kids. Isn't that a shame?"

Kim Benioff recalled nothing about Buster Ewing, but the daughter's name sparked an interest. She set down her fork, pulled the newspaper toward her and studied the article.

Later, while driving to work, Kim Benioff had kept thinking about the real estate agent who had tipped investigators to their first solid lead. Emily Ewing's call had been put through to the Joint Special Operations Task Force, and Benioff had been the one to interview her. She had then alerted Lieutenant Stephens, and within minutes she and four other members of JSOTF were on site, securing and searching the house on Redrock Road, with that weird, newly constructed wall that was meant to hide access to the basement stairs.

They had descended into a grim, cramped space. Benioff recalled dim light and a dank odor and holes in the low ceiling, where something had been unbolted.

Less than three hours later, she learned that a tactical team had tracked the renter, Randy Vanderholt, to his job at the mall. He didn't put up a fight. He led them back to his house on Tevis Ranch Road, and Tilly Cavanaugh was found imprisoned there, in a different basement, less cramped but just as grim.

Alive. Naked and traumatized, but alive.

They'd found no sign of the other girls, but if Vanderholt hadn't taken them, who had? Everyone was frustrated that the trail was going cold. By now, it was arctic.

Benioff had intended to do some research just as soon as she checked her messages and e-mail, but her day had gone sideways. Only now, late in the afternoon, has she had a moment to flip on the lights in the computer czar's office and sit in his oversized chair, following up on an idea.

She knows it's not much. Investigators had cross-referenced registered sex offenders with homes with basements long ago, but since Vanderholt hadn't been netted in that particular search, she wants to go back and dig deeper.

Ordinarily, she would ask another officer to do this kind of search. But their head geek, Drew Eubank, is off on another gambling trip to Vegas—or is it Reno? And Tom Montoya is also taking his allotted vacation, off hunting with some buddies. It seems to her that Montoya and Eubank always seem to screw up and schedule their vacations at about the same time— *men!*—so once again, Benioff is on her own.

She's not a forensic computer analyst, but she's no slacker, and after ten minutes of keying and scrolling, she's certain that this search has already been done. Still, she has never seen a report. She allows herself ten more minutes, hyperaware that her regular workload plus that of her absent team members is stacked on her desk.

Forty minutes later, she's still at it.

Her eyes are starting to blur. She senses another dead end and groans, aggravated by the idea that she's merely retracing steps. Finally, she sends a few pages to the printer. She rolls her shoulders to ease her cramped muscles, remembering that she still has to work on an unfinished report from yesterday afternoon. Stiff from sitting, she gets up to fetch the pages, finds a yellow highlighter, and spreads them out on the desk.

She stands while scanning the printouts, looking for—what? The pen's felt tip hovers like a gull over an ocean of data.

Nothing . . . nothing . . . more nothing . . . and then something.

She scowls and studies. The felt tip dives to the page. Again. Three times.

Suddenly too warm, she takes off her jacket and sits back down at the computer, where she keys in a new search.

Zip.

She tries another approach, and what appears puzzles her. She narrows the focus, backtracks, starts again, and stiffens, studying the information on the screen.

Has this already been investigated and discredited, or has it been overlooked?

Benioff scrutinizes what she has found, a chill prickling her skin.

Meanwhile, the electronic surveillance expert who privately calls himself Duke is seated in his control room, following her every keystroke.

FIFTY-FIVE

The stupidity of it all sets Duke's teeth on edge. After all his efforts, that meddling twat and that idiot Orr-ca are ruining everything. And the worst part is, he let himself believe that he'd already skated past this particular juncture.

After getting away with Vanderholt's killing, he'd begun to imagine he was safe. But then came last night's panicked phone call from J.J. Orr.

Duke had answered the phone with ice in his voice. "I told you never to call me. When I want to speak to you, I will be the one to place the call."

"But this is an emergency, man," Orr whined. "Someone was just here, snooping around."

"Who?"

"Some girl with weird hair."

"In a Jeep?"

"Yeah, how did you know?"

"What did she do?"

"She drove up to the front and just sat there, you know, looking at everything."

"What did she see?"

"Nothing, don't worry."

"Did she walk around the house?"

"No, she just sat in the Jeep, staring. But don't worry, I scared her off."

"What did you do?"

"I scared her off."

"You scared her off *how?*"

"Well, don't get mad, because—"

"Not with a gun."

"Well, uh, now—"

"Idiot."

"Yeah, I know, but—"

"What kind of gun?"

A sigh. "Just a little rifle. A .22."

"That's very stupid of you, Orr-ca."

"Yeah, I know, I'm sorry, okay?"

It was unforgiveable.

A lesser man might have smashed his fist through a wall in frustration, but Duke had stifled his anger and set to work, assessing the situation.

It had taken him years to perfect and implement his plans—vetting and training his keepers, researching and masterminding the elegant snares with which to trap his girls—was it possible that it was all now teetering on the verge of collapse?

He had been so careful. He had remotely fed the proper data into the computers at work, which of course went as planned. He had covered his tracks. But he hadn't expected Kim-bo to be quite so persistent. Or so inventive.

He stifles a nicotine craving, checks the time, and stays glued to his chair in the control room. With a new sense of urgency, he taps into his most informative devices and begins a series of tasks, checking them off his list, one by one. He also attends to the history of Edgy Reggie's GPS signal, tracking her to the sheriff's department—not good—but now she's parked outside the Cavanaughs'.

Careful monitoring reveals that he still has the upper hand. Still, it's clear that Orr-ca must to be dealt with, and having an exit strategy already in place doesn't make it any easier. Such a waste.

He places the call, and Orr answers on the first ring.

"Orr-ca, how many guns do you have?"

"Uh, I don't, uh . . . just the one."

"Don't lie to me."

"Honest, just the one rifle is all. I know better than to lie to you."

"All right. Listen carefully and I'll tell you what I want you to do."

A pause. "Okay."

"Are you listening?"

"Yeah, I am."

"All right. I want you to take that rifle out back and bury it under the woodpile."

"You're kidding."

"You know that having a gun is a violation of your parole."

Silence.

"You know that, don't you?"

A soft groan. "Yeah, I'm aware."

"So, I want you to bury it. Do you understand?"

"Under the woodpile? How am I supposed to do that?"

"Don't make me lose my temper."

"Okay, okay. I'll, uh, move the wood pile, I guess, bury the gun, and then move the wood pile back, right?"

"That's correct. And when are you going to do that?"

"Um, pretty soon, I guess."

"What did you say?"

"No, I mean, I could start right away, but, you know, these short winter days, it's getting dark kinda early."

Duke says nothing. He waits.

"But that's no big deal," Orr says quickly. "I'll get started right away, okay?"

"And why is that?"

"Because you'll be checking up on me."

"That's correct. And when do you think that might be?"

He sighs. "It could be any time."

"So get to work."

Duke doesn't really care about J.J. Orr's parole—not anymore—but he doesn't want the moron armed, either. Besides, it will serve his purpose if Orr-ca is tired and sore and moving slowly when he arrives.

He rises, locks the control room door behind him, and strides through his house to the kitchen. He will need protein in order to accomplish what he must during the next few hours. What he really wants is a nice, thick prime rib, slathered with horseradish, but there's no time. He grabs three protein bars and a Red Bull and sets them on the counter. Then he steps into the room where he keeps all his guns and ammunition and puts on a pair of latex gloves before loading his Glock.

FIFTY-SIX

Reeve, would you like some more stew?" Mrs. Cavanaugh offers.

"Oh, thank you, but I've had more than enough." She takes a last bite of cornbread and surreptitiously checks Dr. Lerner's text message, holding her cell phone under the table:

Flying back now. See you tonight.

The message seemed terse the first time she read it; it seems more so now. Not a word about how things went with Terrance Moody. Not a hint of optimism, which is very unlike Dr. Lerner.

Tilly leans away from her brother and whispers into Reeve's ear, "Come to my room when you're finished, okay? I have something really important to tell you."

Reeve says okay and sips from her glass of milk. The warm food is making her drowsy. Remembering her manners, she excuses herself from the table and thanks Mrs. Cavanaugh for the delicious meal. "My mother used to make cornbread like that," she says, and suffers a sudden image of her mother crying in the kitchen, after the cancer had spread to her bones and she could no longer cook.

"You've been such a great help with Tilly," Mrs. Cavanaugh says. "I wish we could bring you to Fresno with us. Promise you'll fly down with Dr. Lerner?"

She drapes an arm over Reeve's shoulders to give her a brief hug, and Reeve allows this, giving a quick nod before breaking away to rinse her dishes and load them in the dishwasher.

A minute later, Reeve finds Tilly in her room, busily folding clothes and placing them in a suitcase. "There's not much to pack," Tilly says, gesturing. "Nothing fits anymore. And I hate going out to shop."

"I noticed."

"After we move, maybe it'll be better."

"Yeah, I think so. Plus, you'll be getting nice, new clothes for Christmas, too. Lots of them."

Tilly flashes a rare, impish smile. "Yeah, and guess what!"

"What?"

"I have big news," Tilly says teasingly.

"What is it?"

"You'll never guess," she says, going over to her dresser and opening a drawer. "It finally happened." With a squeak of excitement, she spins around, holding up a package of sanitary napkins.

Reeve pastes on a smile. She says all the right things, all the kind, sisterly things that she imagines one should say. But images are spinning through her head, ideas clicking, and she can hardly wait to excuse herself and call Nick Hudson.

The sky opens up and it starts to rain as Reeve heads out of town. She fumbles with the windshield wipers, accidentally veering left so that the Jeep's tires hit the warning bumps of the median. She swerves back into her lane as a big semi draws alongside, sending up clouds of spray, forcing her to slow down. She grips the wheel hard, driving white-knuckled. The interstate descends and straightens briefly at the bridge crossing Jefferson Lake, but the swooping turns resume as the freeway climbs in elevation. Afraid she'll miss her exit, she stays in the slow lane, caught between two big eighteen-wheelers as northbound traffic carries her deeper into the wilderness. The asphalt becomes a slick blur. Road signs flash past. Feeling lost, she vows to take the next opportunity to exit, and suddenly she's off the freeway, down an off-ramp, onto Old Cedar Road.

Relieved, she pulls into the weed-choked parking lot of the abandoned gas station and tries to get her bearings. She checks the map on her phone against the map she snatched from Emily Ewing's office.

Keenly aware that Hudson still hasn't returned her call, she equivocates for a long moment. The engine idles, the windshield wipers beat. She starts keying in a text message:

> Nick: Sorry, but I'm going back to find that place where I was shot at. Don't worry and don't be mad. I'll just find the address and take a picture.

Holding her breath, she hits "send."

The instant Tilly had so proudly shown her that bright package of Kotex, an image of blowing trash had flashed through her mind. She was sure—or almost, anyway—that mixed in with all the paper and rubbish blowing around that cabin, she'd glimpsed the distinctive plastic wrappers from sanitary pads.

Maybe it meant nothing. Maybe the man with the rifle had a wife or girlfriend. But why had he shot at her?

The image of the gun makes her shudder. *I have a right to protect my property!*

Rain spatters on the windshield and she sits gripping her phone, willing Nick to call her back, wondering if she can manage to retrace her route. She closes her eyes, trying to recall every detail about that cabin. It had an unusually solid-looking foundation—concrete all the way around, it appeared—with mesh-covered vents. And wasn't it creepy that the house on Tevis Ranch Road and that old cabin in the woods both appeared to be surrounded by the same type of new chain-link fence?

She clicks on the dome light and studies the map again. When she thinks she has her bearings, she shifts the Jeep into gear and eases onto the road, but as she accelerates, she notices the yellow glow of the icon warning that she's low on gas.

At that moment, her phone rings. She answers the phone without thinking to look at the display, keeping her eyes on the road, assuming it will be Nick Hudson calling in response to her text message.

Instead, she hears the familiar rasp of a voice from her past: "Hello, my little cricket."

Her bowels twist.

"You've been in the news, Regina. Tell me, how are my puffies?"

Her mouth goes dry.

"I see you're in Jefferson," Daryl Wayne Flint continues. "Nice hair."

She inhales sharply. "How did you get my number?"

She waits, but there is no response. Her phone beeps, and when she checks the display she sees the yellow words: *No service.*

FIFTY-SEVEN

Al Krasny makes sure he's the first to enter the room. He needs to set up his computer and arrange his thoughts. Some of his methods might seem old-fashioned, but he can still whip together a pretty fair PowerPoint presentation on short notice. He's not out of the game yet. Never mind that this tip came from that smug little hottie, Kim Benioff. He took her info and ran with it. He did the cross-referencing and found the real stuff. He rushed it to the DA, who persuaded the judge, who issued the warrant. He's the lead investigator on this case, and he damn well deserves to get the credit.

While he plugs in cables and tinkers with setup, young people begin entering the room and taking seats at the conference table. They barely acknowledge him, no surprise. Lose a little hair, put on a few pounds, and you become invisible. Especially to females.

Krasny finishes his setup and takes a seat at the head of the table. With each new arrival, the buzz of expectation rises. He listens to their excited exchanges, but ignores the rising tension, assuming a posture of authority.

"Listen up, people!" Lieutenant Stephens bursts through the door, followed by a tall, athletic woman carrying files and a bulldog of a man that Krasny recognizes as Federal Agent Barry Coulter. "This is what we've been waiting for. We've got an ID and we've got an address."

The room falls silent. Fingers stop drumming, knees stop jiggling.

Stephens addresses those around the table: "You are the elite force, and we're here to brief you and set you loose. Special Agents Barry Coulter and

Yolanda Martin will be taking the lead tonight," he says, gesturing at the two FBI agents who are standing off to the side. "But first, Krasny, are you up?"

"Yep, I've got it," he responds, clicking keys.

"Good. This is Al Krasny, everyone, a top investigator with the DA's office. He has a few things to show you."

Krasny stifles an urge to correct the lieutenant—Not *a* top investigator; *the* top investigator—as he stands to face the room.

Before he can begin, Lieutenant Stephens says, "You all know that our searches of convicted child molesters and sex predators didn't get us to Vanderholt. So one of our team, Kim Benioff . . ." he looks up and scans the room ". . . who's not here, of course, because she's not tactical, came up with some information that Krasny refined. Isn't that right, Al?"

Krasny sucks in his stomach and inflates his chest. "I took what she provided and went with another approach. I cross-referenced the names and keyed into a timeline, looking at the release dates of certain parolees with related priors, and then—"

"Krasny," Stephens interrupts, "we don't need all these details, we need you to get to the point."

"Right, okay. So I kept drilling down, checking gun registrations and weapons violations."

"Looking for our shooter," Coulter observes. "Smart."

Krasny beams.

"Okay," Stephens prompts, "so tell us what we've got."

"I've located one individual that fits all parameters."

"Only one?" someone asks.

"That's right, and here he is." Krasny clicks his remote control and steps aside as a mugshot appears on the screen at the front of the room: a pale, lumpy face with a bulbous nose and bulging, startled eyes.

Everyone leans forward, scrutinizing the man's image.

"Our suspect is J.J. Orr," Krasny continues. "Forty-one, six feet, two-fifty. This guy isn't a registered sex offender, but he's an ex-con, like Vanderholt. Served five years on multiple counts of fraud and embezzlement."

"An accountant," someone snickers.

Stephens shoots the offender a look. "Might seem like a load of vanilla, but that means he's smart enough to hide what he does."

"You thought Vanderholt was just a carjacker," Krasny snaps. "Remember that."

"Tell them the rest," Stephens prods.

"Orr owned multiple weapons, including high-precision rifles, prior to his arrest. And he's not just your average Joe with a gun. He was sharpshooting champ at a gun club in Yuba County four years running."

Agent Coulter whistles.

"And there's more. Uh, deeper background found that Orr was arrested for rape ten years ago."

"But you just told us he's not a registered sex offender," Agent Martin points out.

"He's not. The charges were dropped, but that shows tendencies, which is what we were looking for." This was part of Benioff's contribution, but Krasny has no intention of mentioning that. "There's a peeping Tom charge, too."

"Early indicator," a woman in back grumbles.

With a click of the remote, Krasny replaces the mugshot with a map. "This is the place J.J. Orr was paroled to," he says, and the eyes of the team members follow as Krasny plays the beam of a laser pointer across the map, stopping at a spot circled in red.

Lieutenant Stephens says, "This is a solid lead, people." Nodding at Agent Coulter, he adds, "Barry, you'll take it from here?"

Stephens moves to one side to make room for Coulter, who steps to the front of the room and takes the laser pointer from Krasny, who stiffly resumes his seat.

"Okay, team, we've got our plan ready, so listen up," Coulter says. "Our target is approximately thirty miles northwest of town. This location is not far from where Tilly Cavanaugh was found locked in Vanderholt's basement." The beam hovers over another spot, circled in black, then dances back. "Rural operation. Looks like old-growth pine forests, right? But keep sharp. This whole terrain is pocked with abandoned mines."

"Jesus, you think those girls are stashed in a mine shaft?" someone asks.

"Could be. So keep your eyes open." Coulter nods at Krasny, and with a click the map is replaced by a satellite image. "We've got two adjacent structures, a residence and barn," he says, circling with the beam. "We'll use a two-team approach, and Agent Martin will be heading up the search."

Coulter nods at her, and Yolanda Martin sets two stacks of color-coded folders on the table in front of a man with the physique of a basketball player, who checks the names and starts passing them out. "We're split into red and blue teams," she says. "Blue for the soft approach to the front; Red geared up and deployed early to cover the sides and back."

Coulter continues in his gravelly voice, "Consider this boy armed, got it? Red Team, keep to the trees and approach from the north, where there are fewer windows." Indicating paths with his laser pointer, he adds, "And be stealthy."

"The weather works to our advantage," Martin says. "But odds are, this guy's our shooter, so keep that sniper rifle in mind and keep your heads down."

"What's our transport?" a man asks, frowning down at his open file. "A horse trailer? Seriously?"

"It's not as weird as it sounds," Coulter says. "The smaller structure's a horse barn. So figure two in the truck, ten in back. Best we can do."

"Perfect for all you studs," a woman quips.

"Load of manure, more like," the man mutters back.

"Okay now, both teams," Coulter continues, "we've got warrants ready, but you get any heat, we're authorized for smash-and-bangs. Subdue the target and any accomplices with necessary force. Go with flash grenades and hard rescue tactics. Find those girls, or any remains, and secure the scene. Got it?"

Agent Martin checks her watch. "Time to get moving."

"Okay, go for best case and stay smart." Coulter surveys the room. "Your team leaders have the schematics and they'll bring you up to speed while you roll. Let's gear up!"

He claps his hands and the Hostage Rescue Team stampedes out the door, leaving Al Krasny alone in a room where tension lingers like smoke.

FIFTY-EIGHT

It's raining harder now and Reeve turns the windshield wipers up to full speed. Dusk deepens as the sun fades behind the mountaintops. She keeps her eyes on the road, searching the shadows for anything she recognizes.

A sick knot tightens in her stomach every time she lets her mind drift to the phone call. She swallows and resolves not to obsess about Daryl Wayne Flint. He has already consumed too much of her life. She will change her phone number as soon as she can. Dr. Lerner will contact the authorities in Washington, and that will be the end of it. Simple. No problem.

Now she must focus on what lies ahead. Because fear is paralysis, fear is the enemy.

The road starts to climb as darkness falls. The way seems familiar, and Reeve begins to sense that she's following the right trail. She grips the steering wheel and begins to sweat, recognizing the switchbacks, the steep, slow curves up the hill, even the jarring bumps and potholes.

She forces herself to scan the roadside and watch for the confirmation of the dead raccoon. After a time, she begins to doubt herself, but then there it is, caught in her headlights, still lying swollen on a patch of dirty snow.

She knows she's getting close and unconsciously speeds up. Anticipating what she must do, she shuts one eye, so that it can start adapting to the coming darkness. At the moment she spots the top of the rise, where the road turns and abruptly flattens, she takes her foot off the accelerator and kills her headlights. The night closes in around her.

Her light-adapted eye helps her distinguish the textures of gray foliage and blue-black road. The tires shush on slick asphalt as she tops the rise and turns toward the cabin. She eases off the gas, hoping the Jeep's engine noise won't attract attention, hoping she can find somewhere to park.

As she approaches, she hears something odd. Music.

The Jeep creeps forward and the music intensifies, pounding rockabilly. Through the rain and the trees, she sees a bright swath of light and strains to see, easing the Jeep forward, less afraid now of its noise. The driveway is up ahead. The music grows louder and the light grows brighter. She sees the rusty mailbox with the scrawled name *Orr*. And at the moment she rolls past the long driveway, she gapes at a strange tableau: The battered van is parked at the end, angled so that its headlights are illuminating a man in a yellow slicker, working in the rain, stacking firewood.

FIFTY-NINE

Music blasts out of the van in the driveway as Reeve's Jeep rolls past the house, unlit and, she hopes, unnoticed. The road dips a few yards beyond, and the Jeep's speed increases, but she resists the urge to put her foot on the brake, afraid of flashing telltale lights. She lifts her eyes to the rearview mirror, sees the last of Orr's house diminishing behind her, and steers around a downhill curve to the left.

When she checks again, there are no lights anywhere, so she risks clicking on her low beams, searching for a place to pull over. The windshield wipers beat back and forth. A yellow "No Trespassing" sign flashes up ahead, where a dilapidated gate straddles an overgrown driveway. The Jeep's wheels splash through a ditch as it edges off the asphalt and stops.

She clicks off her beams, turns off the ignition, and the music behind her trickles into the silence. She drops the key onto the passenger seat and looks around, wondering what to bring with her. Her plan of taking photographs with her cell phone camera now seems ludicrous. She can't risk the flash, or even the glow of the screen.

Reeve rubs her empty palms together, thinking, then rummages in the glove box, where she hopes for a pocketknife, but finds only a small flashlight and a four-inch screwdriver. Not much, but she slips them into her pockets, one on each side, so they don't knock together. She zips her jacket tight, turns up her collar, and eases out of the Jeep until her boots meet the ground.

Just one quick look around, she thinks, shutting the door gently. Then she turns, splashes through a puddle, and starts jogging up the road.

The glare up ahead cuts a weird green-blue wedge through the night as she crests the hill. The house looms in dark counterpoint to the bright music. She stops to scan its windows, watching for movement, wondering where the man keeps his rifle.

The rain dribbles down her neck. She shudders, steps off the road, and moves closer.

Keeping an eye on the van, trying to see past it into the backyard, she slips through the gate, and begins creeping up the driveway. Closer, closer . . . she glimpses a yellow smear of movement and stops, thankful for her dark clothes.

The wind whips the trees and their limbs wave a spooky dance in the glare of the headlights, but the van blocks her view of whatever the man in the yellow slicker is doing. She crouches low, slowly moves forward, and gravel crunches underfoot at the same instant the music stops.

She freezes and her pulse jumps in her throat as the man walks toward her. She searches vainly for cover. Cold rain drips off her head into her eyes. Why did she come here? What is she trying to prove?

He reaches the van, opens the driver's side door, and climbs inside. His face is hidden, but his yellow poncho glistens beneath the dome light, bright as a lemon drop.

A fresh CD starts up, brassy and loud. The man climbs out of the van, visible for a second before his yellow hood dips out of sight. Then, after a long pause, Reeve hears the *clunk* of wood on wood as he returns to his task.

She exhales and looks back toward the gate, tempted to return to the safety of the Jeep and the warmth of her hotel room. Nick Hudson's warning taunts her—"*you're out of your depth*"—and she stops.

Now or never. Shrugging off caution, she moves forward, keeping the van's bulk between her and the man who is busy at the woodpile. She moves stealthily, gauging distances as she angles toward the front of the house, which seems empty, with black, lifeless windows.

She creeps up next to the van, pausing in its shadow, and orders her thoughts: Grab the rifle. Watch for people. Find the basement.

What if she startles someone inside? Better to move slowly, or to make a dash?

Her fingertips brush the van's wet side as she hears engine noise coming in fast behind her. She glimpses headlights and drops to the ground, scooting under the van, pressing her belly to the cold ground, not daring to look up as beams sweep the yard.

The other vehicle crunches up behind the van, stops. The headlights switch off, the engine dies. A door opens and slams shut.

SIXTY

Six of the twelve trained and fit members of the Hostage Rescue Team spill out from the back of the horse trailer, gear on, a quarter mile shy of the target. While they hike toward the house, the rest drive slowly on, Agent Yolanda Martin riding shotgun, an agent named Harris at the wheel, and four others geared up and ready in back.

A few minutes later, the Red Team radios that they are in position. Harris steers expertly around a corner and maneuvers up the rutted driveway. He parks the pickup in front of the house, with the horse trailer strategically angled toward the barn.

Agents Martin and Harris, wearing loose civvies over their body armor, climb out and approach the front door. Martin carries just a few sheets of paper in her hands, while the rest of the Blue Team takes their positions in the shadows around the barn, guns ready. The Red Team is already in place, watching the back entrance and rear windows, out of sight.

Martin, knocks, waits.

A porch light comes on and a gray-haired man cracks open the door. His gaze flits from one face to the other.

"Sorry to bother you, mister," she says, trying to sound casual, "but we've got a horse we need to sell. Heard that J.J. Orr might be interested? Is he here?"

He gives a quizzical look, opens the door wider. "Well, I don't know where you woulda heard that."

He takes a step halfway out the door to peer between them at the gleaming horse trailer parked in his driveway. Martin watches his hands. One rubs his chin, the other goes to his pocket.

"Last thing I need is another animal needs feeding," he says, stepping back inside.

Martin hears the implication, winces. "You're J.J. Orr, sir?"

"In the flesh."

"You have a son, sir? Is he here?"

He snorts. "I kicked him out. Junior's a lot more trouble than feeding a horse, I'll tell you."

SIXTY-ONE

Reeve stays rock still. The music beats overhead and the galoshes of the man stacking the wood—Mr. Orr, probably—step into view.

"Hey, see there? You didn't need to check up on me." The voice has a high, nervous pitch. "See? I'm restacking it, like you said."

Footsteps crunch on the gravel to her left. "Good job, Orr-ca," a deep voice says.

The cheerful bluegrass music reaches a crescendo, then stops.

"Hey, you don't need that." Orr's nervous voice sounds loud in the sudden silence.

"Let's go take a look."

The galoshes don't move.

"I said go."

The music starts up again with a mournful tune. The galoshes turn around, and from beneath the van, Reeve watches both men march toward the woodpile. Raindrops flash through the van's headlights and splash in puddles as they walk. The man with the deep voice wears black, heavy boots and has a long, slightly pigeon-toed stride.

As Orr approaches the woodpile, the other man says something she can't make out. Orr spins around so the two men are facing, and now Reeve can see almost all of him, his bulbous nose, his weak chin, his ample waist. Rain drips off the yellow slicker and his fists knot in wet leather gloves.

The other man takes a stance in his heavy boots, and his voice rumbles out like a bass line. Orr responds, his voice higher, pinched. Back and forth. Fast, indistinct, arguing.

From beneath the van, Reeve cranes her neck to see whether anyone is coming out of the house to join the fight, but sees no movement, no light except the van's headlights reflecting in puddles.

She turns back to see the big man stride up to Orr, who shrinks away, his face twisted in fear. Fiddles wail overhead. The big man steps closer and smacks him hard on the chin with one gloved hand. He wears a black, hooded poncho. Other than that, Reeve can only see his wide back and the huge handgun he holds at his side.

The music suddenly drops away. She hears "—the girl—" and sees Orr glance furtively toward the house.

A hard shiver goes through her.

The music starts up again, singers drowning the men's angry voices in the opening chorus. She swallows. She wants to scream, wants to cry, but pushes herself up onto palms and toes, then spiders out from beneath the van.

SIXTY-TWO

Reeve rises into a crouch and sprints away from the music and the men, dashing through the shadows toward the house. She's across the yard and onto the porch in a flash. She glances back, sees no one, and finds the door unlocked. It creaks open and she moves quickly into the dark house.

The room seems empty. An eerie light plays on the ceiling, backwash from the outside glare. Not daring to flip a light switch, Reeve fishes the small flashlight from her pocket and clicks it on, casting its weak beam around the room, searching vainly for the rifle.

A gunshot explodes outside, the loud blast jolting her bones.

She's frozen by an animal instinct, but then shakes herself, forcing her feet to move, stumbling through the house, flinging open doors and whispering fiercely, "Hello? Anybody?"

Toward the back of the house, she finds a sturdy door locked with a padlock and pounds it with the flat of her hand. "Anyone there?"

A voice responds, "Who is that?"

"Hannah? Abby? Is that you?"

"It's Hannah." The voice comes closer. "Who are you?"

"Where's the key?"

"He's got it. What's happening?"

Reeve rushes to the back of the house, where beams from the van stab through the windows, illuminating overstuffed trash bags strewn across the floor. She gropes along the wall, searching for a key rack, scanning countertops. The inane music continues to gush from the van. Out the side window, she sees Orr slumped and bleeding against a stack of wood and longs for a weapon, thinking bitterly of the puny screwdriver in her pocket, wondering if the other man might—

Another earsplitting blast shakes the walls.

Reeve spins around and rushes back to the locked door. "Hannah, Hannah! Is the key on a ring? Hung somewhere? Did they jingle?"

"No, it's a single key, I'm pretty sure. Hurry!"

There's movement at the back porch and the light seems to flicker. Hannah mutters incoherently. Reeve squeezes her eyes shut, trying to think.

She shakes herself, lifts up on her toes, and drags her fingertips across the top of the door frame until she touches metal. She plucks down the key, pinches it between her fingers, and fumbles it into the lock, wrenching it right and left until the lock pops open in her trembling palm.

She pulls the lock from the hasp and opens the door. A single bulb illuminates a small figure and Reeve gasps, seeing her own ghostly image in the pale girl caught in that dim wash of light.

Eyes wild, Hannah pulls a blanket tight around her. "Is he dead?"

"Come on, hurry!"

As Hannah steps into the hallway, heavy footsteps sound on the back porch. Reeve turns to see a backlit figure looming outside. Hannah moans as Reeve quickly shuts the door and snaps the padlock into place. She tosses the key, and with a rush of adrenaline, scoops the girl up in her arms and sprints across the floor. They are out the door and onto the porch in a heartbeat. Strident banjo music pours from the van, blocking out all other sound as Reeve carries the girl down the dark steps and sets her on her feet.

"Don't look back," Reeve warns, but as they dash through the rain toward the gate, she glances once to where Orr is sprawled against the woodpile, eyes open, blood rinsing off his yellow slicker.

They make the gate, turn on asphalt, and rush downhill and away from the cabin, Hannah hobbling on bare feet while rain drenches them like a baptism.

Hannah wears Reeve's jacket and the heat is cranked up all the way, but she's still shivering.

"I need to get you to a hospital," Reeve says, trying to sound in control as she navigates down the steep turns. She checks the rearview mirror. "We're not being followed, at least."

"What?" Hannah wrenches around to peer through the back windshield. "Can't you go any faster?"

Reeve has no idea where they're headed. Her first priority is to put distance between them and the cabin. Now, after ten minutes of this bumping, winding road, they seem to be going deeper into uninhabited wilderness. The windshield wipers beat back and forth. The low gas icon glows yellow.

"Check my cell phone again, okay?"

Hannah fumbles with the phone. "No service yet."

Something up ahead glints in the Jeep's headlights. A stop sign. Reeve breathes silent thanks and turns onto a road with honest-to-god white lines painted down the middle. She accelerates while Hannah pulls down her visor, angling the mirror so she can watch the road behind them.

"Are you getting warm yet?"

Hannah shakes her wet hair, then wraps her legs in the blanket and tucks them up on the seat. "Who are you?" she asks, peering at Reeve with a strange intensity. "How did you find me?"

Reeve takes a deep breath and struggles to come up with answers. By the time they find the freeway, Hannah has stopped shivering.

"Feeling better?" Reeve asks.

"Yeah, I guess."

"I need to get you to a hospital."

"No, I want to go home, not to a hospital," Hannah says firmly. "Please? Just take me home, okay?"

The Jeep splashes through the night, and midway across the bridge over Jefferson Lake, the yellow gas icon on the dashboard begins flashing red.

"Okay, I'll try," Reeve replies distractedly, searching for signs of a gas station up ahead.

They cross the long bridge and the freeway angles up through the forest, seeming to climb toward the clouds.

SIXTY-THREE

Before spending time with any of his girls, Duke usually calls her keeper on a cell phone that he uses only for this purpose. The phone chronicles every visit. It's like an electronic diary. He had to destroy the phone he used to contact Vander-dolt, but he has the other two phones with him. He plans ahead.

With Tilly out and blabbing, and now Hannah inexplicably missing, he has no choice. Still, the very idea of the coming sacrifice is like a knife twisting in his gut.

It's raining steadily when Duke pulls up in front of the house where he has secured the girl with Simon Pelt. He parks his vehicle and puts on supple black gloves made of lambskin.

This time, Duke hasn't brought his own special sheet or his toy box. Instead, he carries only his favorite Glock.

Before getting out of his vehicle, Duke unfolds a fresh black poncho and carefully slips it on. It will protect him from the rain and the blood spatter.

He climbs the porch steps with his heavy boots and knocks, all polite.

Simon Pelt opens the door and his eyes go wide. "Hey man, I'm sorry, but she's not ready. I wasn't expecting you."

He sees the Glock.

"Hey man, what's going on?" Pelt puts up his hands, walking backwards, stumbling.

Duke leaves the door open and follows him inside. He orders Pelt to sit on the sofa.

Pelt is blubbering, but Duke doesn't listen. He looks around and positions himself behind an ottoman, where his pants and boots will be protected from the spatter. Then he aims, fires three well-placed rounds in Pelt's chest, and watches him die.

This time, there's no reason to collect the casings.

Killing the girl would be counterproductive, Duke has decided, so he leaves Abby Hill locked in the basement. He checks the time and pulls the front door shut behind him.

He carefully removes the poncho, refolds it, and puts it in a plastic bag before getting back into his vehicle, taking off his gloves, and driving off through the rain, taking a shortcut toward his next destination.

The silence he leaves behind drenches the house and fills the basement, where it floods against Abby's ears.

She had braced herself the moment she recognized the heavy tread of the man's boots. Listened to the floorboards creak, the muffled exchange of words, the sharp bursts that could only be gunfire. A fearful pause, and then the man's heavy tread, leaving.

Now, curled up on the cot, hugging her knees to her chest, she is awash in a profound and terrible stillness. She waits, knowing that her caretaker is dead, that she is abandoned.

Entombed.

She moans once—a sad, low sound—and shuts her eyes to listen hard for any hint of movement. She cannot hear the rain, the house is locked in silence, and her terror beats like a drum.

SIXTY-FOUR

Hannah Creighton's family whirls around her, and Reeve huddles on their living room sofa, feeling that she has stepped out of a rainstorm into a hurricane. A weeping, joyous opera has unfolded—punctuated by ecstatic six-year-old twins and three barking dogs—while Reeve has rolled through so many emotions that she's literally dizzy. It's almost like watching her own personal history being replayed, and it's all so damn weird that it can only be called cathartic.

But this is not the time or place for Reeve to share this observation. Dr. Lerner is caught up in his own whirlwind, coming out of Hannah's bedroom with one wet-eyed parent or the other, heads bent in conversation. Patting backs, murmuring reassurances. And barely giving Reeve a word, despite that she was the one who insisted he be called.

"He's a psychiatrist," she'd repeated to the Creightons. "Which means he's a medical doctor, an MD, and since she doesn't want to go to the hospital—"

"He might be the best of both worlds," Mr. Creighton had said to his wife. "Don't you see, honey? He could be exactly what Hannah needs."

So, they had called Dr. Lerner, who had rushed straight over from the hotel. And now he's in his element, dealing with an emotional crisis, the kind of man who knows how to ask the right questions, a trained physician whose tone soothes, whose presence comforts. And gradually, the entire household seems to slip past shock and joy, settling into a hushed thankfulness.

Hannah's return is a kind of miracle. And Reeve, who has delivered her, is hugged and thanked in an almost reverential way. She has never been on the receiving end of so much gratitude.

Now she rests alone on the sofa, cocooned in warmth and compassion. She closes her eyes and drifts. Her breathing deepens, heavy with fatigue.

And then phones begin to ring, and her trance wavers.

She hears voices—whispering, harsh, urgent—and she sits up, wondering what is wrong.

Dr. Lerner takes his cell phone into the kitchen.

Mrs. Creighton grasps her husband's arm and they confer, nodding sharply, before disappearing through their daughter's door.

Reeve gets to her feet and heads toward the kitchen, where Dr. Lerner pockets his phone and looks at her with a pinched expression.

"Brace yourself," he says, "all hell is about to break loose."

"What? Why?"

He opens his hands in a helpless gesture. "Protocol."

Jackie Burke was the last person Reeve expected to see, but the moment the prosecutor bursts through the door, accompanied by four uniformed officers, it becomes immediately clear that the spell of sweet reunion is about to sour.

Two intense female officers drag black rolling luggage behind them as Mr. and Mrs. Creighton show them down the hall to Hannah's room. The two somber male officers carrying large briefcases say nothing while Jackie Burke stalks over to Dr. Lerner, who ducks his head apologetically and leads them to a room at the other end of the house.

Everyone ignores Reeve, who is left standing alone in the living room, looking from one door to the other, pinching her damaged hand.

She considers calling her father. Or Nick Hudson, who still hasn't responded to her text.

When the doorbell rings, she's the only one nearby. Opening it, she finds two unsmiling men in dark suits. The shorter, more muscular of the two asks, "Reeve LeClaire?"

She nods and steps aside so they can enter.

But they don't budge. "I'm Special Agent Barry Coulter," he says, holds up his badge, "and this is Investigator Krasny. We have some questions for you."

SIXTY-FIVE

Officer Kim Benioff was at her desk, making a late snack of stale cashews and cold coffee, waiting to hear some news, when Agent Barry Coulter's ID finally flashed on her cell phone. She clicked it open and said, "Hey, rumors are buzzing here. What's going on?"

Agent Coulter grunted. "You're still at headquarters?"

"Yep. Call me a workhorse. So what's the scoop? You got him?"

"No, damn it, didn't you hear?"

"What happened?"

"We were wrong from square one. Raided the wrong damn house."

Benioff muttered curses while Coulter summarized their botched raid on J.J. Orr's father's place.

"Listen, there's no time for finger-pointing," Coulter said. "We need you to come over here, talk to somebody."

"Who?"

"We have a witness."

"What?"

"While we were storming that goddamn empty barn, a civilian found Hannah Creighton."

"What are you talking about?"

"Listen, this is highly sensitive. Keep it quiet, but we need to act fast. And we need your help."

SIXTY-SIX

Anger ticks inside her like a clock. A video camera on the ceiling watches Reeve with its accusatory lens while she sits and fidgets and reviews, trying to imagine what she's done wrong. Instead, she keeps hearing banjo music and seeing blood on a yellow slicker.

They had loaded her into the back of their car like a criminal. As they'd edged past the ambulance coming up the driveway, she'd protested that Hannah didn't want to go to a hospital, but they ignored her and sped downtown, where they set her down in this stark room. She was not finger-printed or charged with any crime, but no one would answer any of her questions, and they confiscated her phone.

By the time Officer Kim Benioff and Agent Barry Coulter enter the room, Reeve is brimming with self-justification. She scarcely waits for their questions before launching into her story: The drive to Orr's house, the man with the gun, the padlocked room, Hannah in her blanket, the sprint to her car. When Reeve has told them every detail that could possibly be important, she stops talking and looks from one set of eyes to the other, waiting for exclamations, or congratulations, or some kind of credit.

Instead, she is given pen and paper and asked to draw a map.

The instant she has finished, Agent Coulter snatches it up and bolts from the room. Benioff follows. But a few minutes later, she returns with a balding hulk of a man, saying, "This is Investigator Krasny."

"We've met," they grunt in unison.

The two sit facing her, and Benioff says, "We appreciate your coopera-tion, Miss LeClaire, but in relaying the events of tonight, you've been skip-ping something important. We need to know exactly how you came to believe that Hannah Creighton was at that particular address. We need to understand each and every step."

Reeve glances up at the dark lens in the corner, wondering who is watch-ing. Tilly's secret burns inside her. "Well, uh, you know that I was kid-napped, and that Dr. Lerner is my therapist, right?"

"Yeah, sure." Krasny leans forward, his forehead shining. "But what we're wondering is how Dr. Lerner got you involved in all this."

"Oh." She looks from stern face to stern face. "I'm working with Tilly Cavanaugh's family."

"As a kind of mentor, correct?" Benioff says.

"You have no training and no official status," Krasny says roughly, "so what is your role here?"

Reeve's chair seems unsteady beneath her. "No, uh, you see, Tilly's fam-ily asked to talk with me. You know, as a survivor of kidnapping."

Benioff sighs. "We understand that. But how was it that you went from talking about your own victimization—"

"And recovery. That's the point."

"Right, okay, but let's be clear," Krasny says, removing his jacket. "We don't have much time."

"So tell us," Benioff urges, "exactly how did you go from responding to a request that you speak with Tilly about your own personal experience, to ending up at a crime scene, witnessing a murder?"

"Well, I . . ." She swallows. The air in the room is like a furnace.

"This is getting us nowhere," Krasny grumbles, rubbing his forehead with one broad hand. "We need answers, and we need them now."

Her throat is like sandpaper. "Um, could I have some water?"

Krasny exhales loudly and Benioff shoots him a look. They know she's stalling, but they're polite. They get some water.

She's handed a plastic cup, and she sips, holding the cup in both hands. Worrying about whether the murderer is the same guy as the dirty cop. Trying to think of any way to protect the promise she has sworn to Tilly. And keenly aware of the lens pointed in her direction.

"Okay, I'm done being nice." Krasny slaps his thighs. "We need details, missy, and you're going to be sorry if you don't cooperate."

Benioff looks at him sideways, tucks a curl behind her ear, and leans in. "Tell us: How did you find Hannah?"

Krasny brings a fist down hard on the table. "And how the hell did you find J.J. Orr?"

Benioff rocks back. "Krasny, for god's sake! You're the one that botched the address. Don't take it out on her."

"But she can't—"

"I'll take it from here," she says curtly. "Go get some coffee."

"Fine!" He shoves his chair back and gets to his feet. "But for the record, I did nothing wrong, and I'm not taking anything out on anybody."

Benioff sits with arms crossed and watches him stomp out the door, then folds her hands on the table and says gently, "What you did tonight was very brave. You must be exhausted. I understand that you'd probably like to call it a night, go home, get some rest. But we still have questions, okay? And we need you to help us put things together."

"I, um . . ." She wonders who is listening and tries to shuffle her thoughts, but they spill away from her like slippery cards. "Um, do you know if Hannah's okay?"

"She's at the hospital. She's in good hands." Benioff pauses, peering into Reeve's eyes. "But we need you to remember that Abby Hill is still out there. She could still be alive."

The events of the past few days roil inside her. Emily Ewing. Otis Poe. Mister Monster. With a glance at the lens on the ceiling, Reeve whispers, "Is there somewhere else we could talk?"

SIXTY-SEVEN

Every member of Texas Hold 'em turns off his cell phone before the band takes the stage, even on a weeknight, even in a rowdy beer joint like The Pony Express. They mostly do covers of their favorite country artists—crowd pleasers—but they also like to present a few originals. The late-night crowd seems to favor the newer songs by Nick Hudson. And the manager, a former ski champion named Roxie, pays attention.

The bar is nearly full, and cash is flowing as fast as the beer. Locals who frequent the town's busy music scene—many of them musicians themselves—make a point of stopping in whenever Texas Hold 'em is on the bill. More than a few are of the opinion that Vegas and Hollywood are missing out, and friendly bets are waged on how long it will be before these boys quit their day jobs.

When the last note is played and the applause has quieted down, the bar starts to empty out. The drinkers pay up and the smokers head outside.

Roxie's policy is to make sure that each member of the band gets a fresh glass of their preferred beverage at the end of the final set. And she takes personal pleasure in handing a glass of Jack Daniel's on the rocks to Nick Hudson.

He has taken only a few sips when he checks his cell phone and shakes his head. "Damn. Eight calls, ten messages."

He cups his phone to his ear as Roxie hums, "Mm-mmm, aren't you the popular one?"

Hudson winces once, twice, then pulls the phone away from his ear as if scorched. Muttering curses, he thumbs the phone several times before dropping it into his pocket and snapping shut his guitar case. Barely saying good-bye to Roxie, he bolts out the door.

SIXTY-EIGHT

Wednesday

It's after midnight by the time Kim Benioff manages to contact the small, select group that Agent Coulter wants. She sets up in the same briefing room that had been overflowing earlier with the adrenaline-charged Hostage Rescue Team.

Crime scene analyst Myla Perkins is the first to join her, carrying a large, steaming mug in one hand and a thick file in the other. Jackie Burke enters a moment later, carrying a briefcase and looking just as crisp as if she were stepping into the courtroom, followed by her assistant, Nick Hudson, who looks scruffy and smells of whiskey.

Benioff checks her watch as they cluster at one end of the table. When a tall woman strides in, Benioff introduces Special Agent Yolanda Martin, and the two tip their heads together for a brief, hushed exchange.

At that moment, Agent Barry Coulter bursts in, his expression grim. "Thanks for coming, everyone. You all need to catch up, and we have to act fast." Gesturing, he says, "Agent Martin is a Hostage Rescue Team leader, and Myla has been running crime scene." To them, he adds, "You two know more than anyone, so feel free to correct me if I get something wrong."

The two women nod, and he spreads papers and photographs across the tabletop. Speaking quickly, he recounts the botched raid on J.J. Orr's father's place.

"We found a cantankerous old man and an empty barn," Yolanda Martin grumbles. "That was it."

"Okay, but this is where it gets cockeyed," Coulter says, putting up his hands. "In the meantime, we apparently had a *civilian* tracking down our target, who's the old man's son, an ex-con named J.J. Orr, *Junior.*"

"No kidding, a civilian!" Myla Perkins says.

"A young woman by the name of Reeve LeClaire," Coulter continues, "who was apparently at the scene when Orr was shot, and somehow managed—"

"Wait a minute," Hudson interrupts. "Reeve was there? She saw the shooter?"

"Right. Let me back up," Coulter says. While he gives a barebones account of Hannah Creighton's rescue, Hudson keeps muttering, "Holy shit," and, "I can't believe this."

"It's surprising, I know, but get over it. We have work to do. The thing is, she couldn't see the shooter's face, unfortunately." Coulter glances down, checking a printed sheet. "She states that she was hiding under a vehicle and only saw him from the back. Describes a tall man wearing a black, hooded poncho, carrying a large handgun. That's it."

"Before you ask," Myla Perkins says, displaying another set of photos, "I've been to the location and processed parts of the scene. It's all panning out just like the witness described."

"We just missed him, too," Yolanda Martin mutters. "Orr's body was practically still steaming."

"Okay," Coulter continues, "first Vanderholt was taken out, now Orr is dead. Two perps executed with two different weapons, right?"

"Right, but it's likely we're talking about the same shooter," Myla Perkins says. "Or at least, that's our working theory. Because, check this out." She lines up two photographs on the table. "This is Vanderholt's place," she says, pointing. "And this is Orr's. Note that the girls were held in basements with identical locks on the doors."

Someone groans as the group studies the photographs.

Coulter addresses Jackie Burke: "You came here straight from the hospital, right?"

"Right, Hannah Creighton is safe and alive and being treated, although we practically had to drag her in the door."

"Okay, bring us up to speed."

"It's not pretty." Burke sets her briefcase on the table and summarizes the events of the past few hours. "Hannah's recovery is the most important thing, of course, but now we're at a crossroads. Because there's evidence that both Hannah and Tilly suffered abuse by the same man."

"This does not leave this room," Coulter warns, looking from face to face.

"Wait a minute. What are you saying?" Hudson asks.

"That there is someone else involved," Burke says. "I talked with both girls, individually, and they each described another man, another abuser, who is apparently the instigator behind these two kidnappings."

"Or maybe three," Yolanda Martin says, "if we can find Abby Hill."

"That's correct," Coulter says. "This guy's a serial kidnapper who works with subordinates. He's organized, high-functioning, and clearly dominant."

"Like a mastermind of some kind?" Hudson asks.

"Correct. Vanderholt and Orr weren't bright enough to coordinate all this themselves. Successful abductions with no witnesses. Prolonged captivity. Secure locations." He shakes his head. "We're looking for a sexual predator who's pretty damn smart. And I'll tell you, he's a criminal of a type I've never seen."

"Wait. Jackie, you said both girls described the same man. This was tonight?" Hudson asks.

"Right after I talked with Hannah, I talked with Tilly," she responds.

"But how come Tilly didn't come forward with this days ago?"

"We'll get to that in a minute." Coulter turns to Burke, saying, "Jackie, please speed through this. Focus on the girls and the abuse and wrap up."

"Right. Okay. It gets worse. This guy burned both of these girls repeatedly." She splays photos across the table and they all stare at close-ups of small, round burns in distinctive, matching patterns.

"Cigarette burns," Myla Perkins observes.

"Same thing with Tilly?" Benioff asks.

"Same thing. This is Tilly's arm," Burke says, pointing, "and this is Hannah's. The scars are virtually identical."

"Holy mother of Christ," Yolanda Martin breathes.

Coulter claps his hands. "Okay, look around and you might notice that there is a disproportionate amount of estrogen represented in this room."

"For a change," Myla Perkins says.

"It's intentional. And you'll know why in a minute, because this is where I need your help." Coulter nods at Benioff, saying, "You found the link between the residences using that list, right?"

"What list?" Hudson asks.

"Emily Ewing's list," Benioff says to him, "which she gave to Reeve LeClaire, which you took from Reeve."

"That list? But it was—"

"On your desk, cowboy. Pinched it while you were out singing."

"Let's not get distracted, people," Coulter interrupts. "The point is, that list shows important information about both places—Vanderholt's and Orr's—that we hadn't found earlier. We've analyzed those elements, done some tracing, and found that both residences were purchased by the same LLC, set up in Reno, by an attorney named Justin Yow."

"Reno?" Burke mutters. "A shadow corporation of some kind?"

Coulter puts up a hand. "Our field agents there had some trouble tracking him down, but they finally got ahold of Yow about"—he checks his watch—"about forty-five minutes ago. The preliminary report is disturbing, and we'll be notified the instant they get confirmation."

The individuals in the room exchange puzzled glances.

Leaning forward and putting his palms flat on the table, Coulter says. "We're here to focus on this guy. To find Abby Hill, or her remains, if we can, and to get this guy pronto, tonight, before he knows we're on to him." He says to Burke, "You have a judge lined up for warrants?"

"Standing by."

"Okay. Both victims attribute their burns to the same sadistic son-of-a-bitch and describe the same suspect: Dark hair, brown eyes, tall, smoker, with a tattoo of barbed wire circling his left bicep."

Something catches in Benioff's throat.

At that moment, Agent Coulter's cell phone rings. He flips it open, listens for a moment. "You're sure? Same guy bought all three houses?" He nods at Yolanda Martin, who nods back. "Okay, we're secure, I'm putting you on speaker."

He sets the phone in the center of the table and a metallic voice says, "We talked to Yow and we're looking at his files. The short version is, you've got a dirty cop."

SIXTY-NINE

For the third time in several long hours, Hostage Rescue Team leader Yolanda Martin approaches a dark, low-profile structure in a rural area. The storm has blown past, and a brisk wind sends clouds scudding across the sky. Treetops whistle, branches chatter against a metal shed, and Agent Martin, alert to the fact that their target is a trained killer, is glad for the noise.

She squats with her Kevlar-vested team in the brush outside, using hand signals to direct two sets of agents to advance around the sides of the house, while another pair takes cover behind the SUV parked in the carport. One man checks the vehicle, putting a palm on the hood, and signals that it is cold.

She waits thirty long seconds, then holds up three fingers and counts down—two, one, go!—and sprints to the door, flanked by two men. They burst inside at the same instant the side door crashes open.

The living room is empty. The armed team rushes from room to room, adrenalin pumping, trigger fingers ready, and makes sure the kitchen and laundry room are also empty.

At Martin's signal, four team members move down the hallway, one agent taking position at each of the closed doors. Everyone pauses, weapons ready, listening. The crackling silence is worse than gunfire.

At her nod, the men kick the doors open.

An instant later, a voice from the first room calls, "Got him! He's down!"

More agents crowd through the doorway and, one by one, slowly lower their guns.

"Christ, you're kidding me," one grumbles.

The body is sprawled sideways in an office chair, an ugly mess, with blood and brains spattered on the computer screen, down the wall, across the rug.

"Oh shit, he sat here and ate his gun?"

"Here's the Glock," the first man says, pointing at the gun with the toe of one black boot.

"There's the casing," says another, nodding at the floor.

"Hey, check this out," says the first, pointing.

A sheet of paper neatly lined up on the corner of the desk has only two printed words: "*I'm sorry.*" Beside it rests an open map of Jefferson County, black Xs on three different spots.

Agent Martin cranes her neck, studies the map, her heart racing, then straightens and taps the first man's shoulder. "Okay, we're done here. Back out, people," she says. "Leave the scene uncompromised. But stay frosty. We've got one more location to check out. And this time, let's hope to God we find a live one."

SEVENTY

It's nearly daylight and Otis Poe is exhausted, but he's thrilled to be here, the sole reporter walking the halls of St. Jude's Hospital, scooping every other news outlet. He can hardly wait to tell his girlfriend.

The emergency staff at St. Jude is abuzz with the news: Both Abby Hill and Hannah Creighton have been found alive!

Abby Hill was discovered at a remote location and choppered in, Poe has learned. One nurse gushed to him that the rescue helicopter descended out of the sky "like a bright, avenging angel," and Poe can picture the whole scene: the chopper settling down on the pad atop the north wing, the hospital staff rushing out in a coordinated ballet, unloading the gurney, rolling the awake and blinking girl quickly through the winter air to the waiting elevator.

He knows that both girls are already resting comfortably, and that both are shockingly pale. Abby Hill, he's told, is especially thin.

"Found in the cellar of some goddamn Unabomber mountain shack," mutters a trauma nurse. "I know all about it," she adds, "because I saw her brought in."

The hospital staff is electrified by rumors. Everyone says the girls are suffering from malnourishment and dehydration, as well as sexual trauma. Those in a position to confirm the actual details about their physical conditions aren't talking, but someone claiming to know says that both girls have suffered similar burns, a pattern of round scars, clearly made by cigarettes.

"Oh my lord," one nurse whispers to another, "like they were branded! Can you believe that?"

Poe soaks up every detail.

He got a tip and arrived early, just after Abby's family burst into the hospital, wild with relief. He wishes he could have seen how they laughed and cried and hugged their daughter to them, careful of the tubes feeding into the girl's veins, alarmed by her bony protrusions and animal smells.

While both girls are getting topnotch medical treatment, Poe has learned that their kidnappers are already cooling in the morgue. He doesn't have the two men's IDs yet, but soon he'll collect all those details.

For now, he can only speculate that the Hostage Rescue Team used plastic explosives to breach the doors, that the kidnappers were killed in firefights, that the girls were found shackled, crying. But he needs specifics. He needs confirmation.

He's especially confused about Hannah Creighton. One EMT swears that she walked in through the emergency room entrance with her own family, and that she had somehow found her way home. But how could she have escaped? Poe can't even begin to get his head around that one.

He tries to sneak down the hallway to the ICU, but a stiff-backed, uniformed guard blocks the door, snarling, "Don't even think about it, man."

Poe backs off, turns, and decides it's time to go. He already has plenty of news to fill his blog, plus a hundred column inches for the newspaper. By this time tomorrow, if he pushes, he could have almost enough to finish his book. But he's got one more source to check with before calling it a night. His best source. Someone who supplies him with information that is nothing short of golden.

The e-mails have a masculine tone, but he suspects that such inside stuff can only come straight from police dispatch, and since everyone holding that particular job is female, it's Poe's guess that the tone and the screen name, Duke, are pure misdirection. But that's fine with him. Otis Poe would never betray a source, no matter what Jackie Burke seems to think.

Anyway, he has a lot of investigating and a lot more writing ahead of him. And then, if all his hard work pays off, maybe his girlfriend will forgive him, decide he's not so bad, despite his obsessions. Maybe she won't move out. Maybe he can even persuade her to accept that ring.

SEVENTY-ONE

Two Days Later

Reeve LeClaire ignores her mid-morning cup of hot chocolate, studying Otis Poe's long, front-page article in the *The Jefferson Express*. "It's all so bizarre," she says, massaging her temples, "it makes my head hurt."

Dr. Ezra Lerner reaches over and absently pats her shoulder while reading the news on his cell phone.

She and Dr. Lerner have retreated to a quiet corner of the hotel lobby, away from other guests, well out of earshot from the lounge's blaring television. They have checked out of their rooms and have their luggage packed and ready. Every couple of minutes, one or the other finds a startling bit of information and makes a comment.

"Look at this," Reeve says, pointing at the article. "Can you believe it? They found a rifle in his closet, the same one used to kill Vanderholt."

"Is that right?" Dr. Lerner glances at her newspaper and continues scrolling on his phone. In a moment, he says, "Oh, here it is. And they found another weapon. The pistol that he killed himself with, apparently the same one used to kill the other two kidnappers, J.J. Orr and Simon Pelt."

"A cop." Reeve shakes her head. "And he almost got away with it." She takes a sip from her cup and muses aloud, "I still don't know how they finally found him. What gave him away?"

Dr. Lerner raises a finger, asking her to wait, then looks up and says, "There's a reference here to surveillance. Could be cell phone records, GPS. They've got all sorts of ways of tracking people these days."

"He was smart, wasn't he? In a creepy, diabolical way, I mean. Pairing up with ex-cons who were pedophiles, but still weren't registered sex offenders."

"Diabolical is the word. He thought of everything. Hyperorganized."

"And hypersadistic."

"The odd thing about him," Dr. Lerner says, setting his phone aside, "is that a narcissist of this type wouldn't usually opt for suicide. It just doesn't seem to fit."

Reeve gives an exaggerated shiver, as if trying to shake off the whole experience. "I keep thinking about those girls. Being kidnapped, raped, and held captive is bad enough. But to have two abusers? That's off the charts."

He gives a grunt of disgust. "It is hard to comprehend. The ex-cons apparently had everyday control. Food and water, basic survival. But as despicable as their primary captors were—"

"At least they weren't as bad as that scumbag cop, right? Not just a power freak, but also a hardcore sadist."

"Such incredible cruelty, so many layers of trauma." He shakes his head and continues reading. After a moment, he looks up at her. "I'm surprised to see your name here."

She makes a face. "Poe and I made a deal. Interview me, using my old name, and leave the girls alone."

"Détente?"

She sits back. "What do you mean?"

"Between you and the press."

"More like a brief thaw in the Cold War."

Dr. Lerner cocks his head, gives her an appraising look. "Do you realize how much you've changed while we've been here?"

"Can you believe it's only been a couple of weeks? Man, I'm exhausted."

"I'm serious. You've made real progress."

"I guess." After a beat, she leans toward him and adds in a conspiratorial tone, "Hey, now that I think about it, I even did my homework, didn't I?"

His forehead knits in confusion. He looks tired, and she realizes that he has been working nonstop, talking with law enforcement, consulting with the girls' families, making arrangements for his next trips, while also juggling the demands of both his clinical practice and his professorial responsibilities in San Francisco. Plus, the ongoing problems with his son.

"Let's see," he says, rubbing his bloodshot eyes. "During our last session, right?"

"Remember the assignment?" she prods. "I actually succeeded in making an intimate connection with another human being."

"Ah. Yes, you certainly did."

"But who would have guessed that I'd be bonding over scars with another survivor, eh?" She gives him a quick, dimpled smile.

"You did a remarkable job with Tilly, far beyond what anyone expected," he says, tapping his chin. "But while I understand the ethics of protecting shared confidences, I may never completely forgive you for hiding things from me."

She rolls her eyes. "I've been thoroughly admonished for that. Jackie Burke called again and practically skinned me alive over the phone. That woman's a terror."

Dr. Lerner casts a look toward the door. "She and Hudson should be here any minute. Anyway," he continues, turning back to her, "before they get here, I wanted to discuss two things with you."

"Shoot."

"First, about Flint's hearing: I wanted to apologize for not having been better prepared."

"What? That's not your fault. Terrance Moody blindsided you."

"He did, but I should have guessed he was up to something, especially after his appearance on *60 Minutes*."

"Dr. Ick likes the limelight. It's not your fault that the hearing didn't go well."

"But I let you down. And when the judge's decision is completely discretionary—"

"Now just stop it," she interrupts. "How could anyone guess what Moody was up to? Or that he would bring Daryl Wayne Flint's mother along to the hearing? I mean, what a drama."

"True, Dr. Moody has never staged anything so elaborate for an annual review before. He probably went to work months ago with this plan to influence the hospital's recommendations to the court." He sighs, shaking his head. "But still, if I'd paid closer attention, I could have presaged that—"

"Come on, nobody can *presage* Moody. He's as freaky as Flint is."

"But clearly, he had his whole strategy planned out. I should have anticipated this."

Reeve exhales loudly. "So Flint's mother wanted to get her poor demented son's security status reduced. And she did. End of story."

"Still, I feel I've let you down. Especially with Flint calling you."

"That phone call wasn't your fault."

"But it should never have been permitted. It's a violation that—"

"Even with a lowered security status, it's not like they're going to let Flint just stroll away, is it?" She puts up her palms. "Enough about that, okay? You said you had two things to discuss. What else?"

He takes a moment, changes his tone. "I wanted to suggest that you think about applying for classes next semester."

Her nose wrinkles.

"Don't look so sour. Just think about it, okay? You have a special aptitude for this. And I think we can both acknowledge that you have some choices to make about your future."

"Choices about . . ."

"About how you want to continue."

She raises her eyebrows.

"Don't look so surprised. You've clearly begun a transition. And you already understand more about captivity syndromes than my best graduate students. Better than some PhDs, in fact. I know you've been reading the journals, some of the literature, but I want you to dedicate yourself to actual study. Do some analysis. Write some papers. Develop your natural insight."

Reeve looks at him for a long moment, unblinking.

"Will you at least consider it?"

She gives a noncommittal twitch of her shoulders. At that instant, her cell phone rings. She checks the display, says, "It's Tilly," and gets up from the table. Walking away with the phone to her ear, she asks, "Hey, are you on your way to Fresno?"

"Nope. Our trip's postponed till tomorrow," Tilly says. "Are you still in town?"

"Just about to leave."

"Well, I wanted to ask if you could come by. For lunch, maybe? Could you?"

"It's hard to pass up your mother's cooking, but are you sure she won't mind?"

"The thing is, I'm making something for you."

"For me?"

"Well, I mean it's nothing, really. Just a small gift. But it's your colors, I think."

Reeve flashes on Tilly's lurid version of *The Scream,* wondering what colors the girl imagines would suit her.

Shades of black, perhaps.

She's says good-bye and is about to pocket her phone when, all at once, she aches to get back to San Francisco. She misses her dad. She misses the Bay. She misses Persie. Acting on impulse, she calls Anthony's place.

He answers on the first ring, and she barely has time to say hello before he starts talking nonstop: "Reeve! Hey! Where the heck have you been? Persie is begging for your company. She says the crickets I give her aren't half as tasty, which makes no sense at all, since they're from the same exact supplier."

She laughs.

"You better come get her quick, 'cause I've had a dozen customers offering sacks of gold for her. They're not bothering her, or anything," he adds quickly. "I've got her in the corner, just like you wanted. But, hey, I think you owe me a beer for keeping her safe and warm, right? Are you back in town? When can you come by?"

"Anthony, whoa, slow down. Persephone is very sensitive, you know. The vibrations from all that chatter will freak her out."

"Ha! I'm the one that told you how sensitive she is. You kept saying she was covered with *fur,* remember?"

When Reeve returns to the hotel lobby, she is sobered to find Jackie Burke and Nick Hudson conferring with Dr. Lerner. She hasn't spoken to Hudson since he snatched Emily Ewing's list away from her and told her to back off. She still feels a bit raw, especially after having ignored his advice and ending up smack in the middle of exactly what he'd warned her against. She tenses, preparing for some kind of rebuke.

Instead, he clasps both her hands in his, holding them warmly. "Here she is, the mighty avenger."

She blushes, trying to think of an appropriate response, feeling self-conscious. When he drops her hands and the conversation resumes around them, she is only half-listening.

After what seems only seconds, she is pulling her luggage behind her as they all exit the warm building into the gusting winter air. The good-byes and thanks blow past her, she waves over her shoulder and heads toward her Jeep.

As she is loading her luggage, Nick Hudson hurries over. "I wanted to give you something before you take off," he says, handing her a brightly patterned CD.

"What's this?"

"Just some tunes for your trip."

"Texas Hold 'em?" she says, studying the CD in her hand.

"Yeah, my band. You like country music?"

"Uh, sure. You're in a band?"

He gives a shrug. "Hope you like the lyrics. I wrote a couple songs my-self."

She tries to think of something clever to say, but barely manages to stammer her thanks, adding, "Well, I hope they're fun songs, good driving music."

He looks at her, shakes his head. "A man has a right to be sad." Then he touches her cheek and says the last thing she would have expected, "Why do the pretty ones always have to leave?"

SEVENTY-TWO

After feasting on homemade lasagna and hot sourdough bread, Tilly pulls Reeve into her bedroom and shyly offers her a small square box wrapped in blue foil.

"Open it."

"Gee, this is my day for gifts," Reeve says, with a stab of regret at having nothing to give in return. She removes the wrapping, opens the box, unfolds the pale blue tissue paper, and lifts out a beautiful necklace made of shining beads, some as small as BBs, some as big as grapes.

"Do you like it?"

"Wow, it's gorgeous." Reeve holds up the necklace of amber, gold, white, and glittering crystal. "You really made this?"

A small shrug and a shy smile. "Put it on."

Reeve holds it to her chest as Tilly secures the clasp at the back of her neck, and they both turn toward the mirror. The beads sparkle and glow with inner fire.

"It looks great on you."

"Thank you so much. You really think these are my colors?"

Tilly beams at her. "Because you're the light. LeClaire means light, doesn't it? That's you."

Dark clouds are blowing in by the time Reeve has refueled the Jeep and is speeding south on Interstate 5. She eases her foot off the accelerator and lets the cruise control lock in at seventy-five mph. It will be late by the time she gets home. Too late to pick up Persie, too late to return the Jeep to her father. Tomorrow will have to be soon enough.

The unincorporated edges of Jefferson straggle out and disappear behind her, giving way to rolling hills and undulating pastureland. Cows. Horses. Distant mountaintops chewed off by angry clouds. The sky starts to spit and she adjusts her windshield wipers, trying to find the right setting.

She feels hundreds of miles away and far outside her old life. A new year is right around the corner. She'll return to a city she loves during a season when the palms are laced with holiday lights. She resolves to be kinder, more outgoing. She'll show her family that she can be a warmer person, the kind that doesn't flinch away from hugs. She will accept invitations and wear clothes other than jeans. She will try to be more normal.

And then what? College again? The idea sparks little enthusiasm, but maybe it's smart to consider the advice of people she knows and trusts for a change.

Time is like driving down this freeway, she thinks. A convoluted path behind, an unseen ribbon ahead, each moment just an inch of rubber on a wet surface.

So philosophical, she scoffs. Better to focus on something real.

The rain intensifies and traffic suddenly tightens. She hits the brake pedal, slows, comes to a halt behind a truck that blocks her view of what is up ahead. The Jeep idles. She yawns, rolls her shoulders, and Nick Hudson's CD catches her eye. She fumbles to open the package while replaying those last moments in his company, the sweet way he touched her cheek.

Why couldn't she see that coming? Was he especially hard to read? Or, when it comes to men, is she simply doomed to perpetual cluelessness?

A siren wails in the distance, coming closer, and traffic begins edging to the side of the road. The semi in front of her eases forward, then stops, and her cell phone begins to ring as the flashing lights of the ambulance throb past. She fishes the phone from her purse, but doesn't recognize the caller. Wrong number, probably, but she answers.

A male voice says, "Hello, am I speaking to Reeve LeClaire?"

"Who is this?"

"I'm very sorry to bother you, but I'm Ernest Hill, Abby Hill's father."

"Her father? Oh. How is Abby doing?"

"Listen, I know it's an imposition, but we've heard about you on the news, you see, about how you helped Tilly Cavanaugh, and we were wondering if you might be able to meet with Abby, if you have any time at all. I'm sorry to pounce on you like this, but would you mind coming by? Might that be possible?"

"Well, I don't really think I'm the person you need, Mr. Hill. Abby needs the help of a professional, like Dr. Ezra Lerner. I can give you his—"

"But he's left town now, you see. And the thing is, my wife feels that a female who, uh, understands the situation would be better for our little girl, at least for today. Please excuse my saying so, but the thing is, we may not want to hire Dr. Lerner because we've heard about a female psychiatrist in LA who sounds terrific. But she can't get up here for a few days, unfortunately, and in the meantime, we've been hearing so much about how you helped with Tilly that, if you can possibly make time, we would be really very grateful. Could you just come by and talk with her? Could you? Even for just a few minutes?"

Reeve eases forward in the slow lane. "Well, I'm sorry, but I've just left town. I'm actually on the freeway headed south."

"Oh, I see. . . . I'm sorry to hear that."

Reeve overhears half of a comment that he makes to someone else, presumably his wife.

He comes back on the line and speaks with an edge of pleading in his voice, "Would you consider turning around and coming back? We'd pay you, of course, whatever you need. How far south are you?"

"Well, I'm—"

"The thing is, we're afraid that Abby's suffering from shock, you know, that post-traumatic kind," he says, his voice choked with emotion. "We love her very much, but we're just not equipped, my wife and I, to handle this sort of thing."

The Jeep crests a hill and she sees the ugly clot of traffic up ahead, a multitude of red taillights bleeding color along the wet asphalt. She sighs. "Well, I'm not so very far out of town, I guess, only a few miles, but I'm afraid I'm stuck on the freeway."

"Has there been an accident?"

"Apparently. I can't quite see it, but—"

"Do you see any road signs? Perhaps I can help."

Reeve spots an exit up ahead. She equivocates for a moment before telling him, "There's an exit sign up ahead for Turnbull Ferry Road."

He explains that she's not far from their house, maybe fifteen, twenty minutes. As the traffic edges ahead and she gains a little speed, he continues, "Could you spare just a few minutes of your time? If you could just meet with Abby, talk to her, let her know that she'll be okay, that she can get past this. It could make a world of difference."

Reeve finds it impossible to say no.

"So, where are you now?" he asks.

"I'm on the exit, and I see a sign for Johnny's Mini-Mart."

"Okay, I know just where that is. There's an easy way for you to backtrack, and you're just a few miles away."

He gives her detailed directions and she hangs up, wondering if Dr. Lerner is right about her "special aptitude" for helping fellow kidnap survivors. Maybe she should suck it up, go back to college and get her degree, like her mother wanted. Maybe there's a way to turn her twisted history into something useful.

Thirty minutes later, following Mr. Hill's directions, Reeve crosses a bridge and heads northeast under a blackening sky. She winds along an old highway, then turns off and follows a two-lane road that runs parallel to the railroad tracks. She proceeds slowly, checking the small map on her phone at each stop sign. The navigator indicates a right, and she turns onto Riverside Drive as the sky opens up with heavy rain. The windshield wipers splash back and forth, and she tries to glimpse the river that must be pushing against its banks somewhere behind these suburban homes, with their neat fences and manicured lawns.

Farther along, the well-tended subdivision gives way to older, more eccentric homes that are harder to see, sprawling beyond thick trees or at the end of long driveways. There are no streetlights. And the river that appears on the edge of her map still isn't visible.

Her headlights glare on the wet pavement as she swerves around a fallen tree branch. She double-checks the address, figuring she must be close.

She resolves that she will give the Hill family her full attention for an hour, tops, and then make her excuses and get back on the freeway. It's such a long drive and she's so tired that she's already worried about the time. She won't get home before midnight. And she dreads the idea of driving for hours in the dark, in the rain.

The Hills will understand. She'll tell them that she has promised her father she's on her way.

Farther still, the road narrows, fences lose their paint, and lawns turn to untamed lots of thick brush and tall pines. The wet gloom thickens and the river remains out of sight. The few street signs are shot through with bullet holes.

At last she finds the address, a number branded into a post. She stops outside the broad, painted gate, noting with relief that there are no news vans. The Hill family has found a refuge.

She rolls down the window and punches the button on the intercom to introduce herself.

The man's voice says, "Come on in," and the heavy gate rolls open.

SEVENTY-THREE

Duke sees her coming. He has been watching her progress on one of his screens, thanks to the trusty little GPS locator, still emitting a signal from its hiding place inside the Jeep's bumper.

The irony of it all couldn't be better.

Duke has already sent congratulatory e-mails to half a dozen individuals, including Otis Poe, who is gleefully blogging about his upcoming book. And to Kim Benioff, who is still in shock over all the sordid revelations about the man she once considered a friend, the late Tomas Montoya.

It has worked so sweetly, Duke's teeth almost ache.

His three insipid keepers are history. His three spoiled pets have been returned to their weepy families. And Montoya, that grinning ape, has been very conveniently eliminated.

The pressure is off.

Setting up Montoya had worked like a dream, even better than planned. The big lummox seemed genuinely flattered when Duke stopped by out of the blue "to show him something on the computer." As if they were more than just fellow smokers, as if they were buddies. As if Drew Eubank, the department's computer wizard, might actually believe that Tomas Montoya had the intellectual capacity to follow anything more complex than a basic download.

It had played out exactly as he'd imagined, with Montoya sitting at his computer, keying in any nonsense he was given, while Duke stood behind, quietly putting on his gloves and slipping the weapon out from beneath his coat.

Just before putting the pistol to Montoya's temple, Duke asked him to tilt the computer screen just a bit, and as Montoya raised his right hand out of the field of spatter and close enough to the muzzle so that it would catch a fair blast of gunpowder, Duke fired.

A suicide. So neat.

It was simple to press Montoya's fingertips onto the Glock, then drop it to the floor, and put the phony suicide note and map in place. Next, he dropped the cell phones that had been used to call Pelt and Orr in a drawer. Once the M24 sniper rifle with a few boxes of cartridges were stashed in Montoya's closet, he was done. Out the door and gone without leaving a single loose thread.

Now the only shred of evidence linking Duke to any of this particular set of crimes is his damned tattoo.

He rolls up his sleeve and considers for the hundredth time the dilemma of either having it removed or having it altered. He hates it. But it was a stroke of luck when Montoya had come back from his Mexican vacation with photos.

"A tattoo, man? Really?" Duke had scoffed.

Montoya had turned sheepish. "Just the one. Hurt like a snakebite, I'll tell you."

And so, with Hannah Creighton barely two weeks past losing her virginity, and the other girls not yet in his sights, Duke had been forced to act. He made a quick trip out of town, gritted his teeth, and got an identical tat. Because Montoya had always been his choice of patsy. Right height. Right coloring. Right build. Right IQ.

Duke had set it all up in advance, planning every move, right through the fake ID he'd used when signing legal documents with Yow in Reno.

Montoya's voice, of course, could not be duplicated. And there was no way to completely fool his keepers, regardless of their low brainpower. But Duke had taken care of all of that.

Dead, dead, dead, and dead!

He paces, lights a cigarette, takes a long draw, then exhales the smoke, regarding the smooth, white, cylinder between his fingertips. Now that Montoya has been taken care of, he can switch back to his regular smokes and stop buying Montoya's brand. He was careful to plant cigarette butts with Tom-Tom's DNA, but he's sick of these damn Marlboro Lights.

Duke's main problem is that his sexual needs have been neglected for far too long, but—he steps to the window, watching for the Jeep's head-lights—a solution is glimmering on the horizon.

This is his chance to gain some benefit, some compensation for every-thing he has sacrificed. His keepers. His girls. And every painstaking step in setting up Montoya, from hacking his computer, to copying his damn tattoo.

The toughest decision was whether to let Abby live, but Duke has no doubt that he made the logical choice. It served his purpose. It lessened the heat on him, while confirming the psychological profile he'd so carefully crafted for Tom-Tom Montoya: The corrupt-but-cornered cop eats his gun, or whatever.

Everyone in authority had behaved just as Duke had predicted. They'd expressed the briefest shock before breathing a collective sigh of relief, sat-isfied that the evil predator was dead, delighted to give themselves credit.

Was this tidy box of poetic justice too neat to be believed? No. Officials never second-guess the luck that saves the cost of a trial.

He takes one last suck of his cigarette and extinguishes the butt. He has had enough of children, with all their bloody whining. He hungers now for someone a bit more seasoned, and so has improvised this diversion with Edgy Reggie.

And afterward? On with his next plan. He chuckles at his own ingenuity.

No more children from Jefferson County. That raises too much heat. In-stead, he'll take a few trips up to Oregon, cruise the streets, pick out a coed or runaway. Any girl even an inch into adulthood will raise far less fuss than an underage target. And hookers, of course, disappear all the time.

In the meantime, Duke will pursue this personal project on the side. A bit impulsive of him, perhaps, but he has everything ready. He has cleaned and oiled his gear. He even has a pan of cocoa prewarmed on the stove.

He pictures how it will go: Little Edgy Reggie will come in, eager to help with poor Abby. He will be anxious and apologetic and—what?—grateful! Yes, so grateful that she has come to see his traumatized daughter. He will say that his wife and Abby are together in her bedroom, just down the hall, and that he was just about to bring them some hot chocolate. Would she like a cup?

He will worry that it's not hot enough and ask her to take a sip. And once she has swallowed and told him it's fine, it's delicious, he'll escort her down the hall.

When they get to the door, he will continue the charade, knocking and calling out, "Reeve is here, sweetheart," stalling, letting the drug enter her blood stream, watching for that telltale slump, that first stumble.

Maybe she'll even giggle, tell him she's feeling woozy.

It will be so easy. He'll open the door and sweep her up and lock her down. The handcuffs are ready.

Duke peers through the streaked window and watches Reeve's headlights glinting through the rain. The beams jerk and sway as the Jeep makes slow progress toward him, bumping along the driveway, growing brighter.

At last, she has arrived.

He is erect with anticipation.

He watches her park the Jeep in the carport next to his Chevy Tahoe, just as he'd instructed. He hears her car door slam. Slowly, he stirs the pan of cocoa on the stove, turning down the gas so that it doesn't burn.

SEVENTY-FOUR

Mr. Hill?"

"Call me Ernest," the man says, opening the front door and showing her inside. He thanks her for coming, takes her jacket.

"Abby and her mother are in the back," he says, gesturing vaguely. "I was just making Abby some cocoa. Would you like some?"

"Yes, thanks, that would be nice."

He leads, she follows. The house is so dark and quiet it seems cavernous. The living room appears clean, but what's that lingering smell? She pauses at the dining table and sets her purse on a chair before entering the kitchen, which is functional and well-equipped, with a wide butcher-block surface and a sturdy rack of knives. There are no feminine touches that she can see.

He lifts the pan from the stove and pours equal amounts of the steaming liquid into two red mugs set out on the counter. "I hope it's okay," he says, handing her one.

She sips the chocolaty beverage. "It's perfect," she says. She takes another sip so that the mug will be less full and easier to carry. It's tasty, but there's something off.

It's just the odor of cigarette smoke, she tells herself. You need to get over your prejudice. Smokers have a habit, an addiction that is hard to break.

She glances around. The kitchen opens into what appears to be a utility room, with a washer and dryer near a side door. There are windows but no curtains. "You have a nice home," she says, trying to be polite.

He smiles at her and lifts the other mug. "Let's go back to Abby's room. They'll be so glad you're here."

He turns and exits the kitchen, and she follows him through the house, thinking he looks nothing like his daughter. He's tall, while Abby is petite. He has black hair and caramel coloring, while Abby is blonde and fair.

The hallway is gloomy to the point of being funereal, and she wishes he would turn on a light. His boots are loud on the hardwood floor.

She realizes that she's exhausted, far more tired than she believed, and wonders whether it's safe to drive all the way back to San Francisco in a storm. Maybe not. She should probably stay in Jefferson for one more night.

He stops outside a door at the end of the hall and calls out that Reeve is here. His voice is deep and rough and oddly familiar.

The mug of cocoa grows heavy in her hand.

They wait, but there's no response from inside.

She leans against the wall.

He's patiently holding the red mug, watching her.

Still, no response from inside. It's very quiet.

He's watching her with a smile that morphs into a sneer. "How is it? How's the cocoa, Reggie?"

Fear pulses through her. She looks at the liquid with alarm, hurls the mug at him, and spins away, fleeing down the hallway, bouncing off walls.

She pushes herself to run, feeling clumsy and slow, like running in a dream. He snickers close behind as she stumbles through the living room on heavy legs. She lurches into the kitchen, spins, sees the knife rack, and snatches up a big one.

She whirls to face him. The blade glints in the air between them.

His eyes are wary, but his chest is a huge, plaid target that expands and contracts as he breathes.

She lunges at him, slashing. He steps back and she misses but recovers quickly and, waving the knife, backs into the utility room.

He follows and she strikes again, stabbing at him, the point of the blade piercing his jeans and cutting his thigh. He howls, knocking the knife aside and smacking her across the face so that she staggers backward, bumping hard against the washing machine.

He's on her in an instant. He grabs her by the hair and cracks her cheek against something hard. She whirls and flays, knocking things to the floor, grabbing a jug of bleach and swinging it around. She aims for his face, barely misses his chin, and scrambles away. She's reaching for the doorknob when she feels the necklace tighten around her throat. She thrashes, the necklace strangling her, digging into the soft flesh under her chin. She spins around, elbows sharp, and suddenly her feet are out from under her. The necklace snaps as she falls, the beads bouncing and rolling away as her skull smacks hard on the tile.

He seizes her by the neck and hauls her to her feet. She skitters sideways, gasping for air, punching but not connecting, kicking and thrashing and hastening the effect of the drug that is racing through her veins.

SEVENTY-FIVE

By the time they reach the back room, she's barely struggling.

She weighs less than he would have thought, small and feather-light.

He sets her down on the cot, stretches her out, and begins to undress her. He pulls off her black sweater and black bra and tosses them on the floor.

He studies her skin. Her nipples are the color of milk tea, topping firm, small breasts veined with pale blue. Her skin is etched here and there with the pink-white memories of old mutilations. His fingers touch the round, crenulated burn marks that dot her forearms, and then linger over the matching, whorled spots on her shoulders where she was electrocuted by Daryl Wayne Flint.

He murmurs to himself that virgins are overrated.

She moans as he removes her boots and socks and slips off her jeans and panties. He admires her there, small and feminine and spread-eagled on the mattress. Reverently, he traces the strange, shiny scallops on both thighs. Bite marks, he decides. He examines the rings of scars around her ankles.

He flips her over and admires the pattern of scars on her back, long, feathery strips left by a whip, no doubt. He pictures a fresh pattern of burns on her buttocks, now unmarked.

With effort, he restrains himself from unzipping to explore the deeper contours of her body. Later, when she's alert and frightened, it will be so much better. And afterward, when he's ready to go again, he'll take his time adding his own marks to the map of scars on her skin. But not now, not when her eyes are rolling back in her head. Fucking a girl in this state is akin to masturbation, barely better than fucking a dead whore. He likes to watch the fear light up their eyes.

He handcuffs her to the bed frame, noticing the fine scars that bracelet both wrists. He stares at her for a long moment, imagining what he'll do when she wakes, and then he closes the door.

He gets a bathroom towel, cleans up the spilled cocoa in the hallway, tosses the towel in the laundry hamper.

He carries the mugs back to the kitchen. The one she threw is chipped.

The house has slipped deeper into darkness. He turns on lights, sets the mugs in the kitchen sink and fills them, along with the pan from the stove, with soapy water.

As he squats to gather up the items spilled across the floor, his jeans constrict painfully and he jumps to his feet, cursing. His leg is bleeding. He'd nearly forgotten about the knife wound. Spying the knife, he snaps it up with a grimace and tosses it into the sink.

Duke heads to the bathroom to tend to the cut. It surprises him that she managed to stab through his jeans, but it's not a deep cut. He wipes off the blood, and it takes only a minute to clean and bandage his wound. Satisfied, he zips up his jeans and returns to the kitchen.

He cleans the blood off the tip of the blade and slips the knife back into its slot, shifting the heavy knife rack farther away from the counter's edge.

He lights a cigarette and moves to the side of the house, where he stands at the window and smokes while gazing out. He studies the Jeep, still visible in the deepening twilight. He has already figured out how to dismantle and dispose of it. He'll have to cut off the roof and hood with a torch before whittling the body down to manageable chunks. Then he'll sink every last bit—windows, bumpers, chassis, every nut and bolt—deep into the river, piece by piece.

But he'll keep the battery. And the tires.

It will be an interesting project. How long will it take? Five or six days? It doesn't matter. Nobody's going to look for it here.

Besides, didn't his new pet just announce to the whole, television-viewing world that she wants to disappear? A smile twitches at the corners of his mouth. He loved seeing that particular clip on the evening news. What a bonus. And now Reeve's disappearance is well under way. He has prepared just the spot for her final vanishing act.

Before Montoya's body was cold in the morgue, Duke was wrapping a chain around an old tree stump not a hundred yards from his house. He hooked the chain up to the Chevy Tahoe's tow hitch, locked the hubs, revved the engine, and yanked the stump out of the soaked earth. Now it rests on its side, mud-caked roots clawing the air, balanced on the lip of a deep, new cavity. A very convenient grave. In a couple of days, when he's finished with her, he will dump her body in, hook up the chain again, and yank the old stump back into place.

The cold weather will hide the stink of decomposition, and by spring, she'll be nothing but compost.

He inhales deeply and savors his own brilliance.

When things calm down, even before the New Year, he will have his next girl in place, locked in the newly prepared basement. But this time, the search for a target will be carried out in a different state. No more tedious monitoring of local family dramas and dull suburban chitchat. Targeting a runaway eliminates so many problems. Some anonymous girl, with no history, no melodrama, and no family crying to the cops.

Thanks to Duke's innate talent for long-term thinking, his new keeper, Fitzgerald, is already in place. He's a better selection than the others, carefully vetted, an ex-con who is steady about keeping appointments with his parole officers. A smarter man than Vander-dolt. A more reliable man than Pelt. A more hardened criminal than Orr, who wasted far too much time coddling his girl. As a bonus, this new keeper has had a recent visit from the sheriff's department, so now he's clean and forgotten and off any list of suspects.

The next abduction will be trickier, more of a challenge, but perhaps that will be a nice change. He and Fitzgerald will drive up to Oregon together—in separate vehicles, of course—to scout out the appropriate victim. Fitzgerald will handle the part with the most risk, the actual kidnapping, and then smuggle the new girl south, where the new house is ready and waiting, bought using a different phantom corporation, a different attorney, and a fresh ID.

Duke takes a deep drag on his cigarette. His plan is nothing short of inspired. It's flawless.

Something streaking across the back yard catches his eye. He scowls out the window, watching as that same damn yellow tomcat slinks out of the bushes, shoots through the rain to the carport, and stops on the dry concrete beside Reeve's Jeep.

The cat pauses to lick its fur before boldly striding up to the front bumper, where it sniffs the vehicle's tires. It rises up on its hindquarters and places its big front paws just above the hubcap, as if intending to climb the tire. Then it drops to all fours, and in one smooth bound it's atop the hood.

Duke clenches his jaw, watching the cat lower itself and settle onto the warmth of the Jeep's hood. He glances behind him. His air rifle is just where he left it.

Keeping an eye on the cat, he steps backward, reaching for the gun, and is slightly off balance as the soles of his boots come down on the slew of colorful beads that scattered across the floor during his fight with Reeve. He scrambles, boots kicking underfoot, rolling and sliding off the beads as he struggles to regain his footing, but he's a tall man who slips and topples hard, banging the floor with his skull.

SEVENTY-SIX

In her dream, Reeve is holding a big, black pistol, struggling to shoot Daryl Wayne Flint, but she's so tired and weak that she can barely lift the heavy gun.

It explodes in her hands and she's awake.

Her hands hurt. She's groggy and the room is spinning. She's lying on a hard mattress. How long has she been asleep?

Her aching arms are stretched above her head, and the moment she tries to move she feels the cruel bite of the handcuffs and knows that she's been recaptured by Daryl Wayne Flint. A hot, liquid panic swims through her. She wrenches vainly against the cuffs and gags on the realization that she is naked. Stripped. Handcuffed. How many times have her nightmares returned to exactly this?

Something oily rises in her throat and she knows she's been drugged.

She clenches her fists and moans, then bends her knees and digs her heels into the mattress, shoving her head toward her hands, bending her arms, pulling and pushing until her hands touch her face. Her eyes roll. The room tips woozily.

She angles her mouth toward her hand and jams her fingers down her throat until she gags. Her stomach retches but comes up empty. She tries again. Her stomach knots and spasms and expels a warm liquid that soaks into her hair.

She coughs and lies there, panting, fighting for clarity. She dully remembers the man and everything shudders into place.

She takes a deep breath, forces her eyes open and tries to focus. She inhales, exhales, testing her ribs. Her tongue explores her sore cheek, her split lip. She stretches and flexes. No broken bones, no obvious wounds.

Her hands are cuffed tightly, the chain looped through the metal bed frame, but she has some mobility. At least she isn't fully restrained.

She stares wildly around the room, which is small and spare, with no furniture other than the bed. Everything appears dusted in a gray, dim light spilling from the window above the bed. There are no bars.

She sees her clothes wadded on the floor, her sweater, her bra and panties and jeans. Her boots. An impossible distance.

She lifts her legs over her head, folding at the waist until her bare toes touch her fingers, and her mind grasps at a single hope.

In one smooth move, she swings her legs off the bed, rolling and flipping over onto her stomach, and manages to kneel on the cold floor with her arms pulled taut above her head. Her wrists twist painfully against the unforgiving cuffs.

She grunts as she scoots away from the bed on her knees. Angling toward her clothes, she lifts up on her toes, straightens out horizontally, and stretches as far as she can, reaching blindly with her feet. She grits her teeth, yanking against the cuffs, and barely touches denim with the big toe of her right foot.

She stretches and grits her teeth, trying to grip the fabric with her toes. Her muscles quiver and she collapses in frustration, panting. Maybe another approach, maybe . . .

She twists her hands in the cuffs and firmly grips the bed frame. Bracing herself on the floor, she strains, trying to move it.

It doesn't budge.

She wrenches harder, swallowing tears.

Nothing. It's bolted to the floor.

Exhausted, she flips over and sits on the hard floor, calculating the tantalizing distance between her and her target. She takes a deep breath, extends her arms flat on the bed, puts her weight on her shoulders and lifts up, straight as a plank. She walks out on her heels as far as she can, stretching, her arms straight and rigid as she reaches out and traps the hem of a pant leg under one heel.

She drags it toward her, muscles burning. It comes slowly, the cuffs biting into her wrists as the jeans gradually unfold.

She sits briefly to ease the strain, swallows, repositions. When she lifts up again, she clamps both heels on the pant leg, traps the fabric, yanks once, and collapses.

The pants are closer now, and from a sitting position she can stretch out and pull the denim with her feet, tiptoeing along the seam, dragging her jeans toward her with small steps. The jeans come inch by inch, spreading out until the waistband snags, catching on one of her boots.

This will be tricky. She licks her lips and pulls gently, using her jeans to drag the boot toward her. Slowly . . . slowly . . . until the boot falls over with a muted *clunk,* the sole facing the wall.

Muttering *please please please,* she keeps pulling . . . and the jeans keep inching toward her. . . . Then the boot sticks to the floor. She groans, but the jeans come closer, dragging along a single black bootlace.

Her eyes water. She flips over, stretches out straight again, grunting as she reaches vainly with her toes for the bootlace. Rigid and shaking with effort, she crabs sideways and touches the lace, stabbing at it with her big toe. She has it, then it's gone, then has it again.

Her palms are slick as she grips the bed frame and her muscles burn as she drags the lace toward her, but then the weight of the boot resists and she realizes with alarm that she cannot let the lace snap away. Carefully, she eases off.

Holding her breath, she repositions again so that—yes!—she grips the lace with her toes and steadily pulls the boot toward her. Slowly, slowly . . . it makes a small scraping sound on the floor.

Eyes clenched shut, she pulls steadily with her right foot until she feels boot leather brush against her left shin. She collapses and sucks in air. Quickly, she flips over and sits on the floor. Then, carefully cupping the boot with both feet, she bends at the waist, lifting the boot over her head.

Her legs quiver. She feels the tickle of a bootlace on her forearm, cranes her neck back to watch. Carefully lowering the boot, opening her palms, crunching her abs, lowering the boot toward her grasping fingers—*Now!*—she drops the boot into her open hands and clamps tight.

Gasping, she struggles back onto the bed. Her wrists suffer her weight, the handcuffs biting as she clutches the boot and scoots up, up, up to the head of the bed, maneuvering on her back until her face is angled toward the toe of the boot. She wriggles into position, opens her jaws wide, and clamps the boot solidly between her teeth.

The fingers of her right hand crawl up the laces to the boot tongue, searching awkwardly for the rigid place and the slit. *Focus. Locate the spot.* Her fingernail touches metal. Carefully, she pries and wiggles the handcuff key. It loosens. She tugs at it slowly. It comes free, she has it, but then it slips and she cries out, fumbling to catch it, clasping at it, pinning it tight with the little finger on the numb edge of her damaged left hand.

Her skin is slick with sweat. She coughs, but manages to hold the key still.

Concentrating hard, she shifts the key bit by bit until she manages to reclaim it with the fingers of her stronger hand.

Carefully, she nudges the key around, maneuvering it until it seems to be pointing in the right direction. Sweat drips into her eyes and she holds her breath, straining her wrists into position, squeezing the key in place, intent on not letting it slip away as she gets it lined up with the keyhole. With effort, she slides the tiny bit of metal forward and inserts it into the lock. Then, wrenching her wrists awkwardly, she turns the key . . . more . . . a little more . . . and feels the small metallic hiccup as the cuffs click free.

SEVENTY-SEVEN

Duke stands over the kitchen sink, seething with an anger so intense he can scarcely think. He presses a bag of frozen peas to the swelling lump on the back of his head, feeling that he has lost track of time, wondering how long he was out. One thing is crystal clear: He will make her pay for this. For this, and for every single minute of trouble she has caused, and worse. He'll make her pay for everything. For those stupid beads, which caused him to fall. For Vanderholt's idiocy. For the loss of Tilly and Hannah and Abby.

And most of all, for stabbing him in the leg and making him bleed.

His head fills with cold calculation as he catalogues all the implements of pain he has waiting in his control room, stashed in his box of toys. What can be horrible enough for this interfering little twat?

And there it is, right before his eyes: The rack of knives. Sweet.

He tosses the bag of frozen peas in the sink and pulls the largest knife from the rack. Yes, won't this terrify her, this big carving knife? He will become her worst nightmare. He thumbs the sharp blade and places the long knife on the counter.

One more? His fingers move from one handle to the next, and then he selects the smallest. He pulls it out and turns the wicked blade in the light: An efficient tool, sharp as a scalpel, with which he'll turn her skin to scrimshaw.

He carefully wraps the smaller knife in a kitchen towel. Then he grips the impressive knife in his hand, feeling its balance and weight, and carries both knives from the kitchen.

He goes to collect the rest of his gear, imagining how this girl's past tortures will pale in comparison, how anything Daryl Wayne Flint devised will seem like a childish game in the face of the pain he'll inflict.

He can hardly wait to hear the screams he'll carve out of her.

Reeve sits on the bed, rubbing her wrists, feeling small and exhausted and woozy. The horror of her situation wavers before her for a moment before the certainty that the man will return knots in her stomach. She forces herself upright.

She tries the door, but it's locked, of course. She breathes in and out and tries to focus. There's no water, no toilet, no bedpan. He's not intending to keep her here long term. Her mouth goes dry. How long until she'll be missed? Two hours or two days, it makes no difference. No one will look for her here, no one will connect her to this man.

Who is he?

She pushes the thought aside. *Concentrate!*

The room has a sinister familiarity, yet feels less oppressive than a basement. . . . It's above ground. . . . *The window!* She scrambles up on the cot and finds the window framed in place, without a latch. Her fist pounds the glass once in frustration before she stops herself, afraid of making noise.

Her heart thrums in her ears. She hears something and freezes. His footsteps clomping down the hallway, closer.

Think!

She can see nothing but night outside the rain-spattered window. She searches the room for a weapon, her head swimming. A boot? The handcuffs? What does she have now that she didn't have in Daryl Wayne Flint's godforsaken basement?

The footsteps turn and fade as she scrambles off the cot and assesses each item: a window, a sheet, a mattress. A door opens and closes. Muffled noises come from somewhere deep in the house, something heavy thuds.

Hurry!

Seizing on a plan, she drops to the floor, assessing the cramped space beneath the cot. This could work. She pushes her clothes under it, placing her bra where it will be handy.

The sheet comes off the cot in one swift movement as she rises. She drapes it over her shoulders, then snatches up her boots and climbs back atop the mattress. Bracing herself, she raises one boot above her head, aiming the heel, bringing it slowly to the window, gauging the distance. She swallows, turns her face away, raises the boot high, and swings it hard and fast, smashing through the windowpane, which shatters in a hail of splintered glass.

She knocks loose a few remaining shards as she impulsively hurls the boots out the window into the darkness, and then tosses the sheet across the windowsill, as if for protection from the jagged glass. She quickly pulls one last perfect shard from the frame, and then she's off the cot, onto the floor, flattening herself, scooting under the bed as the man's heavy footsteps stop outside the door. Momentarily shifting the wedge of broken glass to her left hand, she uses the cup of her bra to get a tight grip on it with her right. The shard is roughly the size and shape of scissors. With the bra as protection, she wields it like a weapon.

The key snicks in the lock. She holds still, ignoring the carpet of broken glass, praying that her ruse will work.

If he doesn't believe she has escaped out the window . . . if he looks under the bed . . . *Don't hesitate. Attack the instant you see his eyes.*

The door bangs wide. A glare of light. He roars like a bear and his huge boots clomp into view, inches from her nose. She doesn't breathe. The piece of glass gripped in her hand seems futile, but she holds it tight, listening to him curse, watching his boots stomp sideways.

Strike fast. Get him in the eyes. Stab him in the throat.

Suddenly, he pivots on the balls of his feet and rushes away, leaving the door ajar.

Releasing her grip on the jagged shard, she scuttles out from beneath the cot, oblivious of the broken glass gouging her palms and knees.

A door slams. He's outside searching for her.

How long until he figures out that his prey is still inside? Three minutes? One?

With no time for clothes, she is out the door, dashing down the hallway and into the living room, trying to orient herself, working out the contours of the house, uncertain where to turn. Her keys are in the Jeep. She can't hope to outrun him, barefoot and in the dark, but the Jeep can save her. She'll crash through the gate and find help.

It sounded like he went out the front door, so she sprints past it and heads toward the side door. She's through the house in a flash, into the utility room, her bare feet treading on grit and stray beads. She's about to grasp the doorknob when she freezes. Her own reflection blanches in the glass, and she realizes that she's illuminated like a fish in a bowl while he's roaming around outside. She drops to the floor, feeling trapped and panicked.

What if he's between her and the Jeep? She needs a weapon, something, anything. . . .

She curses herself for not having thought to keep the glass, but she can't go back. Glimpsing a dark area to her right, she scuttles over on hands and knees. With no windows here to worry about, she jumps to her feet, searching, and what she finds makes her gasp: a gun cabinet.

She turns the knob and the cabinet door swings open. It's a whole damn arsenal, a full array of gleaming guns, their barrels neatly vertical above an orderly row of tins of gunpowder.

She snatches up what she recognizes as a shotgun, murmuring, "stopping power." It feels heavy and foreign in her hands.

She hears a noise and turns just in time to see the man open the door. It swings wide and she stands motionless, hoping he won't see her. For a heartbeat, she imagines that he'll charge into the house and she can slip away behind him. . . . But then his shoulders turn and his eyes shine and his body seems to swell.

She grips the gun with both hands, trying to remember Tilly's brother's instructions, and thumbs off the safety. Aiming at his chin, she clumsily pumps the shotgun and watches his Adam's apple roll up and down.

He pastes on a sour grin. "You don't even know if that thing is loaded."

"Your face just said it is."

He scoffs. "What are you going to do? Shoot me?"

"Maybe." She licks her lips. "Who are you?"

"You have no idea, sweetheart."

Dr. Lerner's words echo in her head—*a narcissist wouldn't opt for suicide. It doesn't fit*—and she inhales sharply.

"Put the gun down, kid. You don't know what you're doing."

The gun feels slick in her hands. Blood, she thinks. From the broken glass.

"Take off your shirt," she says.

"What?" He scoffs. "Listen, put down the gun. You can't even aim."

"I don't need to be accurate, I just need to be close." She takes a step toward him, and almost imperceptibly his features shift. "The shirt," she says. "Take it off."

He unbuttons his shirt while rolling his eyes as if it's a game, shedding the fabric slowly, exposing clavicle, chest hair, abs . . . until the shirt slides off his shoulders and reveals the inked ring encircling the taut muscle of his left bicep. He gives the tattoo a sideways glance, then meets her eye.

Her stomach constricts. "I know who you are."

"You think so?" He smirks. "Are you going to call the police?"

She glances involuntarily toward where her purse waits on a chair.

"Go ahead. Call."

There's no way she can get her cell phone and place a call while keeping the shotgun leveled at him. They both know it.

"I had plans to cut you, but it looks like you've already done the job," he says mockingly. "You know you're bleeding, right?"

She shifts her foot and feels something wet and sticky beneath her toes. The gun should make her feel powerful, but it only feels heavy. Every moment is like sinking deeper into soft wax.

He watches her weaken, utterly confident that he'll regain the upper hand. He knows she can't manage that shotgun. He's got the trigger pull adjusted tight, and she sure can't aim, not with the lame way she's holding it. Seems like there's something wrong with her left hand.

He makes a tsking sound. It's a nuisance that she's dripping blood on his floor, but he knows how to clean up blood.

"That was pretty clever, that bit with the broken window. The sheet. Your boots. It took me a minute to figure it out."

Realizing he's trying to distract her, Reeve tightens her finger on the trigger. The barrel wavers and his eyes follow the zigzag of the gun.

"Hey now, Reggie, be careful with that."

She raises the shotgun and swallows. She has to do something besides stand here and talk. "Put your hands on your head."

"What?"

"Hands on your head. Do it! Okay, now turn. Slowly . . . That's right, go on." She doesn't prod him with the gun barrel, doesn't dare get that close, so she's relieved when he turns and steps forward. She moves in behind him, keeping the gun pointed at his spine, reminding herself that she is the captor, he is the captive.

"Stop right there," she says, surveying the room. She wants him where she can keep an eye on him. Not on the sofa . . . not by a door . . . Her eyes focus on a single upholstered chair that is just a U-turn from where she found the guns, near the corner, pooled in the light of a lamp. She chews her lip, looking from the chair to her purse. She can rest the shotgun on the table while getting her phone. She can manage.

She directs him toward the chair and he does exactly as he's told, following along the wall and slowly easing down until he's seated.

"That's right. Now, put your hands behind you."

Again, he does as he's told. And sitting in that pool of light, half-clothed, he appears suddenly vulnerable. She has an overwhelming desire to let her guard down, but takes a breath, shakes it off, and sidles around the table to her purse, saying, "I know who you are."

"I doubt that."

"You kidnapped Tilly, and Hannah, and Abby. Who else?"

He shakes his head.

The gun barrel wavers and she tightens her grip. "I should shoot you just for Tilly."

"You don't want to do that. It's not in your character," he says, shifting his weight to the back of the chair where he has stashed the handgun. He knows exactly where the Colt 1911 is, and he figures it will be simple to overpower her while she's fumbling with the phone. The shotgun has given her an irrational sense of infallibility. He can pull the Colt from between the cushions and aim before she even has a chance to react. Perhaps she's lost so much blood that she's not thinking clearly.

He almost chuckles, thinking, Edgy Reggie is losing her edge. But he's careful to keep the smile off his face while he watches her rest the shotgun on the table.

She keeps it pointed at him with her finger on the trigger while using her left hand to open her purse.

"You're the sniper that shot Vanderholt," she says.

He sneers. "A mercy killing."

"And Montoya was framed." Her mouth has gone dry and her voice sounds strangely gruff. "You killed him, and you killed those other two guys."

"Why would you think that?" All he needs to do is keep her talking.

"What about Emily Ewing? You killed her, too, didn't you?"

"That stupid woman with the high heels?" He laughs while extending his hand between the cushions behind him, finding the handgun hidden there. He pinches the handle grip with his fingers and smoothly guides it into his palm. "She tripped and fell into that fancy koi pond, a victim of ridiculous shoes."

"How do you know that?"

"Read it in the paper."

"That wasn't in the paper."

He smirks at her, his lips twisting into the same kind of loathsome, arrogant grin that Daryl Wayne Flint used to wear. An urge to kill him boils through her. She imagines shooting him smack in the mouth, right through those disgusting yellow teeth.

He recognizes that look. "If you're gonna shoot that thing," he says calmly, "you better watch the recoil."

"What?"

"It has a nasty kick."

It works like a charm, just enough of a distraction so that she glances down at the shotgun, and in that instant he's pulling out his weapon in a swift motion he has practiced a hundred times, getting the drop on some imaginary intruder, swinging the pistol up and forward in a smooth arc, taking aim and squeezing the—

BOOM!

The shotgun blast fills the room and the Colt flies from his hand as gunshot rips open the wall behind him. Knocked off her feet, ears ringing, Reeve barely hears him shout as he jumps up, his eyes focused on the pistol on the floor. In that instant, he bumps the lamp, which teeters and falls as if in slow motion, light splashing down the wall, illuminating the cavity where the sheetrock has turned to dust, where the back of the gun cabinet has splintered, where rifle butts jut through like broken teeth. He jerks toward the lamp and cries out as Reeve glimpses the ruptured tins of gunpowder. The lamp shatters on the floor and flames erupt with a hot bright *whoosh!* as heat and light explode through the room.

SEVENTY-EIGHT

Duke's closest neighbor, Maggie Shaw, has never been one to meddle. Live and let live and leave me the fuck alone, that's her motto. If teenagers want to race down the road in their souped-up cars, she doesn't care. If some drunk tosses beer bottles out the window, or some kid shoots BBs at a squirrel, it makes not a lick of difference to her. She has sturdy, barbed wire fences posted with plenty of "No Trespassing" signs, and as long as intruders stay off her ten-acre property, she's not going to confront another living soul, much less call the cops.

But damned if that isn't some kind of racket! She shuts off the blare of the television and listens to what sounds like gunfire—Jesus! like a god-damned war!

She bolts out of her chair, across the living room, and out onto the porch. The door slams behind her as explosions rip through the night and she jerks to a halt, staring off in a southerly direction while the detonations crescendo and then abruptly cease.

Maggie Shaw stays fixed in her bedroom slippers, gaping toward the old Eubanks' place, wondering what the hell could have set off such a blast.

Gas? Propane? A meth lab?

Her heart pounds while she stands there in the cold, listening hard, trying to hear past the dripping eaves and spattering rain, watching what looks like a smoky-yellow glow, appalled to think that this time she'll have to call 911.

SEVENTY-NINE

Reeve staggers to her feet and stares around wildly. The house is howling, ablaze. Clouds of thick smoke fill the room while hungry blue flames lick the ceiling. She spins in panic, choking on scorched air, searching for escape. The floor bucks as she's blasted by detonations of heat, and the horror of her situation clamps down so hard she swoons under the certainty that she's about to die.

She falls to her knees and scuttles away from the inferno as fast as she can. The world is on fire but the floor seems slick as ice. Where is the man? She can't see. She hits a wall. Wheezing, feeling like a rat in a maze, she scrambles along it, knocking against furniture and catching on electrical wires.

Here's a corner, a hallway. Blinded by smoke, she gets to her feet, coughing, and stumbles away from the fire. If the man is following, she can't see him. Her shoulders bang against walls. Smoke stings her eyes. Here's a door ajar and she pushes into the room and stands there, gasping. It's cooler here. She sucks in air rank with sweat and smoke and finds the light switch. No power.

She lurches forward in the dark, groping, and smacks into something hard. A desk? Yes, here's a keyboard . . . another keyboard. She hurries on, deeper into the room, blindly feeling in front of her, finding monitors and equipment and more desks stacked with so many computers that she fears she's going in circles.

Now smoke is pouring into the room. Why didn't she shut the door? She chokes in despair and keeps going. There has got to be a window somewhere!

Coughing, she crashes into a rolling chair, bounces off a table, turns, and window glass gleams before her. She bumps into another desk and quickly sweeps computer monitors and equipment off the surface. They clatter and smash on the floor as she climbs unsteadily onto the desktop.

The stink of smoke intensifies. Her throat burns. Gasping, she reaches up and fumbles along the windowsill, sliding her fingers along the glass. She gropes for the lock, struggles with the mechanism. It clicks, and the glass slides open with astonishing ease.

Fresh air rushes in, carrying the sound of sirens in the distance as Reeve puts both hands on the windowsill and boosts herself up, balancing on the edge before she tumbles out naked into the cold and welcoming darkness.

EIGHTY

Wearing coveralls and carrying a fire extinguisher, Maggie Shaw climbs over the fence and charges through the brush toward her neighbor's burning house. She arrives just moments before the fire truck screams up the driveway. Shouting, she hurries over to it and grabs the sleeve of the first fireman she can, insisting that she just saw a naked woman jump out the window.

When they search, they find her in the carport, smudged with soot and smeared with blood, sitting cross-legged on the ground beside an open suitcase, dressed in sweats and bloody socks.

"He's in there!" she rasps, waving a wounded hand.

It takes the paramedics a few minutes to coax the young woman into the ambulance. Her voice is raw and she seems disoriented. When she tries to explain what happened, they tell her to take it easy. Her respiration is shallow, her pulse is racing, and they diagnose smoke inhalation and shock, just for starters.

Firemen, doctors, and cops ask questions, and Reeve does her best to answer—tongue thick, throat scorched—while drifting in and out. She feels hot needles and cold hands. And as her pain evaporates, she dimly recognizes the same quality of drug that was injected into her that night years ago in Seattle, after she was pulled from the trunk of Daryl Wayne Flint's crumpled car.

When she opens her eyes again, she is safely in the hospital.

"Hey there."

She looks up at Nick Hudson, who is sitting in a chair at her bedside.

"How are you feeling?" he asks.

She lifts off the oxygen mask with a bandaged hand. "You know what happened?" she asks hoarsely.

"Yes, but it's over now, and you need to rest, okay?"

She coughs, troubled eyes searching his. "He's dead?"

"He is. Most definitely."

"I didn't kill him, did I?"

"No, the fire did that."

"They're sure?"

"One hundred percent."

She sighs heavily and he reaches over to stroke her forehead, then helps her replace the oxygen mask. She closes her eyes, her breathing deepens, and she surrenders to a heavy, dreamless sleep.

When Reeve next opens her eyes, Nick Hudson has vanished. The stink of burnt hair fills her nostrils and she realizes the oxygen mask is gone.

She slowly sits up, looks around, and tosses off the covers. Her legs are marked with cuts and bruises and burns, and bandages are taped around her knees and both feet. She stares, thinking: *Damn. More scars.*

She swings both legs over the side of the bed, stands gingerly, and hobbles two steps across the room to a bouquet of long-stemmed yellow roses. Clumsily, she lifts out the small white envelope tucked among the blooms. Even with her bandaged fingers, she can feel something small and asymmetrical inside.

She opens the card and finds a key taped beside a note that reads:

I hope you never need one of these again, but just in case . . . Nick.

She stands very still, regarding the universal handcuff key in her palm, weighing what to say to Nick Hudson.

He answers her call two minutes later, and she thanks him for the roses. "They're gorgeous. And thanks for the key."

"Promise me you're not going to need it."

She coughs a laugh.

"How are you feeling?"

"Like I've been chewed on by a very large dog."

He chuckles. "Well, your voice is sounding pretty good, a lot better than when you gave your statement."

She's momentarily confused. She can scarcely remember talking to investigators after the fire. "It was recorded?"

"I've listened to it twice. Pretty wild stuff, I've gotta say," he continues. "The arson guys are like kids in a candy shop."

The yellow roses briefly morph into flame and she blinks away the image.

"We're finding out things about this guy you wouldn't believe. I mean, first off, did you hear about your Jeep?"

"Is it all right?"

"Sure, and it's released from evidence already. But here's the thing: We found a GPS tracker under your bumper. We think he planted it there."

"What? He was tracking me?" The thought makes her skin crawl.

"Apparently you weren't the only one. And you're right that he was a cop."

As he tells her some of what they've discovered about Drew Eubank, the computer wizard and surveillance expert who orchestrated the kidnappings of Hannah, Tilly, and Abby, her hands start to hurt. She realizes she's strangling the phone with one hand and clenching a fist with the other.

"Nick," she interrupts, "this is too much to take in."

"Oh, right." There's an awkward pause. "Sorry. I shouldn't unload all this on you while you're in the hospital."

"No, that's okay." She glances at the roses.

"But anyway, uh, I'm glad you called, because I wanted to ask: Do you think you'll ever come back to Jefferson?"

She hears the underlying meaning and pictures Nick Hudson's kind eyes, his tempting mouth. She fervently tries to imagine being with him as his future unfolds: going to law school, bringing bad guys to justice, strumming his guitar and writing ballads. . . . It suits him, but she shakes her head. "I'm sorry. You're an amazing guy, but we both know it wouldn't work. I could never fit in here."

A pause. "Well, sure. You belong in San Francisco. Jefferson must seem pretty dull."

"Dull?" She scoffs. "Don't I wish? But I need to get home. I'm tired."

"Sure. I understand. It must be exhausting being you."

"What do you mean?" she asks, trying to subdue the edge of defensiveness in her voice.

His reply is gentle. "Reeve, honestly, no one would ever accuse you of being ordinary."

She replays this conversation a hundred times while driving home, clutching the wheel with bandaged hands, fighting her regrets. She drives for hours without stopping, and when her hands throb from gripping the wheel too hard, she rests them one at a time, stretching and flexing, knowing that they will heal, that the tender pink scars will thicken, toughen, fade, and turn numb.

Her head aches, her heart aches, but at last she crosses the Bay Bridge and exhales a sigh of relief. It seems like months since she's been home.

The city appears etched in radiance. A bright moon shines overhead and the Ferry Building is aglow as she turns onto the Embarcadero and cruises slowly along the wide, familiar lane, marveling at the tall palms sparkling with holiday lights.

ACKNOWLEDGMENTS

So many people helped carry this novel from my hands to yours that it would take an entire book to thank everyone properly, but I'll do my best to keep it short.

I count myself lucky for having many smart and talented friends, and I'm particularly grateful to those who kindly read versions of my manuscript. A thousand thanks to Jeffery Deaver, Dr. Robert Jones, Cynthia Maas, Peggy Newell, Chips O'Toole, and Professor Emeritus John Williams. Another thousand thanks to the Decatur Island Writers, Authors All: Rachel Bergman, Karen Engelmann, Lynn Grant, and Marisa Silver.

Huge thanks to Michael Neff and his Algonkian workshops for helping me cultivate this story, plus five stars of gratitude to my critique group at AuthorSalon.com: Kari Pilgrim, Jennifer Skutelsky, Francis Vandenhoven, Scott Young, and especially Lois Gordon.

I owe my deepest gratitude to those who helped sharpen my writing skills over the years, notably Jeanne Mackin, Rahna Reiko Rizzuto, and Rebecca Brown, my superlative advisors at Goddard College. A wink of thanks also to Robert McKee and to Tom Jenks.

I owe a debt of thanks to retired police captain Ben Reed, Jr., to Dr. Bruce Gage, program director and chief of psychiatry for Washington State Prisons, and to Emmitt Booher, all of whom helped shed light on certain areas of expertise. (All errors are my own; please grant poetic license if you can.)

This novel would never have made it beyond chapter one without the enormous help of Dr. William Powers. It would not have seen print without my excellent agent, Liza Dawson. And it would have been a much lesser book without my superb editor, Hope Dellon, along with Andrew Martin and the terrific team at Minotaur Books. A deep bow of gratitude to you all.

Boundless thanks to my fabulous family. Mom, Dad, Mark, and Dianne, your unfailing love and support mean the world.

Thanks also to the citizens of beautiful "Jefferson County" (you know who you are). Please accept my apologies for fooling with your region's geography.

And lastly, dear reader, my thanks to you for choosing this book.

RESOURCES

Here are some important resources if you need help or information:

- National Center for Missing & Exploited Children: 1-800-THE-LOST (1-800-843-5678) http://www.missingkids.com/ or http://www.ncmec.org
- National Domestic Violence Hotline: 1-800-799-SAFE (1-800-799-7233) http://www.thehotline.org
- National Human Trafficking Resource Center / Polaris Project: 1-888-373-7888 http://www.polarisproject.org
- National Missing and Unidentified Persons System: http://www.namus.gov
- Office for Victims of Crime: http://www.ovc.gov/help/index.html
- The Elizabeth Smart Foundation: http://elizabethsmartfoundation.org/